MISS VENEZUELA

Also by Barbara Wilson

Novels:

Ambitious Women

Murder in the Collective

Sisters of the Road

Cows and Horses

Translations:

Cora Sandel: Selected Short Stories

Nothing Happened, by Ebba Haslund

MISS VENEZUELA

Barbara Wilson

The Seal Press

Many of these stories previously appeared in the collections *Thin Ice & Other Stories* and *Walking on the Moon*, published by Seal Press.

Library of Congress Cataloging-in-Publication Data

Wilson, Barbara, 1950-
    Miss Venezuela / by Barbara Wilson.
        p.   cm.
    ISBN 0-931188-58-X : $9.95
    1. Women--Fiction.   2. Lesbianism--Fiction.   I. Title.
PS3573.I45678M5   1988
813'.54--dc19   87-35112
                                                                           CIP

Cover illustration and design by Debbie Berrow.
Text design by Clare Conrad.
Composition by The Typeworks, Vancouver, B.C.

Printed in the United States of America
10 9 8 7 6 5 4 3 2

Seal Press
P.O. Box 13
Seattle, Washington 98111

CONTENTS

MISS VENEZUELA

The Investment

Una was her name. Una Eunice Huckle. She was the only thin person in a family of fat slobs and she had a real live monkey besides, though Susie never did get to see it.

It started when Susie's father decided to invest in real estate. Of course it was all pretty small potatoes. He didn't become a large scale developer or a slum landlord or anything like that. He just bought some land in a place down the coast and had a duplex built.

It was very exciting.

Every Sunday the four of them, Susie's mother and father and her little brother, John, would pile into the blue '56 Chevy with the *I Like Ike* sticker on the bumper and head off down Pacific Coast Highway to see the progress made that week. On the way her mother and father discussed what they would do with the rental money while Susie quietly tormented her brother or read from her birthday book, *Favorite Poems, Old and New*.

There were signs all along the highway advertising housing developments. "Come Visit Our Beautiful Model Homes"; "Complete Community"; "VA Loans, Easy Payments."

Rossmoor, Eagle Heights, Harbor Hills, Glenhaven—all these names were like poems to Susie, flashing by outside her window. She was disappointed sometimes to think that she lived in an ordinary house on an ordinary street with no fancy name at all.

"Someday," she often heard her father say, gesturing out

the window at the stretches of fields and farms and dunes, "this is going to be one big city, from L.A. to San Diego."

Whenever he said that, Susie always felt a chill go up and down her spine; it was frightening and stirring at the same time.

"Where will all the cows go, Daddy?"

"In the future, we won't need cows anymore. You'll be able to push a little button in your kitchen and just hold up your glass. Milk! Made right there."

"Your daddy's joking, Susie. There's plenty of room for cows and people, too," her mother said.

There were some cows in a field near the duplex site and sometimes Susie visited them, but mostly she liked to play in and around the building area. First the trees were cut down and then there was a big hole in the ground. One Sunday they came to find that the concrete had been poured, smooth and white like snow in a rectangle shape. After that, the outlines of the duplex went up in wood, and they walked through the rooms, through doors and through walls, like ghosts. Susie collected little odd-shaped pieces of wood and formica for her dollhouse; John pretended his chunks were trucks and cars and raced them around and around, making noises.

What Susie liked best about the building was that it wasn't just one house, but two. Both were exactly alike, like Alice's house in *Through the Looking Glass*. When the walls went up, she would make John go in one of the units while she went in the other and follow her from room to room.

"I'm in the first bedroom now," she'd scream.

"I'm too."

"I'm in the kitchen now."

"Me too."

The walls were pretty thin and good for hearing.

When they came to find the linoleum down one day Susie wanted to know why the duplex had linoleum instead of wood floors like they had at home.

"Linoleum's cheaper," her father told her.

"Are they going to be poor, the people who live here?"

"No, they won't be poor. . . . But some people don't have as much money as us. Young couples, for instance, starting out. They need something less expensive."

"They're going to pay *us* to live here," Susie shouted. "This is *our* house. We have two, no, *three* houses now."

The roof was on one Sunday and then the stucco men came and made it look like a sand castle. Afterwards it was painted a cheery yellow color with white trim. There were bushes planted all around the duplex and finally a faint breath of green over the lawn where they'd put in the grass seed.

And then one day they came and it was all done. Everything. It was hard to remember that a while ago it had just been a bunch of trees. It looked as if it had been there forever.

That day they had fried chicken and potato salad and Kool-Aid in one of the new kitchens that smelled like paint and a little still like sawdust, and Susie's father said, "All we have to do now is find some people to live here."

"I hope they'll be nice," said her mother.

Her father showed Susie the advertisement in the paper and then the phone calls started. Every evening her mother or father had to drive all the way out there to show the duplex to people who might want to live there. When they came home they were tired. Something was always wrong with the people somehow. Susie began to sense worry in her parents' voices when they talked about the duplex.

"Do you think we built in the wrong area?"

"The land was so cheap, but it's not exactly a middle-class community."

"I'm afraid they wouldn't keep it up."

"They had two dogs."

"No, we don't want dogs."

Finally a young married couple with a baby moved into one of the units and her parents grew more cheerful. And one night her father came home with the news that there was another family interested in the other unit.

Susie's mother was against them. "Three children, Jack! The place only has two bedrooms."

"I know, I know. But it's not really our business, is it, if they don't mind being cramped. The man moved his family out here from Nevada looking for a job, got one and then was laid off. He's just found another. They're pretty desperate for housing—they've been living in a motel since they arrived."

"You're too soft-hearted, Jack, they'll just be trouble.... Do they have girls or boys?"

"Three girls. The oldest one is nine, Susie's age. I can't help it, Emma, I feel sorry for them."

Susie was listening and took her father's part. "I want them," she said. She liked the idea of a girl her age living in the duplex. It would be somebody to play with when they went down there.

"I suppose it will only be temporary," her mother said uncertainly.

"Just until he gets back on his feet."

The Huckle family was already moved in the next time Susie and her family drove down to the duplex. They seemed to be expected; the Huckles were dressed in their Sunday best and had cookies and potato chips to offer, as well as beer for the adults.

Susie couldn't believe it. They were huge, all of them except the one girl, Una. She wanted to say something nasty to John, like, "Lucky they don't have much furniture, they can use each other for couches," but her mother gave her a pinch that meant *be polite.*

The duplex unit looked really tiny now with so many people, so many fat people, in it. Mrs. Huckle, in a sleeveless floral dress that made her arms bulge out like boa constrictors eating rabbits, shuffled around, pushing cookies at them and introducing her daughters.

"This here's Bernice Almira, and Dorothy Jolene, and here's my oldest, Una Eunice."

The younger girls looked a lot like their mother. They were wearing dresses without any waist and their little thick legs were stuffed into faded old tennis shoes. They scuffled and bumped each other and looked at their hands and said hello in squeaky voices.

Una Eunice was different. She was almost taller than her mother and was as thin as a chair leg. Her face was long and bony with a straight nose and wide mouth. She looked more like an adult than any child Susie had ever seen. Una too was wearing a dress, but it hung on her like ruffled curtains and was cinched around her middle with a wide black patent leather belt.

She didn't say hello. She said, right at Susie, in the snottiest way, "I've got a monkey."

Everybody looked at Mr. Huckle, a tall, red-faced and unhappy man with a stomach that hung like pillows over his belt. He coughed.

"She does have a monkey," he said finally. "But it's not here."

Susie's mother murmured a little anxiously, "You know we don't allow animals . . . that's just one of the things we decided. . . . "

Mrs. Huckle looked like she was going to bash Una. She whined, "Her uncle owns a pet shop and gave it to her. But we made her give it back before we left Nevada."

"It's still *mine*," Una said resentfully.

"Everybody should have a monkey," laughed Susie's father in his friendly way.

"Can I have one, Daddy?" John wanted to know.

"Susie," said her mother. "Maybe you and John and the girls could go outside and get to know each other."

Susie didn't like Una pretending to show them around.

"I was here before you," she said. "I remember when this place was just a hole in the ground."

"Who cares?" said Una, taking out a pair of dice from her pocket and jiggling them in her palm. "This is nowheres, anyway. This isn't Nevada."

Susie was stumped for a minute. She didn't even think she knew where Nevada was. "Well, I have my own bedroom at our house. And besides, this is *our* duplex where you live. We could live here ourselves if we wanted to."

"No skin off my back," said Una, squatting and shaking the dice out on the sidewalk.

Susie was intrigued. She watched Bernice Almira and Dorothy Jolene go tittering off into the bushes beside the duplex and start to play some pretend game with twigs and dirt. They looked like Tweedle-Dum and Tweedle-Dee with their little chubby legs and round faces. John was ignoring them, rolling his truck down the driveway.

"How come you're so skinny and they're so fat?" she asked, staring fascinated at Una's long fingers shaking the dice.

A look of cunning appeared on Una's little adult face. Her eyes were the funniest shade of green, like limeade or something cool and artificial.

"Cause I'm adopted. This isn't my *real* family," she explained haughtily. "I was a gypsy when I was born. That's why I have a monkey."

"You aren't a gypsy," Susie said, half-believing it all the same. "Gypsies don't have blonde hair."

Una tossed the dice carefully. "No skin off my back."

"How come you always say that?"

"Cause I don't care. I don't care what you think."

After a minute Susie said, "When are you going to get your monkey back?"

Una saw that Susie meant to be friendly and leaned back on her heels. Her green eyes went dark and thrilling. "Soon as I get old enough I'm gonna find my real family. They'll be out sitting around their campfire, just waiting for me, and I'll come up and say real quiet that I've finally come back. And they'll know it's me cause I'll have my monkey with me. They'll just have been waiting for me all these years, and soon as I come we'll go around the world like in a circus. We'll have trained elephants and wild jungle tigers and lions and I'm going to be their acrobatic and walk on a tightrope and fly through the air. Everybody will scream, they'll be so scared I might fall. But I'll never fall, never ever. Never," Una repeated with intense satisfaction, rolling the dice.

*

"Well," said Susie's mother when they were back in the Chevy and driving away.

"I think they'll keep the place up," said her father. "They seem pretty reliable."

"They sure are fat," said John.

"Except Una. She's adopted. She's really a gypsy and she's going to be an acrobatic when she grows up and goes back to her real family."

Susie's mother sighed. "It's really sad, isn't it? I don't know. It just seems sad to me somehow."

They didn't go as often now to the duplex, only once a month to collect the rent. After the first time, Susie's mother didn't come anymore. She said something about it depressed her too much. John didn't like to go either, so after awhile it was just Susie and her father making the trip.

Every time it was the same. They went inside and had cookies and then Una and Susie went out while her father talked to Mr. and Mrs. Huckle and had a beer. Every time Susie asked Una about her monkey and every time Una told her about her gypsy life to come. Then they played games with Una's dice just like real gypsies.

One day, driving home again, Susie's father seemed quieter than usual. He said, "You like Una a lot, don't you, Susie?"

"I guess I never met anybody like her before."

Her father drove on silently for a moment. The poetry signs of places were all around them. Then he said, "Una's father lost his job this week."

"How come?"

Her father shook his head. "It's hard to explain. Sometimes businesses hire a lot of people just for a while. To do something they need done right then. But after it's done they don't need the people anymore, so they let them go."

The sign for Rossmoor flashed past. It was one of Susie's favorites. It showed a man and a woman smiling in front of a bright blue door. "Live the Good Life at Rossmoor," it said.

"Can you lose your job?"

"Oh I could. Sure. But it's not likely. I have something my company needs, that not many people have. It's what I went to college to study."

"Didn't Mr. Huckle go to college?"

"I guess not."

"He's not so smart as you, is he, Daddy?"

"Maybe, maybe not. That doesn't mean he shouldn't be able to find a job."

Susie thought about this a little.

"I'm going to college, aren't I?"

"You certainly will if you want to."

"Will Una go?"

"Una seems to be a very intelligent young girl. A little given to daydreaming possibly. . . . "

"She's going to walk the tightrope in her real family's circus and she's never going to fall, she told me so."

Her father laughed, then sighed. "It's hard to stay up there sometimes," he said.

The next time Susie and her father went to collect the rent from the Huckles they found the duplex very still and dark with the curtains drawn. After a long wait, Una came to the door. She looked very pale and skinny in her cinched-in dress. Her face was frightened and haughty at the same time.

"My parents had to go out. They're sorry, but could you come back next week."

"Certainly we can," her father said cheerfully. "No problem."

But driving home he would hardly say anything.

The next week nobody answered the door. It was scary, somehow, to see the drapes too tightly shut. They went next door to the young couple's unit. Frank the husband was watching TV and his wife Marianne was feeding the baby a bottle. Susie's father asked politely if they had seen Mr. Huckle lately.

"Sure," Frank said. "He's always at home now. Isn't his car out in front? I thought I heard them all just a while ago."

Susie's father thanked them. As he and Susie went by the door to the Huckles' unit she saw him look down at the keys in his hand. Then they went and got in their Chevy. Mr. Huckle's old station wagon was parked right in front of them.

"It can't go on like this, Jack," Susie heard her mother say later that evening.

"He's bound to find a job soon."

"You told me Frank said he was always there. He can't be looking very hard."

Her father just looked miserable.

Susie was sitting in front of the TV with John, but she was reading her book of poems. She had found one she liked, about a bird. She didn't understand it very well, but read the lines over and over:

> *"Like one in danger, cautious*
> *I offered him a crumb*
> *And he rolled his feathers*
> *And rowed him softer home*
>
> *Than oars divide the ocean*
> *Too silver for a seam*
> *Or butterflies off banks of noon*
> *Leap plashless as they swim."*

Susie wanted to ask what "plashless" meant or tell them that somehow this poem reminded her of Una, but her mother was talking again, very quick and soft.

"Jack, please be reasonable. How can we pay our loan back if we can't even collect the rent? We're not rich. Do you want me to talk to them? I can."

"No," her father said finally. "It's my fault. I'll do it."

A few days later Susie looked out the front window and saw all the Huckles getting out of their station wagon in front of her house. She charged out to greet Una.

"Come on," she shouted. "I'll show you my room."

Una was dressed in the same dress she always wore. She almost smiled when she saw Susie but then her face went stiff and grown-up. She looked at the rest of the Huckles, lined up against the car like heavy bowling ball pins. The wagon was loaded to the brim with boxes; there were even mattresses piled on top.

"Can't," she said briefly.

"Yes you can, can't she?" Susie appealed to Mr. Huckle.

"All right."

Delighted, Susie grabbed Una's hand and pulled her along back to the house.

"Lo, Una," said Susie's father, coming out on the porch with the newspaper still in his hand. He stared past them at the Huckles as if they were the last people he wanted to see.

Una gave him a fierce stare but allowed Susie to drag her into the house.

There was so much Susie wanted to show her friend: her dollhouse, her row of books, her chest of toys.

"This is all yours?" Una asked suspiciously.

"Come on, sit down on the bed." For some reason, the first thing Susie pushed at Una was *Favorite Poems, Old and New.* "This is what I got for my birthday. It's poems."

Una looked at it without interest. She stared around at the gaily wallpapered room with its shiny maple furniture for a minute, then went to the window.

"Read this," Susie persisted. "It's about a hurt bird, and butterflies."

"We're going to Nevada," Una said. "I get to have my monkey back."

"What? You can't leave. You live in California now. You live in our duplex."

"We can't live there now. Your dad is making us leave."

Susie joined Una at the window. Out on the sidewalk Mr. Huckle was talking and raising and lowering his hand in a jerky way. All Susie's father was doing was nodding. He was still in his business suit from work and looked much younger than Mr. Huckle in his white tee shirt and khaki pants, with his belly drooping out between them.

The two girls watched as Susie's mother joined them on the sidewalk. She too looked young and thin next to the shabby fatness of Mrs. Huckle and her two daughters. All of a sudden Susie looked at Una in her old floppy ruffled dress with the patent leather belt. She didn't understand why she felt so bad. She felt exactly like the look she could see on her father's face, shamed and impatient and sorry all at once. She didn't understand why Una had to look that way and why she didn't want to read the bird poem and why they were going to Nevada. She felt sorry she had even asked Una to come in and see her room.

"No skin off my back," said Una, turning away from the scene on the sidewalk. It was terrible; Mrs. Huckle was crying and clenching her pocketbook and Bernice and Dorothy were sobbing too. Mr. Huckle was shouting and Susie's mother was looking around nervously and Susie's father was just standing there.

Una began to talk very fast, her green eyes getting hot and cold at the same time. "When I get my monkey back I'm going to teach it to do billions of tricks and we're going to go on TV and I'll be so rich I'll buy a huge house and a million dresses and everything I want."

"I thought you were going to be an acrobatic? When you find your real family."

"You stupid," Una shouted suddenly. "They are my real family." Una stared at her and all around the room with hatred. "You think you're so good just because you live here. Well I'm going to live in a house a million times bigger than this, and I'm going to—"

"Una," said Susie's mother, coming to the door. "You're going to have to leave now, dear. You father's getting ready to go."

"Yes, ma'am," Una said and walked stiffly past her. Susie tried to follow.

"Susie, I think you should stay in here for now."

"But Mom." She was passionate. "I'll never see Una again."

Her mother shook her head. They both went to the window and watched Una get in the car, squeezing her thin body in among her sisters and all the boxes. They saw Susie's father standing helplessly on the sidewalk, the newspaper still in his hand. Then the station wagon with its load of mattresses and people was gone.

"I'm sorry, Susie. I'm really sorry. It's our fault, I know that now. We were never meant to be landlords, to have that kind of power over people. We just don't know much about people less lucky than ourselves."

"Una said they *are* her real family."

"I know."

She made a move to embrace her daughter, but Susie broke away. It was the worst thing she had ever felt, this knowledge rising in her, like butterflies in the pit of her stomach, that people were different from each other and that some were not lucky, and that all her life, starting now, she was going to have to watch people like Una walk on a tightrope and, sometimes, watch them fall.

Starfish

Kevin and Kate sat on the beach, waiting for their uncle to emerge from the sea. It was late in the afternoon of a hot day, that time when the salty sparkling grittiness begins to disappear, to be replaced by a windy white calm. Most of the crowds had disappeared, limping burnt and tired back to their cars. The beach had been transformed and so had the ocean. It was no longer a green mobius strip rippling frothily end over end next to the shore, but something enormous, endless, stretching to Japan and China, a solid if permeable world full of mysterious things that never saw the light of day.

Their Uncle Jeff from Michigan had a harpoon and a snorkle and was somewhere inside the sea, searching.

They had watched Lloyd Bridges in *Seahunt* so they knew how people in black rubber gear let themselves be lowered down off boats; they had seen on television the expressions under the face masks, the bubbles that signaled fear or astonishment. They had seen in black and white enormous schools of fish surround the diver like leaves swirling in autumn; they'd known when he was in danger from sharks and other fish with sharp, gaping mouths.

Now Uncle Jeff, a social worker and an artist, who was visiting, their mother said, to forget something that had happened to him and who didn't have a job, was inside the ocean looking for what he might find.

On the shore Kevin and Kate discussed this.

"The big fish don't live here, they live way out. He won't

get a big fish," said Kate authoritatively. She was nine and could swim like a fish herself; whenever they went to the beach she would stay in the water the whole time, making it part of her. Making it belong to her.

"He *might*." Kevin, ever hopeful, lived in a world of possibility that his sister could not jar him out of, only use to her own advantage when she wanted to tell stories.

Now she changed tactics. "A big fish will hook on to his harpoon and take him miles and miles away, to the place where the big fish live. It's an underwater castle made of red coral with a beautiful lawn of shells and statues all around of mermaids. The plants are wavy and the pictures on the wall change all the time because they're just coral frames and anybody who wants can swim into them and sit and be a portrait."

"He'll be the king."

"No! He'll be a prisoner until he marries a fish, but at first he won't want to do that. He'll say, 'She's too slimy and her eyes are bulging out,' and they'll put him in a jail cell until he says yes."

"Will they have babies?"

"Fishbabies! Yuck! But maybe they'll be cute. They'll have his head and her tail and they can swim all day and never go to school. They can come and visit us."

"Then he'll be the king."

"But he must pay the price," Kate said. She liked how that sounded and said it again. "He must pay the price."

At long last they saw the snorkle coming towards them and their uncle fighting the waves at the shore. When he rose they saw his pale upper body with a streak of sunburn on the shoulders. He was carrying a mesh bag filled with something and was huffing.

"Look," he said, and spread his catch out for them on sticky wet black sand. There were five starfish, white and pinkish on the outside, with tiny bead-like suckers on the inside and a feathery little gate in the center.

"Did you harpoon them?" Kevin asked.

Uncle Jeff laughed. "No, I just picked them up. They're still alive. See?"

The starfishes' small gates wafted gently. They were so crisp and hard to be taking breath.

"We'll take them home and boil them and then put them out to dry."

Kate had done that once to some shells, but after whoever lived in the shells had already gone away. The starfish had no place to go.

"Can't we put them back?" she suddenly asked.

"But they'll be so pretty," said Uncle Jeff. "Once they're dry."

Their mother was expecting fish for dinner, not starfish for decoration. She said they couldn't use any of her pots to boil them, the starfish would just have to dry up on their own on the patio. Uncle Jeff sighed and said they would be better if they were boiled, to take away the smell, but then he took some newspaper and put them on it. They were probably already dead then. He cleaned the sand off them and said they would be nice as paperweights. Their mother said, "Oh Jeff."

Once Uncle Jeff had been an artist. That was in the old days when he was young. He went to the Art Institute of Chicago and painted watercolors. Afterwards he put the paintings in Grandma's house in Illinois and one day a storm came and then a flood and all the pictures floated around in the basement and dissolved. Then he got a Masters in Social Work and became a social worker. His job was to go around and interview pregnant women on welfare. He also had to drive a taxi then and that was too much. In the middle of the story somewhere he got married to a lady who was mean to him. That's what their mother said anyway. Their father said he had had a Breakdown.

Now he didn't work and lived with Grandma and everything would be all right if he just took his pills.

Uncle Jeff was handsome and tall and knew a lot of things. He said different things than their parents and he didn't agree with them. "Polly," he said to their mother, "There are other ways of looking at the world."

What other ways? That was what Kate wanted to know. In school last year they had studied about the Navajo Indians. They made a hogan in their schoolroom and the boys went out to the playground to hunt and the girls stayed in to grind corn with little stone pestles. The Navajos believed there were spirits in the world, dead people's spirits and animal spirits. They had a man who talked to the spirits and gave them what they wanted to put their souls at rest.

Uncle Jeff talked to spirits too. Kate had heard him at night in the living room where he was sleeping on the couch. He had conversations with nobody and sometimes he cried.

"He can't get over her," she heard her mother telling her father.

"But it's been over a year now," said her father. "When is he going to pull himself together?"

"If he just takes his pills. Mother said he's all right if he just takes his pills."

Kate felt them watching Uncle Jeff. They watched him when he ate and when he drove the car. They asked him where he was going. "Out for a walk." They asked him how he slept, her mother asked him if he was taking his pills. "Yes, Polly."

They never asked him what he thought. But Kate asked him.

"Who are you talking to, Uncle Jeff, at night when you can't sleep?"

"Ghosts," he said and smiled. "People whose voices I hear in my head."

"Is it God?" Kate's mother had told her that in the Bible God talked to people, to Abraham and Samuel.

"No, I don't think so," Uncle Jeff said.

Uncle Jeff didn't go to church with them. He read the paper and smoked. He took the car and went on drives or around the neighborhood walking. Their neighbor Mrs. Hood told their mother that Uncle Jeff was talking to himself when he went by her house. Their mother said, "He was fine until his wife left

him. The doctor said it created a kind of break with reality.
But he takes pills for it."

The starfish had dried but they had a terrible smell. Suzy
the dog got ahold of one of them and carried it around the yard
and tore the leg off it. It was rotten and a little powdery.

"You should have let me boil them, Polly," said Uncle Jeff.
His voice was calm but angry.

"I can't just turn my life upside down for you, Jeff," their
mother said, and she was angry too. "I want you to throw
those starfish away, they're not coming inside this house."

"Fine," he said and then he started screaming. "You and
Mother, you're both the same. Always telling me what to do,
always watching me. That's the reason you're glad Harriet left
me. You couldn't stand me having a different life than you.
You couldn't stand me leaving the church and painting, you
couldn't stand me living alone in Chicago with my friends and
studying, you couldn't stand Harriet being an actress, what
she stood for. You want everyone to live like you, safe and
stupid and narrow-minded in your stupid narrow-minded
church."

"Jeff," said their mother dangerously. "Have you taken
your pills?"

"No, I haven't fucking taken my pills," he shouted and
stomped out the door.

That night he talked worse than ever to himself in the living
room. He was talking to Harriet, Kate knew now. Harriet who
was an actress and who had left him and made him break with
reality. His voice rose and fell and he cried, and once her
mother went in to try to say something, but it was like he
didn't hear her.

In the morning he was sleeping or lying there and wouldn't
get up. Kate and Kevin went and looked at him on the couch.
His lips were dry and there was a powdery white dust at the

corners. His eyes were blank and had nothing behind them. It was like he had turned into a ghost.

He lay there all day and late in the afternoon an ambulance came to get him, to take him back to Michigan, said their mother, who had talked to Grandma on the phone and agreed it was all because he didn't take his pills.

The starfish sat for a long time on a shelf in the garage and gradually their smell got fainter and fainter. Their family went to the beach a few more times that summer and Kate stood in the waves shoulder-high and let them rock her. Out in the ocean the big fish swam and carried prisoners away to their rock coral castle and posed in frames when they wanted pictures, but the ocean was a flood that carried things away and Kate never went very deep. She always wanted to see the shore.

Crater Lake

" **M**ount Mazama was once an icy peak that towered 12,000 feet over the Oregon landscape for perhaps millions of years. Then one day, about 7,000 years ago, it blew, spreading darkness and ash as far away as Canada. Pumice, magma, and ash poured out and down through the valleys. When it was all over, the top half of the mountain had collapsed in upon itself, creating a chasm six miles across and 4,000 feet deep. This isn't actually a crater but a 'cauldera.' A cauldron."

Kate's index finger trailed the water anxiously. She was careful not to lean too far out of the launch as the guide made his speech. The blue color of the lake was as unreal up close as it was from the ridge looking down, as artificial as the water on a printed map of the world, awash with tiny letters like ship-wrecks: Pacific Ocean, Arabian Sea, Arctic Ocean. Once she and Kevin had played a game with their old globe: closing their eyes they'd spin it, each in turn, stopping it with a sharp punch of the finger. The town of Snowdrift in Manitoba, Guagdougou in Upper Volta, Dargan-Ata in Uzbek. It was difficult to land in Iceland or New Zealand, impossible to find Hawaii or home in the dark by chance. Most often the finger marked a watery grave.

"The lake's unusual color comes from its remarkable clarity and the way the sky not only reflects the water but penetrates it. The red and orange wave lengths are absorbed by the water molecules; the blue and green lengths are transmitted through the water, bouncing from one molecule to another in a process known as backscattering. Crater Lake holds more than four cubic miles of water; it's the deepest lake in the United States and the seventh deepest in the world, at 1,996 feet."

The guide ended with a joke to cheer them up. "Some guys having trouble with the wife get ideas out here. But don't even think of it." He putt-putted the little launch nearer the shore.

Kate looked across the boat at West, her father, and he winked. It was her cue to smile, not to think of anything bad. Of wives falling endlessly away from life through blue water. Of mothers.

It was the first time Kate and Kevin had been on a vacation alone with their father. Their mother had died in March; it was now August, the end of August, the end of the summer season.

They'd driven up from Southern California, past places like San Luis Obispo, San Simeon, Big Sur, San Francisco, to the Redwood Country, the Oregon Caves, the Rogue River. It had been a week or more of motels, hamburgers, signs that promised exciting sights miles ahead, and soft, splintery trees you could drive through.

The Chevy station wagon was packed with everything they might need, and Kevin and Kate took turns sitting in front with their father. Day after day, mile after mile they sang "I've Been Working on the Railroad" and "Michael, Row the Boat Ashore." Kate knew a lot of songs from fifth and sixth grade and the sound tracks of "Oklahoma," "Music Man," and "South Pacific," too. West knew some old Army songs: "Over here. Over there." Kevin mostly remembered Christmas carols. They sang those a lot too, especially "Jingle Bells."

They told all the knock-knock jokes they remembered and then they made them up. All the ones Kevin made up didn't make any sense, like:

"Knock-knock."

"Who's there?"

"Mary."

"Mary who?"

"Mary Derry."

Then Kevin would go off into peals of laughter, and they would join him, helplessly, even while protesting that that wasn't how it was supposed to go. But after a while it became a standing joke with them, and when they were tired, when dark was coming on and they were hungry and looking for a motel, they would do the knock-knock joke about Mary Derry. Mary Derry was their next door neighbor's daughter and Kate and Kevin's babysitter.

And sometimes West would say things like "The Winter family is okay, that's for sure. We're a real team. The Winter family is going to make it, all right."

Now they were at Crater Lake, in the lodge, and Kate even had her own room. True, it was tiny and connected to her father and brother's much larger one. But it was still private. And the waiter in the dining room called her Miss. Kate wondered if he guessed their family tragedy, if he wondered where her mother was, if he saw that Kate had bravely taken up her place as the woman of the family, and if that was why he was so polite to her.

Lately Kate had started to see herself from the outside. To stand a little apart from herself and look over, casually, to see the kind of impression she was making. Wherever she was she would find someone to notice and then imagine that they were watching her. She had already found two people in the launch, and they were partly the reason she was trailing her finger in the water and smiling bravely at her father.

One was a woman in her fifties, with short, no-nonsense gray hair and a tweedy coat and skirt and a cane by her side. Kate had decided she was a novelist and that she had never married, but went around by herself observing people in order to put them into her books. Whenever this woman glanced at her Kate tried to look both modest and interesting.

In many books that Kate had read the young girl went on a vacation with her family and then met a rich, elderly, eccentric woman who took an interest in the girl and left her money or gave her the encouragement to live an artistic life. The women in these books had suffered in life and were in a position to understand suffering in others.

Kate wanted a mentor.

So far, she hadn't met anyone, back home anyway, who was like that. There were the mothers of her friends in the neighborhood, and two of her mother's friends who took turns driving them to Sunday school. There were also two of her father's women friends. Mrs. Fletcher was older than her father, and Kate and Kevin had secretly laughed at her for trying to be so nice to them in order to marry their father. The other woman was named Patti and this summer they'd been over to her house a couple of times for dinner. Kate didn't like her at all. Patti had a pug nose and a frosted French twist and the most insincere smile Kate had ever seen. She could never be a mentor. She was too young and too stupid and her house was filled with Danish modern furniture with nubby orange upholstery and gilt cupids on the walls holding plastic ferns and she served them dinner on TV trays in front of the television.

West had never asked Kate or Kevin if they liked Mrs. Fletcher or Patti. They were just friends from work who had them over for dinner. It didn't mean anything. There was something about tragedy that included a lot of dinners out.

The only interesting thing about Patti was that she had a son named Carl. He wasn't exactly cute though. He was six-four (he said) and skinny. He had reddish-brown freckles and the same color eyes and hair and white teeth and pitted skin from acne. He ignored Kate and Kevin the times they were over, and just went in and out of the house, saying, "See you later, Mom."

Kate wondered when she would begin to be attractive to boys. The second person she had noticed in the boat was a boy about fifteen, with his parents. He was dark-haired, blue-eyed, straight-nosed, and romantically sullen; he looked like he didn't want to be here at all. Kate hoped he would notice her own indifference to life. Later, perhaps on the climb back up to the ridge where the hotel was, he would come up behind her and say, "What are you thinking?"

And she might say something about God. Or about death.

She might say, with a quiver in her voice, that she had been thinking of that cold March day when they had buried her mother on a windy hillside overlooking the Pacific Ocean. . . .

But, disturbingly, another, clearer memory inserted itself in Kate's reverie. Of going to her homemaking class the day after the funeral and sitting around the table with the three other girls before class. One of them had asked if she'd been sick, and Kate had suddenly been unable to speak. She had clutched the yellow excuse slip in her fist, moved it slowly towards the girl. Under "Reason for Absence," it read "Mother's Funeral."

The girl took the slip and read it and passed it without a word around the table. All of them looked horrified and disgusted rather than sympathetic, as if Kate were pulling something over on them. She'd felt it so strongly that she had, for a moment, almost believed that she'd made it all up, a particularly vulgar, stupid joke that no one was going to laugh at.

She'd choked back tears then, had wanted to run from the room, had remained sitting, staring down. She'd felt accused, as if it were a nasty habit she was born with—to exaggerate misfortune, just push it a little too far so that others distrusted her rather than felt for her. She was melodramatic and somehow false, puzzlingly false. For the emotion was true at the bottom—it just got distorted coming out. The intonation, gesture; something gave Kate away, made people disgusted or embarrassed instead of comforting.

She'd seen that look a dozen times in the last two years. Passed between adults over her head, from teachers to students, from friends to friends.

As if Kate were showing off. Or as if she were playing with something ugly or forbidden. "Put that death away now."

What was it in her that kept wanting to take it out of its hiding place again and again, to touch it with the same mixture of horror and fascination, to display it slyly around to everyone?

The only two people she didn't feel that way around were her father and Kevin. They never had to talk about it, because they knew. They had been through everything together, down to the final day, when the black limousine came to their house and took them to the funeral parlor where they had sat in the balcony, like Kings and Queens at the opera, looking down on all the crying people. The sickly smell of flowers had been all around and a lamenting organ had played a lot of hymns. And someone had spoken, but Kate couldn't remember a word of it. She and Kevin had held hands and their father had bent his head and moaned and sobbed. Afterwards everybody left the funeral parlor and the three of them had to go to the coffin and look one last time.

It was awful. No one should have to do that. Look at their mother dead. She had make-up all over her patched face and her eyes were shocked under their closed lids. She didn't look one bit peaceful, she only looked strange and unfamiliar and as if she had given up and gone away, scared and alone.

The guide was telling the myth of the lake now, as they cruised up under a massive bulkhead of hardened lava, Llao Rock. The Klamath Indians, the People of the Marsh, once known as the Ouxkanee, lived between two mountains, between Good and Evil. The good place was Mount Shasta, the beautiful white mountain where the god of the upper world, Sahale Tyee, lived. The bad place was Mount Mazama (where they were now), where Llao, the god of the underworld, came up from time to time to shoot sparks into the air and rumble ominously and scare everyone.

One day the two gods began to fight and Llao threw burning rocks at Sahale Tyee, which fell upon the Klamath Indians. The elders thought the rain of fire was a punishment on them and their people for their wickedness and so they climbed the peak and leapt into the flames. Then Sahale Tyee was touched and sorry and angry too, and he drove Llao back down to where he belonged. The mountain fell in upon the Lord of Darkness and sealed his door. He was never seen again and the crater filled with quiet water.

"The Indians never came up here after that," added the guide. "It kind of gave them the creeps. It took a white man to discover the lake on June 12, 1853. John Wesley Hillman. He was looking for the Lost Cabin Mine; he came up here and looked down. He called it the Deep Blue Lake. The lake kept being discovered and given other names until Crater Lake finally stuck. It became a national park in 1902 under President Roosevelt."

Kate could see why the Indians hadn't much liked to come up here. It was kind of spooky in a way, to be floating over this blue blue water that went down into the earth so deep but was still above the sea. Even the names of the islands in the lake were eerie: Phantom Ship and Wizard Island. And the breeze that came up from the lake was icy even in the sunshine. There were still little patches of snow on the peaks around them.

Suddenly there was a commotion at the back of the launch. Somebody's kid had dropped something in the water. What was it? No one heard and then everyone did. His mother had been letting him play with the car keys, just to keep him happy. And now he'd dropped them, just like that, into a lake almost 2,000 feet deep.

That night was their last at the lodge. Tomorrow they were leaving early and taking the faster way home, two or three days of steady driving on the freeway. Before dinner Kate and Kevin went walking, collecting things to take back home: pinecones, pretty pieces of wood, specimens of dried lava. Kate had it all planned out: they would make a little museum when they came back, a kind of panorama box. They'd make two cones, one white and one black, and the black one would have its top punched down. . . .

"I get to do that, punch it down. With my fist," Kevin interrupted.

"Okay," Kate allowed. "Then somehow we'll get a cup or something and put some blue water in it, with food coloring, and then we'll stick it in there, with tape or something."

"We can make eruptions," said Kevin. "We can get firecrackers and put them inside the cones."

"No, the eruptions are over. The lake is peaceful now."

They stood looking at it. The sun was setting, making gilt-edged crimson and purple cloud-ribbons in the sky; the lake was turning golden too. From this distance it looked like a cauldron of boiling gold. The white bits of unmelted snow were like flecks of metal thrown up around the lake's steep sides.

"It's lava," Kate screamed suddenly. "It's going to boil up and over the sides and catch us if we don't run."

Kevin stared open-mouthed.

"Run," she screamed, tearing past him and back to the lodge. She was laughing and screaming at the same time. Kevin ran after her, getting into the spirit. "It's erupting, it's erupting," he shouted.

They ran until they came to the lodge door. The lady with the short gray hair was just coming out, leaning on her cane. She smiled at the two of them.

"Playing a game, dears?" she asked pleasantly.

Kate blushed. She remembered she was too old for this kind of stuff.

At dinner West said they could have whatever they wanted. He urged them to choose expensive things they'd never had before. Kevin still only wanted a hamburger, but Kate picked roast duckling with orange sauce. West had a Manhattan before dinner and then wine because it was the last night.

The drapes in the dining room were open on a sky that was still light purple. Kate could see the reflection of the three of them. In the window she saw she looked older. Her face didn't look so round and chubby; it looked like it had cheekbones and mystery. Her hair with its cowlick was soft and full, not just messy, as usual. She was wearing the blue suit she'd worn to her mother's funeral. She looked like an adult, a young lady. The waiter called her Miss and served her first. She exaggerated her movements, did dainty things with her mouth.

"Dad," said Kevin. "Kate keeps looking at herself in the window."

"I am not." Kate flushed and stared at her salad, took another roll.

West seemed preoccupied. He asked if they'd been having a good time on the trip. He said, "The Winters are all right." Kate glanced at him in the window. He'd lost weight, but his classic, fleshy features and cleft chin were still strong. His wavy brown hair combed back and smooth with Brillcream made him look very handsome. "Yeah, yeah, the Winters are a good old team." He seemed like he was nervous. He didn't even notice that Kevin was picking apart his food in that weird way he had, as if inspecting it for termites.

"That was funny," Kate said. "When the keys fell in the lake."

"Very funny for them getting home," said West.

"They're probably still falling, don't you think? Falling all that way to the bottom?"

"Maybe."

"Knock-knock," said Kevin.

"Who's there?"

"Crater."

"Oh Dad, why doesn't he learn?"

Kevin looked hurt. "Well, I know how, I just don't want to."

"You don't know how. Your jokes are stupid."

"They are not."

"Yessir."

"Okay, kids. That's enough," said West. "Look, I've got something to tell you."

They looked at him attentively. He seemed almost scared, like he didn't know how to begin.

"You know Patti," he said. And then, "We're going to get married."

They didn't say anything. Kate's duckling came. The golden sauce was like lava covering its brown limbs. It looked like it had been trying to run away and had gotten caught. It made her sick. She couldn't eat it. Tears started coming out of her eyes, falling faster and faster.

"You kids need a mother," he said. "I need a wife. Patti will be good to you."

"She will not," Kate burst out. "I hate her."

Kevin said, "I hate her too."

"That's ridiculous," said West. "You don't even know her. She's, she's . . . a wonderful cook."

"You liar. You Hitler," said Kate, hardly able to speak.

West was shocked, then stern. "Don't you dare talk to me like that. I'll decide what's best for us. You're just a child, Kate, you can't even comb your hair straight."

"I can cook. I can cook liver," she said. "I iron your handkerchiefs." She started sobbing. She saw the little pile she made of his handkerchiefs every Sunday, how she damped them with the sprinkler and opened them out carefully on the ironing board, ironing so that the edges were straight and exact. Then she folded, ironed again and folded until the handkerchief was a perfect small square.

"That's not the point, Kate," his voice softened. "You do a lot. But you need a mother."

"I *have* a mother," she said. "She's just dead."

But he went on as if he hadn't heard her. "The last years have been hard for the Winter family. We've got to start over, make a family again. You're growing into a young lady, Kate, you need some help there. Kevin's just a little boy, he needs a mother too. This doesn't mean we're forgetting anything, it just means we have to go on."

His voice had fallen into a rhythmic pace, as if he were saying what he'd rehearsed.

Kate started pulling apart the legs and wings of her orange duckling. She still couldn't eat, but it helped to do something. Her mind was boiling. Would they have to go live in Patti's house with the Danish furniture and gilt cupids? It was too small. And Patti with her fake smile and pug nose, what would she be like if you got to know her? She wasn't like a mother.

"You shouldn't marry Patti if you want to get married," she said. "You should marry Mrs. Fletcher." She hadn't thought she liked Mrs. Fletcher all that much but suddenly she seemed a lot better than Patti. She was nice at least. She was cozy and warm and called them sonny and Katey and had photos all around her house of her dead husband, Bill. It came to Kate that they hadn't seen her all summer.

West was astonished and amused. "I thought you didn't want me to get married," he said.

"I don't," she said frantically. He made it sound like she'd lost a point in a game. "I mean, but if you have to get married, someday, you should marry someone nice."

"Patti is nice."

Kevin's tears had stopped, though he was still looking at Kate for cues. "Will Carl live with us too?" he asked.

"Yes. And we'll move to a bigger house."

"Will Suzy come too?" Suzy was the Winters' dog.

"Yes . . . "

Kate couldn't stand it. They were talking as if it had already happened, as if the decision were over. They'd never had a chance to decide. You couldn't just say, here's your new mother, that's all, now everything's going to be different. She was crying so hard she couldn't see straight, she couldn't eat, she couldn't speak.

The waiter came and looked at their plates. West motioned that he could take them away. In the glance he gave the waiter Kate saw the same complicity about her difficult, exaggerated, melodramatic behavior that adults were always giving each other. Adults, but never before her father. There was a roaring in her ears, as if a chasm were opening all around her, as if she were falling.

"If you do this," she whispered, "I'll hate you forever."

"You don't talk to your father like that, Katherine."

Frightened of losing him, of his anger, she choked out, "I'm sorry."

"That's better," he said, with an encouraging smile. "Now, what do you say to a hot fudge sundae?"

The ride home was uneventful. Kate sat in the back seat the whole way, reading and staring at her father's neck. He told some stories at first, tried to get them singing, but it was no use. Finally he just drove. As fast as he could. Back home. Back to Patti.

After the first morning Kevin asked if he could get in the

back seat too. West looked hurt but said okay. Kevin and Kate played some games by themselves and Kate read to him.

"Aren't we even going to have any knock-knock jokes?" West asked once, in the middle of the Sacramento Valley, on the second day. "Come on, Kev, let's have Mary Derry at least."

"Don't want to," he said, possibly offended that his punch line was so well-known.

"I have one," said Kate suddenly. Her chest felt tight and filled with something hot and liquid.

"Great," said West, beaming. "Let's hear it."

"Knock-knock."

"Who's there?"

"Death."

A pause, then, quietly, "Death who?"

"Just death, that's all."

"Very funny, Kate," her father said after another pause. "Very goddamned funny."

How to Fix a Roof

When my cousins and I were little, Aunt Jane and Ma used to joke that we kids had been exchanged in the cradle. They said I should have belonged to Aunt Jane, and Carrie and Darryl to Ma. I always reminded them that I was younger than my cousins, so how could there have been a mix-up?

When I got older I started to understand.

Not that I don't like my mother. I love her better than almost anyone, but she's different from me, or I guess I'm different from her, since she was here first. I mean, look at her: she's tiny and jumpy and always has a quick put-down and an opinion or two or three or a hundred on everything. She wears glasses and has wiry brown and gray hair that she sticks behind her ears when she's thinking. She's organized and political and involved in every cause that comes along, and as far back as I can remember, she's always been like that. Dad's sort of the same way, though he's quieter, and they get along in what Aunt Jane calls a "neurotically wholesome" way.

Aunt Jane's divorced, like I'd probably be if I was forty-eight and not fourteen. We're tall and red-haired and stubborn and we can't get along with anybody, even though underneath we're pretty nice people. Ma calls us "moody." That's her way of getting back for being called "practical." I used to ask her what she meant by "moody." She always said, "Your Aunt Jane."

Aunt Jane is an artist, though, like I want to be, and I think it's good for artists to be moody. I mean, they have to sit and plan out what they're going to do, and they can't always be worrying about how many people they invited for dinner and what to feed them, or who to call if the toilet gets stopped up, or what new awful thing the government is plotting. It gets in the way of their concentration.

That's what Aunt Jane says when Ma tries to talk her into something, like going door to door to stop the arms build-up, or making cookies for a bake sale to benefit somebody. "I have more important ways to spend my time, Madeleine," she says. "And don't bother making me feel guilty either."

Cause Ma is good at that. "More important things than peace?" she shrieks.

I tried to tell Ma once that carrying picket signs interfered with my concentration too, but she told me I was too young to have any concentration and what kind of world did I want to grow up in anyway?

When I go over to Aunt Jane's house she leaves me alone. I go right to my part of her studio and start laying out my paints. Her studio is in the attic, the whole length and width of the old house that Ma and she grew up in and that Aunt Jane has lived in on and off during her whole life. It's so quiet up there and you can see across the lake to a little island where Aunt Jane and Ma used to picnic as kids, and the sunlight comes in, through the big glass windows that frame one whole wall. We can work there for hours and then, when it gets dark, we'll take our pictures downstairs and prop them up against the sofa (which is spotted with paint already so it doesn't matter) and discuss them.

Aunt Jane cares what I think, she says I have a good eye for color, unlike Ma who asks me, "Is this punk or what, these plastic pink shoes and where'd you get that purple sweater, good god, with your red hair!" After we're done looking at the paintings, Aunt Jane has a glass of Scotch and I have some milk and sometimes we eat smoked oysters and cheese and crackers, which is all Aunt Jane has around.

Sometimes Aunt Jane tells me stories and they're always different from the ones Ma tells me. Ma's version of her early life is that she was a good student and wanted to become a nuclear physicist but then she met Arnie (my dad) and he was a radical and a pacifist so she realized she should do something else. Like cause trouble. To hear her talk you'd think she never was a kid at all or had any fun because she was too worried.

But Aunt Jane has other memories. Like how Ma got sent home from school for putting tar on the teacher's seat and how she used to hang out in the bathroom rolling her hair for hours. And also how the two of them were always together in the summer, swimming and rowing to the island for picnics and trying to catch fish with safety pins.

Ma has never denied any of this, but she sighs when I bring the stories up and says, "Oh that was so long ago." And she says that Aunt Jane should never have moved back to that house after Grandma died because there are too many memories... and besides, it has a leaking roof, it always did, and someday Jane'll fall down those attic stairs and break her neck like Grandma (Grandma just broke her hip, but then she got pneumonia in the hospital, so Ma considers it the same thing).

What I like best though is when Aunt Jane tells me stories of her life before she came back here, when she lived in Paris and Tokyo and Los Angeles, "when it was still a nice city, hardly smoggy at all."

"I wish I was an artist in Paris," I said.

"But I was never an artist there, just a bum, we were both bums, it was lovely." Later on Harry, my ex-uncle, got a job in Tokyo with the government. "Never marry a bureaucrat," Aunt Jane warned me, "even when they appear to be a bum at first."

"I'm never getting married," I said.

"Good girl."

Ma always says, "Oh, you'll grow out of *that*."

In Los Angeles Aunt Jane started to paint and got a little famous, she says because of her red hair and her mean personality, but also I think because of her work. Even Ma is proud of her, in her way, especially since Aunt Jane moved back to our city. "Jane Delorio?" I'd heard her tell someone. "She's my sister."

She's my *aunt,* I thought, and then felt ashamed. It was like I was happier to be connected to Aunt Jane than my own mother.

Because I don't want to make Ma jealous, a lot of times after I come home from Aunt Jane's I make a special effort to help her address envelopes and make phone calls. But my heart just isn't in it. I'm too excited thinking about the painting I finished and what Aunt Jane said and all the things I want to do in life and all the places I want to go.

Sometimes Ma looks sad and says, "I suppose you won't be hanging around here much longer, will you? You'll be off to New York or someplace in a couple of years."

When Aunt Jane suggests that I study in New York I get thrilled, but when Ma says it, I feel guilty. "I could go to art school here," I tell her.

"I don't want to hold you back," she says, but I know she's thinking of Carrie and Darryl, my cousins, and how they're such loyal and unimaginative kids, even if they're not half political enough, that they'd never think of leaving town except for a vacation to Hawaii.

Carrie is getting a graduate degree in the School of Engineering and Darryl has a job in a bike co-op. We used to row out to the island when we were little, but now I hardly see them except on holidays. Ma says they are very bright, but I think they're boring. Aunt Jane sometimes gets mixed up and calls them "Carryl" and "Darrie."

I had just started the ninth grade when things changed. Even though it's only been a few days now, everything seems different. Maybe if I write all the changes down first it won't be so hard later on to explain them. Ma calls this prioritizing but I don't know what's most important so I'll just make a list.

1. Ma went to jail.
2. Aunt Jane fell down the attic stairs and broke her ankle.
3. A big storm blew away some of Aunt Jane's roof.
4. I learned something useful.

You see what I mean about prioritizing? This is sort of the

order everything happened in, but some things happened in-
dependently and some things happened because of other
things.

Everything was important.

But to start out, I'd have to say that having Ma in jail was
the most exciting thing. It's because of something she did last
summer, when she and a bunch of her friends were arrested
for "resisting arrest." At the time I wondered how, if she were
really resisting, she could get arrested, but I guess the judge
didn't see it that way.

"The Constitution allows for peaceful assembly," he said at
the trial. "There were hundreds of people at this demonstra-
tion, most of whom dispersed without incident. Only five of
you decided you had to make an issue of it by striking members of the police force."

"I'm never going limp again," shouted Ma unexpectedly. "I
wish I'd given him two black eyes. Calling me an old lady who
should be home knitting!"

So on top of two weeks for resisting arrest she got another
one for contempt. The judge said she should be ashamed of
herself.

Aunt Jane sat beside me at the trial, groaning loudly and
muttering, "Madeleine you fool," but when I asked her
whether she thought Ma was a disgrace to the family, like the
judge said, Aunt Jane said, "Certainly not. I'm very proud of
her. He's the one who's a disgrace."

She told me I should stay with my dad in his hour of need,
but as soon as she got home she fell down the attic stairs and
broke her ankle and I had to go over there anyway, which is
what I really wanted to do.

I don't think Dad has ever known an hour of need in his
life. He's too busy going to meetings and there are even more
of them since Ma went to jail. He's pretty happy about the
whole thing, he says it reminds him of the Sixties.

But anyway, Aunt Jane was in a terrible lot of pain from her
ankle and the doctor said she had to stay off it for at least two
weeks. Fortunately both Carrie and Darryl happened to be in
Hawaii so it was up to me to take care of her. I brought over all

my stuff and started baking cookies right away. I have made thousands of cookies in my short life, mostly for Ma's benefits, and consider it one of my great accomplishments, next to basketball and painting.

I thought it was going to be wonderful staying with Aunt Jane and having her all to myself for two weeks, and after she ate some of my chocolate chip cookies she thought so too. We planned how we would turn the living room into a studio and rig up her easel so she could paint sitting down. It was too late to do anything about it that first night though, especially since we'd eaten so many cookies, so we decided to wait until the next day.

Just as I was lying down to go to sleep upstairs I started to hear the wind getting really loud. The big trees near the house were howling like wolves with sore, cracking throats. The windows rattled and clattered and an unfastened one in the bathroom kept banging open and shut. Then the rain came down, sheets of it like thick, hard plastic with a knife edge, cutting slashes in the night. Slash, crash, bang, rattle, boom. I liked hearing all the noises, curled up under Grandma's quilt, snug and warm. I even heard the lake a few blocks away, slapping like thunder on the shore.

When I woke up the next morning it was still raining, not so hard, more like the usual Northwest blecko. I could have almost forgotten about the storm except that when I came running out to the bathroom (being as usual late for school), I saw a stream of water gurgling down the attic steps. For a minute I just watched it, fascinated by the artistic way it pooled itself up on each step before making the next descent, like a waterfall in a Japanese garden—then it occurred to me that so much water wouldn't just come from anywhere except an overflowing bathtub or the sky, and there wasn't a bathtub in the attic. There was only Aunt Jane's studio.

Or what had been Aunt Jane's studio. I couldn't believe that I'd slept through what must have happened up there during the night. There were overturned chairs and boxes; the easel was lying on its side like a fallen scarecrow; there was a pool of rainbow-colored water an inch deep in the middle, with sketch-boats sailing back and forth in the wind. There was a gap the size of the couch in the roof and it was letting in the rainy sky like there was a shower nozzle up there.

I didn't even stop to think. I rushed crazily down the wet stairs screaming, "Aunt Jane, everything's ruined. The roof is gone, the roof is gone. Your paintings are *ruined*."

"If I hadn't been taking codeine," said Aunt Jane later that day, "you would have given me a heart attack."

I couldn't understand what was wrong with her, why she just opened her eyes and looked at me like I was somebody in a dream.

"I thought you were a dream," she said. "I wish you had been."

Finding I couldn't wake her I raced back upstairs to try to save whatever I could. It seemed hopeless at first. Even the paintings hanging on the walls were damp; even the sketches lying on the still upright table were soggy and mushed together. Still, I did what I could; I started staggering down the slippery steps, the heavy canvases in my arms. It was only when I dropped one that Aunt Jane woke up.

"Rosa!" I heard her call. "What's going on up there?"

This time I was more careful. "Uh, nothing, Aunt Jane. Just a little . . . rain."

In trying to pick up the canvas I somehow pushed it over the bannisters of the main staircase. It settled with a final crash at the bottom of the stairs, right where Aunt Jane could see it.

"Flaming Venus!" she gasped. I thought she was cursing maybe, but it turned out to be the name of the poor painting, a prizewinner she was getting ready to ship to a museum in Dallas. Soggy Venus would have been better now.

"Aunt Jane," I said, appearing suddenly to prevent her making any fast moves of rescue or anger. "Your roof's leaking."

"It's always leaking," she said, attempting to stand and falling back with a cry of pain. "But why are you throwing my painting around?"

"I mean, it's really leaking this time. I mean, it's sort of gone."

That whole morning is a bad memory. I ran back and forth, trying to save as many paintings as possible, while Aunt Jane rolled around like a wounded cow on the sofa and shouted directions. "Don't drop anything!" And then she would cry, "Oh, why did I break my ankle? Oh, why didn't I get that roof fixed? Oh, why why why do these things happen to me?"

I wished so much I had Ma to call up. She would have been mad and blamed it all on Aunt Jane, but she also would have known what to do. I kept trying to think of what that would be.

"Maybe you should call somebody, some roof-fixer," I said, on one of my trips down.

"I don't know any."

"Look in the Yellow Pages!"

But the next time I came into the living room with a wad of sketches and a five-by-six canvas, she was still sitting there, carefully sponging droplets of water off the heavy dried oil surface of "Window on the Skagit."

I was glad she'd stopped groaning but I still wanted some help. Plus she'd never asked me about my paintings (they were mostly okay). I hardened my heart. "Well, what'd they say?"

"I can't call," she said abstractedly. "I can't concentrate."

"Oh here," I said, grabbing the phonebook from her side. "I'll call."

"I can't stand talking to those kind of people anyway," she muttered. "I've never been able to deal with them. That's why I have an agent. Oh god, what's *she* going to say?"

"Résumés, retirement, rockeries, roofs, roofings. There are millions of them."

I started dialing at random.

"Hello," I said. "We need a roof, I mean, the old one blew away and it's a terrible mess."

"Tell them I don't have much money," Aunt Jane commanded.

"We want it done cheap and as soon as possible."

Aunt Jane yelled in my ear, "Right away."

"Friday?" I said. "Can't you come today? No, I'll try calling some other places."

"This would have to happen when your mother's in jail," said Aunt Jane.

"Well, it did," I said. "So it's up to us."

But really it was up to me since Aunt Jane was back to dabbing at and murmuring over her paintings. Finally I got a roofing person to agree to come over in the early afternoon.

"By that time we could fix it ourselves," said Aunt Jane, who still thought she had a right to an opinion. "Are you sure it's as bad as you say, Rosa? I have some big plastic bags in the basement . . . maybe you could just get on a ladder and stick them in the cracks . . . "

"You must be crazy," I said, hearing Ma's voice come out of my mouth."

The roofers showed up about two in the afternoon. By that time I'd moved everything in the studio down to the living room. It turned out that only one painting (that Aunt Jane had never really liked) was badly damaged, but Aunt Jane, instead of being glad, just got more and more distracted. "The work of months," she kept saying. "The work of years."

She was completely into it, and I couldn't help remembering how Ma always said she was too dramatic.

"I don't go around punching cops, Madeleine."

It wasn't that I didn't like either of them being dramatic, but for the first time I started wishing for a little sense and know-how. I was an artist too. How come I got stuck with the details?

The roofers were two guys in overalls and punk band T-shirts. One of them I knew from a long time ago. He'd been a friend of Darryl's in high school and had gone swimming with us in the summers. Aunt Jane didn't remember him at all, but

he remembered both of us. His name was Shawn, and his partner's name was Bill.

"I'm glad you finally got here," said Aunt Jane bad-
humoredly. "Thousands of dollars worth of art has been
ruined."

"It got ruined in the night," I added, so they wouldn't feel
it was their fault.

"We'll see what we can do," said Shawn cheerfully.

"I'm not spending a lot of money on this," warned Aunt
Jane.

"We can give you an estimate," Bill said. "These are sure
beautiful paintings."

But that just got Aunt Jane started again. "Why me?"

I went upstairs with them, trying to excuse my aunt. "It's
only that she broke her ankle yesterday, and my mom went to
jail and everything . . . ."

"I saw that in the papers," said Shawn. "An inspiration."

I beamed. "Yeah, she's alright."

They both whistled when they saw the roof. The hole
seemed to have gotten wider since I'd last been up there; it was
the size of a Volkswagen now. Luckily the rain had almost
stopped, but the pool in the middle of the room hadn't gotten
any smaller.

"These old houses," sighed Bill. "Nobody ever keeps them
up."

"I remember playing up here," said Shawn. "How old are
you now, Rosa? Seventeen, eighteen?"

"Fourteen," I said.

He looked disappointed. "Well, Bill, what do you think?"

Bill shook his head. "We can throw a patch on her, but it
won't hold long. The whole roof looks rotten to me."

"Don't call it her," I said.

"That's right," said Shawn hastily. I thought he had im-
proved a lot in seven or eight years. He used to be one of those
skinny boys with glasses. Now he had a gold ring in one ear.
He didn't look like a bureaucrat, or a bum either.

"Alright, Rosa," grinned Bill. "We'll need our ladder and something to get rid of this water first. You want to help?"

"Six dollars an hour," I said. I might be an artist, but I knew my value. Even if I'd never fixed a roof before.

We worked the whole afternoon, draining the water from the floor and putting up plastic over the hole. I showed them right away that I was just about as strong as they were and that I had some good ideas too. I learned a whole lot and liked it too. The only bad part was realizing that Aunt Jane was going to cause a stink over how much money it would cost to fix the roof.

"She's not very practical," I told them. It was an understatement.

"Two or three thousand dollars! But I'm only an artist. That's as much as I make in a year sometimes."

"But you must have insurance," Bill said.

We were all back in the living room, surrounding the sofa where Aunt Jane lay like a martyr with her foot in a cast and a moody look on her face. "Oh shit," she said. "I was planning some kind of trip in the spring. Why do these things have to happen to me?"

Once I'd thought it romantic that Aunt Jane had had so many things happen to her. I'd always compared her, favorably, to Ma, who was more likely to make things happen. For the first time I started to wonder what was wrong with Aunt Jane anyway.

We all just sat there and then Bill and Shawn got up to leave.

"Well," said Aunt Jane. "What can I do? I'm crippled, my work of half a lifetime has vanished—I might as well destroy myself financially too."

"We'll start in the morning," said Bill, and Shawn smiled at me. "And if Rosa wants to keep helping. . . . "

"Rosa's an artist," said Aunt Jane. "She doesn't know anything about roofs. She's like me."

"I could learn though," I said, wondering if Shawn would

give me a ride to jail to visit Ma. She'd probably like him, if she didn't think he was too punk.

Already I saw myself a famous artist. With a roofing business on the side.

Looking for the Golden Gate

SAN FRANCISCO—(AP) Edwin Kreuz' charter flight to San Francisco made a brief stopover in Bangor, Maine last weekend and he mistakenly got off the plane, spending three days in the East Coast town before realizing that the Golden Gate was nowhere to be found.

"Alles okay," pronounced the beaming Kreutz, a Bavarian brewery worker, at one point after he arrived on the West Coast Friday.

I

In the travel bureau, color posters of America never show the middle states, the Midwest of the great immigrations, Minnesota where your nephew lives. The posters only show one coast or the other; you have your choice of skyscrapers or cable cars. All the posters show the ocean. You must fly over the ocean to get to America. In America many people live by the ocean, perhaps most of them.

Bridges, what a country for bridges. Vast bridges over water, steel plates and girders connecting islands, peninsulas, promontories. In the posters the sun catches the steel of the bridges; they arch over the bays and harbors, making civilization possible, spreading civilization along the coasts.

In the posters the water under the Brooklyn Bridge is dark. The skyscrapers loom ahead, sharp-angled, windows mirroring the life below, dirty, intellectual, hard. New York City is the financial center of the world, the travel agent tells you.

And if you love plays and art. . . . You shake your head. Culture you can take or leave. You want a good time. Germans have been mugged in New York City. Not two years ago, a neighbor of yours was beaten up in his hotel elevator. The hotel was in Times Square. New York City has too many tall buildings, too many dark streets, the water underneath the bridges is brown and cold.

But California! One poster fascinates you: tiny white sailboats scudding under the Golden Gate; in the background, a hillside of pastel houses. The pleasantest sort of vertigo grips you when you gaze at this picture. You first saw it on your way to work at the brewery. Monitoring the pressure of the vats, you dream of sailing in that harbor, while the red-gold bridge hangs over you like a constant, fixed star in your navigation.

"Ach, Kalifornien," says the travel agent, and the very word is like a swarm of true sunshine in the cool fluorescent office. "It is more expensive to fly there, but very much worth it." And he hums as he fills out the papers: *"Kalifornien, hier ich komme. . . . "*

II

The charter flight is late boarding. You wait in the lounge of the Munich airport with some of your fellow workers. They toast you again and again with beer, envious, ribald. With their help you are imagining a California girl who will be golden and warm in your hotel bed. They press relatives' addresses on you, requests: Send me a backscratcher from Chinatown; I want a beer stein that says California; and for me, a girl. And me. And me.

Your brother and his wife arrive to bid you farewell. Their son lives in Minneapolis and they have been to see him twice. They have visited New York and Chicago too. They think your trip to Calfornia frivolous; you can hear them whispering to each other, "Going to California on his salary. He should visit Karl, he hasn't seen him for years."

Pfft, what do you care for your nephew? And as for your salary, hmpf, no wife, no children. It's your own business what you do with your money.

You try to explain, "The Golden Gate, the Golden Gate."

Your friends turn the words into a bawdy refrain, "Open up those pearly gates."

Your relatives counter soberly with advice about America. "Wear your moneybelt. Remember to tip, service is not included. Don't get drunk."

These last words of caution are already too late; you're sodden by the time the plane is ready to take off. *Wiederseh'n.*

III

More drinks in the plane, you lose count. A brief talk with your neighbor, a woman visiting her daughter in Los Angeles. You'd be glad to chat further, but you see her draw away. She is drinking coffee with sugar and pitchers of cream. What the hell, you don't want to be offensive, you have your own thoughts. You stare out the window. Ocean, nothing but ocean. You think: a plane is a kind of bridge, a moveable bridge, a movement bridging. . . . It is getting darker and you are very tired. It seems to be night for a long time.

IV

Something is happening. You have arrived.

"You can get up," says your neighbor. Everyone is getting up. Most people have already left the plane. Panicky, stumbling, still drunken (after all these hours, and with your strong head), you grab your flight bag and exit.

The darkness smacks you. Can San Francisco be so cold? And dark? You cross the runway to the lighted terminal. It is very small, smaller than Munich's. But you're in no state to compare. You want to keep sleeping. Must find a hotel, you think. Dazedly, you find yourself leaving the terminal. Lucky you only have your flight bag, no suitcase to worry about.

No one stops you.

It is only later, walking the highway outside the terminal, that you wonder about customs. You'd heard so much about customs—bringing in, bringing out, declarations and duties. Your passport is unstamped with the sign of entry, its crisp empty pages flat against your heart.

V

It's no use, you're too tired and the hotels of San Francisco are as distant as the stars above. How they glitter in the sooty California sky. No cars pass you or you might hitch a ride. The highway rolls through fields and pastures. Why not? Not since you were a child have you slept outside.

VI

You wake in the middle of the field, clear-headed, the birds singing; it's spring in California. Your flight bag pillow doubles as a saddle and you are a cowboy out on the range. The Wild West at last. You half expect your horse to be feeding over the rise. She will whinny and warn you of Indians. . . .

Yawning awake, you remember your flight. It seems a little incredible to you now that you just could have walked off like that. What happened to the rest of the passengers? Never mind. San Francisco's wonders beckon. Open up your pearly gates.

Back on the highway, you catch a ride in ten minutes.

VII

"How are you?"

"Beg pardon?"

"Pardner? Hah, I'm fine, *pardner!*"

"Say, wher'ya from?"

"Would you repeat it, please?"

"Where-are-you-from?"

"I am from Germany. *München.*"

"German, eh? What brings ya to Maine?"

"Would you repeat it, please?"

"I came to see the Golden Gate."

"Oh. . . . Right. Say, can I drop ya anyplace special?"

"Would you . . . "

"Where-are-you-going?"

"I must a hotel find, please."

"Right. Howard Johnson's okay?"

*

VIII

You sign your Cook's Traveler's Cheques with a flourish and are shown a room with a double bed, TV and bath. Who said traveling was hard? What does your brother know? Your English is sufficient to get you a hearty breakfast at the hotel restaurant. The waitress even brings you a beer, though she can't help glancing at her watch.

"It's only nine o'clock, Sir," she begins.

"I never have beer without breakfast," you try to explain, making a joke that only occurs to you later.

If only your friends could see you now. Here in California, in San Francisco, while they trudge off to the brewery.

When the waitress comes back you ask politely:

"Where is the Golden Gate please?"

"Where's the what?"

"The Golden Gate, the Golden Gate?"

"In San Francisco, I believe, Sir."

She is trembling for some reason. She is very young. You try to modulate your voice.

"Can you not tell me the direction I must follow or street car I must go with to find the bridge?"

"I didn't catch all that, Sir.... "

Losing patience, you shout, "The bridge! *Die Brücke!*"

"The bridge?" She is clearly terrified. She points out the window behind you and a little coffee splashes onto the floor from the full pot in her other hand. "There's a bridge a few miles away, Sir."

You note the direction of her fingertip. West. Good. Excellent. "Thank you, Miss."

You don't forget to tip.

IX

The best thing to do is to procure a map, you decide, and are pleased with your astuteness. A map will solve all your troubles. You walk along the streets trying to find a shop that will sell you one. San Francisco is a strange city. Sometimes they say, "Sorry, no maps." Sometimes they just shake their heads. Sometimes they use the puzzling word "bangor."

"Bangor." What does this word mean? You try looking it up in your dictionary without success. A colloquialism perhaps? Meaning, "I'm sorry?" or "Not today?"

You keep on walking westwards, finding a restaurant where you lunch on beer, beef and potatoes. What was a mild spring day has turned gray and sullen. By the time you've paid your check and left a tip it's pouring. You buy an umbrella on your way back to the hotel. Your first American souvenir.

X

There is a new waitress at the hotel restaurant that evening. She is older and friendlier, talkative even.

"Ain't this weather somethin'?" she says as she brings you the first of many beers. The name embroidered on her uniform reads "Bev." She is thick-waisted and mustachioed, more like your brother's wife than a California girl, but she has a kind face.

"Rain like this where you're from?"

"I am from Germany."

"Say, that right? No wonder you're drinkin' this beer like it's goin' outta style. Tell me, how does American beer compare with your beer over there?"

"It is good, good beer." Watery, pale, tasting like piss and chemicals, it's terrible. But you are too polite to insult her country.

"You really think so? Don't care much for beer myself. Vodka's my drink."

"Vodka's very good and nice. Can I buy you one glass?"

Bev snorts cheerfully. "Here? You gotta be kiddin'."

She brings you another beer. "You must be quite a traveler to have gotten all the way up here. Mostly we don't get too many tourists until summer."

"Yes. I like it."

"Bangor? Well, I thought so once myself, came from a small town and Bangor looked pretty damn big. But times change. I'm ready to move on, only I don't know where. If I'd been smart, I could've saved my money and gone traveling like you. I'd like to see New York City. Would you believe I've never even been out of this state? I've always thought I'd fit in better someplace like New York City. My kind of people, you know what I mean? I'm the type that likes to stay up all night partying. Never take drugs, wouldn't touch 'em, but I do like to drink, yes I appreciate a good time. And Bangor being what it is, well, all I'm saying is, a person needs to move on, see things, meet different people.... You're kinda like me, I bet. But why you chose Bangor I don't understand. Maybe it seems kind of exotic to you, but lemme tell you.... "

She has lost you. You smile and nod, listening to the strange rhythms of her speech. She is coarse-featured and familiar-looking. Her shoulders are broad and strong, she is large-bosomed.

Bev intercepts your glance and breaks off her monologue.

"Say, you staying in the motel?"

"I have a room, yes."

"Well, what do you say I bring a bottle of vodka up tonight and you can tell me all about that country of yours?"

She is not the California girl they promised you, but they will never have to know.

XI

Bev is gone when you wake up with a terrible hangover. Maybe it's jet lag, you tell yourself. Whatever it is, you can't get out of bed. The hotel room sags around you, impersonal, foreign. How far you have traveled from home. You got up for work six days a week for the last thirteen years. Now, in a strange city, there is no reason to leave your bed. You sleep through your second day in San Francisco.

Someone knocks and whispers your name, but you don't remember the words to respond.

XII

You start up out of bed on the morning of the third day, confused and frightened. All night you have dreamed of a bridge like a conveyor belt, moving barrels of beer from one side of the bay to the other.

Your face looks unfamiliar in the bathroom mirror. Your

watch has stopped.

You are wasting your precious vacation.

The young waitress in the restaurant timidly asks if you would like a beer.

"*Nein,* coffee."

Don't get drunk, resounds your brother's voice in your ear. You've lost time, you haven't seen the Golden Gate yet. Every time the waitress comes to your table you ask her, you plead with her, to tell you where the bridge is. She can only shake her head.

"I don't know what you mean. I don't understand you."

Your voice rises uncontrollably, "You must help me."

Everyone turns to look at you. The manager, who has just arrived, is apprised of the situation by the young waitress.

"Where's Bev?" you are shouting now. She will help you. She will understand.

"It's her day off," says the manager sternly, taking your arm. "Now please Sir, don't cause a disturbance or I'll have to call the police."

You're out on the street. It's raining.

You must find a map. One of these stores must have a map. There is something wrong with your mind, with your tongue. Your English worsens with every encounter. Will no one understand you? All you want is a map, is a sign, is a wave in the right direction. You can find the Golden Gate if someone only points the way.

XII

The police pick you up at the city limits. You are standing in front of a sign that says: WELCOME TO BANGOR, MAINE. Pop. 33,168. They think you are hitchhiking. You think you are dreaming. They think you are drunk. You think you are crazy. You have just realized the enormity of your mistake. You are so shaken that you feel no relief. Someday, you think, as you get into the car, you will be able to laugh about this.

*

XIV

On the last day of your visit, they take your photograph with the Golden Gate Bridge in the background. You, an ordinary German, a brewer, have been made an honorary citizen of San Francisco. You have been given chopsticks, backscratchers, beer steins and trolley cars, books and maps and posters in return for telling and retelling how you could have made such a blunder, how you looked and looked for the Golden Gate in a small inland East Coast city.

You don't have a California girl to take back on the plane. Sightseeing has kept you too busy to meet any, you tell yourself. But you have lots of other souvenirs. You had to buy another flight bag to hold them all. Your original bag only had room for an umbrella and an empty vodka bottle.

Earthquake Baroque

"At the transept, if you looked into the choir, the big round columns were manly and lovely. How big and manly!"
"A Visit to Chartres," Paul Goodman

1. *A Previous Conversation*

"Sometimes," she said, "I feel like an anthropologist in my own culture."

"Huh? What are you talking about?" he asked. They had just finished watching a movie on TV, made from a well-known novel. The climax was holocaustic and hip; at the end Joanne Woodward hung herself in a jail cell, Paul Newman packed up his suitcase and left town.

"You know," she said, " ... the patriarchy ... "

"Oh, that again. ... " He couldn't deny that he had been moved by the film; it appealed to his own self-destructive tendencies. "What the fuck can I do?" he muttered.

She just groaned.

They stared at each other from across the room. Her bitterness was confused by longing; his longing was confused by fear.

2. *Approaching the Cathedral (his version)*

"What the fuck do you mean I should've noticed the way the tower had shifted, the way the cathedral 'sagged,' the way the plaster had crumbled off, so that the stone was showing? Well, of course I fucking noticed, but so what? Weren't these churches made to last? They gave this style of architecture a name for godsakes, I read it in the guidebook, here: 'Earthquake Baroque.' They meant it to withstand time, nature, everything. And anyway I was hurrying, I didn't have time to notice, there were so many damn beggars. All women? Yeah, I guess they were all women now that you mention it, but so what?

"You're saying I should've looked up, noticed the *sky*, had a *feeling*...."

"Oh yeah, you can say that afterwards with all the newspapers to back you up. 'Experts predicted.' Oh sure. They never bother to tell us when and where *exactly*, to warn us... The sky, why should the fucking *sky* tell us anything? I, for one, don't believe in earthquake weather.

(Pause) "Besides, I wasn't even in the cathedral when it happened."

3. *In the Cathedral (what she saw)*

Like a dutiful tourist she visited the cathedral on their second day in the Mexican city. It had taken centuries and billions of pesos to construct; therefore it must be worthy of note. Dozens of generations had given their money and their labor to it; nevertheless they had died before seeing it completed. Yet she, having contributed nothing, could, by virtue of being born at a certain time, walk leisurely up and down its transepts, looking and not looking, curiosity her only emotion.

Curiosity and, yes, relief; no men would approach her in this house they had built in honor of their god.

The principal materials used in the construction of this place of worship were marble, stone, gold and iron. It was very cold, in spite of the heat outside. It was quiet and solemn, in spite of the chimes that throbbed rhythmically overhead and around her like a heartbeat. The heartbeat of God? she wondered. But she was not religious, merely curious. She took

her time and admired, though coolly, the altars of beaten gold
with their reliefs of pillars, scrolls, bouquets, frames, pros-
ceniums and cupid heads. Jutting out at angles from the
golden altars were plaster saints and Jesuits, dressed sedately
in browns and grays, their faces pale, ascetic, starved, yet im-
modest all the same. Who could remain humble, elevated so
high above the rest?

She sat and stared at the altars, lost in their decorative size.
The rest of the cathedral, to her heretical eyes, appeared
strangely like a zoo. Every chapel, and there were at least five
on each side of the cathedral, was caged off by a hundred-foot-
high iron grate with scrollwork and emblems at the top. Inside
the cages were specimens of piety: Jesus primarily, looking
like a pacing tiger, and sometimes Mary.

There was one terrible cage containing a tableau of a plaster
Mary, limp hand outstretched, eyes hunting the sky through
the stained glass windows. A placard named the situation
"Nuestra Señora de la Soledad," Our Lady of the Solitude. The
message, as she understood the Bible, was that Mary was
grieving over the loss of her only begotten Son. He was safely
out of the cage.

While Mary looked a little like Joanne Woodward before
she hung herself in the jail cell.

4. *After the Earthquake (comparing notes)*

"Fuck! So you really were in the cathedral during the
earthquake, my god! I got there earlier in the day, couldn't
find you and left again. What was it like, what happened?"

"I was standing in front of one of the chapels when the
ground started to shift—people ran back and forth, nobody
knew what to do. I crouched down—a plaster saint crashed to
the floor right beside my head. I heard the organ, groaning. . . . "

"Fuck. . . . "

"I know the cathedral was built to last—'Earthquake Baroque,' I read it too; all the same, as the trembling continued,
candelabras fell, fissures opened up in the marble floor, an

iron grate was bent like a soft wire fence, you should have seen it, right in front of me... flakes of gold big as this flew through the air.... "

"Fuck! What did you do then?"

"I stole something."

"You *stole* something, at a time like that, from the *cathedral?*"

"Don't you see, it was meant to last forever, but it didn't ... and it won't...."

"I think you're fucking crazy.... What did you steal?"

She has placed Our Lady of the Solitude near the window of her bedroom, the window that looks out onto the sea. Mary's plaster face is still grief-stricken, but now her eyes search the horizon.

She is waiting for earthquake weather.

In the Archives

The last time I went to the basement of the library to deliver the goods, Sammy hefted my papers in one hand and pointed an admonishing finger at me: *Let's get to work, girl; not much here for a six-month period.* She smirked, but suddenly I was back in the fifth grade with Miss Chickalee, trying to explain why I didn't have my report on the Navajos. She didn't accept my excuses any more than did Sammy: *You're a bright girl, Nell. This should have been a snap for you. I know you're not interested in the Navajos, but it's something you need to know. Besides, you've got to learn to work whether you feel like it or not if you're going to make anything of yourself in this world.*

Sammy is a funny name for a librarian, and for her. She's heavy, unlike the bird-like Miss Chickalee, but she has that same squint of unthwartable and almost obscene curiosity. She presides over the dungeon damp of the archival lower depths in an executive mu-mu which hits her log legs mid-calf and is zippered to her neck. Surprisingly, she isn't that much older than I, but I always feel I should call her Miss Something-or-other. I am timid and obsequious under her authority, even though I keep telling myself she's just an ordinary person: as intelligent as I am, but with a different kind of intelligence. After all, we both graduated with honors, steamed through college right to graduate school, laying brick after brick upon the edifice of success.

I am a success, aren't I? Or why would she want my papers? I am the one who's going to be famous, aren't I? So why should she have the power to judge me, why should she be able to make me feel ten years old, a bad child who hasn't done her homework?

I've been having trouble, some trouble . . . concentrating, I told Sammy reluctantly. I didn't say: I've been following the soaps on daytime TV . . . One day I did nothing but walk the alleys downtown . . . Some days I don't even get out of bed. I just lie there and eat cashew nuts . . . .

Sammy assumed a sympathetic, conspiratorial air. She pretends to be so interested in the creative process. *It just fascinates me,* she often says, vulture-like. *When did you first decide to be a writer? Had you always written or did you just start one day? What made you start? I'm so envious, I think it must be wonderful. We're so lucky to have all your early poems and drafts . . . it's not often we can collect the whole* oeuvre, *from the beginning.*

I am a brick in her edifice. She has only been down in the archives five years, but already she's looking ahead. Seeing her own fame, her perspicacity. How she will be congratulated, looked up to by all the young archivists for picking a winner and getting her under her thumb. How did you know that Nell Golden would be the next Emily Dickinson, the next Sylvia Plath? Modestly Sammy will gesture to the files filled with everything I've ever written and assume a hushed tone, *I just knew . . . something about her . . . .*

She told me a story once, during the first flush of our acquaintance, when I was trundling in all my first notebooks, my college efforts: *We have a graduate student here working on the notebooks of Roethke. He's working on a thesis showing Roethke's development. You wouldn't believe how discouraging it is for him, Nell! You see, Roethke didn't always date his notebooks. Can you imagine how difficult it is for this poor fellow to follow Roethke's development when he's not sure which notebook follows which?*

They will know all about my development, because all my notebooks are dated. Sammy sat down with me and made me date them. The first one is from my junior year in college. It is filled with imitations, shows my enthusiasms, influences, excesses. I did Wallace Stevens for six months and then went through a confessional stage: Lowell, Sexton, Plath. A year later, as a senior, I began to find my own voice. Soon after, I started to publish, though it wasn't until I was twenty-eight that my first book came out. Of course I wanted to be famous, expected it, but it wasn't with a sense of Duty to History that I kept everything. I'm only like my mother, a packrat, whose house is filled from the basement to the attic with twine-bound faded dailies, and still garish *Times* and *Newsweeks*, with suitcases packed for evacuation and for memory with long underwear and old tutus; whose drawers are crammed with recipes, stringballs and tin foil left over from the war effort; whose garage is a museum of car parts, and whose mind is a compendium of clichés and wisdom from the year of her birth.

I kept my notebooks because I keep everything. Because I don't like the act of throwing away.

If I think about that side of myself, I can almost understand the life of a librarian. Dedicated to pigeonholing, to classifying, to saving for a rainy day. When I was twelve my father gave me a desk that he had built himself, carefully, laboriously. How I loved that desk! It was all cherry wood, built like a rolltop, but without the rolling lid; still, with twelve or fifteen of the most amazing little cubbyholes. I put something in each one: a seashell from my aunt's trip to Fiji; a silvery dove feather I found at the park; a list of books I wanted to read (*War and Peace, The Grapes of Wrath*); a cunningly carved sandalwood box; a miniature copy of Shakespeare's sonnets. And sometimes on rainy days, I would play with my desk for hours, dusting, rearranging—what I used to think of importantly as "putting things in order."

I do like desks with lots of drawers, I like file cabinets, I love alphabetizing. I put my recipes in a little box, and when I make lists, I number the things to do or to buy and draw circles around the numbers. But that is only one side of my character and I suspect it is rapidly dying. I haven't been to the laundromat for weeks and my dishes are all piled in the sink; my plants are withering, letters go unanswered, and my library books are long overdue. I haven't made a list in ages because I no longer have Things To Do.

A few weeks ago, I woke up more inspired than usual and decided to take out some old poems and work on them, one of them in particular. I had three drafts of it so far, but the latest one didn't grab me anymore. I went back instead to the first draft and began to scribble on it, changing a word here and there, trying out a new stanza at the bottom of the page. When that page grew crowded and unintelligible, I retyped it, then I made a few more changes and typed it over again. I got up from the desk pleased with myself and went and made a cup of coffee. The song of the poem kept chiming in my head, how perfectly it had come together. Dum-de-*dum*. Yes, I was a poet, I was a good poet; it was a perfect poem.

But coming back to my desk I saw the five sheets of paper, each with part of the song, part of the poem, and I felt a terrible despair. How could I show the progression of the poem? Should I number them and then on the third draft make a note saying, "Refer to first draft"? Sammy was not interested in the end poem, only in the steps leading up to it. She didn't love the song, only the process. Only I knew the process. Slowly I ripped up every sheet except the last and stuffed the scraps into the trashcan. Peacefulness overtook me, along with a feeling of petty revenge: You'll never know, I thought, you'll never know.

When I first got a call from Sammy, inviting me to deposit in her poetry vaults, I was ecstatic. I had been chosen, confirmed. I was only thirty, after all, and had only published one book, to sparse and muted acclaim. It's true that I'd received a grant and with it, some recognition, and my poems were now appearing in some of the better places.... Still, so were hundreds of other people's poems. We were all young, all good poets, but.... But I was being picked out for posterity. My work was considered good enough to reside down in the fireproof, vandal-proof vaults of the university library. That meant they had faith in me! I would be great; they thought I would be a great poet someday, me, Nell Golden!

For months I walked on air; I delivered to Sammy every-thing I had; I said casually to friends: *Whew, it's a relief not to have to tote that stuff around anymore. I have so much closet space now, and I don't have to worry about fires anymore.* My friends and relatives were admiring, my poet friends envious. I could see the question in their eyes: Why did they choose you, why not me? I rose in their esteem, I basked in it. I was going to be a great poet. It was confirmed, I had been chosen.

But then, subtly, things began to change. My grant ran out and I was back to waitressing part-time. Rejection letters that I'd always taken in stride now began to pain me. Why wouldn't *The New Yorker* take these poems? Didn't they know my work was in the university archives?

My first book had been published by a small press; thinking myself above that now, I sent my second book manuscript to the big publishers. It was rejected at five places, without com-ment. *Oh well, there's always that small press,* I said cheerfully, but they rejected it too. I had to burn their letter, it hurt me so much. In carefully worded language they intimated that it was not as good as the first manuscript; they had the feeling I was not doing anything different. "The first book was amateurish in ways, but still exciting. These poems lack your earlier spon-taneity, without being necessarily better crafted."

I didn't have the heart to send the manuscript out again. I began to avoid my poet friends. Whenever I saw one of their poems in *Antaeus* or *The American Poetry Review,* I closed the review immediately, so I could say, *No, I didn't see it.* My own poems were still appearing in reviews and magazines, but I didn't seem to be progressing. The same places that had pub-lished my poems five years ago were still publishing them. But? What if they stopped taking them? They could stop at any time, and then where would I be?

I don't know how to write a better poem, I thought. I don't know how to write anything different from what I'm writing now. And yet I couldn't think of giving it up, not now. Being "a poet" was my identity. My friends, my family, the whole goddamn world saw me as a poet. I'd made them see me that way. When I could have had an escape, gone into teaching, for instance, I had proudly said, *I'll never teach. Those who can't, teach. Teaching warps the creative process. I'm a poet and only a poet.* So I had worked at odd jobs, waitressing, clerking, planting trees. In order to keep my identity as a poet safe. In order to stay free of the academic swirl. And now I had no other identity to escape into. Could I suddenly say, *I'm a waitress?* A thirty-two-year-old waitress?

When I first began to write poetry, I never believed for an instant that I would not be famous. And yet, that wasn't my only motivation. Far from it. I only wanted to write. I was so amazed that I *could* write. The words poured out; when I got up from my desk sometimes, I wanted to fall down in prayers of thanks. *Finished. Well done. Perfect.* Not bragging, just acknowledging . . . something that had appeared on the page.

But now, when I sat down at my desk, I felt a cold sweat: *Who would publish this poem? Would anybody publish it? What if nobody published it?* My friend, Sandra, had a series of poems in *The American Poetry Review*, a full-page spread, a flattering photograph, and she wasn't in the archives. *APR* had never taken any of my poems. *Where should I send it then? Would anybody take it?*

Sammy called me *We haven't seen you for a long time,* she said with a touch of sternness. *Where have you been keeping yourself? I'm dying to see your new stuff.*

I'll bring it in, I promised, and then procrastinated. When I finally made it down to the archives, it was with a bunch of failed poems, a small pile of papers that Sammy weighed in her right hand like a fishmonger handling a dead trout. She didn't know that they were failed poems, that they were bad poems, that they didn't move, and that they would never be published anywhere—anywhere that mattered. She only saw, or felt, that there were not many of them. Not much for a six-month period.

I watched her guiltily, feeling small and powerless across the room from her, a punishable student or an AWOL private. Yes, that day she looked more like a brigadier general than an elementary school teacher. She was dressed in an olive-drab mu-mu with red ribbon epaulettes. Sammy stared from me to my papers with beefy cheerfulness, as if awaiting an explanation for my misbehavior. I could almost imagine that she had a stick in her top drawer, or a firing squad in her closet.

Never had I felt the weight of the library press down on me with such vehemence. Above us rose six stories of book shelves, the square blocks of civilization, crowded together incestuously, magnificently, threateningly. Everything that had ever been thought worthy of being preserved. How could I dream of adding to that weight? There was already too much. The library pressed down upon me like a giant steam-iron, flattening my tiny presumptions, my obvious failures.

Sammy's office had bright travel posters and humorous cat prints, but no windows. At that moment, however, I imagined that I could see right through the walls into dank archival catacombs filled to the brim with scraps of paper from the trashcans of obscure writers. Why hadn't it occurred to me earlier that there was something sinister in all this preservation, that the archives were in fact a morgue for writers waiting to be reclaimed by posterity? Or at least by another generation of graduate students.

If the library pressed down with the weight of established, leatherbound thought, the vaults multiplied without reason around me ... there must be thousands of rooms beyond this neat little office ... echoing with all the sentences that had never been finished, all the poems that had been abandoned, all the letters that should have been forgotten, all the notebooks that should have been burned.

I could hear the vaults echoing. Or was it my voice?

I want them back. I need them back.

What, Nell?

My papers. All of them. Please.

Nell, Sammy said, surprised and displeased. *You signed a contract. Don't you remember?*

But I still own them, I said. *You're just keeping them for me.*

No, Nell dear. You own the literary rights, but we own the papers themselves.

Give me them back, I said, my voice rising alarmingly in the cool, still basement office. It was echoing somewhere, I knew it.

I'm sorry, I can't. They belong to the university. In spite of her military girth, Sammy was just like Miss Chickalee at that moment, the voice of authority and far-seeing wisdom.

I can't write, I muttered, trying to keep my tone down, trying not to hear the echo. *I can't write anymore. It's all bad, and you don't even know it. I don't want to be writing for you anymore, I want to be writing for myself. I don't want to think about myself as a poet, I want to be a poet.*

Sit down, Sammy commanded. I sat, a mistake, as I felt even tinier across from her massive desk, her massive form. She put the papers into one of her drawers and locked it. *Now tell me what's wrong.*

I tried. I tried to explain that since the archives had decided to collect my papers, I had become self-conscious and afraid. That I was competitive and angry at other poets. That I was terrified of failure. I tried to explain as well as I could that I was choked up, constipated, by the idea of someone reading and judging everything I wrote, finding me wanting. I calmed down because I thought she was listening and understanding. I was rational, or so I thought, persuasive. *If I could be free,* I said, *with nobody expecting anything, I'm sure I could begin writing again. Good poems.* I promised that I would will the university all my papers when I died. I promised that I would personally give Sammy a copy of the will. *But not before I die, not now.*

When I was finished, Sammy's look of sympathy lingered, like the eyes of a dead person that have to be closed. *I understand, I understand,* she murmured consolingly. *I've heard that all writers go through something like this at one time or another. It's called writer's block, isn't it? Believe me, I understand. But you'll get over it, writers always do. They go through a bad time and then they're all right again. You will be too. Meanwhile, you have to understand our position. We've put a lot of time into classifying and keeping your work. It's part of our program to find and save the work of up and coming writers. We can't just give your papers back to you because of a sudden whim of yours. A whim that is bound to pass sooner or later. Think of it this way, Nell, we're saving you from yourself.*

But the papers are mine.

Mine, mine, mine, came the echo. Mockingly. As if anything were yours after you wrote it down. If you gave your work away in a Devil's bargain, you could expect the Devil to keep it. No use complaining afterwards that the bargain wasn't fair. That you didn't want to live forever. That you'd rather have your old life back, thank you, and let fame take care of itself.

Only Sammy wasn't even the Devil. She was just a responsible librarian with a job to do, protecting the work of up-and-coming young authors from their own self-destructive tendencies.

They belong to the university, Sammy said firmly and looked at her watch.

She shouldn't have done that. *All right,* I said, drawing a deep breath and standing up, remembering how the heroine of my favorite soap dealt with betrayal and death. *You have my early work, and you know and anybody who's interested will know, what kind of a poet I was before I was thirty-two. But neither you nor anybody else will know anything about me after today—because I'm going home and destroying every notebook, every poem, every* scrap *of paper with my handwriting on it. And I will never give you anything again.*

I slammed the door on Sammy's shudder, again as my favorite heroine was wont to do, and took the elevator up out of the basement. I had to leave the early Nell Golden down in the archives, a hostage to my getaway, but I think by that time I was glad to get rid of her. She was no longer a faithful accomplice, but a dangerous liability with her greed and ambition.

She couldn't write worth a damn, either.

Drive-Away

This is an old nightmare. You are driving and you come to a bridge. It is high and arched, you can't see the end of it. It spans a body of water. You want to get to the other side. At a moderate speed you ascend. There are no other cars. Your hands grip the wheel, you could not stop the car if you tried. The arch of the bridge is too high, it has something wrong with it, you can't see the end. As you reach the top of the curve, you see what you have always known—that this bridge breaks off in the middle. You are in the passenger's seat, there is no driver. You can't stop, you don't know how, you are falling, falling.

There is a bridge something like this between the states of Washington and Oregon over the Columbia River.

You're on a trip alone, you're driving down the whole West Coast by yourself. You're driving a drive-away car for a man who lives in Seattle, a man who plans to spend a month in San Diego on Business. He wants his Cadillac with him, but he needs to fly. He has entrusted his car to a drive-away service—to you. To drive-away isn't strange. Hundreds of people do it every day.

But you're afraid of driving.

You know nothing about cars. You only got your license last

year at the age of twenty-five. After that triumph (mixed, for the test took place in a Northwest thundershower; you hadn't been able to see out the window; you were unable to parallel park for nervousness), after that triumph you have never really driven again. You have no car, you believe in public transportation, you never want to go anywhere anyway.... You proved yourself last year; now you can show your driver's license for identification. You don't have to make up stories anymore ("I'm an epileptic." "My whole family died in a terrible car wreck, I was the only survivor." "I'm sorry, I haven't driven since my last suicide attempt.").

In this society, it's taken for granted that everyone over sixteen can drive. You once got through life by pretending that you too could drive. It was only out of pride, or more likely embarrassment, that you finally got your license. So that when it really came down to it, when a friend said, "Hey, why don't you take my car and run to the store for a bottle of wine?" you wouldn't have to explain, "I don't have a license," or elaborate a psychopathic tale ("I was the cause of a fifty-car collision on the L.A. freeway at rush hour. Dozens of people died. It was night and the sirens wailed for hours. The whole world was flashing red lights. I wore a neck brace for a year.... ").

Now that you have your license you can legally, theoretically, jump in anyone's car and streak over to the grocery store. Theoretically. Instead you become more devious ("Let's walk instead, I need the exercise." Or, "I'm not really in the mood for wine."). It's not because you can't drive, or that you don't have your license now. It's because you are still afraid. You'd rather be driven or not go at all.

But now you're driving down the coast in a maroon-colored Cadillac convertible equipped with stereo and even a tiny foldout bar, which contains individual bottles of alcohol, a flask of tonic water, olives and swizzle sticks. Why are you doing this? It's one thing to get your license, it's another thing entirely to prove yourself by driving somewhere. Your hands grip the wheel.

"You're a good driver," your driving teacher told you in the course of the lessons. "You're very cautious. There's no need to grip the wheel."

You had paid for the lessons, you were trying to be cool. How could you tell her, "I have a sense of vertigo, a terrible sensation of powerlessness behind the wheel. I feel that anything might happen. I need something to hold on to."

This trip alone begins when you tell a new friend (someone who doesn't suspect your history, someone who says he thinks you're a strong woman) that you are planning to visit your family in Southern Calfornia. You say you'll go by bus or train.

"Hold on," he says. "Why don't you get a drive-away car?"

He has driven away lots of cars himself. It's a great way to travel, according to him.

You say you're afraid you'll get tired driving all that way by yourself.

"Maybe I could go with you," he suggests. "I really need to get away. I have a friend in San Francisco I'd like to see."

Infatuated, you agree. Why not? you think daringly. The idea grows on you. The two of you in campgrounds by Oregon rivers. Drinking coffee in truck stops, telling your life stories (editing out certain phobias of course). A double bed in a hotel room overlooking the Golden Gate Bridge. You have to get over your fear of cars, you tell yourself sternly. You just need more experience. What better way to gain self-confidence than to drive down the coast with a man who believes you're strong?

It's all set. You're scheduled to pick up the drive-away car. Then, at the last minute, he can't get off work.

"I'll take the bus," you say, enormously relieved. Your family is expecting you, you can't wait.

"Why not do it anyway?" he urges. "It'll be cheaper, you already have the car, you can take your time, go where you want...."

You can't tell him you're afraid, that torture would be easier than this test of endurance. He has such a good opinion of you. And you do want to be the woman he imagines—tough, challenged, strong. You even want to be that person for yourself.

You leave Seattle in the early morning, hoping to beat the traffic. Not understanding traffic patterns, you find yourself in the midst of the early morning rush of Boeing workers. In the gray dawn many cars have their lights on. It takes a while to find the right switch. The wipers go on. You turn them off. Then you notice that it's raining. You turn the wipers back on. This occupies you during the stop-start of the traffic. Stop. Start. You've never driven a car with power steering and power brakes before. The car you learned on demanded more vigorous handling. You aren't used to patting the brake. You jerk the car forward and back. Sweat collects in the hollows of your body, you fumble at the heater switch. It's off. You feel so damn conspicuous in the Cadillac. Everyone knows you're a horrible driver, a woman out of the comic strips. Stupid bitch, the man in the rear view mirror is mouthing.

After Boeing field the traffic clears out. For a minute at a time you're the only car on the freeway. You relax, think, I really am doing it. Then a car passes you (you're only doing forty), and the fears grip you again: that you aren't real; that you're dreaming; that a human being has no right to be in a metal box moving out of control.

You pass the turn-off to the airport. Oh, if only you were flying to California. You love airports, their aura of space, intrigue and money. You could be strapping down your belt and leaving the earth now, watching Seattle recede through the clouds. Compulsively you reach for your seat belt. Yes, it's fastened. Only two hours in the air and you could be in California. Instead you have three days before you. Driving this car is like flying, you assure yourself. If you were in the passenger's seat, you'd certainly enjoy it. It's the responsibility that gets to you, the knowledge that it's your brain, your synapses which tell this death machine what to do.

Cars pass you, left and right, reminding you to speed up. You're glad they lowered the speed limit to fifty-five. You wish they would lower it even more, to thirty. That should be fast enough for anyone, shouldn't it? More economical too. In Los Angeles where you grew up, the speed limit was sixty once, but everyone drove faster. Out past the city limits you'd been in cars going seventy, eighty miles an hour. Like the wind.

How could you have grown up in L.A. without learning how to drive? It's impossible. It took a car to get anywhere. You'd grown up in the back seat. Remember the long drives your family took on Sundays, to the deserts, up into the mountains, down the coast?

Unsummoned, a picture of the back seat of your parents' car pops into your mind. The seat is plump and blue and woven. You and your younger brother draw an imaginary line down the middle of the seat. "Cross this line and I'll hit you." "OW!" "You crossed it, so that's what you get." "Barbara, stop hitting your brother." "He asked for it, he crossed the line!"

The car doors to the back seat have their handles taken off. They are smooth, round knobs. You can't get out of the back seat by yourself.

Ambulances make your father pull to the side of the road. Cars pass slowly by the wrecks, passengers and drivers craning their necks guiltily. "Don't look, kids."

Traveling the freeway back and forth from Sunday excursions, you sometimes see as many as three or four accidents. "Don't look, kids." Your parents look and for a few miles they have nothing to say.

Who drives? Your father. He's very careful. He has never been in an accident, he has never even gotten a parking ticket. Your mother is different, she is nervous driving.

One of your father's favorite stories: The day after your mother got her driver's license, she pulled out in front of an oil truck. It was our first car, we couldn't even give it away after the accident.

Your mother laughs in the passenger seat, her credibility totally destroyed. She only drives to the grocery store now.

Another memory: How your father flings an arm across your chest if he has to brake suddenly. The jerk, the dreamy sense of being protected.

Or, your father driving quickly over the bumps in the road, chuckling, "We're on a roller coaster, kids." Bouncing on the seat, you please him by your little gasps of terror.

But these memories get you nowhere; you alone have responsibility for your life. That's the trouble, you don't want responsibility for your life. You want to be driven around everywhere, forever.

In justification you think, now wait a minute, I have done some difficult things, I have shown courage. Yeah, what? Well, I went to Europe by myself, learned languages, got jobs, hitchhiked alone. . . . You're really proud of that, aren't you? You like it when people say, "You went to Europe alone?" You love that. Oh yeah, verbally, you're pretty clever, aren't you? You could get yourself out of any situation. Too bad you didn't get out of this before it was too late.

But I went glacier-climbing in Norway, didn't I? Climbed up one of the tallest mountains in Northern Europe with an ice pick.

You know very well that that was a mistake. When you saw the size of that mountain and the way your friends were preparing to scale it, you wanted to run away. It was only your lack of Norwegian that forced you to go on. They practically had to drag you up some parts.

Face it, you have no sense of physical courage. You see death in every risk.

There is death in every risk.

You're afraid of dying by your own hand. You'd rather somebody else killed you.

Signs flash by. Only sixty miles to Portland. It's still raining. The road is smooth and almost empty. The Cadillac glides under your touch. Press down on the accelerator a little more, get up to sixty, you won't get caught. The faster you go, the faster you'll be there. Won't it surprise your father when you drive up to the door? Faster. You won't get caught. You're in control. Is this why people like driving so much?

Ed loved driving. Ed is the man you lived with for two years when you were nineteen and twenty. He thought you were crazy. Perhaps you were crazy. You didn't do much but write poetry and read and try to teach yourself languages. You worked at a Taco Bell during the afternoon. He knew what he was doing. He was going to school. He was going to be an actor. He became an actor.

He didn't want you to take drugs for fear you might flip out. You were also convinced you might flip out. You asked him to teach you how to drive because your father never would. He shook his head firmly. The implication: You're too unstable to even drive down a city street. You might kill a dog or a child. And then where would we both be?

He had his mother's car. You were immobile. You read Proust in the original and waited for him to come home and drive you somewhere. You were crazy about him, you found a horrible kind of thrill in being so dependent, like Marcel. Still you fantasized sometimes about leaving Ed, sometimes about taking a driving lesson. Eventually you did both.

Remembering him, you flip the radio on. He never drove without music. You hear that it's past noon. You've been driving without stopping for hours and you're suddenly exhausted.

Signs tell you that you're about to leave the state. You can't recall the landscape you've passed through. The Columbia River divides Oregon and Washington. One state down. But your sense of exultation fades as you consider the bridge. Trembling, you pull over for a rest before crossing. You are convinced you can't make it.

You crawl into the back seat, investigate the bar. The urge to down a tiny bottle of Scotch is irresistible. From the safety of the back seat you consider feminism and alcohol. They aren't helping you cross this bridge. The old fears are too strong, the more so because you don't understand where they originated. You have lied for so long.

"Why do you need to drive?" asked your father. "You have boyfriends."

"You'll run somebody over, you'll go out of control someday," warned Ed. He used to drive you over bridges in Southern California. You liked to hang out the window looking down at the blue water, up at the blue sky—rock on the radio, Jefferson Airplane probably. Effortlessly you soared over the water—in the passenger's seat. You didn't have to prove anything.

Why did the idea of proving yourself become important? Especially to a man you hardly know? You can do other things well. Your fear's legitimate. People die by the thousands on the road. Why do you need to drive and add to their number?

Because—I've lied for too long.

I don't need to drive, I've gone without driving for years. What I need is to understand my fear. There's nothing really wrong with being afraid of driving. What's wrong is wanting to be driven, expecting to be protected.

You get back into the front seat and start the car. You have had this dream before. It is an old nightmare. You are driving and you come to a bridge. It is high and arched, you can't see the end of it. It spans a body of water. You want to get to the other side. At a moderate speed you ascend. There are no other cars. Your hands grip the wheel, you could not stop the car if you tried. The arch of the bridge is too high, it has something wrong with it, you can't see the end. As you reach the top of the curve, you see what you have always known—that this bridge connects to land on the other side. You are in the driver's seat, you can't stop, you are safe and you are driving, driving.

Pity

"Once you find a surrogate mother, it is essential to gain all the information about her physical and emotional well-being you can. Speak to her family physician about her medical records. Of utmost importance are diseases which may be transmitted to the child or endanger the pregnancy —diabetes for instance, or schizophrenia."
—*from a newspaper article*

. . . But she wouldn't look at me, couldn't perhaps, I was moving so quickly so high above. It was a black night, not pure black though, more the color of a velvet tuxedo beginning to mildew. The ground sent up waves of cold, it might have been permafrost . . . over it, like an old army blanket, grew lichen and a kind of phosphorescent blue fungi. There, in the middle of it, she lay numbly, out of my grasp, not hearing my cry, head turned away, not looking at me. *The wind roared through the vacuum, tearing me away.*

She is twenty-seven, a graduate student in English at the university. Her specialty is William Blake. She will use the $8,000 to finish her doctorate, to write her dissertation. $8,000 is the going rate. I keep picturing her at home or in the art library, surrounded by reproductions of Blake's watercolors and tempras, his filmy, muscular angels drawn upwards like water vapor, his human sufferers chained and anchored to the ground. Yes, at home; for instance, in front of a smoky autumn fire, reading, making notes, growing full and round with "my" child.

I have never met her, and I agree that it is not a good idea, but I know her application by heart. Sandra Joan Godwin. Parents and grandparents still living. No sickness in that family, no cancer, no liver/kidney/heart disease, no diabetes, no broken bones, misshapen limbs, no mental illness of any kind, not the least little phobia. She is one of six children; there are numerous cousins. Three of her older sisters have families. Not a miscarriage or a mongoloid among them.

Is it possible? An entire family—four generations—with so clean a bill of health? They're Anglo-Saxon, needless to say, white, middle-class—the men tend to business, the women to stay home with the burgeoning families. Most of them live in Iowa. Sandra is the first in the family to go beyond four years of college. The transcript of her interview states that: "I am close to my family but I've only seen them a few times since I moved here four years ago to start graduate school." Does she worry about them finding out? I can't imagine that she has told them what she means to do.

We know so much about her; she knows nothing of us except that we are middle-aged and can't have children. But we can pay.

In another world I might have to give her *my* application, or Paul's, for after all, it's between them. . . . Yes, I've thought often of sending her a letter, explaining my situation, the reasons I want, I need to have a child . . . it would make it all less commercial somehow. But do I expect altruism then? For her to take pity on me? That's too complicated, uncomfortable; better leave it a cold business transaction. Rent-a-womb. Syringe a bit of Paul's seed into her uterus and simply let it grow . . . we pay all the medical expenses . . . she lets us adopt the baby . . . she takes the money and writes a book on Blake . . . and none of us ever meet. Except me and Paul of course.

I could never give her my application, put my own medical history down on paper for a stranger to read . . . I could never do it . . . write the word "hysterectomy," for example. And

then there's my whole family, practically, in and out of in-
stitutions . . . .I have wonderful stories to tell when I'm in the
mood, like the one about Uncle Timmy tossing his boyfriend
out the window . . . but I must admit, it looks cold on paper. I
too have supported my share of shrinks, more perhaps because
they're the only ones you can talk to these days than because. . . . Still, I have sometimes wondered how any of us
would make it without Valium.

I'm giving the wrong impression, I see; what kind of a
mother will *she* make? A damn good mother! I'm almost forty,
but so what? Thirty-nine's not an impossible age to be a
mother, it happens all the time. "The mature mother," etc.,
etc. And as Paul said, in his charmingly sententious, profes-
sorial way, "We have so much to offer a child. . . . "

Well, laugh, but it's true. Why else have we garnered the
fruits of a successful academic career (his) if not to bestow
them on a child? Clothes, dollhouses, fire engines, books, perhaps a horse, certainly a bike, and when he or she graduates
from high school, a car and a college education. A trip to
Europe, even graduate school, why not? I feel lavish today.
Without a child we have nothing to spend our money on.

You see what a cynical tone I'm taking, believe me it's only
out of despair . . . .There are so many reasons that we want a
child. . . . To begin with, we've wanted a child for years, almost since the day we got married. (Isn't that why one gets
married?) We waited patiently, secretly rather relieved that I
didn't get pregnant *right* away, like all the other graduate students' wives. That took me up to the age of twenty-six, when
Paul received his Ph.D. and the doctor found a benign tumor
at the mouth of my uterus. He decided to remove the whole
thing while I was still under the anesthesia, just in case. Just in
case. We thought of adopting, and waited and hoped for years,
but they always passed us over . . . I wondered if it was my history, but couldn't the adoption people see that it was not having a child that was making me crazy and that I would be perfectly all right if only I could fulfill my function as a mother, if
only I had someone else to care for, if only I could be a
mother, I would, I know it.

*

This is not a robbery! The child leaps to me of its own free will.
Look how it stretches out its tiny arms — as if to say, I am yours
now, Mother. *And it is plain, as she lies in her shroud below me*
(we fly by like a hurricane) that she is only momentarily tired; she
will have more children, as many as she wants. Only — why won't
she see the connection between us? Why does she turn her head
away? As much as I call to her . . . is she crying? No, you can't
have the baby back! Don't cry, my darling, be glad for me, be glad
for me. Take pity . . . please.

Today is the day they performed the insertion on Sandra.
Paul says nothing but I can tell from his face that he suffered
something of an indignity. How stuffy he is sometimes, with
his bow tie and bald head; no, not quite bald, and that makes
it worse — those few gold-gray strands leaking across his shiny
forehead like so many rivulets of dirty water. Yet he maintains
his dignity and his perseverance, in spite of all odds, in spite of
me.

He has his routine and it suffices him. In the morning he
gets up early and makes himself a cup of chocolate and me a
cup of Sanka. He reads something, a literary journal or a
novel, while he's dressing (which he does very deliberately; he
knots his bow tie himself). Then, off to work. . . . In the evening we take turns preparing dinner (his concoctions are
simple but delicious, crêpes or omelettes; mine are messy and
highly seasoned); after the news, he retires to his study to read
and grade papers. While I, while I. . . .

I have wondered, working myself up indignantly, as if I
were viewing a soap opera and were not myself the concerned
party, "Why doesn't he leave me? I thwart him, I give him
nothing, I hate him and he knows it."

Habit is it? Pity? I couldn't stand that, not from him, poor
creature. No, I couldn't stand to be pitied by a man. A woman
yes, a woman's sympathy could be very sweet. She might
know what I feel; him, never.

And yet of course we do get along in a horrible kind of way,
the way of all married couples. We choose our subjects care-

fully; we have our jokes; we make allowances.

There is someone at my back, someone with my exact measurements. My mirror or my mimic. It is almost as if we are joined at the hips, riding through the air like Siamese centaurs. My double is not blind, but he never sees what I see. For instance, the woman lying on the ground, whose child we bear away in our swift flight—he doesn't see her. How she is anguished, almost dead with grief and longing for her baby, he doesn't see that. He does not look down. The molting blackness around us is not black to him. *The consistency of his vision allows him to perceive light everywhere. Cheerful, matter-of-fact. . . . I am driven, he thinks he is driving, and we are both mistaken.*

All has gone well though Paul says nothing. My sources indicate that the seed has taken and that Sandra is indeed pregnant. Five weeks pregnant. They say she is remarkably healthy and has experienced no morning sickness. I wish I could say the same for myself. My headaches are coming back; I've had to lie down and keep quiet a great deal. Paul seems concerned but refuses to talk about the baby because he believes it upsets me. Doesn't he understand that the baby is the only thing I want to talk about? We need to get everything ready! Paint the nursery, begin the trust fund, buy the toys, find a pediatrician. . . .

"Keep happy, keep yourself occupied," he says quickly, before he goes off to the university in the morning. But my occupations have long ago disintegrated into pastimes, into nothing.

"Why don't you take up painting again?" he hints.

"I can't compete with Blake," I tell him snobbishly.

"What an attitude," he tries, jocularly. "What if everyone thought like that? What if I thought like that?"

"You should," I tell him, knowing however, that the damage was done long ago.

And now, suddenly, as I lie in bed (useless to rise and make my headache worse), I have become convinced that Sandra was not chosen at random, but that Paul knew her and wanted to have a baby with her. Why else was her application on top, why else did he discreetly push her name at me? Healthy, intelligent—maybe it's all made up. Was there a real insertion instead of a clinical one? I search his face in my mind.

At the same time I know this thought is unworthy of me, of us, and that Paul loves me and only me. To have stuck with me through everything! It will be our baby because we willed it, no one else's. We will adopt it from Sandra and it will be *mine*.

—Still, I've decided to watch her, to make sure nothing happens to the baby, also to assure myself that there's nothing between them. It won't be hard, I know she spends most of her time at the library. It will give me something to do; that should please my husband.

I saw Sandra today in the art library; I knew it was her because she had the Blake books spread out in front of her. She is tall and rather thin-skinned, the sort of brunette with lots of little moles and freckles. Her lashes are long, she has blue eyes and wears enormous hoops in her ears. Her front hair is pulled childishly back by barettes. She looks younger than twenty-seven.

I managed to have a few words with her under the pretext of wanting to look at one of her books. It's just as I suspected, she is more interested in Blake's paintings than in his poems. She plans to do her dissertation on one of his illustrated manuscripts, the *Marriage of Heaven and Hell*.

Trembling with deceit I turned the pages of one of the books to show her my favorite painting, "Pity."

I quoted Sandra the lines from "Macbeth" that Blake was illustrating:

"And pity like the new born babe
Striding the blast or heaven's cherubim hors'd
Upon the sightless couriers of the air
Shall blow the horrid deed in every eye
That tears shall drown the wind. . . . "

It is a murkily marine-colored painting with the mottled effect characteristic of that period of Blake's life. At the bottom of the painting is a woman lying as if dead or terribly tired. She is in a shroud which covers her feet and leaves her shoulders and arms bare. Her hands are clasped over her breasts. Golden hair coils in a profuse and sculpted pillow. Wearily or in pain her brows contract; her eyes roll.

Still, the main interest of the painting rests in the upper half of the picture, in "heaven's cherubim hors'd," receiving the "new born babe." The two cherubim are back to back flying through the ominous night on two blind horses. The horses fill the page horizontally. Their tails and manes flow in movement, their nostrils flare in the wind. The arms of the second cherub, whose back is turned to us, mimic the horizontal stream of the horses, yet because of the cherub's downward curving palms, the hands serve to contain the horses' flight, to compress it within the realms of the painting.

The cherub in front is crouched in a typical Blakean posture, massive, androgynous, hair shooting up and off to the side like a fountain beaten back by the wind. Her (I always think "her") well-muscled arms reach down to hold the baby, though *hold* is not the right word, so lightly do they touch. The new born babe is at the center of the composition, the nucleus. Hardly a child except in size, the little being is fully formed, robust and almost burly. His tiny toe rests on a finger of the cherub. His head is thrown back and his arms open wide, as if to embrace her.

When I wrote my art paper on Blake I was struck by the measure and balance of this extraordinary composition; that isn't what moves me now. It's the expression of the two women, the one on the ground so exhausted, hurt and distant, the other so loving and full of compassion. She holds the child but her attention is directed only to the woman lying still as death. One feels that an exchange has transpired. The baby has surely left the woman on the ground of his own will and desire, yet the concern of the woman moving away is for the real mother. The woman takes the child as she is meant to, but she looks back, she looks back.

"This is just how I imagine a child being . . . adopted," I

whispered to Sandra in the library.

Sandra looked at the book with calm eyes. "Yes, perhaps," she said.

Her pregnancy wasn't showing enough yet for me to make any reference to it, but I continued, staring at the reproduction:

"Of course, what's beautiful about this painting is that it expresses the possibility of connection, the possibility of giving and receiving joy in this world. Blake knew that 'the most sublime act is to set another before you.' But how hard it is, how much compassion we must show. The painting illustrates that perfectly. Not in the conventional way—of course you understand that . . . ."

Sandra stared at the painting and then at me. "I guess I see what you mean." But there was hesitancy, and perhaps the beginnings of irritation in her voice.

I thought sadly that she must think me crazy. Perhaps I should tell her that I was onto her? *We have a common bond.* Mention Paul—but that was too obvious, and why bring him in? While I gazed at her, memorizing her face, her expression, thinking—so, my child will have freckles and blue eyes, Sandra suddenly got up and went to the shelves, murmuring something about needing another reference work. I saw her thread her way silently through the stacks to the exit.

Slowly the anesthesia wears off, wears down; I come half alive, my mouth full of dried nettles, my eyes like glazed saucers. The world swims in and out, blue and green, very dark, velvety. All the lower parts of my body, beginning in the middle of my spine, feel dead. No bleeding, no aching, nothing to remind me that I have borne a child. Abandoned, too tired to cry out, I only know my baby is not with me. I don't remember what papers I signed so long ago that brought me to this place.

Tonight I went into Paul's den and confronted him with my discovery.

"I've seen her," I said. "I've talked to her."

"Who?" he asked impatiently, still looking down at the papers on his desk. There are apparently very few things I do that irritate him, but he hates for me to bother him when he's in his den. He was wearing his embroidered slippers and the Japanese dressing gown I gave him so long ago, and what is left of his hair was tangled.

I put out a hand to straighten it. . . . Forty-two this year, I thought . . . it's too late to have children . . . we're both too old for a child now . . . if only this had happened ten years ago. . . . He pushed my hand away. My sudden overwhelming sadness made me, as usual, take a caustic tone.

"Sandra Joan Godwin," I spit out. "Who else?"

"Godwin . . . " he muttered, pretending to be puzzled. "You mean, the girl who's doing the Blake . . . ?"

"I have no name.

I am but two days old.

What shall I call thee?

I happy am.

Joy is my name," I quoted slyly. "Yes I saw her in the art library and talked to her. Your lover, the mother of your child."

"What! Betsy, what are you talking about?"

"Oh, I know your ways—pretending that it will be *our* child, that she is only a surrogate womb. You say we'll adopt the baby and it will be ours then, but it won't, it will be yours and hers . . . I'll be left out . . . you'll leave me . . . Barren, barren, barren."

"Betsy, you're overtired, getting excited, you know it's not good for you. Come on, come on, let's go lie down and take something."

"Yes," I said, sobbing, but calm or deadened underneath, looking down at myself from high above, flying by. "Yes, all right, I'll lie down," giving in to him once again, wanting to believe him, his pity, not believing him, never. "Tears drown the wind," I cried over and over.

*

I am cold, a wet wind is blowing, as if the very sky sobbed for me. Voices in the wind envelop me like the sheets they have wrapped about my body. A woman's voice, sounding like my voice, compassionate and loving even as she steals from me. "Mine, mine, mine," I want to cry, but I can't force the words through the slack opening of my mouth. I can't see her, I try to imagine her, the woman who is taking my child—she resembles the nurse with the vast bosom, the arms like muscled pillows, who gently forces medicine through my lips. "Sleep," she murmurs. "Sleep."

Because of the scene with Paul I am back in the hospital. Now, in a lucid moment, I can see that it's for my own good. I must reserve my strength for the baby when it comes. I believe it's four months along now, but it may be five. I lose track of the time.

Whenever Paul comes to visit, I ask eagerly after Sandra's health.

"It will be all right," he says, pulling the strands of hair over his forehead. I realize we have never been happy together; still, I couldn't bear it if he left me.

"Please don't divorce me," I beg over and over. "We'll adopt it, won't we, and then we'll have a child, our own. It doesn't matter *how* it comes into the world, does it, as long as it's ours?"

"No, it doesn't matter," he says. "No, I won't divorce you.... Rest now, Betsy, take your medicine."

He brings me books on Blake, the only thing I can stand to read. I have memorized the aphorisms of the *Marriage of Heaven and Hell* and can quote them by the hour. Most often, though, I look at Blake's painting, especially the one of the two women with the child like a pinprick of light between them.

"The possibility of joy," I tell Paul. "Given and received. Do you see it?"

*

"Come back, come back ... " but my mouth won't open.

Too far away now to hear her even if she should call. I have taken her light, her little life from her, out of her. Someday we will understand this separation.

Disasters

L ate winter had become one long ice storm. In December and January snow had fallen over the New England countryside, deeply molding the landscape into valleys and hills of comfortable softness, quiet as the pictures in a children's story book. But in February the weather began a course of ice storms. Day after day sleet fell, then froze. Ice lay in a heavy crust over the earth, only to be smashed again and again with the weight of frozen falling things—tree limbs and telephone poles. Life was in abeyance except for these accidents; everything was on the surface, frozen in patterns.

He was waiting up for her, as she had half hoped, half dreaded he might be, in the kitchen, the only warm, bright room in the house. He was sitting at the big oak table with a large book open before him.

"So, how was the first night?" Malcolm asked, too eagerly, looking up as she came in.

"It's good to be home again, that's for sure." Laurel's overalls were covered with a fine, pastel-colored dust; her arms and back ached unbearably. She sank into a chair opposite Malcolm, taking what comfort she could in the warmth of the room, in the tawny glow the oil lamp cast over the books and newspapers piled on the table. She *was* glad tonight that she had him to come home to, glad for his red plaid flannel shirt, his jeans, his fair skin and early-graying hair softened and made golden by the light—glad for all things comfortable and familiar.

Malcolm made her some orange spice tea from a box the same color as the lamp, while she rested her head on her arms. "What was it like?" he asked again.

"I've decided I can stand it for six weeks," she tried to smile. "The pay's all right, more than I made as a clerk, and if I'm careful, I won't have to work again until summer. . . . But Malcolm, oh god, it's awful."

He placed the cheap tin teapot between them and sat down again. He stared at the open pages of his book intently for a moment before closing it.

"*The Titanic*," Laurel read, upside-down. "What are you reading that for?"

"I was looking for something else at the library when I found this section that had all kinds of books on disasters—a whole row of them. Christ, they were all there: shipwrecks, earthquakes, tidal waves, eruptions—you name it." With a kind of shame-faced animation Malcolm patted the pile of luridly illustrated books under the lamp. "I checked out as many as I could."

Laurel read the titles out loud slowly: "*The Wreck of the Memphis; The Morrow Castle, Tragedy at Sea; Alive! Story of the Andes Survivors; Catastrophe! When Man Loses Control; Death on the Ice.*"

Another of Malcolm's crazy obsessions, she thought wearily. He'd been going to the library every few days the whole winter. First it was novels, then history. He'd slipped briefly into the occult and then out again into the natural sciences. At this rate he would exhaust the library's entire stock by spring; it wasn't very large. All day he sat at their kitchen table and read, going out only occasionally to take a walk. Since the beginning of the ice storms he hardly did even that. He had given up drawing and hadn't been to his studio in weeks.

She didn't want him to think there was anything accusing in her tone, though. She smiled, "I can't believe it. That library has about three volumes of poetry—by people I've never heard of—and then they have all *these* books. A whole row of catastrophes?"

Malcolm flipped his book open again. "It's really pretty in-

credible, I mean, when you read these things you can't help
wondering what it would have been like. . . . Imagine being on
the Titanic. What a ludicrous series of mistakes, except for the
way it ended. The men sinking while the women went off in
lifeboats. . . . Laurel, I'm sorry, I wanted to hear how your
first night went."

"Now that was a catastrophe. God," she sighed and stared
down at her overalls. "Look at me. I'm covered with the
stuff." She brushed futilely at the pastel dust, which only
served to embed it more thoroughly in her clothes. "And my
shoulders are killing me." She made shrugging movements, as
if to throw off an enormous weight which continued to press
down upon her. "Well, it's awful, it's the most awful thing
I've ever done, what can I say? The mill is a beautiful old
firetrap—windows up to the ceiling, small panes from the last
century. It's about 110 degrees in there with the presses all going. The noise is deafening. You can hardly hear yourself
think—talking with anybody except in the breaks is out of the
question. . . . I did talk in the breaks, though, and. . . .

"Oh, Malcolm, the funniest thing—the woman who was
showing me the ropes, Paula, asked me if I'd just gotten out of
school. Well, when I think 'school,' I think 'college,' right? So
I said, no I'd dropped out last year after one quarter of graduate school. But she meant *high* school. Well, how old *are* you,
she asked me. Twenty-four, I said. You're kidding, she said,
you don't look more than eighteen or nineteen. How old are
you, I asked her. She looked about thirty-five or something.
Twenty, she said."

Malcolm laughed appreciatively along with Laurel, but continued after she had stopped and sighed.

"All the women—there are about eight of them—look that
way, sort of pudgy and beat-up. There are only two men, a
mechanic and a supervisor. Some of the women were talking
about their children at break. I think they all have kids. I bet
they're all only twenty or so. Can you imagine?"

Neither could very well. They sat and drank their tea in the
lovely cantaloupe glow of the lamp. Rousing himself, Malcolm
said encouragingly, "Well, now you know how they make but-

tons. . . . "

"Oh, it's interesting all right." Laurel livened up slightly and ran her fingers through her frizzy hair. "We each have our own workspace, see. On one side is the press, a huge monster that comes together like two steam irons with little button-sized doo-dads on the meeting surfaces. On the other side of me is a kind of trough, filled with small, round, nascent buttons. They're soft and powdery and look like Sweet Tarts — it's very tempting to want to eat them. So then you grab this big wooden mold with two layers, the top one punched with button-sized holes. You scoop up the Sweet Tarts and jiggle them around until they fall into the holes. Then you turn around to the press, put the whole frame in square, squeeze its sides so that the buttons fall through onto the little press doo-dads (they have little spikes on them to make the buttonholes). Then you turn on the press so that the top part of it comes down, and *voila* — lots of little laminated hot Sweet Tarts, that you sweep off." Laurel shrugged her thin shoulders painfully again. "It really kills your back, that wooden frame is heav-*ey* — and it kills your hands and forearms from squeezing the frame." Laurel made squeezing motions. "You know what? Paula, that woman who taught me tonight, said in a week or so I wouldn't be able to open jars anymore. My thumb muscles develop differently or something."

Malcolm looked at her helplessly. "Maybe you shouldn't do this kind of work. Maybe you could find something else."

Laurel stood up and swung her arms back and forth. "I couldn't find anything else in this town that pays as much. We get a differential for swing shift, you know. No, I can stand it. They can. Christ, one of them's been there for three years. And it'll only be six weeks or so." She almost added, Somebody's got to work . . . but that wouldn't have been quite fair. His unemployment benefits still had several weeks to go.

She went into the bathroom adjoining the kitchen and began to run the bath water. "I'll put Epsom salts in, that should help," she said.

"Good idea," Malcolm paused, then opened the Titanic book again.

"And you know what else, Malcolm?" Laurel asked suddenly, coming naked to the bathroom door. "Those hot buttons fly *off* and *burn* you. The women wear sleeveless shirts because of the heat and their arms are covered with little round welts. They even have the buttonhole marks on them, like real buttons fastened to their skin. But I'm going to wear long-sleeved shirts, I've decided, even if I sweat to death!"

She disappeared again. Malcolm closed his book and looked at the clock. It was two a.m.

The nice thing to do would be to go in and scrub her back, but he didn't feel like it. He felt somehow that it was his fault she was hurting, that she'd had to take this job. Which was ridiculous, they'd agreed a year ago when they first met, that they would remain self-supporting.

A year ago. . . . He'd been finishing up his graduate studies in sculpture at Rhode Island School of Design; Laurel had been trying to decide whether or not to drop out of her Master's program at Brown and really devote herself to poetry.

Malcolm got up and moved towards the bedroom. He couldn't remember now whether he had encouraged her to quit school. Now that he looked back on it, he thought that college had been the most wonderful part of his life. A steady stream of ideas, all the best influences, trips to New York occasionally, the prospect of a show. At the time though, he'd been eager to leave; perhaps he'd unconsciously swayed her, too.

Yes, it was hard to remember, now that everything was so changed, what it had all been like. When art had seemed the right choice for him, the only choice.

Malcolm got into bed, shivering with the cold, and thought about their first apartment. It had been small and sunny, on the third floor of a building in downtown Providence. Too small, not like this big old house. Laurel hadn't written much poetry there after the first months, after he'd finished up his work at the college studio. She'd read a lot, he'd read too.

Studios were expensive to rent; besides, he'd needed a rest, a new perspective. For too many years he'd been competing, been pressured. It had been time to rethink his ideas, to find out if he had any of his own.

When a friend of theirs had told them about this small town in the Connecticut countryside, where people would rent you their barns for practically nothing if you fixed them up to use for studios, he'd jumped at the idea of moving. Laurel hadn't been quite so enthusiastic.

But she had come. She couldn't blame him. He wouldn't let himself feel guilty about her; he already had enough to worry about.

Malcolm drifted off to sleep on the far side of the bed.

In the bathtub Laurel was crying quietly. That morning she'd gotten a letter from her friend, Sally, who had finished graduate school and was now teaching at a small college in New Hampshire. The letter was wildly enthusiastic: she loved teaching, the countryside was beautiful; she was in a writing group; she had just met someone who wanted to publish her book.

It wasn't fair, Laurel cried. She was just as good a poet as Sally—not that she begrudged Sally her success—but here Laurel was, out in the sticks, with nobody to talk to about writing and Malcolm going crazy, and now she was working in a factory.

The summer had been wonderful; she remembered writing Sally a letter just as full of enthusiasm. They'd found this fantastic old house to fix up and Malcolm had worked on converting a barn into a studio and Laurel had written three or four hours every day. They'd gone berry-picking and swimming in the pond, had picnicked often and made love at least once a day.

They'd been happy.

But in the fall they'd both had to get jobs. Malcolm found a high-paying one with a bunch of boat-builders and had made enough in three months to get himself through the winter.

She'd had to be content with clerking in the five-and-dime, telling old ladies where to find the embroidery thread, making only five cents over minimum wage.

She'd stopped writing, had begun to forget that she ever had. Malcolm hadn't helped. When she'd suggested returning to Providence, he wouldn't hear of it. To fix up his studio for nothing? He was only waiting till he got laid off in December so he could go back to sculpture full time.

She could have gone back by herself. But instead she'd quit her job in November and hung around, waiting for things to get better.

And for a time, around Christmas, things had gotten better. She'd been able to write while he was out of the house and it had been fun to return to Providence for the holidays and be admired for their pioneering spirit.

The water was going cold on her. She just couldn't go back to that mill job tomorrow. And what could she write to Sally, how could she offer her congratulations in the right way? What was she supposed to say? "Malcolm fixed up his studio but can't seem to do any work. Instead he sits around all day and reads books on disasters. I ran out of money again and have started working in a button factory. Pretty soon I'm going to have little red welts all over my arms and won't be able to open jars anymore.

"Isn't life wonderful?"

"So Betsy came back from the telephone with a murderous look in her eye and said, 'Someone tell Don I'll be right back,' and rushed out. We all stared at each other. Which one of us could tell the *foreman* that Betsy had just *left*, in the middle of the shift? And we didn't even know why. Well, Molly, the pretty fat one with the alcoholic husband, must have told him something, she's a sweet-talker. Then, about half an hour later Betsy came back. 'I guess I fixed *her*,' she said when she went by. I couldn't leave my machine to ask what happened, but during our next break, Betsy told all of us that when she'd called home earlier, a *woman* had answered the phone. So she hung up, rushed over there, grabbed a kitchen knife out of the drawer and *cut* this woman on the *ear* before her husband could stop her. Then she turned around and left again—Malcolm, are you listening to me?"

Malcolm looked at her sullenly. The way she went on and on about these women of hers. Every night she came home as wound up as a top and always with some new story to tell. Sometimes it was horror stories about something at the factory—an overhead fluorescent light had broken and spattered the floor right next to someone's feet. Sometimes it was a major revelation like the fact that Paula had actually taken out a subscription to *Ms.* magazine after hearing Laurel talk about it. Sometimes it was just feverish, wound-up talk about anything and everything.

Lately Malcolm had taken to going to bed before she came home; her intensity, sometimes verging on tears or hysterical laughter at the way these women lived, was too harsh after an evening spent reading. But tonight he'd forgotten the time, engrossed as he was in a particular book about mining disasters. He wished she would stop; he wanted to finish it tonight.

"I just can't understand," Laurel burst out, "how you can keep reading those books, day after day, week after week. Malcolm, it's sick, it really is, to be living secondhand like this."

"I suppose you think I should go make buttons with you."

"Anything would be better than this, this sitting around reading about disasters and catastrophes. And you don't have to be so nasty. I hate the job, but these women are teaching me more about life than you can get from a book."

"Laurel discovers the proletariat."

Laurel grabbed up one of the books, slammed it open on the table and began to read: "*The next day, as thousands gathered on both shores to watch, local officials began searching the river for the bodies of the dead. With the primitive diving equipment then available, it was three days before they even found the wreckage of the train. Recovering the bodies took much longer. Seventy-five people had been on the train, and there were no survivors, but only forty-five of the bodies were ever found.*"

"What, *what* can you possibly get out of that? A book like this is just lists. It has no context, no meaning, it's just senseless horror. Do you *feel* anything when you read about these people, on their way somewhere, who ended up dead in the water? I mean, what's with you?" Laurel's voice sounded painfully in her ears. "Do you imagine you were there or something? Does it give you a thrill? Or are you just some kind of vulture, feeding off these experiences because you never have any of your own?"

Malcolm stood up shaking. "Give me that book."

For answer, Laurel threw it across the room, into a stack of dirty pans in the sink where it made a frightening clatter.

Malcolm seemed to advance on her, to raise his arm, then as she shrank back into her chair, he passed by her, slamming each door of the house as he went through it.

"Malcolm," Laurel shouted, running after him. "What's wrong? Won't you tell me what's *wrong?*"

But the last door, the one to the bedroom, was locked.

That night while Laurel slept fitfully on the living room couch, Malcolm threw open the windows so that the icy rain chimed in, and dreamed of train tracks breaking off without warning, of ships sinking without a sound. Sometimes he was a passenger, screaming and crying for help with the rest; more often he stood somewhere slightly above and away, full of horror, knowing that there was nothing he could do to save anyone.

By morning he was feverish, trembling. The carpet around the two windows was soaked; wind had blown chunks of ice across the room. Some were very large, they almost seemed like icebergs, and he in a boat looking down at them. He closed the windows and got back in bed. Then he rose and looked out the windows again. The sky was as dark as a bruise, full and fat with menace, ready to storm.

Laurel came once to the door and tried the knob, but she didn't call out to him. He waited until he heard her go out, then he got up to make some tea. But he felt weak, his head ached badly and he could hardly see to read. Although he wrapped himself up in a blanket, shudders still ran through his body. After half an hour he took his favorite book, *Catastrophe! When Man Loses Control*, back to the bedroom with him. Carefully locking the door, he fell into a light and uneasy sleep.

When Laurel came back from shopping the bedroom door was still locked and no sound came from behind it. She was by now more angry than concerned. All night she had wept on the couch, wondering whether to leave him. She realized she had been miserable since coming back from Providence in December. Now she wondered furiously why she'd bothered to come back at all. Obviously Malcolm didn't care if she were here or not, if he was going to sulk like a little boy the first time she took him up on his obsession. And it *was* crazy, reading all those books. She'd been patient long enough. It had passed the point of giving him space to find himself. Christ, she'd moved to the country with him, given up her friends, work, everything she needed, to be with him. So *he* could find himself, so *he* could become a great sculptor. And not one piece of work had he done. He'd been sitting around like a moron since early winter, letting himself drift deeper and deeper into a depression that he was unwilling to share or to talk about. She bet he didn't even miss her while she was at work, she bet he wouldn't know the difference if she were gone forever.

It was fucking time to put a stop to this. She'd give him another few weeks, until she was ready to quit her job. If he hadn't given some sign before then, she'd go back to Providence, or maybe even New Hampshire. She didn't need to put up with this shit.

When it was time for Laurel to leave for work, she gathered up all the books on the table and stuffed them in the closet. Let him sulk as long as he wanted. Things would have to change.

Stepping outside to wait for Paula to pick her up, she was

aware of a change in the weather. For several days it had been clear and crisp, icy underfoot but bracing. Last night it had sleeted and it looked as though another storm were coming up. The sky grew darker and darker, while the wind bit through her parka with an angry vengeance.

"Christ, it's cold," she and Paula agreed. And laughed. "Lucky we're working in such a warm place."

Paula was one person who would be sorry to see her go, Laurel thought. The twenty-year-old mother of two, who had dropped out of high school to get married and who had been working at the mill almost two years, had completely changed Laure's ideas about working class women, even about friendship. Paula had an eager, hungry way of questioning Laurel without implying that there was something that she, Paula, lacked. If I've done one thing by taking this job, Laurel thought, it's been helping Paula see that there's a larger world than this town. And Paula had been good for her too, Paula with her constant phrase, 'I'm not taking any shit'; her tips on beating the system and fucking over the foreman and his impossible quotas. Paula knew how to throw her press out of whack when she needed a cigarette without it looking suspicious. Paula wasn't afraid to say to the foreman after the accident with the fluorescent light, 'I'm not working in this place another day unless you get some wire mesh under those things.'

Laurel would miss all the women, she realized, going into work that day. Younger than she, they were stronger and harder. They knew how to stand up for themselves. They were vital in a way that the refined clerks at the department store had never been, much less the people she'd known in Providence. And they'd accepted Laurel, for all her education and pretentiousness ('A poet?' Betsy had said and left it at that). She would miss them.

The storm broke midway through the evening, in a burst of thunder and lightning. Laurel's press was positioned opposite the tall, tiny-paned windows so that she saw the first streaks of blue and silver in the black sky. A few minutes later a rolling blast of thunder shook the glass and hailstones blossomed like firecrackers. She and Paula glanced across at each other and grinned. Anything was excitement in this place.

"Let's just hope we can get home all right," Paula shouted above the noise.

"Oh, it can't last very long," Laurel screamed back. What did she care if she got home or not, if Malcolm still had the bedroom door locked?

But the storm, instead of abating, grew wilder and wilder. Lightning flashed every few moments, until the accompanying thunder began to seem like another huge press outside, groaning with a billion-ton weight. Could the earth even stand up to this constant barrage? It was almost as if they were under enemy attack, a kind of winter blitz.

Now inured to the rhythm of her machine, Laurel filled her mold mechanically, shook it and hefted it into the press without thinking about it. She was just turning to fill the mold again when suddenly it was dark. A woman screamed in the abrupt silence.

"Everybody stay where they are," the foreman said loudly, too loudly, for with the presses stopped, the mill was only a drafty, echoing cavern.

Laurel put her mold down where she remembered the bin was and called cautiously over to Paula, "Paula, did the power fail or something?"

"Lightning," Paula said. Relief swelled her voice into a laugh. "Well, that was sudden, wasn't it? Suppose we get a break now?"

Laurel giggled as relief poured through her too. She heard the others laughing and sighing around her in the dark, still standing obediently at their presses.

From the direction of the office a bright light appeared. It was the foreman, Don, with a battery-powered lamp.

"Everybody all right?" he called as he came toward them.

"Jesus, Don," Paula drawled. "Do we have to keep standing here?"

"I guess not." He halted uncertainly and let the women make their way over to him instead. "Nobody hurt? Who screamed?"

"I did," Martha admitted. She was a small blonde woman who had always looked too fragile next to the heavy machinery. "But I was just surprised, I guess."

Suddenly they all began to talk. Had a lightning bolt knocked out just the mill's power, or was it the whole town? Don went over to one of the windows and they all followed him. Where the lights of the town usually blinked, up and down the hill, all was dark.

We'll see how Malcolm likes this disaster, Laurel thought. She half-hoped that there were no candles in the house, that the oil lamp was out of oil. A certain giddiness had overtaken her along with the others. It was like a recess from school, this unexpected coup by the weather, and it left her feeling charged with hilarity, now that the first fear of the dark had gone.

The mechanic, Al, now appeared. "Seems to be the main power station," he said laconically. "No sign of fires or anything."

Hail and sleet still shook the big building, while the blue lightning continued to flash in beautiful morse code across the wall of windows. Laurel felt that their small group was very tiny in the cathedral-like gloom of the mill. How helpless we are, really, she thought. Our world is based on everything going according to plan. But it takes so little to bring it to a halt.

"I'll get my radio," Betsy offered and stumbled over to the lockers. She turned it on as soon as she got it out, so that across the room, preceding her, came a faint trickle of sputtery slow waltz.

"Get the news, can't you?" Don said, impatiently trying to recover his authority. "See what happened."

Betsy fiddled with the dial. A man's voice crackled briefly before it died away.

"It's an old radio," Betsy apologized.

"Here, give it to me," Paula said, but she had no better luck. The only station that seemed to hold was the one playing the waltz. Don tried, and so did Al. The others seemed content not to know.

"How long do you think we should wait?" Martha asked.

"At least half an hour," Don said sternly. "It might be nothing, the lights might come right back on."

There was silence for a moment and then a renewed wave of giggling.

"What are we going to do here in the dark?" Paula asked. Betsy had fiddled the dial back to the waltz station. Provokingly it boomed louder, not drowning out the rattle of hail and clash of thunder, but underlining them rhythmically. It was a Strauss waltz, reminiscent of glittering ball gowns and long tails, of marble staircases and dazzling chandeliers. Laurel thought she had never heard anything so incongruous, or so wonderfully appropriate. The music was a reminder of one of the highpoints of a very civilized civilization. It came to them in the dark, out of the past, as sweet and luxurious as a technicolor movie.

"Well, we could dance," Laurel laughed. It seemed to her the funniest thing she had ever said.

"I'm game," said Paula. "Christ Almighty, I used to take dancing lessons off the TV." She held out her arms to Laurel, who swept exaggeratedly into them.

So, for the next delirious few minutes, the group of workers paired off into waltzing couples and careened around the dim, silent mill to the strains of the "Vienna Waltz." Even Don and Al gave in and got into the spirit.

When the waltz had ended, they all stopped in gales of laughter and agreed to call it a night.

"God works in mysterious ways," Paula told Laurel in the car, driving slowly through the icy, unlighted streets. "It's a miracle to be off work at nine o'clock."

When the lights went out Malcolm was only vaguely aware that something had happened. So feverish that he hardly knew where he was, he only gradually began to understand that there had been a qualitative change in the atmosphere. He'd been lying in a drugged sleep for hours with the light on, rousing himself at intervals to try to read. It had begun to seem very important to him to continue reading. Laurel had challenged him by calling him a vulture. No, not vicarious, he thought wildly. This is my work. He couldn't remember how he had first come to be interested in disasters; he thought now that it must have been a kind of preparation for his art. That was it, he was trying to understand how things could go wrong and so suddenly. We're living on the surface and underneath, he thought, trying to force his mind to work, things are *there*. It seemed to him that for the first time he was beginning to see an order in the universe, an order in disorder, in randomness, and that was what art was, wasn't it? It would help in his art, help him to begin creating if he could only understand what that meant.

Dozing and shivering, he kept trying to arouse himself to read and take in more facts. Over and over he read the lists of shipwrecks, mining disasters, and train collisions from his book. This book was wonderful, it had everything. It had been put together by the editors of the *Encyclopedia Britannica*. What did Laurel mean, there was no context? The whole world was the context, the whole of civilization and its attempts at order was the context for things going wrong, for man, as the title said, losing control. He knew about losing control, he had lost it. And there was a context for that, the context was his whole life, patterns he had been living, thinking that they meant something, that he was on his way to something. Now he saw that what had happened to him was unforeseen, but not an accident. It was a breaking through, a breaking down of the old patterns, so that something else might emerge. It had been the disaster books which had helped him to see that. Laurel, with her emphasis on discipline and results, just like his professors, was blind to the horrors and wonders of the breaking through. They thought that art could be planned, that everything would be taken care of . . . and it couldn't.

He woke and didn't know what time it was. The light in the room was off; everything, in fact, seemed to be darker. Except for the lightning which shot at frequent intervals across the sky and illuminated the room furtively, everything was dark. Malcolm couldn't remember having turned off the light. He

struggled up and groped for it. It took him a long while to realize that the light was for some reason no longer working. What
had gone wrong? Stumbling to the window, his brain on fire,
he saw that there were no lights anywhere. He thought perhaps that he was dreaming, yes, that he was dreaming a disaster, he didn't know which kind. Was he in a mine, had the
power failed, was water beginning to fill the shaft? He didn't
know. He tried to think it through, but there was nothing to
give him any clues. I'll go through the house, he decided
finally, and if the rest of the lights are working, I'll know. He
wasn't sure what he would know, maybe only that he wasn't
dreaming. He opened the bedroom door and went into the
living room. It was too black to see anything at all; he couldn't
remember if this was a place he had actually lived. If so, where
were the lamps? He knocked something over and heard the
crash of ceramic. That awakened him briefly from his stupor.
I'm sick, he thought, I'm very sick.

"Laurel," he called. There was no answer. He became irra-
tionally afraid. Why wasn't she here? Why was it so dark? Was
he really dreaming, was he really in a mine? Were the shafts
filling with water? He thought he heard the sound of water,
rushing and lapping.

"Laurel," he screamed, but he knew he was in a mine and
he had to get out fast. He had to get out because otherwise he
would die, he would be drowned, suffocated, smothered.

How could he get out? Wait, this was his house, wasn't it?
There were doors, there was the front door. He opened it and
stood staring at the black sky, the torrential downpour of rain
and sleet. He couldn't go out there. But the water, the water
was roaring behind him, around him, his feet were already
wet, the mine shaft was filling and he had to get out.

Malcolm began to run.

There wasn't a single candle lit in the house when Laurel
said good-bye, still laughing, to Paula, and got out of the car.
Probably gone to sleep, she thought. What if he had locked
the door again? I'll break it down, she told herself. Her good

mood gave her energy. No matter what he says, she thought, I'll demand that we get it out in the open.

But why was the front door open? Christ, the hall carpet was soaking wet.

"Malcolm," she called angrily. "Malcolm!"

She crashed through the house to the kitchen and lit the oil lamp. Then, carrying it carefully, she retraced her steps to the bedroom. That door, too, was open. The bed was rumpled but there was no one in it.

Laurel was at first confused, then terrified. Where could he have gone on a night like this? Then it came to her—he had been worried and had gone to the mill to meet her. It was all right, he had been worried, he had gone to find her, he still loved her. And she loved him. When he came back she would tell him about the waltzing and how she felt about Paula's friendship and how they could change their lives if they tried, if they tried hard enough.

Malcolm's body was found the next morning, near the pond. He had not been killed immediately when he fell and hit his head on a stone, but the effects of exposure on his already weakened body had sufficed. No one was sure whether he had been unconscious from the blow or whether he had tried to keep on going. His hand was frozen around a branch he might have tried to use as a kind of prop.

"He had no shoes on, he was wearing his pajamas," they told Laurel. "Do you have any idea why he was out there?"

Paula sat beside her, holding her hand. It seemed funny to have police standing in the kitchen, funny to see the sun pouring in this morning as if the storm had never been. It glittered on the icy rooftops out the window, smooth and unbroken.

It didn't make sense to tell them about the fight or about the shelf of catastrophes in the library, or that their isolation out here had had something to do with it or that Malcolm had found he had no ideas once he got out of school. She could have told them that Malcolm was afraid he wasn't good enough, that she was afraid, too, but had something else to sustain her, women like Paula and Betsy, for instance, who remained real to her when everything else went flat.

Laurel clung to Paula's hand, the hand that could not open jars but could give comfort to a friend, and wondered why she and Malcolm had never done that for each other. It was too late now.

"He was unhappy about his sculpture, his art, it wasn't going very well," was all she could say. Like every disaster, which breaks through a pattern and becomes part of the pattern, the reasons for it seemed clear only after it had happened, though no less mysterious.

Thin Ice

Kate woke upright, still traveling. It was early morning now, just past dawn; the sun eked out a brightness in the flat winter sky. The train was passing through Montana. She knew it was Montana because of the cattle. They were the first thing she saw when she opened her eyes—fragile, tiny, black and all shades of brown, stoically pawing the ground under their hooves, standing in forlorn clumps of three or four, pawing, stamping, methodically and desperately stamping through the icy plain to get at the grass underneath.

Kate was stiff everywhere: shoulders, back, eyelids, tongue, heart. She might be in Montana but for a moment she couldn't remember why.

The wedding. Her younger brother's, only brother's wedding. She hadn't seen him for two years and now he was marrying a woman no one knew in a remote town in northeastern Montana. Kate stretched, remembering the last time they'd met.

"Just passing through," Kevin said. He'd called from the Seattle Greyhound station and asked if he could spend the night. He wouldn't say where he was going; why. He had a furtive, youthful moustache and long, greasy brown hair. He must have been twenty then; he was four years younger. His eyes were as blue as she jealously remembered. "What a cute little boy. And those eyes!" ladies on the street and Mother's friends would coo. No one had cooed over Kate; she was a scowling and pugnacious child.

They'd stayed up all night drinking beer and talking about their childhood. The next afternoon, when Kate got up, he was gone.

Now Kevin was getting married, and at the last minute he had invited her to come. Kate blinked back tears and stared stubbornly at the cattle on the thinly iced Montana plain; she watched them break up the ground they stood on.

She was the only one to get off at the stop. The train was twenty minutes late and there was no one there to greet her. Kate stood in the one-room station for ten minutes wondering what to do. Did everyone really know everyone in small towns, like the novels always said they did? But she didn't even know the name of the bride-to-be. Her brother had neglected to tell her that.

"Kate!" There he was, they were.

Her name was Patricia and she looked about fourteen, blonde, petite, anemic under a fading tan. They were both wearing flannel shirts and down jackets. Kevin's hair was shorter and he had no moustache. He suggested immediately that they go have a beer.

"Dad couldn't come?"

"No," Kate said. Kevin looked disappointed. What did he expect? When he'd only dropped them each a line three days ago? It was Christmas time, the flights from L.A., where their father lived, hopelessly booked up. Kate could only come because the Hiawatha Express happened to stop here for two minutes en route to Chicago.

"How was the trip?" This from Patricia, shyly.

"Great. I've never been in Montana before. . . . "

She and Kevin smirked. "Not much to see, is there?" said her brother. "We've been going crazy the last week."

They were half-way through the town by now. It consisted of four blocks of stores and taverns and a few gas stations.

"We've been spending most of our time in here," said Kevin, leading the way into a bar.

The walls were covered with a static zoo of animal trophies. While Kevin went to order a pitcher, Patricia pointed out the curiosities. A two-headed calf. A monstrous wolf. An antelope.

"Did you grow up around here?" Kate asked politely. She really wanted to ask what Patricia had been doing in Florida and how she'd met Kevin, or if they'd met in Florida at all . . . Florida was the place Kate had heard from Kevin last. He'd been scuba-diving, he wrote on a hotel postcard, for a living.

Patricia shook her head. Her hair was the color of a manila envelope; it was cut very short and pushed behind her small ears.

"No, Tunisia," and she added, "My father was a sergeant in the Air Force. He's retired now. They live out at the old Air Force base."

Kevin came back with the beer. Kate wanted to cry: you're too young to get married! She felt absurdly old across the table from the two of them and had to keep reminding herself: I'm only twenty-six.

Patricia tossed off a beer in two swigs and stood up. "I'm supposed to get the flowers," she reminded Kevin matter-of-factly. And to Kate: "I'm sure you guys have a lot of things to talk about. I'll be back in a little while."

"How old is she?" Kate whispered to her brother when Patricia was gone.

"Eighteen," he said, as if it were the most natural thing in the world.

They finished three pitchers, just the two of them. They didn't talk at all about the recent past, what they'd both been doing for the past two years, in Seattle and in Florida, or wherever Kevin had been. For them, still, the strongest connection was their childhood, the golden time, "before . . . ," "before Mama . . . ," "before Mama died. . . . "

Kate didn't tell him, for instance, that she was on unemployment. She mentioned briefly that she was writing for a newspaper. She didn't tell him it was radical and feminist, she didn't mention her nonexistent salary.

What they talked about was the Christmas they got the Monopoly set; how they played it for four days straight, getting up at five in the morning to continue a game their parents had forced them to abandon the night before.

"You always used to cheat me though," Kevin said, smiling. "You thought I was too little to understand."

Kate laughed indignantly. "I did not. Remember how I'd share my hotels with you when you were losing?"

"You *loaned* them to me. That's a real different thing."

When they had stopped laughing, he asked shyly, "Remember the stories you used to tell me when we washed dishes together? The Feeble family who used to go down the kitchen sink drain to have adventures?"

"You still remember them? Nancy and Jack Feeble?"

They had shared the same room when they were small, they had run away together (to a nearby park), and traded plans for the future with utmost seriousness; she was going to be an actress, he would be a race car driver.

They were fairly drunk by the time Patricia came back. The wild animal busts stared down at them, Kate thought, like magic totems, mournful, distant.

"Look at that one," Patricia said, pointing out a small, long-eared, long-snouted specimen above the pinball machine. "It's a jackalope." She and Kevin both laughed. "A cross between a jackrabbit and an antelope."

Kate regarded the trophy with drunken seriousness. A freak of nature. Tragic. It was only later that they told her the animal was an invention of the bartender's.

They drove twenty miles to the Air Force base through a flat white countryside. In spite of the cold, there wasn't much snow; only ice, everywhere. The base, Patricia remarked, was being phased out since the end of the Vietnam War. Once it had been a thriving, self-sufficient (with the help of the government) community. Now only a few reservists and their families lived here, according to Patricia.

"But if your father's retired," Kate began.

"They get to live in the house for free, just to keep it up," explained Patricia. "They keep thinking of leaving, but they haven't decided where to go. We went to Florida in the Winnebago but they didn't like it much."

Kate looked quickly at her brother. Would this be the beginning of an explanation? But he said nothing.

The family was at the door to greet them: mother, father and two younger children. There was a heavily decorated and lighted Christmas tree in the window. The TV was on in the background. The Winnebago was parked in the driveway.

The wedding was scheduled for the following morning. Kate wasn't sure how she was going to make it through the intervening time. After a dinner of dry roast beef, white bread and chocolate pudding with Redi-Whip, Kevin and Patricia had retired upstairs. Kate was left alone with the family in front of the TV. They watched two games shows and one sit-com in a silence broken by well-meaning questions directed at Kate during commercials. Just as she felt she was going to pass out or start screaming, Patricia's father invited her out to take a look at the Winnebago. They put on their coats and boots and crossed the frozen lawn.

"This is the sink, look, real running water from the tank." Patricia's father turned on the faucet for her. He opened the cupboards where the dishes were all restrained by elastic bands.

"Have you traveled much?" Kate asked. "I heard you drove to Florida."

"Yeah, I didn't think much of Florida. Jews everywhere you went," he said. He was a sleek, round-eyed little man, his arms firmly muscled under a polo shirt, his hair crew-cut. "Next winter I plan to drive to California with the family. I'm retired, you know. I can go anywhere."

He showed Kate the beds, four of them. "Two people got to sleep together," he explained. Then he added, "I've been living in the Winnebago since we got back from Florida. My wife and I aren't getting along too well these days."

After a few minutes Kate excused herself and walked across the lawn. She kicked at its glittery surface in imitation of the Montana cattle. Patricia's father didn't follow her inside and none of the family seemed to expect that he would.

*

December 23, 8:42 p.m. (by digital clock)

I've never tried to live through a longer evening. I can't believe that I'm here in Montana, in the middle of nowhere or close to it, responding to questions about my life. "Unmarried at twenty-six." God, do they make me feel old.

December 23, 9:26 p.m.

... I know, I know, I know there are homes like this all over the country. But it's different thinking of Middle America related to me. They have me in the nine-year-old girl's room. She has posters of David Cassidy and John Travolta on the walls. She has a horse collection marching on two window sills. She showed me how to use her record player, showed me the records she puts on before she goes to sleep at night. I tried to get her to take it all with her, but she's sleeping on the couch in the living room and, "They all hate David's singing."

The junior bed sags dismally under my weight. There aren't enough covers. Luckily I brought my sleeping bag. Trying to read ... I hear the family moving about; the mother's having last minute consultations with her daughter about the reception. Patricia is moaning that "It will be too small. All my friends have moved away." I expect the mother to counter, "Sorry 'bout that!" (She has used this phrase constantly since I arrived. Tartly. She must have been an impudent young girl. . . .) But instead she begins a long monologue about her own wedding, too long to repeat here and not very interesting, but all the same, I listen and listen.

December 23, 10:09 p.m.

What a difference age makes when you're young. I was the first-born, Kevin the baby. Both had advantages; still, I think I exploited mine better. Even before our mother died, I usually got my way. I was so damned wily, my brother so trusting. I suppose I thought it could go on like that forever . . . his trust. Today I remembered something I didn't tell him. A story with a moral, or no moral. . . .

Our family belonged to a beach club in Southern California. It had a pool where Kevin and I took swimming lessons, a gym and a private beach. One parent or the other would drop us off there on Saturdays for our lesson, with explicit instructions not to go outside the bamboo fence of the private beach, in other words, to the ocean. But I loved to swim in the sea, or rather, to just stand in the waves and be buffeted about, pretending to be a mermaid or something At that age, Kevin didn't like the ocean much; it was too dark and cold, he said. He only followed me to the water because he could make better sandcastles with wet sand. Our parents didn't know we were down there, of course . . . they would have been furious, and Kevin and I had a solemn pact not to tell them.

One afternoon, while building one of his sandcastles Kevin stepped on a rusty nail embedded in a piece of driftwood. He cried out, but there was very little blood. We looked at the puncture.

"I know. I'll go get you a band-aid," I said.

So I marched up to the lifeguard station and asked for a band-aid.

"What happened?" The lifeguard wanted to know.

"Oh, nothing much. My little brother stepped on a nail, that's all."

The lifeguard looked suddenly concerned. "Was it rusty?"

"Rusty?" I wondered what was wrong. Why didn't he just give me a band-aid? "A little maybe."

"Are your parents here?"

"Yes," I lied, hoping he wouldn't ask to speak to them.

"Well, go tell them what happened. Tell them to take your brother to the doctor right away for a tetanus shot."

"Ten-nis?"

"Tetanus," he repeated. "To prevent lockjaw. Wait, maybe I should talk to them."

"No, I'll go tell 'em. Right away!" And I raced off. What was lockjaw? Did it mean you couldn't open your mouth anymore? How serious was it?

Kevin was dribbling wet sand over the castle.

"Did you get the band-aid?"

"No," I said. "They didn't have any more." I looked carefully at his mouth. The lifeguard was probably just trying to scare me. I couldn't tell our parents how Kevin came to step on a nail. That would mean the end of the ocean.

"It doesn't hardly hurt at all now," Kevin asserted. He stood up to get more wet sand in his pail. He was so thin that his trunks hung around his hips. His eyes were as blue as the deepest summer ocean. I had never loved him more.

I've never told Kevin about the tetanus shot he should have had. Wonder if he remembers that day?

December 23, 11:15 p.m.

People would call me "little mother" after our mother's death. For six years, until I went away to college, I was the woman of the house. And I was satisfied. I liked cooking, liked cleaning, liked dispensing advice. I felt threatened by my father's girlfriends, though the relationships never came to anything. He almost got married once, but then the woman decided she couldn't cope with two children. She was pretty young. I think my father was really in love with her; he sort of gave up after that.

The three of us made real efforts to be together sometimes; we'd take trips in the station wagon, all singing at the top of our lungs, go to football games, make popcorn and watch TV. After I left, everything fell apart. Dad and Kevin just couldn't be together. And I was off at college, smoking dope, reading Camus, learning about sex and politics. I'd come home for holidays, but I wasn't much interested in. . . .

There's something else I thought of on the train trip, an early memory: Kevin, my baby brother, the day they brought him home from the hospital. I was four. I stood on a chair to reach the crib and tried to stuff a piece of chocolate candy into his mouth as a welcoming gesture. I was heartbroken that he didn't want it, that he burst out crying.

Kate woke up groggily on the morning of her brother's wedding, having stayed up half the night beginning a journal that she would never continue back in Seattle. In the bathroom she met Kevin, shaving.

"They're having breakfast downstairs," he said.

"You coming?"

"Not hungry."

Kate nodded, wishing he would look at her. But he stared fixedly into the mirror, scraping at his lean cheeks, his blue eyes dark as his Levis.

She went downstairs and had bacon and cornflakes, and instant coffee with Cremora. The TV was on, the Christmas tree lights blinked feverishly, sleet was falling on the flat plain that stretched outside the windows. The family was eating breakfast in front of the TV, except for Patricia's mother, who was doing her hair at the dining room table with three mirrors propped in front of her. Kate had carried down the camera that a photographer friend had lent her, a very exotic, expensive camera, and was trying to load it. She'd thought she might attempt some interesting, candid shots of the members of the wedding.

"Need any help?" asked Patricia's father. He was wearing his bathrobe and had the Sunday paper spread all around the sofa. His eyes flicked to the TV every time there was a burst of canned laughter.

"No, think I got it," Kate said, inwardly cursing her lack of technical expertise. She should have brought her own camera, the kind with the cartridge, where all you had to do was press a button. Now, did you thread the film through this slot or that one?

"I had a great camera, picked it up in Japan once. In the Air Force," explained Patricia's father. "Traveling like we did, we picked up things for a steal. Course we had to leave most of them behind. Let me tell you about our villa in Tunisia."

And he launched into a long story about a Tunisian rebellion or revolution that had ravaged the countryside and forced the family to hide out at the base, leaving their villa to be plundered.

Every time Kate began to be interested in what he was saying, Patricia's mother would break in from the dining room.

"Walt, stop boring poor Kate with your boring stories."

"No, I'm inter—"

"She's interested, Judy, she's a journalist for godssakes. She needs to know this stuff."

"Actually I'm not a political writer, I mean international politics. I write book reviews occasionally for a—"

"I don't care, Walt. Tunisia was an awful, dirty place. Tell her about the rats and the niggers that would steal everything that wasn't tied down. That's why we don't have those vases and things now.... No, don't tell her, this is a wedding day after all.... "

After several of these exchanges, during which time Kate resolved to go to the library as soon as she got back home and to look up something on Tunisia, Patricia finally came down the stairs and put an end to the bickering. She was wearing her mother's wedding dress and a tiara in her dull gold hair.

"Look at Trish!"

Her little sister came over and hugged her. Her brother jostled her tiara. Her father stood silently. Her mother sighed. This was the moment Kate should have taken the candid shot. Unfortunately, due to the Tunisian uprising, the film was not yet in the camera.

"Kevin will be down in a minute, then you can use the bathroom, Daddy." Patricia's tone was gentle and matter-of-fact. Kate began to see what Kevin saw in her.

Kate drove to the church with Kevin and Patricia, wearing her blue velvet suit with the camera over her shoulder. She felt as if she were going out on a story. Objectivity cheered her up. She was an observer, she was not involved. She was merely a spectator to the human condition.

They drove through the white swirling wind to the base's chapel and community center. From the back set Kate noticed how nice they looked, how they hardly talked, how they touched not at all.

Of course, she thought, amazed that she hadn't thought of it before. Patricia was pregnant. It was a shotgun wedding. That's why the mood was like this. Should she make them stop the car, have a heart-to-heart talk about the future? Tell them about rising divorce rates? Tell them what happened to children from broken homes? It's all a mistake, kids.

"The road's like a skating rink," Kevin complained.

"Maybe we won't get there," Kate tried to joke.

"Oh, we'll get there," smiled Patricia, adjusting her tiara.

Two bridesmaids in yellow bore Patricia away with cries and giggles, while the minister led Kevin off. Kate was left to wander around in the community center, taking her candid shots. She got one of Walt standing pensively by a window, staring at his watch; one of the little sister, skipping with a basket of flowers; one of Patricia's friends waving around a blue garter; one of herself in a mirror.

After a while she grew bored and filed into the church with the rest of the guests. She remembered that the relatives and friends of the bride were supposed to sit on one side, those of the groom on the other. Luckily no one was paying any attention to that rule; otherwise Kate would have been completely alone.

She wondered suddenly, painfully, if their father had tried to come after all. Had he ever liked Kevin? On the telephone he'd sounded more disgruntled than anything. "Montana, getting married in Montana? Isn't that just like him? No, of course I can't get a flight. . . . "

The ceremony seemed briefer than the weddings she recalled from her youth. Kevin forgot his lines and had to be prompted. Patricia's "yes" rang out like a spoon tapping a glass. Then it was over, before Kate had had enough time to reflect on the institution of marriage as a whole, what it meant, what it could possibly *mean*, to stand up in front of a crowd of people and recite some tired old words and promises. In spite of herself, however, she was moved, close to tears . . . "in sickness and in health. . . . " Mother had been sick two years before she died.

The professional photographer posed Patricia and Kevin in front of the altar. Kate realized that this was the first time she had seen them kiss.

Outside the wind howled over the Montana plain and chunks of ice knocked against the stained glass windows like uninvited guests.

Kate was by herself in a corner of the reception hall, quietly getting plastered with her own stolen bottle of champagne, when Kevin found her.

"Hi." He was also somewhat drunk. His hair was rumpled and his bow tie askew. He looked very handsome and very young.

"Having a good time?" he asked.

"Oh, moderately. How about you?"

"I'm glad it's over."

"Are you? I don't know, I feel kind of sad. Now you're actually married."

"Yeah, I know. Crazy, isn't it?"

Kate saw Patricia, her dull gold hair smooth under the tiara, watching them from across the room.

"How do you feel?" she asked her brother.

"Fine. Oh great. Yeah, I'm fine."

"Kevin, why'd you do it?"

He looked bewildered. "Why? Oh, I don't know, seemed like the right thing to do."

"Is she pregnant?"

He looked even more bewildered. "No, oh no, not that."

"Then?"

"I just wanted to. I met her, I liked her. We get along, you know. I guess I was just lonely."

"Are you going back to Florida?"

"Florida? Nah. I lost my job scuba diving there. I was unemployed when I met them."

"Them?"

"Yeah, I was hitchhiking and they picked me up in their camper."

"And you came back with them to Montana?"

"Yeah. Crazy, isn't it?"

Patricia came over. "Kev, I have some people I want you to meet."

"Congratulations," Kate told her. "You look great."

"Thank you." She paused and stared with great warmth and desperation right at Kate. "You wouldn't believe how many stories Kevin has told me about you. Sometimes I think his childhood was the only thing that ever happened to him."

"Yeah, sometimes I feel that way myself."

"We did have a pretty good time then," Kevin said softly.

Patricia took Kevin's arm. "We're planning to visit California and see your dad. I'm really excited about seeing where you grew up."

"At least it's sunny there," said Kevin and drew a laugh. They moved away to meet Patricia's friends.

Kate finished the bottle of champagne just as it was time to go. The hall had only been rented for a couple of hours.

It was brilliantly sunny when Kevin drove his sister to the train station the next morning. It was Christmas. They didn't talk much at first; they were both hungover. Patricia was still in bed, asleep. Kate hadn't been able to say good-bye to her.

It had snowed during the night; the drifts by the roadside were scalloped by the wind. The sun hurt Kate's eyes.

"Reminds me of sand dunes," Kevin said, pointing. "Remember how we used to roll down 'em when we were kids?"

"Kevin, why do we always talk about the past?"

"That's the only time we ever spent much time together, I guess," he said uneasily, glancing at her.

"Sometimes I've thought you hated me and Dad."

"Sometimes I have." Kevin was driving more slowly now, eyes squinting against the glare. "You both tried to boss me around all the time. Maybe you didn't realize that, but you did. I hated it. And after you left for college, it was really bad. I was only fourteen, you know. Dad wouldn't let me do anything. He was always restricting me, punishing me, telling me I wasn't like you . . . and why wasn't I like you?"

"And I was wasting his money smoking dope in the dormitory," Kate said, but Kevin didn't smile.

"It made me mad, him always wanting me to do what you'd done. Read more, get better grades, stay at home more, go to college. It made me sick. I did a lot of things I did because I wanted to be different from you."

They were getting near the town. The gas stations appeared, then the taverns. Kate felt her stomach contract; she had wanted to talk, but not here, not now. She was too close to leaving, to beginning her own adult life again. She wished she'd never brought the subject up.

But a kind of anger had come into Kevin. He didn't look at his sister; he shielded his eyes from the morning sun and hunched over the steering wheel, saying, "I don't know why the hell I got married, I just did it. Maybe it will be terrible, I don't know. Maybe it'll be great. I'm just doing it. I didn't want to invite you and Dad, you know. Patricia made me. She's into the formalities, see? The wedding was her idea, the bridesmaids, the reception. She was shocked that I wouldn't invite my only two relatives . . . and then Dad couldn't even *come*."

"I'm glad I came," Kate said, rather feebly.

"I'm glad you did too," Kevin said and looked at her for the first time. "Only, you shouldn't have acted that way."

"What way?"

"As if you were too good for the whole situation. I know Patricia's family is fucked up, but all the same they're good people and you didn't treat them right."

"What did I do?"

"Just little things, you might have thought they didn't notice, Kate, but they noticed. The way you said, 'I never eat white bread.' The way you went off by yourself at the reception and drank. They were hurt. You've always been like that, always thought you were better than other people. I sure can't see you on a newspaper going around interviewing people."

"They say I have a good eye for detail," Kate tried to joke.

"A good eye, but no heart."

"Oh, shut up. What about you? What do you know about

love or anything like it? You don't love Patricia, I can tell that much."

Kate was suddenly sobbing. They turned into the train station parking lot. They had ten minutes.

"She loves me," said Kevin quietly. "That's something."

They got out of the car and opened the trunk to get Kate's suitcase.

"Why did she ever die, Kevin?" Kate found herself asking. But that wasn't right, what did their mother's death have to do with what they were now?

He looked at her dumbly. He was crying too.

The train arrived. It was only due to stay two minutes. There was so much Kate had to tell him.

"Will you come and see me?"

He nodded. "Yes, we will."

"There's someone I want you to meet."

"Are you getting married?" He was grinning now, in relief.

"No, I'm not getting married. You're the only one who'd do something crazy like that."

They hugged. Kate only reached the middle of his chest.

She stood on the train steps. "Kevin! Remember the rusty nail on the beach? I almost killed you because I. . . . "

The train was moving. Kevin said nothing, but stood and watched as it gathered momentum. For ten minutes at least Kate saw him on the platform, waving, growing smaller and smaller. In winter the Montana plain is very flat and white. You can see back, or forward, a long way.

Stalingrad

Round One:

It was the last day of her visit and the Panzer tanks had thrust deep into her country. In lightning maneuvers she found herself surrounded and eliminated, while he pressed on to Moscow, to Leningrad, to Stalingrad. If he occupied any of these cities for more than two weeks, he would win. Her only hope was to hold out until winter, when the heavy snow would overcome him, when his supply lines would falter, when her replacement troops would arrive in greater and greater numbers.

In the kitchen his wife, Fran, was washing last night's dinner dishes, very silently.

Jeff rolled the dice and got clear weather for October. He rapidly occupied Minsk and Smolensk, with heavy losses on her side. In spite of his hangover he was intense, exultant, boyish still at thirty. It was times like this that he reminded Kate most of her brother, Kevin; both of them blue-eyed, brown-haired, more than handsome—familiar.

"If the weather holds I'll be in Moscow before Christmas."

"We've only got two hours before my plane leaves," Kate said. She was finding it hard to get into the spirit of the game; it had something to do with Fran so quiet in the kitchen. Fran thought war games were sick; she had said so, brusquely, when they got it out.

"I wish you wouldn't encourage him," Fran had said. "He

never plays these things anymore."

Kate never played them either, except with Jeff. Her own lover, back in Seattle, had been jailed for resisting the draft years ago. When they'd moved in together, she'd clandestinely deposited "Gettysburg" and the "Battle of the Bulge" in the trash. Peter would be appalled if he saw her now, massing her troops around Moscow, protecting her railroads, plotting survival in a fight to the death.

She couldn't help it, she felt responsible for Fran's resentment, especially since for the first time they'd had some good talks, had acknowledged a warmth for each other. The usual awkwardness around one of Kate's visits had vanished. They'd discussed their jobs, their friends, books and politics... and Fran had finally admitted that she felt all right about Kate's older, still confusing claim on her former lover, Jeff. Kate had told her all about Peter; Fran had asked her advice about Jeff.

For Kate to jump an hour ago at Jeff's suggestion that she play a game of "Stalingrad" with him, "for old time's sake," had been wrong. It was a betrayal of those confidences, that new friendship.

Jeff bent over the honeycombed mapboard and totaled up the number of his attack factors. His brown hair fell into his eyes and he pushed it back. "Five to one—defender eliminated. That's you, Red." He grinned.

I've always loved him, it's just different, Kate thought.

"You wait," she threatened, blocking Fran from her mind. "Your time's coming."

Attacks:

"When we first got married," Fran had said, pouring herself another glass of wine last night, "I thought he'd do everything he said he would." Her straight blonde hair had swung unhappily around her freckled face. "I was so young... this winter he didn't do anything but sit around with his friends and drink beer. Talking about baseball, dope and car parts. I hate them. Why is he so easily influenced? He's not like them. He could be a writer. At least he could write."

Fran was a graphic designer, working for an advertising agency, rising fast, making big money now. She'd been supporting Jeff for the past six months.

"It's like he wants to fail. When I talk to him about the future, how he sees himself when he's older, *I'm* never in the picture. Instead he's in some hotel room somewhere, like his father, drinking and alone. It doesn't even seem to scare him."

"I think it's just a stage," Kate had tried to reassure her. "I mean, he did get a book published. It's not his fault they remaindered it. I'd be depressed, too. He'll get back on his feet. He's always been that way."

"Is Peter like that?" Fran had wanted to know—blonde, earnest, young. Her family was well-off; she had been embarrassed about being a virgin, Jeff had said.

"Well . . . no. But then, he's not a writer. He just goes to work and comes home and then goes to meetings. He thinks about the world situation a lot." Kate had faltered slightly. Peter's seriousness sometimes weighed on her. When you came right down to it, Jeff had been fun to be around most of the time, propounding his crazy ideas, taking up any dare, with no regard for propriety or safety. Like Fran, Kate had worried about him; he could be so intense when he was writing, so moody when he wasn't. Peter was a known quantity; he suited her much better. All the same, there were still things to be said for the way Jeff had livened up life back then. He had challenged her in a way Peter never did. He'd shaken up all that she believed in. He had been good for her.

Hadn't he?

History of the War:

Jeff's apartment had been a shambles of dumbbells, paperbacks, stacks of typing paper and beer bottles. On top of the refrigerator, piled high and ragged with use, were "Blitzkrieg," "Afrika Korps" and "Stalingrad."

"You must be kidding," she'd said when he suggested a game the morning after they'd first slept together. "I don't know about you, but to me, war is no game. Vietnam's hardly over and already they're talking about blowing up the Mideast. You can't be serious."

"Take it easy, for Chrissake. Give a little. Think about it. Can't you imagine a situation different from your own?"

"Give in and start believing it's possible? No, I won't believe that."

"It happened, didn't it? This might give you some understanding why."

She had played, and played again, had learned to give herself up to the game and suspend judgment.

Maybe the differences between them had excited her, maybe they'd made her believe that she was experiencing life more fully. There had been the pull of connection, too—she might read Austen and Woolf, organize against nuclear power, play the flute and write sensitive stories—but Jeff was right, there was another world out there. Her brother had joined the Army. And there was Jeff, with his interest in the Beats and sports—the thriller he was writing, full of speed and murder, male things, things that fascinated her, if only because she was so opposed to them.

They had argued constantly even as they changed each other. "Idealist," "Nihilist," "Sexist," "Prig"—the terms flew back and forth for six months. When Kate had finally moved out, shouting that not only would she never live with him again, but she wouldn't live with any man, Jeff had gone away for an extended vacation.

The next time she heard from him he was married. He'd invited her to visit.

Defenses:

"It's not that I don't care about her," Jeff had said as they'd walked along the beach two days ago. "But I can't give her what she needs, stability, a future. It would be better if we split up, I guess."

"You've always been a romantic, thought of yourself as a loser."

"Come on, have I ever pretended anything else?"

They'd talked about their writing. Kate was still working on her first novel, which was taking forever.

"I've got some ideas," Jeff had said, " . . . But I don't know, what's the use? The first one didn't even get any reviews. Hell, I'm never going to be any good, what's the use?"

Once these discussions had sparked anger. Kate had been like Fran then, furious at his fatalism, his apocalyptic romance with the male mystique. She had defended her values, had psychoanalyzed: "Just because your father was a failure and an alcoholic doesn't mean you have to follow him."

Now she'd only said, "You're drinking too much, you know."

He'd changed the subject. "How's Peter?"

Kate had dug her feet into the sand. "It's funny, I feel almost relieved to be away from him. I don't know why. Sometimes I feel like I'm hiding a part of myself from him. I mean, we never get down and talk, never do anything the least bit out of the ordinary. All the things you and I fought about, he takes for granted. . . . He's part of some new committee against the draft. . . . "

"Don't tell me I really corrupted you?"

"Of course I'm against war, I hate it, but it makes me feel funny sometimes. You know Kevin's a sergeant in the Army now."

"He's still in?"

"Yeah, he re-enlisted. He's going to make a career of it. Am I supposed to hate him or something? Peter makes me feel like I should."

She had told Jeff often enough that he reminded her of her brother so that he hadn't needed prompting. "I can bet he doesn't like you coming down here to visit me, either."

Kate had laughed a little. "You're part of my sordid past."

"Fran feels the same about you."

In revolt, they'd grabbed hands as they walked, united by some bond neither really understood.

Replay:

Kate used to play war games, active ones, with her younger brother and their friends. There were only boys in the neighborhood; that made it awkward.

"You gotta be the nurse," they tried to tell her.

"I wanna be a G.I."

"Girls can't fight."

"I can too."

But after a point she had stopped struggling. She had understood finally what they seemed to have known from birth: war was not for girls. Girls could look on or they could go do something else. She had taken up reading.

Round Two:

One of his divisions had become isolated. Kate swept down a railway and eliminated it. She recaptured Kiev, began to bring out her reinforcements. The tide was turning, as it always did. Whenever they played this game, she took the Russians' part.

She always won.

Fran had gone out to the store. In her absence they'd fixed themselves Bloody Marys and Kate was talking about postponing her flight.

Flanking:

Kate had told Fran the night before: "I was always afraid for Jeff. It's like I felt sometimes that I was the last bulwark between him and death. That's ridiculous, of course. I mean, I took care of my brother for years, and that didn't stop him joining the Army. I found out I couldn't be Jeff's mother. I didn't want to be anyone's mother."

"That's what they all want." Fran had been almost vicious, pushing her blonde hair behind her ears. "Someone to protect them while they explore the outer limits. Keep the home fires burning."

"It's hard to stand by, helpless, thinking he might really destroy himself. . . . Not that Jeff is really going to destroy himself," she'd added.

"They just use it, they keep using it so you'll take care of them."

When Jeff first told her he'd gotten married, Kate had cried. She'd said she would never visit. Later she'd realized that was stupid. He should have a chance to live his life with whoever he wanted to. So she'd come down to see him and had been horrified by how young Fran was. That first visit had been awful. Fran had hardly talked, had only regarded her with jealousy and misery. Some old current of attraction had remained between Jeff and Kate; they had almost given in to it.

Only after Kate had started living with Peter had things gone better. And this visit, her third, Fran had opened up. Kate had felt it, and welcomed it—the comfort of confidences, shared experience, support.

They had drunk a little too much. They had touched each other's hands over the table.

"Do you think I should leave him?" Fran had asked.

"Yes," Kate had said. "No . . . I don't know."

Round Three:

Kate was decimating his troops now and it was only January in the course of the war. They were on their second Bloody Mary.

Fran came back from the store, her eyes dark-rimmed and full of resentment.

"Isn't your plane supposed to be leaving in half an hour?" she asked Kate.

"I called and changed it to a later flight. I called Peter, too," Kate added almost apologetically. It was ridiculous, but she didn't want to leave. It was so nice here with Jeff. It was like old times, better than old times.

Fran wouldn't go away. "Who's winning?" she asked irritably.

"Kate, as usual. It doesn't look like I'll ever get to Stalingrad."

"I hate these games," Fran burst out. "I don't know what you see in them."

Jeff shook the dice impatiently. "Intellectual stimulation."

"It's a bad habit," Kate said, nervous. "But Jeff's right. I don't think it has much to do with an actual war mentality. Or maybe it does, I don't know. But we enjoy it, anything that's fun can't be all bad, can it?" She drummed her fingers on the mapboard and stumbled on, staring down, seeing it all before her: the drifts of snow, the bitter winds, frostbite and starvation, digging in. "It gives me a sense of history. I mean, I'd read about the Russian campaign, but this helps me visualize it. I know now why the Germans lost, why they had to."

"You told me last night you were scared something might happen to your brother if there really were a war."

"I can't cut him off," Kate whispered. "I still love him. I want to understand him. Maybe that means understanding war, too."

"The Russian campaign was real, goddammit. Can't you understand that? It wasn't a game. It was a stupid war between Hitler and Stalin that killed millions of people. Generals play these games, men with power, men who could get your brother killed. I can see Jeff playing it, he wants to die. But why you?"

Kate shook her head.

"Franny, would you shut up?" Jeff said. "You've never understood what was between me and Kate."

"Oh, I understand all right. I just don't understand what I have to do with either of you."

"Fran," Kate said, "I'm not trying to . . ."

"Oh fuck off, both of you, just fuck off." She slammed out the door.

Kate half rose, then sat down again. "Oh Christ."

Jeff fixed them another Bloody Mary.

"I don't suppose you'd consider staying down here."

"My sympathies are all with her, you know."

"I know. That's why you're living with Peter."

Kate started to put the pieces of the game away. "I concede."

"Don't." He suddenly came over to her and grabbed her by the shoulder. "I love you. I always have."

"I loved my brother and look where it got me. And him."

"I only married her out of spite."

"Jeff, don't say that."

"You never risk anything. That's why you want to be the Russians all the time. You just sit there and wait for my troops to die in the cold."

In spite of herself she had to laugh. She drank some of her Bloody Mary.

"You've always been a bad influence on me. You get me all confused."

"And Peter doesn't?"

"And Peter doesn't."

"Better go back then."

"I'm going to."

At the Frontier:

In the plane Kate fell asleep and had a dream.

She was in a city under siege and got a message that her brother needed her. He was at the front. Disguising herself as a man, she found her way to his side. He was already dying. His blue eyes brought back their whole childhood, and then some; he was turning into Jeff.

"You have to take my place," he told her.

"I don't believe in war. It's only men killing each other.

You never wanted me to play with you. I don't know the rules anyway."

She took off her coat and wrapped him in it.

"Don't leave me," he said, before he closed his eyes.

"It's not my war, it's not my war. I don't understand. Please. Don't leave me."

A bomb burst, illuminating the battlefield. Suddenly she saw that all the soldiers were women, and that there was no reason to be afraid.

Women never killed each other.

But she couldn't help crying. Her brother was dead. Jeff was dead. "Do they all have to die before it will stop?" she asked a woman next to her.

"Yes," the woman said. "No . . . I don't know."

Sense and Sensitivity

It's not me who needs help, it's the whole rest of the world. The stories I've heard since I first began to see that therapist! I hardly have to mention my once a week visit when I get this, Oh I should be seeing a shrink, too. I just can't cope with blah, blah, blah, and the whole bloody story follows. My own poor problems, if they are even problems, have nothing on theirs.

The therapist, a nice enough young fellow, is a friend of my daughter's, and I'm seeing him on the advice of my daughter, because I was so foolish as to exclaim one day, "I don't understand anything anymore. I don't know what the world is coming to." This cry of dismay, combined with what Stella calls my erratic tendencies, meaning my refusal to take a low-paying secretarial job and my obsessive novel-reading when I should be cleaning house and babysitting her two children, was enough for Stella to set up an appointment for me with Dr. Augustus.

I can imagine how she described me. . . . "My mother has been slowly falling apart since her divorce. Instead of trying to adjust to the modern world, to her new reality, she's retreated into fantasy. . . . Every time I go over there she's reading some nineteenth century novelist, or even worse, Jane Austen. She can hardly be bothered to talk to me. My father left her a lovely house, and she's let it turn into a pigsty. I'm worried when I leave Leaf and Canny there. She lets them do anything. . . . Once I found them lighting matches in the bathroom, they all could have burned to death!"

That part's true and I'm very sorry, but wouldn't an easier solution be not to leave the children with me at all? I love my grandchildren but I don't really want to be bothered with them. Stella was enough. Twenty-five years of marriage was enough. Half my adult life wasted on sparkling kitchen floors and well-balanced dinners. If I only want to live now in the small villages of English literature and look forward, through trials and tribulations, secret elopements and entailments, to the happy endings of the virtuous and just, who can blame me?

Stella, for one. She has modernness like a disease and is determined to communicate it to me. When I say I don't understand her world and don't want to, it only makes her more set on having me enter into it.

Entering into her marriage, for instance. My own situation seems clear-cut to the point of cliché: Bob was regularly unfaithful throughout our marriage and finally, a year ago, when he was fifty, he threw me aside and married the proverbial twenty-three-year-old stewardess. Ho hum. Stella refuses to understand what a marriage can become in twenty-five years, how two partners can be as good as living apart long before they actually separate. "He just threw you away like you were an old trash can, Mom." (I have tried to divest Stella of the habit of "Mom" but in spite of her forward views she still clings to it.) Useless to explain that I am an old trash can, but I don't really mind it. Useless to explain that I like living by myself enough to excuse this terrible insult to my pride. Useless to explain that I don't want to recapture my youth by taking a lover or buying a hot tub or cruising to Puerto Vallerta. Stella can't stand the picture of me subsiding happily and graciously into old age.

Perhaps it's because she feels sometimes like an old trash can herself. Her husband hasn't left her, and in fact I would be surprised if Mickey ever did, but they are living out as curious a tragicomedy as I ever heard of, and honestly, never *did* hear of, until Stella clarified the gory details. I still have trouble imagining how it all came to pass.

Stella came to me crying one day. I reluctantly tore myself away from a fifth or sixth reading of my favorite Austen novel, *Pride and Prejudice,* to ask her what was wrong.

"Mickey is in love with another woman!"

"Oh dear," I said, trying to look concerned. "But it will probably pass, don't you think?" I vaguely remembered that Mickey had had a tendency to fall in love often, especially before Stella became pregnant the first time.

"This is different," Stella wailed. "If he only wanted to sleep with her, it would be different."

I didn't see the problem then, if that was the case. In my experience it had always been the sleeping together aspect which caused the difficulties, though in my time, before everybody was so open, we managed to keep it quiet; the wife asked no questions and the husband told no lies.

"Why doesn't he want to sleep with her?" I inquired patiently. Far be it from Stella's mother to show a lack of interest in the details.

"Well, he does want to, actually, but she wouldn't."

"She believes in monogamy, then,?" I asked, trying out one of Stella's current words."

"She's, she's a lesbian."

"Oh, my goodness."

Then it all came pouring out. "See, Mickey used to know her before she became a lesbian, but they were never lovers, just friends. Then Sarah became a lesbian, but she only *just* became one, so Mickey doesn't know if it's going to stick. They saw each other for lunch and it was obvious they felt this terrible attraction for each other, but Sarah is living with another woman and she's practically a separatist.'"

"What's a separatist?" I asked faintly.

"Oh, Mom. A separatist is a lesbian who for political reasons has decided not to have anything to do with men."

"What was she doing having lunch with Mickey then?"

"Well, she's not a separatist yet, and Mickey is hoping she'll reconsider it. I mean, it's obvious that if she can still feel this terrible attraction to Mickey that she's confused."

"Hummm." To be honest, I had difficulty imagining anyone having "this terrible attraction" to Mickey. He's a sort of skinny, intense man whose only possible charm is in his self-effacing manner. His haunted eyes, which Stella finds so compelling, have always bored me. I had gotten used to Stella's infatuation with him, but I had difficulty seeing that other, possibly more sensible, women might feel the same way. I was interested in this new idea of separatism, though.

"How can these women live in a world without men? I mean, practically? Don't they have to go to the grocery store now and then?"

"They ignore men as far as possible, that's if they live in the city. A lot of them move to the country in communes and become self-sufficient. Anyway, it's not grocery store clerks who are the problem, they can just ignore *them*. . . . The point is not to have anything to do with men on a personal level."

I considered this. Jane Austen had lived in a primarily woman-centered world where her closest companion was her sister, Cassandra. And her novels, too, circle through that female universe of manners rather than action. That was one of the things I found most restful about Austen's work, her detailing of the small lives of women. Yet I, like the author, was always conscious of men in the wings, ready to provide romance, heartbreak, and possibly, a home and a decent income at the end.

"How can I compete with this kind of idealized love?" Stella was moaning. It did seem a problem. Stella, though attractive and still young, had the worn and seedy aspect of the young mother, in spite of her advanced, and supposedly relaxed views. My harried maternity was exactly what had first impelled Bob to indiscretion, not because he thought I was bourgeois, but because he thought I was boring.

"Does he think of this girl Sarah as some sort of challenge?" was all I could come up with. I didn't mean challenge in the ordinary sense of male conquest and domination. Mickey was too much of a political idealist for that. He had recently become involved in what he called a "men's group" and his favorite topic of conversation with me was feminism. Both he and Stella seemed to see me as some sort of latent Betty

Friedan, whose callous abandonment by her husband made her ripe for conversion. Their arguments both amused and irritated me. I was perfectly willing to consider the changes in the world for the better and to reevaluate my years of oppression as a woman, but I wasn't at all interested in their prodding advice about going back to college after twenty-five years and taking up where I left off as an English major. "The only reason I went to college was to find a husband," I used to tell them. "I never gave a damn about studying English literature then and still less now. Wordsworth, ugh."

Nevertheless Mickey had succeeded in convincing me that he was a true believer in the Cause, and I could see that it might be quite a feather in his political cap to convince a potential lesbian separatist that he was just as much a feminist as she was.

"What's challenging about it?" Stella asked glumly. "No, he's in love and it's terrible."

"Are you going to leave him?"

"Leave him? Of course not." Stella's chin rose. "We'll work through it somehow." My daughter has this awful confidence in working through things.

It was conversations like these which convinced Stella that I should see her therapist. I was not convinced, but ever the willing Mom (at least sometimes), I took the appointment date down and went to see him.

It wasn't half so bad as I imagined. In fact, I gradually found myself rather liking the idea of it. While driving to his office I engaged in an imaginary conversation with a god-like being who would answer my worst confusions about this new generation, with its emphasis on getting things out into the open and being sensitive about each other's feelings.

Dr. Augustus (he apparently likes to be called Jim, but that I can't manage) was a tall, thin young man on the order of Mickey, but with a beard and without the soulful expression.

We exchanged a bit of small talk and then he asked pleasantly, "You're divorced, Ms. Campbell?"

"Yes. For a year now."

"How do you feel about that?"

I paused. "Stella thinks it heresy, or worse—not coming to grips with my true feelings, but I would say that I feel fine about it."

"You had been separated for some time?"

"Not in actual fact . . . but since Stella went off to college we had been living . . . at a distance from each other. Neither of us were, how shall I put it, the sharing type. We did not communicate like young people today and we didn't think it necessary. After the first years, our being together was more or less habit. I didn't actually find it that difficult to adjust after Bob left. It was surprisingly easy, in fact."

"It was an amicable divorce, then?"

"Oh, well, these things are always touchy, aren't they? Bob seemed so guilty that I had to play along with a scene or two, but once they were over, yes, it was very amicable. And he was very generous."

"These scenes weren't genuine?"

I hesitated a moment, not sure how to begin. How to explain that they had a core of genuineness, an unexplored anger twenty years old. And that when I accused my husband of lying to me I was not only talking of the present, but of the past, using phrases I might have meant the first time I discovered traces of another woman in his things, but no longer.

"Didn't it feel good to get things out in the open?" Dr. Augustus prodded gently.

"It was too late, you see." Was that a quaver in my voice?

"Sometimes," said Dr. Augustus, "things that don't get said pile up inside and choke off real feeling."

"I've never believed that everything needs to be said," I found myself asserting, while I began to have the strangest, most choking sensation in my chest.

"Why did you decide to begin therapy, Ms. Campbell?"

"My daughter, Stella, whom you know, needs to be understood. In addition, she feels that I'm not living in the real world. She thinks I should be doing something with my life."

"How did she feel about the divorce?"

"Politically or . . . ?"

Dr. Augustus smiled. "Really."

"I think she was terribly angry with both of us. It was one of her myths that we were a happy couple. While all her friends' parents were divorcing, she could depend on us to stay together."

"You never expressed your real feelings about the marriage to her?"

"That's not quite the right way to put it. I had no real feelings about the marriage. I had the habit of it."

"Does Stella see her father now?"

"No, never. That's the political side of it. He's the patriarchal enemy in the scenario while I'm the heroine."

"Would you say that your daughter has a traditional marriage?"

I raised my eyebrows. I wondered how much he knew about lesbian separatism.

He went on without waiting, "Does it seem strange to you that she depended so much on the traditional aspects of her parents' marriage while trying to live an entirely different way herself?"

"Well, strange and then not so strange. Aren't a traditional upbringing and traditional values what give you courage to go against them and try something new? Besides, the whole society's changing and she wants to be a part of that change."

"Do you, Ms. Campbell?" He smiled seriously.

"I'm not sure."

"Well, Mom, how did it go? Did you like him?"

"He seems a very nice young man."

"But did he help?"

"I don't think either of us is quite sure what there is to help. But we did have a pleasant talk."

"So you're going to go back?"

"Oh yes."

It was at this point that friends and relatives began flocking to tell me their stories. They were amazed that such a well-adjusted person as I should be consulting a therapist, when *they* were the ones who had the real problems. Such personal complications as they laid before me I couldn't have believed at first, though eventually they began to acquire a degree of sameness. Love and sexuality. Monogamy, non-monogamy; open marriage, closed; affairs and friendships crossing the gender barrier, the race barrier, the age barrier. Everyone seemed to be either attracted to or sleeping with someone not their legal or supposedly chosen partner.

Was the fabric of society going through some kind of mad shredding machine? I wondered. Was this random coupling and uncoupling, this frenzy to touch and to know as many people as possible, the true harbinger of decadence, Roman-style, or the sign of a totally new social order, dedicated to truth in advertising and freedom of expression, every expression? Whatever it was, it didn't seem to be a thing that people were in control of, or something that they even took much pleasure in. It was more that the options—so many of them—had become so suddenly apparent, seeming to demand action first and then confused scrutiny. "I couldn't help myself," was the commonest explanation. "And now I don't know whether to tell Paul or Susan and have it out in the open or whether just to go on as usual." Or, "Mark just told me that he's having an affair with Carl but he doesn't want that to change anything between us. He says it's making him more sensitive to masculinity. . . . " Or, "It's his first affair with a Black woman and I don't know how Angie will take it. She grew up in Georgia, after all. On the other hand, she *is* fooling around with the kids' babysitter."

Sometimes I heard these stories second or third hand—their parents told me—but just as often it was the parents confessing to peccadillos and lusts. "I couldn't help myself." It began to sound like a contagious social disease, this desire, this need for new and forbidden (but what *was* forbidden anymore?) experience. Or mad creatures in rut, a generation so subjected to instinct that morality had become helpless before its demands. No one wanted rules anymore, everyone, even older people, seemed to want freedom, as much as possible, but no one was quite prepared for the consequences, or even sure whether there should be any consequences.

It was almost a relief sometimes to listen to poor Stella's continuing saga of Mickey and Sarah, prolonged and even courtly, though that "relationship," too, seemed to have its inexorable progress.

As Mickey related the blow-by-blow details to his faithful helpmeet, so Stella passed them on to me. First it was simple meetings, where Sarah had to be extremely careful about running into any of her lesbian circle, separatist or otherwise. She and Mickey met in out-of-the-way taverns and went to drive-in movies together. One night they apparently made the wrong choice of drive-ins. The film turned out to be horribly sexist. On the one hand, the amount of groaning flesh revealed on the massive screen had the effect of making the two clutch for each other's genitals; on the other hand, both Sarah and Mickey were so depressed by the exploitation of the women in the film that they agreed to end their romance. At least temporarily.

"He tells you all this?" I asked Stella, appalled.

"I wouldn't want him to lie like Dad."

"Sometimes," I said, "there are things that ought not to be shared."

"How are you getting on?" Dr. Augustus wanted to know.

"I haven't had much time to myself since I started coming to you," I answered a bit peevishly. I'd been on the phone all morning with Stella's aunt on her father's side, who had insisted on telling me about her affair with an eighteen-year-old boy who'd come to trim the treetops one day. "Now it's not just Stella traipsing over every day with her problems but everyone else I know. They're too cheap to see a therapist themselves, they think they can get advice from me. One of the things I liked most about living alone was making a mess and not worrying about it. Now I have to house clean every day. At this rate, I'll have to get a job to get away from them."

"Would that be such a bad idea?"

"Of course it would. How could I go on with my spiritual development while answering my boss' telephone? Easy for you to say." Yes, I was in a sour mood today. Everything about Dr. Augustus and his office irritated me—his thin, caring face, the ferns and rubber plants littering the wood-paneled den.

"What about political action?" he suggested, hearing in my tone that same undercurrent of incipient revolt that had often made Mickey and Stella urge me to distribute leaflets or lie down in front of nuclear plants.

"Impossible. I'm not a group person. I hate groups even when I support their aims. All I want is to be left alone. Can't anyone see that?"

"Right," he said, giving me a searching look. Then he asked me the same question he'd asked at the first session. "Ms. Campbell, why did you decide to come to me?"

"I wanted to *understand.*"

He paused a moment. "Right. Do you know what I think?" Without waiting for any reply he went on, "I think you understand, I think you understand so well that you're paralyzed into a state of non-feeling and non-action. If understanding is all you want, you don't need me anymore. I think this should be your last session."

"Exactly what I was thinking," I said bravely, though inside I was shattered. Not to come here anymore? Not to trip over his jungle of plants on the way to the chair where I could sit and talk to the only person who listened? "That's fine with me," I said. "Send me your bill."

But my certainty of confusion had been destroyed and even Jane Austen brought no solace. When I came home I unplugged the phone and settled back to reread *Mansfield Park*. More fervently than ever did I wish myself on an English estate, taking tea genteelly and suffering quietly and ironically. Was it so very wrong to wish that the world hadn't changed? I tried to imagine Jane in this society, for instance, sitting in the slip-covered rocking chair across from me with a cup of coffee and a cigarette, consoling me in supple, well-turned phrases.

I tried and failed. Even Jane Austen would lose her famous objectivity, her amazing universal perspective, if she had my life. You could hardly remain objective in this day and age, you were forced to choose up sides. If Jane Austen were alive now, she'd probably be a lesbian separatist.

I plugged my phone back in and started to look up Dr. Augustus' phone number. It had occurred to me that every one of Austen's plots turned on the fact that people kept silent. If Edward had told Elinor about Lucy, if Anne had told Captain Wentworth that she loved him. . . . But I was tired of keeping quiet after all these years. There were things that needed to be said. Instead of dialing Dr. Augustus, I found myself on the line to Bob's office.

I think it was the only time in my life I ever raised my voice to him. Even during our divorce scenes I had kept becomingly distant and cold. But suddenly I was shouting invective at Bob, telling him how he had ruined my life and Stella's. Stella, in fact, would have been proud of me.

"I knew," I shouted over the phone, "every time you slept with anyone. I could feel it on you, coming home after one of those conferences, some woman's touch all over you like a sheet of Saran Wrap. Answering the phone all those years and having someone hang up immediately. The way you suddenly took up golf and then tennis to get out of the house. You were unfaithful for years. Did you think I was stupid?"

"I heard you were seeing a psychiatrist," Bob said smugly, not at all alarmed. "I suppose he told you to let it all hang out. Or was it our women's lib daughter?"

"He and Stella have nothing to do with it," I said. "You ran all over me and I let you. I just wanted to let you know that, after all this time, I finally realized what a pig you are. I hate you."

"What's the point of all this?" he asked, but I hung up.

I couldn't decide whether I felt better or worse for having called him. Having released my long-buried anger, I was proud and uneasy at the same time. Things had been going along so well, with so much dignity and such a feeling of control, before all this started. Like Elinor, like Anne, like every one of Jane Austen's preferred heroines, I had kept my feelings to myself in an excess of good taste and good sense. I had listened to the Mariannes of the world and prided myself on my superior restraint, ignoring the very real pain that comes from repressing resentment.

Now that I'd let some of it out, I felt afraid. Had I forfeited my superiority and my happy ending to any result? Now that I'd begun to have feelings, would I turn out like the rest of them, miserable and confused and cheated, ready to regale the world with my troubles?

Stella came over that night.

"Daddy," she began, "called me and told me you'd had some kind of fight. That you called him up and accused him of all kinds of things."

"It's true," I said gloomily. "Though I don't know what good it did. All that pent-up anger. Stirring up the past. Maybe if we'd talked about it while we were married. . . . "

"And Jim said you'd ended therapy."

"I feel like I've just started."

We sat in silence for a while, unusual with Stella. The room was neater than it had been for many days. I'd vacuumed and dusted and put Jane Austen away on the shelf. No happy ending for me, or anyone, indeed, if there had been such a thing.

"What's the use?" Stella said finally.

"Of what?"

"Of anything. . . . Talking it out, not talking it out. Pretending to work on things, nothing really changing. What's the use . . . of anything?"

I began to get a presentiment of alarm. My Stella talking like this? "Mickey and Sarah?"

Stella sighed unhappily. "They've gone off together on a weekend trip. I guess when they come back, everything will be out in the open. They might even live together."

"Oh Stella."

"I keep wondering—what if I'd taken a stand, right at the very beginning. What if I'd said no, no dice, forget it—instead of trying to be so understanding? Do you think it would have made any difference?"

"I don't know." I thought, maybe we're not so unlike after all, Stella, you and I, both of us willing accessories to the crime, compliant to the very marrow, me by keeping quiet and you by being understanding. The both of us hiding our feelings, hoping against hope for a happy marriage, a happy ending.

We drank coffee, we talked about Leaf and Canny.

"There's always the children," said Stella.

"Yes," I said, remembering how I had clung to my little girl at the hardest times, willing her life to be different from mine. I wondered whether the moral cycle would have swung full circle by the time Leaf and Canny grew up, whether it would be a virtue by then to be repressed instead of open, sensible instead of sensitive, and whether that would save them from what we were going through now.

I thought not. But after all, you can hope.

Emily's Arrows

1. *1969*

His parents kept asking, "When are you going to get married?"

My parents were "disappointed." However, they gave us a used vacuum cleaner to help us set up housekeeping.

I used it faithfully.

I was very married.

2. *Henry Miller and the Taxi Dancer*

At first we were very happy in our rebellion; then we began to quarrel.

Robbo was suddenly after me to get a job, though he didn't have one either. He was going to school on a scholarship which turned out not to be sufficient for the two of us. A nineteen-year-old college drop-out, I sat at home, cleaned and read. I especially read about Henry Miller's enigmatical wife, June, in Anais Nin's diaries.

" . . . *the phosphorescent color of her skin, her huntress profile, the evenness of her teeth. She is bizarre, fantastic, nervous, like someone in a high fever. Her beauty drowned me. As I sat before her, I felt I would do anything she asked of me.*"

Robbo read Henry Miller and it made him horny, but he didn't like it when I faltered on about Anais Nin's attraction to Henry's wife.

One day I ringed my eyes with black eyeliner, like June in

the photograph.

"You look like an idiot. Wash that off," Robbo said when he came home in a bad mood. "Why don't you get a job and *do* something?"

June Miller had been a taxi dancer when Henry met her. She took drugs and lived at the fever point of existence. She carried on with women and everybody.

I said I would get a job when he got one.

It was our first fight and I hated him.

3. *Fast Foods*

A week later we both got part-time jobs at the Taco Bell on Pacific Coast Highway, right across from Shepard's Ambulance. Two or three times an hour the electric doors rose up to spit out a flashing, wailing rescue car. It was harrowing at first, but you could get used to it.

Our Taco Bell manager assured us that "fast foods are the wave of the future. . . . " A skinny, sly man with yellow, erupting skin, Handy had trained in Texas at the Taco Bell School for Managers. He had also been with Kentucky Fried for a while. He was pleased we caught on so quickly to burrito making. He lectured Robbo: "Stick around. You can rise to the top in this biz. Look at me, not much older than yourself. I'm bringing it in all right."

Handy thought Robbo should quit college and go to manager school. He was impressed that Robbo could chop twenty pounds of onions without crying.

4. *Emily*

Emily was the person I most often worked with in the afternoons. She was sixteen or seventeen and was still in high school. She was tall, dark-haired and almost beautiful, except for one thing:

Emily looked as if she had fallen asleep and someone had drawn lines in fine pencil across one cheek; they radiated out from a dimple or scar near her left ear.

"I'm glad you didn't try and brush it off first thing," she told me a few days after we began to work together. "Most people do."

Her parents were bringing a suit against the doctor who had put her face back together after a motorcycle accident. He had left the dirt in.

Emily was metaphysically inclined. The sirens didn't bother her. She believed in karma, reincarnation, afterlife, everything. She was working her way through *The Tibetan Book of the Dead*. During slow times at the counter she read me bits.

She wanted to move to San Francisco when she graduated in June. She took acid every weekend.

"Get back to work, girls," Handy admonished us. "Wipe up that bean goop when there's no customers."

He did not suggest we go to manager school.

5. *(Un)married Life*

was easier with both of us working at Taco Bell, as we ate burritos, tostados, tacos and soft drinks two meals a day.

Nevertheless, as spring began to turn into summer I grew more and more depressed. I cried and read, read and cried. I read every single novel of Henry Miller's to find out more about June, returning always for reference to the first volume of Anais Nin's diaries.

Anais said Henry lied about June, made her into a character, did not touch her true essence. Anais told June, *"You're the only woman who ever answered the fantasies I had about what a woman should be."*

Anais told Henry, *"If there is an explanation of the mystery, it is this: the love between women is a refuge and an escape into harmony and narcissism in place of conflict. In the love between man and woman there is resistance and conflict. Two women do not judge each other. They form an alliance. It is, in a way, self-love. I love June because she is the woman I would like to be."*

"It's not my fault you're unhappy," Robbo told me. *"Do something with your life."*

Do something, always *do* something. He made it sound so

easy. But all my energy had gone into my rebellion, first to in-
itiate it, then to sustain it. I had dropped out and I had moved
in with Robbo. I felt too weak to do anything else. I dreamed
of dramatic gestures, a life at fever pitch, knowing a woman
like June Miller, *being* her—while day after day I served out
beans with a smear of red or green chile sauce and listened to
the ambulances scream.

6. *Emily's Acid Trip*

Emily asked me if I would like to take acid with her one
weekend. First I said yes, then I changed my mind. I had
taken acid with Robbo once and I had cried the whole time.
But I said I would spend the evening with Emily while she
tripped.

She had borrowed someone's apartment as she still lived at
home with her parents. It was one of the barest apartments I
have ever been in; there was toilet paper in the bathroom and
that was about all.

No, it wasn't quite empty. On the bare wooden floor of the
living room were two corduroy bean bag pillows and a big
spool table with a clay pipe and a dish of strawberries, the first
of the season.

We smoked some weed and lay bumpily back onto the pillows.

"You sure you don't want to try it?" Emily asked, taking
two tabs out of her front shirt pocket.

I shook my head. I felt high enough and just fine. I looked
longingly at the curves of the strawberries. "I'm starving," I
said.

"Me too," Emily joked and popped one of the tabs.

I think I was waiting for something to happen immediately.
Nothing did.

We smoked more weed, and I began to eat the strawberries,
holding my greed in check, taking only one at a time, letting
my tongue brush the faint prickles up and down, then rubbing
the berry over my lips so that some of the juice escaped and
stained them, finally breaking into the fruit in slow bites, ex-

posing the feathery white center.

"Whoo! Are you getting into those strawberries," Emily giggled; then, she bent over and kissed me quickly, almost experimentally, on the mouth while I still had one of the berries in my teeth.

I was more amazed than anything to see her face close-up, with that graphite tattoo spraying across her cheek like a comet.

"Don't worry," Emily said, worldly or embarrassed, leaning back once again, out of sight behind the spool table.

I wasn't worried; no, not that. And if she had asked me, I would have said unhesitatingly that I had liked it. She didn't ask though, or say anything at all for a while.

7. *The Reincarnation of June Miller*

Later, while staring at the ceiling, I launched into an animated description of June Miller: "She had tuberculosis, but she didn't mind it. It helped her live a fiery life, that's what she wanted—to burn up, not to be ordinary. She lied about everything, she couldn't help it. She needed life to be interesting. She had affairs with men and women. Anais Nin was in love with her, lots of women were. She believed in Dostoevsky like the Bible. She lived in New York and Paris, she might have been a drug addict, she was very beautiful, and she wore kohl around her eyes."

My voice drifted off. I looked expectantly at Emily, beautiful and drugged, as dreamy as a harem girl in her Indian shirt, with a veil of scars over her expression. Would she be as moved by June's life as I was?

Emily said nothing for a moment; then she ventured in a faraway voice, "Maybe you're her reincarnation. Or is she dead yet?"

I didn't know, to tell the truth. I was taken aback by the question. I found I hardly believed in June as a real person; she was so much a symbol in my mind, though of what, I would have found it difficult to say.

"You know what I'd like to do?" I surprised myself by saying. "Is get some black eyeliner and dance naked around the room."

But right after that I fell asleep.

8. *My Dream (I think)*

I opened my eyes and saw Emily across the room, in front of a full-length mirror I hadn't noticed before. She was naked and could have been dancing, though it was very slow, more like a plant weaving in the wind. She was shadowy and white and lovely, and the thin scars on her face formed a kind of mantilla or a spider's web over her cheek.

I wanted to touch her very much.

I said, in a voice that sounded like my voice, but still odd, "Give me another strawberry, June."

9. *More Sirens*

Then I was awake. I didn't have any idea what time it was.

"Emily," I whispered. "Where are you?"

She was lying asleep and fully clothed, behind the spool table, half on a pillow and half on the floor. I knew I should leave, Robbo would kill me.

I didn't wake her then, but leaned over and brushed her scarred cheek with my lips. It was soft; the dirt lay lightly under the skin.

A siren began its long shriek the minute I stepped out the door. It was only about five blocks to our house, but on the way I had to go past the Taco Bell. Robbo and Handy were just closing up when I got there. They let me in. Handy was friendly and wanted to put me right to work.

"Could you just wipe off that counter?" he asked, giving me a rag.

But Robbo was furious. "What the fuck are you doing out at 2 a.m.?"

I didn't know if I'd done anything to be ashamed of, but I suddenly felt as guilty as if I had. In some vital way I had been unfaithful to him, and everything was different. I didn't even want to look in his direction.

But the doors of Shepard's Ambulance tore open then and spewed out another screaming car, cutting off all conversation long enough for me to think up an excuse.

"I got Dad to drop me off here so I could walk you home," I said, lying as skillfully as June Miller ever had, embracing my deception.

10. *Emily's Arrows*

Emily graduated that June, a few weeks after our evening together, and moved to San Francisco. She gave me a copy of *The Tibetan Book of the Dead* and I gave her the first volume of Nin's diary. We hugged each other good-bye beneath Handy's somewhat disgusted eye, in the back of the Taco Bell where I had been stirring refried beans. I wanted to ask her why she had kissed me or if she had really danced naked before the mirror. Instead I begged her impulsively, "Don't get your face fixed."

She just laughed. "Forget *you*," she said.

Not long after that Robbo and I split up. "I'm tired of masculine/feminine conflict," I told him rather grandly. "Yeah, well I hope you get it together sometime," he returned.

I gave the vacuum cleaner back to my parents and went back to college. Soon I was studying the usual subjects and demonstrating against the war, and had forgotten all about June Miller.

Not quite: years later I fell in love with a woman who had once worked as a topless dancer in New York. She had the same dark-rimmed, world-weary eyes and pouting cheeks as Henry Miller's photograph of June in the *Diary*.

I remember once telling this woman about Emily. I ended my description with something I had never thought of before. "Some of the lines on her face were like arrows."

"Which direction were they pointing?" she wanted to know.

I laughed and shook my head. "They weren't *pointing* anywhere," I said. "Were they?"

Il Circo Delle Donne

The day before I joined the circus I did something perhaps even more out of character. I broke the windshield of two Italian boys who were following me. I was forty-one years old, a housewife and mother of two. I was on my second honeymoon.

The rock hit the windshield with a sound like a flock of birds rising unexpectedly out of the grass, raucous, high-pitched, explosive. Immediately the boys inside began to shout, even before the last cracks had spread, with alarming finality, across the curved front window of their Fiat, and I, a woman who could have been their mother, made a break for it.

I hadn't meant to throw the rock, I'd only meant—but what had I meant? To threaten them? To give them a taste of the same fear they'd aroused in me? Following me like this all over the little holiday town, clutching my arm, gesturing, inviting, suggesting, then getting into their car just when I thought I'd gotten rid of them and creeping after me with their blow-dried, spray-coiffed heads out the window, hooting and whistling. I'd tried ignoring them, had tried explaining, "I'm married," had tried shouting back at them, "Leave me alone"; until finally I'd just stopped, picked up a rock to fit my palm and heaved it in their direction.

The car revved its motor, they were coming after me and now I could no longer pretend I was only strolling vigorously. I started running, tearing down the tree-tented sidewalk as if I were again an eight-year-old girl with a stitch in her side and terror and victory in her heart, two paperboys after her for stealing an evening edition.

I burst into the hotel room. Andrew said, "What's wrong?" I didn't know whether to laugh or cry. My heart pounded harder now I was safe. Surely they wouldn't follow me here but even if they did—yes, I'd had every right. If I were arrested I'd go with a sneer on my lips, refuse to pay damages. I wished they'd been blinded, maimed for life. . . .

"Nothing," I managed. "I had a slight run-in with some of my admirers."

He raised an eyebrow, yawned and forgot it. Of course no one bothered me when he was around; therefore no one bothered me at all. I was just nervous, I could see him thinking. Judith and her imagination. He tried to rouse himself, lay back down.

"Shouldn't have drunk so much at lunch," he muttered.

We'd had four courses and a full bottle of the local wine, to console ourselves for the weather. It was a gloomy spring here in Italy; in fact, bad weather had pursued us for the last month: unseasonal snow in England, floods in Holland, the mistral in Provence. It was hardly, Andrew had reminded me for the fiftieth time in three weeks, like our first trip to Europe, some twenty years ago—a glowing, brilliant time of picnics in the Mediterranean sun.

I sighed and went to the window to check for the Fiat. I suddenly felt ridiculous, ashamed of my temper. They'd been so young, Greg's age. The street was empty under the new-leafed poplars; behind them was the Lago di Bolsena, a smear of gray liquid that was partly water and partly low-lying fog.

I heard Andrew, also sighing, rise from the squeaky mattress. He went to the sink and splashed water on his face, and I could see, without bothering to turn, the widely-spaced gray eyes, bland as the lake, the growing bald spot, the too-short socks that showed his thin, hairy ankles, the polo shirt girdling his accountant's paunch.

"I thought we could take a drive this afternoon," he said, gargling Vichy water. "See the cathedral at Orvieto. What do you think?"

"All right."

God, but I was sick of him.

The Umbrian hills were covered with grape vines and orchards just beginning to flower. It was an old, much-cultivated land, I read in the guidebook. The Etruscans were here first, their grave sites still dotted the slopes; they had been conquered by the Romans in 265 B.C. Later the Christians had built their towns on the volcanic mesas, "as close to Heaven as possible."

The town of Orvieto stood up like a hardened sandcastle in the midst of the sunless, blossoming hills. There was a stone bridge leading to it over a trickling river. Just before the bridge, however, was a flat piece of land with a red tent collapsed on it like a parachute and half a dozen painted trailers. I saw an elephant eating poplar leaves, and several black horses.

"Andrew, it's a circus."

"*Il circo delle donne,*" he read slowly from a banner stretched between two trees. "Circus of Women? Now what in hell?"

As we got closer we saw signs of great activity. Someone brought a bucket for the elephant; someone else walked by with a dog on their shoulder.

"Are they really all women?" I asked doubtfully. The figures were dressed in workclothes, not a low-cut leotard or spangled headdress among them.

"In Italy of all places," Andrew said, driving right past it.

I craned my neck back. "You know, I haven't seen a circus for years. . . . Did I ever tell you I used to dream of joining one?"

"You juggle the checkbook pretty well," he laughed. Need I add, heartily?

"I wish the boys could see this," he was saying half an hour later in front of the cathedral, as he energetically snapped the big rose window and the marble columns etched with tendrils and bas-reliefs.

"They had their chance." For myself I was glad that Andy considered himself too sophisticated, at nineteen, to be caught dead with his parents in Europe, and that Greg's lifeguard job made it equally impossible for him to join us. It wasn't that I disliked my sons, just that I found their teen-age preoccupations increasingly obnoxious. Their obvious desire to be free of me hurt, at the same time it reminded me of my own all-too-brief youthful rebellion.

It was Andrew who missed them. If he wasn't talking about the weather he was mourning their absence. "The chance of a lifetime." "They used to be so excited about going to Europe." They had been, once. So had I. Hadn't we all gathered around the dining room table night after night with the maps in front of us, the guidebooks opened up, planning down to the hour which museum we would visit, which hotel we would breakfast at, which coliseum, church, ruin, resort, spa, beach, factory, parliament building, castle we would take in, and in which order? Long before Andrew and I ever made it, however, the trip had become a joke. Always there was something to put it off. Not enough money, not enough experience with languages, Greg's appendicitis, Andy's drug bust, Andrew's new client. I was the only one who'd never had anything holding me back.

Which is why I'd been dutifully trudging around for the last few weeks looking at cathedrals exactly like this one. If I were by myself I wouldn't be here, I'd be down at the circus tent, watching them set up. Could it really be an all-women's circus? I'd wanted to be a lion-tamer, myself, or a horseback rider. Years and years ago.

My eye wandered across the Piazza to a group of young men in tight rayon shirts unbuttoned to the navels of their hairless chests. Their voices were loud, exhibitive, their gestures full of smoke and contempt. They dominated the old stones of the Piazza; around them, at a careful distance, walked silent women in black dresses, carrying baskets and bundles, their heads down. Andy still expected me to do his laundry when he came home from college. I'd overheard Greg telling a friend on the phone, "My mom says she's for the ERA but she's never done anything with her life."

I started through the wide doorway behind me.

"Wait," said Andrew. Then, "I'll catch up with you."

I hardly heard him, or else I might have asked myself, again, why it was so important that we stick together all the time. Hadn't we spent almost every minute in each other's company for the last few weeks? It was one thing, if you were both twenty-one and just married and desperately in love—as we had been, yes, we had been—to cling to each other like grasshoppers in heat, but after twenty years of marriage and going your own way (Andrew to the office, me to the grocery store, to the PTA, to the swimming pool, to the dry cleaners), what point was there? Especially when you didn't look at anything in the same way and were tired of the very sound of his voice, of his ideas and his fake cheerfulness and his homesickness and his curiosity and his need, and his need.

The cathedral interior was striped in black and white marble, with numerous frescos and carved woodwork. I'd left the guidebook with Andrew; if I'd had it with me I probably wouldn't have opened it anyway. I reserved my cultural interest for my husband's benefit. By myself I lapsed into boredom, a mental lethargy as concrete as the walls of a room in a psych ward, not even padded. I couldn't figure out where I'd gone wrong, or why I'd never done anything in my life except have a family, or why it was only now I felt it.

"Psst," a voice at my side whispered. I glanced over and saw a young boy with a stylized curl on his forehead and the beginnings of a moustache. *"Americana?"*

"Go to hell," I muttered violently and marched in the opposite direction, to where a group of tourists were standing in front of a painted wall. It was the famous fresco by Signorelli, I recognized, having seen its likeness in the guidebook. A vivid and horrible piece of art, it depicted the end of the world, a place of fire and eclipses, earthquakes and murder. In the sky, angels blew long trumpets to wake the dead, who came walking, skeleton by gaunt skeleton, up from the ground. The colors were burnt orange and sooty black, cadaverous green and bruised white. The expressions in the eyes of the damned were hardly different from those of the saved. They all looked hopeless, driven, and, in some crucial way, condemned and abandoned.

"*Signora,*" began a male voice next to me.

I turned, screamed, "Leave me alone," and saw Andrew at my side, totally bewildered by the failure of his joke.

A few minutes later I was walking down the hill to the circus grounds. "I'm sorry," I'd told him. "I've just got to get away by myself for a minute."

I walked quickly, head down as I'd seen the Italian women do, ignoring all comments. Though I refused to look at the men around me I still felt their presence, a malignant and pulsating cancer of maleness, eating away at me. I was afraid to look up, not for fear of what they might say to me, but of what I might do to them. Smash their windshields, smash their faces, make them leave me alone.

I came to the stone bridge, crossed it, joined a few locals at the rope marking the circus grounds. Closer now, I could see that the workers were indeed women, lifting boxes, leading horses and carrying buckets. There was a light rain falling and it sweetened the strong odor of sawdust and animals and canvas. The women were all shapes and ages, from the little girl in overalls and a gypsy scarf tying up her black curls, to the wrinkled midget with a wise face and humped back, to the six-foot-tall black woman in jeans and a sweater. They seemed to be older rather than younger, though, and this surprised me. I always associated the circus with my own youth, had never thought of it as an occupation, as something that adults did. But here was a woman coming past me, in her sixties by the looks of a gray tail of hair coiled around her crown, and carrying a bucket filled with bloody meat.

She smiled at me and asked a question.

"*Non capisco.*" I held out empty hands.

"English?"

"American."

"Ah. And you come to see the circus. The Women Circus?"

Her voice was low, German-accented. Her eyes caught and held me by their sparkle.

"It's wonderful," I said.

"Come inside," she invited, lifting up the rope so I could pass. She had broad shoulders, muscular arms, she smelled of sweat and blood.

I ducked under but hesitated, "I really can't stay. My husband will be wondering. . . . "

She shifted her bucket, waited, said nothing.

I hovered. "You're going to feed the lions?"

"My friends, my children. I am Marianne, the lion-tamer."

To be able to say that so naturally. "Judith Ellery," I murmured.

"Come with me."

"Oh, I couldn't . . . I have to get back."

She shrugged, winked again and passed on. I was still inside the roped off grounds, couldn't make up my mind to leave. I drew a deep breath, sniffed. Why did it seem so familiar to me? I couldn't have gone to the circus more than once or twice as a child, my mother holding my hand, pointing out the animals, assuring me that the tightrope walkers wouldn't fall, that the lions wouldn't eat their trainers. But when I'd told her I wanted to join, she'd laughed. "Wait and ask your husband," she'd said mysteriously.

Other women passed by me, talking among themselves in different languages. None of them asked me what I was doing. I knew I should leave, but when I looked back at the rope, with all the men hanging over it and making insulting remarks, I couldn't. Maybe everything would have been different if I'd had a girl instead of two boys.

Now the tent was going up. It was crimson canvas, very heavy to be supported on such slender poles. Sagging, wavering, slipping, rising and falling. The women shouted to each other, held firm; a lanky clown rushed up to grab a pole . . . and suddenly I was there too. I smelled sweat and sawdust and animal shit, saw the blackness underneath the tent turn to light. I steadied a pole while the woman next to me pulled hard on a rope. She was Indian, her skin the color of warm sand, her hair black as peppercorns.

I saw Marianne across from me as the tent lifted, her two arms raised as if in praise. She smiled at me, shook her head.

I slipped away.

Andrew and I ate dinner in a tiny trattoria, off an alley that was just a stone staircase. For the first time we seriously discussed going home early.

"Three months is a long time to spend traveling," he suggested. "We could still take the rest of the summer off. Rent a cabin by the lake, do some fishing. Even if Greg and Andy didn't want to be there all the time, they could still come up on weekends."

I pictured myself boning fish, hanging sheets out to air, heating water on the wood stove. "I'm sorry," I said. "I keep feeling like I'm failing you in some way." I meant 'failing myself,' but I didn't know how to tell him this.

We held hands over the cluttered table. "We should have come earlier," Andrew said. "We should have made it a regular thing, every four or five years, to come back. I guess we've forgotten how to travel."

I stared, fascinated, at his gray eyes, remembering how I had loved him, when we got locked out of our hotel in Marseilles and panhandled on the streets all night. We had traded dreams, had planned the future. Even if we had children, we'd decided, nothing would stop us from living life to the full. I didn't know I was already pregnant. I looked at the bulge under his polo shirt, at his balding head. When had it happened? He seemed so much older than me. My husband, the father of my children, I reminded myself. I felt nothing now, except the desire to get away.

"It's me. You're all right. I'm a wreck. I don't know—everything gets to me—the weather, the stares, the comments. And yet, I don't even want to go home, it's more than that. . . ."

"It's the weather," said Andrew, waving at the waiter for the check. "The weather is spoiling everything."

Yet the sky was clear by the time we came out of the restaurant. Now that we'd half decided to leave this country, it seemed to be doing its best to please us. The stars were bright, it was almost warm, the windows glittered with chocolates and jewelry. The streets were crowded.

"They look like they're all going somewhere," said Andrew. Then, inspired, "I bet it's that circus. Want to go?"

"I don't know." I thought of Marianne. There were so many things I could have asked her.

"Are you tired?" He took my arm.

"I don't know, I want, I want. . . . "

"It's been a long day."

As we drove over the bridge we saw the lanterns strung through the trees, the big tent glowing like a red lightbulb. I helped to raise that, I remembered, and was silent.

"Sure?" Andrew asked. "All women. It's hard to believe."

"All right," I said suddenly. "Let's go."

It was as magical as the circus had always been, a fairyland of animals and spangles and daring acts. *Il circo delle donne* had only one ring, but there was activity enough, and this time I didn't feel that I was missing anything.

First came Katrina, the ringmaster, wearing a tux the color of a mermaid's glittering green tail. She had short dark hair and a voice that shook the tent walls and yet was impossibly confiding and friendly at the same time. She spoke in Italian so I didn't understand her. Fortunately, each act was also announced with a placard, carried around all sides of the ring by the midget with the wise and shining face.

Elsa *e* Grazia! Highwire artists, so alike they must have been twins, with firm, muscular thighs and arms, not wearing the usual low-cut leotard, but instead, old-fashioned bathing costumes, striped in purple and red. They were so easy and energetic that I only remembered later that they had worked without a net, skipping and sliding along the wire as if it were two feet from the ground instead of thirty.

The Sisters Karenina! Three women with Russian-looking square faces and thick brows. They brought their black Arabian horses smartly around the ring, then leapt on their backs and began a series of stunts, to guttural shouts of "Hei!" and "Ayah!" They did somersaults on the horses' wide haunches, flipped from horse to horse, rode them through flaming rings.

"Not bad," whispered Andrew. My heart was pounding and my palms were wetting through my dress where I had them pressed. I was remembering how I had jumped onto old Betsey's back after returning from the circus that morning and Betsey had herself jumped over her owner's fence, a real circus horse, and run away down the block.

There were jugglers and acrobats, some fine-featured and Asian, others Slavic and springy. They threw knives in the air and made pyramids, spun around the ring like jumping beans. There was a clown named Alphonsine, loosely knit, all bones and rolling eyes under her carrot frizz, perpetually surprised by the failure of her schemes. She had a little dog who followed her everywhere. "Pipi" she was called, a mongrel terrier as big as Alphonsine's black bag, who indeed seemed to live in the bag and only came out to be liontamed or to shy away from hoops.

We filed out of the tent during intermission and found a stand selling sticky candy and espresso. The sky was black and starry as an old piece of carbon paper held up to a lamp. The lanterns glowed green and red.

"I wish the boys could see this," Andrew murmured. "Did we ever take them to the circus, do you remember?"

I shook my head. I could hardly remember the boys, my sons. They seemed to belong to some strangely vague part of my life. Certainly I had borne them and nursed them and bandaged up their knees. I had listened to their troubles in the same way I'd listened to Andrew's stories of his clients. I had watched them turn into men and have no use for me, nor I for them.

"Did you see the way those Russian women jumped backwards onto the horses behind them, that was incredible!"

Andrew agreed. "The European circus is a very interesting tradition," he said. "Long generations of circus families, intermarriages, usually managed by one person. That's why it's so unusual to see something like this. These women must have broken away from the old family circuses to start this."

"What if they were just ordinary women, I mean, housewives or mothers, who just broke away from their lives and did what they'd always wanted to do?"

"Oh, I doubt that," said Andrew. "Think of the training!" He gave me a quick look and laughed. "Why? You're not thinking of joining, are you?" The idea seemed to amuse him immensely. "How could I explain it to the boys? Sorry, sons, Mama has become a horseback rider in an all-women's circus."

'Wait and ask your husband,' my mother had said.

Sheba! A refined, plump matron with gold teeth, sitting high on Jubub, an elephant the size of a truck. Jubub was graciously lumbering, but not without a sense of humor; when she picked up a little boy in the first row and deposited him in a tub of water, her tiny gray eyes seemed to wink.

And then there was Rebekah, the black woman, now dressed in leopardskins instead of jeans, who cheerfully took on challengers and pinned two men to the ground while twirling another in the air, all without seeming effort.

The mood of the crowd, which up to now had been rowdily good-natured, if contemptuous, changed suddenly. A group of men in the back started shouting and one threw a bottle. It took the arrival of the lions to get everyone back in order.

They came, two lions, three, not in cages but on leashes escorted by Marianne, diminutive and gray-haired. This, to me, was the best part of the evening. She had no whip, she did not seem to force or fear them. "They must be really old," said Andrew, a little nervously, but anyone could see they were not, that it was not age that made them bow to Marianne, but understanding. They did not jump through hoops or climb on barrels. They turned over and over in time to the music, let Marianne lie down beside them, let her put her head next to theirs.

It was chilling, it was magical, it was perfect. I stopped breathing several times, I think everyone did.

Then came the finale, too soon, and Katrina thanked us. Andrew stood up. "Very interesting," he said, but he looked as if he would be glad to get away. The lights went up, the crowd shoved out the doors. I saw the women in their black dresses, heads down, following their men out of the tent; I saw men and boys staring at me. I put my head down too.

That night, in the hotel overlooking the foggy lake, I dreamed that two boys were chasing me. I couldn't remember what I'd done or if I'd done anything. I didn't know if I were a child running from the neighbor boys, a mother running from her sons, or a woman traveler running from her admirers. There was no landscape at first, it was only dark, a dark street lit by lamps high above, that cast small round puddles of yellow in front and in back of me. I was terrified, so terrified that I wanted to wake up. Somewhere in my mind was the remembrance that I had the power to stop this horror merely by opening my eyes, as if it were a fresco of the damned that I could turn away from. And yet I felt that if I did wake up, found I was safe after all, that I wouldn't find what I was looking for. And so I continued to run, in my dream, and gradually the darkness took on shapes. Animals. I was in a kind of jungle and the lamps overhead were really eyes, yellow lion eyes, small benevolent elephant eyes, funny winking dog eyes. Oh, of course, I knew suddenly, I'm at the circus, and as soon as I realized that, I stopped running and stood, in full and brilliant light, surrounded by animals and by the women who trained them. There was a great clapping and, unhesitatingly,

I bowed.

I opened my eyes. It was still dark, but I had the premonition of light coming slowly from somewhere outside. I went to the window and watched the sun come up over the lake. It was misty, white, unearthly.

Without making a noise I put on pants and a heavy sweater, took my passport and the keys to the car. At the door I stopped and looked back at Andrew, at a white hairy arm cradling the bald head. A good father, I remembered. The boys will look just like him.

It was about seven-thirty when I reached the red tent. I didn't go up to it yet, but stood by the car in the mist, watching. I saw the woman lion tamer, Marianne, she of the gray, coiled hair and muscular arms, who had been on the other side of the tent as it lifted, who had made friends of the lions instead of fearing them, come out sleepily into the morning air with a coffee cup. She yawned, she raised her eyes to the pale sun, she looked around. In the instant before she saw me I thought of my sons, of Andrew, of leaping on Betsey's back. Then Marianne waved and called, "Come," and, unhesitatingly, I went.

Take Louise Nevelson

"You're in Phoenix,' Christie said on the phone. "Oh my god."

There was less than delighted amazement in her voice. Melissa paused, unwillingly locking eyes with a teen-age runaway in white shorts and scalloped red boots in the opposite phone booth, before she asked, "Is everything okay? I'm sorry I didn't let you know. I thought I'd surprise you."

"You surprised me all right... but never mind, I'll come and get you."

"Are you *sure* this is a good time...?"

"I'll be there in ten minutes."

Half an hour later Christie was at the Greyhound station, explaining nervously, "I couldn't find a parking space."

Melissa, who had spent the intervening time watching the young runaway try to pick up an older cowboy, burst out, "What have you done to yourself? I mean, your hair?"

It was bleached, frizzed and sticking out like a clown's.

"I'm just the same. Oh god, it's embarrassing. When you've known me so long and everything."

"Well, don't worry," said Melissa, hoping for the best. "It looks good."

"It looks like shit, I know. I just got up."

The two friends stared at each other and laughed. Still, it wasn't quite natural. Just getting up at two in the afternoon? Had Christie been sleeping with someone? Was she living with someone? Her eyes were bloodshot and her tanned face dry and lined.

"I thought this was the middle of the school year?" said Christie. She had always been vivacious, but now her clear, ringing voice had a harder undertone. She rattled her car keys unconsciously.

"I got laid off." For a moment the still-fresh pain of it threatened to overwhelm her, then Melissa said lightly, "Reagan says not to worry if the services in your home town fold up. It's the American way to move on. And the Sun Belt's booming, according to him. So what are you doing these days?"

Christie held open the door of the Greyhound station and the hot desert sun exploded like the flame of a cigarette lighter in their faces.

"Selling encyclopedias," she said.

Theirs was an old friendship, forged in a hated sewing class in junior high. Christie, at that time a skinny misfit with long light brown braids and glasses, had only been slightly better at putting in a zipper than her classmate Melissa, a chubby and withdrawn pre-intellectual. Time had changed them both, but not their friendship. They had gone to college together, on scholarships: Christie to major in art, Melissa to study library science. Ten years ago they'd tried to live together in a cold-water flat in Barcelona, an attempt that ended when Melissa contracted pneumonia and Christie went off with a British lawyer.

In the years since they'd written on and off, seen each other twice—once in London where Christie had set up a studio when Arnold left her, and once in the town near Eugene, Oregon, where Melissa had started a job as a high school librarian. Melissa had tried then to persuade her friend to stay in Oregon.

"It's too rainy, too much like London," Christie had said. "I want to go someplace really hot, really different."

Phoenix had been her choice, and at first Christie's letters had been enthusiastic. People were interested in her painting, she might get a job in an art school, she had a lover and was thinking of marrying. . . .

"Oh, him?" said Christie tightly when questioned. "The fucker turned out to be already married."

Melissa could have told a similar story, many similar stories of being rejected: Cathy had gone off with Marsha; Pat had returned to New York; and Debra had finally left her the day before she'd been laid off.

She said, "I'm not involved with anyone either."

"Christ," said Christie, pouring her another cup of coffee in her pure white, sparsely furnished living room. "What a pair of losers we are."

Melissa, settling back in an uncomfortable high-tech chair, couldn't help remembering the self-improvement sessions they'd engaged in all through school. Poring over *Seventeen* and later, *Vogue,* they'd endlessly made each other up and curled each other's hair. Melissa had lost weight while Christie had discovered what bold stripes could do for her thin figure and had gotten contacts. Melissa had decided she was the dark, mysterious type; Christie had learned to be bright and chatty.

"I think nineteen was our high point," Christie recalled.

"We were still hanging in there at twenty-three."

At thirty-three both of them seemed to have returned to the body shapes and faces that their genes had marked out for them at birth: Christie was starvation thin, nervous and pinched around the mouth, a chainsmoker; Melissa's heaviness verged on obesity, especially in the hips. If she looked older than Christie it was only because her short dark hair had streaks of white now. But Christie's new style was hardly any improvement. The blonde frizz around her narrow face gave her the brittle falseness of a beauty shop operator.

From coffee they moved on to a bottle of brandy Christie had in the cupboard; from bitter, recent memories they progressed to thoughts of happier times.

"Whatever happened to those watercolors you did on the balcony in Barcelona?" Melissa wanted to know.

They spread the pictures out on the white rug and let the

smells and sights of the leafy Ramblas, with its stands of flowers, birds and books, drift into the cool white room.

"We thought we had everything in front of us," sighed Christie.

"Maybe we gave up too easily," Melissa said.

In the morning they both had hangovers that they cured with aspirin and a swim in the apartment pool.

"Hey, this is all right," Melissa said, paddling luxuriously in the clear blue water.

"Phoenix has its good points . . . if you stay off the streets."

"You must be doing pretty well at selling encyclopedias if you can afford this place," Melissa said, noticing the deep lanais around each apartment, the bougainvillea flowering at the edge of the pool, peach, red, violet.

"I'm not too bad," Christie admitted. "My manager says I could bring in three or four hundred a week if I put my mind to it."

"Four hundred a week?" Melissa was astonished.

"But you gotta work your tail off." Christie raised herself out of the pool and stretched out on a towel. Her tan was walnut dark and her blonde curls wept into her eyes. "She had me doing TM, you know, meditation, for a while. To get me centered. I think it helped, but I just couldn't keep it up. I'd be sitting there in the lotus and I'd think, This is ridiculous. So now I go back and forth. I don't go out for a week, sit around and read books and sketch and brood—then I get worried about the rent or the phone bill, and I jump in my car and hustle like a little devil."

"It's hard for me to imagine," Melissa said, swimming over to her side, wondering how long it would take to get a tan like Christie's, how long it would take to lose forty pounds. "I mean, you were always a kind of shy person, underneath." For the moment she forgot Christie's acquired vivacity, remembering only their mutual adolescent pain at being called on in class.

"Oh, it's just like playing a part in a play. This company has the spiel all written out for you. You memorize it and learn to anticipate the responses. Depending on who you contact, you don't have to think about yourself at all. Sometimes I get incredibly high from it, getting people to believe me, getting them to want what I'm selling. And besides," she went on half ironically, as if reciting from a text, "this encyclopedia is a quality product. It took ten years and the work of thousands of experts in their field to develop. It has full color illustrations, up-to-date statistics and detailed maps. It's an invaluable resource for schoolchildren of every age as well as for adults. There are even instructions for all aspects of home repair, cooking and sewing. In only twelve volumes you get a complete library as compared to the hundred or so books you'd need to have the equivalent amount of information in your home."

"Sold," laughed Melissa.

"Maybe I should go out today," Christie said, pinching one of her thin brown thighs in a dissatisfied way.

The first week Melissa stayed with Christie was made up of daily swims, drinks on the lanai and dinners out. It didn't take Melissa long to begin to relax. A vacation was what she'd needed for a long time. She refused to think more definitely about her life. She hadn't given up her house in Eugene or her feelings about Debra; she assumed she'd have to go back and fight the lay-off sometime . . . but right now it was such a relief to be just a guest, to do nothing except wake late, swim, drink beer and eat Mexican food. Even Christie seemed to be relaxing. She still smoked continually and drank a little too much, but some of the old, light-hearted energy had returned. She talked about going back to Europe, about giving art classes. Several days in a row she got out her sketchbook and worked on old drawings.

One morning, however, Melissa woke up and found Christie carefully putting on turquoise eye shadow and skin-tight white pants.

"The day of reckoning is at hand," she said. "Off to the salt mines, or rather, the student apartments down in Tempe. I haven't hit them for a few months."

That day Melissa walked into downtown Phoenix. It was about ninety-five degrees in spite of its being only March, and she seemed to be the only person on the streets. The six-lane boulevards were packed with air-conditioned cars, however; their drivers left them only to dash into equally cool shopping malls or the big, pseudo-adobe buildings in the city center.

Perspiring heavily in her overalls and leather shoes, Melissa experienced dislocation's despair for the first time since her arrival. The feeling here was so different from that of the vaporous green hills and pastures of the Williamette Valley, the muted sky and unobtrusive farmhouses and cabins around Eugene. In Phoenix everything was superficial, chain-owned, garish, plastic-shiny—a flat sprawl of gasoline-stinking asphalt on a smoggy dry plain. Melissa had hardly reached the downtown area when she turned back again. She could have cried with longing for the woodsy wet smell of the garden out back, for the small pine bedroom with its view of the hills, for the sound of Debra's voice singing Sweet Honey in the Rock: "B'lieve I'll run on . . . see what the end's gonna be. . . . "

Everything she'd tried to repress about their final argument came back now as Melissa trudged slowly, painfully over the burning bright sidewalks. How Debra had accused her of never wanting to take risks, of constantly lying, of holding them all back by her silence; how Debra had said she would never be a real lesbian until she found the courage to voice it.

"But I don't want to be a *real* lesbian," Melissa had said. "I just want to be me."

It had been the day after Debra left that Melissa had been called into the high school principal's office to be told of her lay-off. He'd said that the school board had decided that the budget couldn't afford a full-time librarian anymore and that they'd asked a local housewife, a former librarian, to run it instead as a volunteer, with two or three seniors to help check out books. He'd presented it reasonably enough, but there was something in his eyes, and those of the secretaries in the office, that had convinced Melissa there was more to her dismissal than mere budget cuts.

She had offered to reduce her hours, to take a pay cut, had even turned a little sour at the end asking why she was the only one being laid off. Yet she hadn't dared to push it further; she was afraid of being accused, publicly shamed. Had they found out she'd been living with a woman, that she'd had an article published in a lesbian journal, that she sometimes went to gay bars? But I didn't go to the lesbian-gay pride march, even though I wanted to, she thought. I was so afraid of my picture being in the paper. I didn't let myself be interviewed about my work at the library for the women's newspaper. Even though I was the one who started the school's feminist collection.

If she went back to Eugene she'd have support for her fight, but did she really want to fight it, especially if it involved coming out to the school, to the city? What if she lost her house, what if they ignored her in the grocery store, what if she could never get another library job?

"You're kidding yourself if you think everyone doesn't at least suspect," Debra had scoffed. "Why not put an end to their paranoia and save yourself an ulcer?"

"No one suspects," Melissa had said. "No one knows anything about me."

She was the dark, mysterious type.

Melissa was quiet that evening and so was Christie. It had not been a successful day, saleswise.

"Money, money, money," she complained. "They all say they don't have any, but they have Calvin Klein jeans and stereos worth a fortune and their Jags and Saabs are parked all over the street. *We* should have been that kind of poor."

Later Christie had a long conversation on the phone with her supervisor and then announced to Melissa, "I'm going to Flagstaff tomorrow; want to come?"

"What's there?"

"A bunch of untouched students, a Ramada Inn, mountain air. . . . " Christie's voice suddenly took on the cajoling note Melissa remembered well. "Come on, it'll be just like our old times traveling."

"You'll have to promise not to leave me in the lurch then."

"Melissa! Have I ever?"

They left it at that.

The next morning they set off before eight, with styrofoam cups of coffee from Winchell's Donuts, in a brackish fog that lifted only to reveal dismal trailer courts, billboards and desert scrub.

"Take Georgia O'Keeffe," Christie said after a while, lighting a cigarette with a determinedly elegant wave. "Take Louise Nevelson. Now *they* have style."

"You think you'll ever get back to painting seriously?" Melissa asked.

"Oh sure . . . but I was thinking more of their faces, their clothes, everything . . . Nevelson all in black, with those riveting, thick-painted eyes, those turbans. . . . You know, *Seventeen* never prepared us for getting older. We need role models."

"That's true," said Melissa, and felt depressed. Christie, in her tight turquoise jeans, lacy Mexican shirt and high-heeled appliquéed boots, looked stunningly sexy this morning. But nothing could disguise the bitter lines around her mouth and the dry look of her blonde curls.

"You can say what you want about selling," said Christie, "but in a way it's been good for me. Makes me get out, keep going. I was really dragging around a year ago, let me tell you. Some days I didn't think I was going to make it."

"Because of . . . ?"

"Randall was the last straw. Up to then I'd still been believing I could make a go of love. Now I just sleep with them and forget it." She stubbed her cigarette out and stared out the window. "But it started with Arnold, that downhill feeling . . . I guess Randall just picked up on it . . . can you believe he told me I was too old for him? He didn't want experience, he wanted a goddamn Brooke Shields."

In London Christie had worn paisley scarves around her

head, and gigantic hoop earrings. She had slept on a mattress piled with mirror-studded pillows and soft sheepskins, had burned incense and smoked hash. Her lovers all had two last names and said "bloody bitch" in fake cockney accents.

"Not that I'm interested in love now," said Christie. "Once I get some real money together, I'll go back to painting. This landscape *does* excite me." She gestured to the unprepossessing cacti out the window, then suddenly asked, "So what happened with you? You've never really said. Did you leave or did he?"

"What?" said Melissa and then, uncomfortably, "Oh, I was left. . . . " She paused, wanting to begin, wondering how, murmuring, "It still hurts."

"They're all jerks, men," Christie shrugged. "But what can you do?"

In Eugene Christie had followed her around to women's bookstores and cafes with mixed china and lace tablecloths. She'd talked art with Melissa's current roommate, Pat, and had read some of the feminist books on the shelf. When she'd left she'd admitted that it was all very interesting, but not really her style, and Melissa had realized that Christie hadn't gotten the idea at all.

Now Melissa shook her head, holding back the words as she had held them back so many times before: I'm a lesbian. I love women. I'm a lesbian.

"What are you so afraid of?" Debra had demanded. "No one's asking you to be separatist." But Debra worked in a women's moving and hauling collective; she didn't understand the pressures of being around men and straight women all the time, some of whom would look at her differently, would distrust and disrespect her opinion, would feel *sorry* for her. . . .

"The main thing," Christie said, "isn't really sex at all. It's a matter of style. Take Louise Nevelson, she's like Hecate. Or Isak Dinesen. Have you seen those Cecil Beaton photographs of her? A real aristocrat."

All that Melissa recalled about these women was that they were terribly skinny, gaunt even, but Christie rushed on. "They *made* themselves look like that, totally unordinary, remarkably beautiful and strange, through force of will. That's all, force of will."

By the time they reached the mountains they were back on their favorite adolescent subject: how to change their self-image.

"I just don't feel attractive anymore," Melissa admitted. "Being this heavy. Maybe it influences how I act."

"You were pretty popular in high school after you lost weight."

Melissa hadn't thought about that for years. She would have been ashamed to admit to any of her Eugene friends that looking attractive and being popular was anything to be proud of. In Eugene all her friends were comfortably bulky too. They bragged about their muscles like longshoremen. She'd enjoyed it, believing she had gotten completely away from the rigid stereotypes of what women were supposed to look like. Now she wasn't so sure.

"In London," mused Christie, "I thought I really had it down. Boy, was I hot shit—a cosmopolitan American artist living with an upperclass British lawyer, excuse me, *solicitor*. We used to go to the ballet and the Royal Shakespeare Company, we took our vacations, our *holidays*, in Mallorca. I was such a fool not to marry when he wanted to. I thought I was being so liberated. . . . I never suspected he would change."

Melissa knew that was the price you paid when you identified with a man; she'd read it, heard it and experienced it herself, but her friendship with Christie made it hard to say out loud. Besides, it *was* sad. In spite of being mad at Christie so long ago for ditching her in Barcelona, she'd still been admiring. "My friend who lives in London, the painter, we grew up together. . . . " It was the image still Melissa wanted to have of her—exciting, worldly, artistic.

The mountains were much more beautiful than the desert. Smoky blue even close up, they suggested Indian myths and magical transformations.

I could still change myself, Melissa was thinking. I don't have to be stuck in this body, these attitudes. Lose weight, get a good tan, invest in some clothes, become a traveler again. Of

course it would take money and she didn't have much of it . . .
but to be free of the expectations, the limitations of Eugene, to
find other friends, another life somewhere else. . . .

"What do you think about trying to sell some books with
me today?" Christie suddenly suggested. "I could give you
some of the easier routes. It'd be a hundred in your pocket, no
sweat."

"Oh, I couldn't," said Melissa. "I'm not dressed for it. . . ."
She was wearing her overalls, an *off our backs* T-shirt and a
pair of worn sandals with socks.

"Nothing easier," Christie laughed. "I've got Mastercharge, Visa, American Express. It would be a pleasure to get
you some new clothes. I haven't said anything, but you've let
yourself go a little. You could be really attractive with a tiny
bit of work."

In spite of herself Melissa was intrigued. Selling, she could
never sell, especially encyclopedias . . . but what had she been
thinking just now about changing her life? Surely that meant
taking some risks. And the money would come in handy,
she'd been spending more than she should.

Flagstaff was small and surprisingly rural. The fresh azure
sky blew through the car windows with the scent of a dry pine
sachet. When they reached the city Christie drove right to the
shopping mall.

"Please," she said, when Melissa continued to protest; "my
treat. It'll be just like old times."

Growing up in southern California they had spent whole afternoons in the local shopping center, going from one store to
the next, trying on wardrobes, discussing them. Green had
been Christie's color, emerald green if she could find it; it
went best with her long, sunstreaked brown hair. Plum or
maroon suited the darker Melissa, they'd decided. It made her
look pampered and wealthy. Melissa had worn Maybeline Velvet Brown eyeliner and mascara, Christie Jade Green. They'd
had their favorite perfumes as well—Chantilly for Christie,
Wood Musk for Melissa—though they'd never been able to afford anything but a spray from the tester bottle.

"This is really ridiculous, you know," said Melissa, but she let Christie lead her inside the most expensive department store, let Christie explain to a haughty-looking saleswoman what they were looking for. It was more than ridiculous, it was embarrassing to admit she now wore a size eighteen. When Melissa put on a dress, her stocky, thickly haired legs looked like a bear's. She tried to explain that even at the library she just wore overblouses and jeans.

"Never mind," consoled Christie. "Have a go at this suit instead."

Finally one of the pantsuits fit and even looked good on her. It was plum-colored and expensive and made her look youthfully mature.

"Don't worry,' Christie said. "none of your friends will see you. But you look fantastic."

Christie bought a pair of designer jeans and a shirt for herself, signing the Mastercharge slip with a disdainful flourish. As they came out of the store she linked arms with Melissa, laughing, "Oh, that was so much fun. I've missed having a girlfriend."

"I've missed you too," said Melissa.

They ate lunch at a pleasant restaurant waving with ferns and had several glasses of wine, while Christie explained all Melissa would need to know about the encyclopedias. It was easy to fall in with Christie, especially while drinking, and to believe she could really do it. Once outside the restaurant, however, as Christie was driving her to the area she was to canvas, Melissa experienced strong misgivings.

"How can I knock on anyone's door? I hate people knocking on mine."

"Don't be silly," said Christie impatiently. "Just remember what I told you. They'll eat it up." She gave Melissa a pat before shoving her out the car door. "I'll meet you at that Ramada Inn over there in five hours."

Even before one half hour had gone by Melissa knew that

she wouldn't have any sales. It was all she could do to merely tap gently on a door. When it opened she felt blank.

"Hello," she said miserably. "I don't suppose you'd be interested in an encyclopedia? . . . Well, thanks anyway. Sorry to have bothered you."

The housing area was made up of small duplexes and trailers. These were not rich students like those Christie had described in Tempe. Beat-up sedans lined the dusty streets and broken toys and beer cans clogged the gutters. Few of the residents, all renters probably, had made any attempt at landscaping; occasionally there were spindly trees, more often there was nothing but some shabby, butt-strewn grass and a few tall, flowering weeds around the buildings. The interiors, from what Melissa could see during the brief intervals the doors were open to her, were just as pathetic: shaggy, discolored rugs or worn linoleum, cracked vinyl sofas and bedspread-draped armchairs, plain plastic tables, beer bottle collections or dusty knickknacks along the windowsills. Each time a door opened she had a glimpse into her own past, her own family's way of life.

If she hadn't know it before, she knew it now. She had traveled a long way from her childhood, from a world where cheap shabbiness was the norm, where people were at the mercy of those salesmen who chose to badger them.

For fifteen years she'd been able to forget all that. A scholarship had taken her away to college; two summer jobs had paid for her trip to Barcelona; she'd been middle-class ever since—no, more than middle-class, free to choose her own life. In Eugene she'd become beyond class, able to be environmentally aware because she had money, able to eat simple, nutritional food because she had money, able to dress unobtrusively because she had money. . . .

Now, standing in front of a peeling pastel duplex with cut-rate organdy at the windows and a rusty lawn mower half-hidden in the weeds, Melissa remembered everything. Was this the reason she couldn't come out? Because she was afraid of losing everything she'd worked for, had come to take for granted? But I've lost it, she reminded herself, without calling myself anything. And Debra, the prom queen from Minneapolis who'd become a proud truck driver, hadn't understood. "Are you still hoping you'll find the perfect man, the man who'll make the decision for you?"

"Debra," she'd pleaded. "I love you, I want to live with you. And I am a lesbian, I just don't want to be publicly identified as one. I don't want to be interviewed. I'm afraid of being fired if they realize how I've spent the library budget."

But perhaps it was true, perhaps she was still waiting for the right man to come along, as her mother continued to assure her he would, as she had hoped, as Christie had hoped, in the poverty of their tiny bedrooms, poring over *Seventeen*.

"I don't even know any men," she reminded herself aloud, just as one of the duplex doors opened and a woman stepped timidly out onto the broken porch. She was very young, dressed in a faded halter top and a pair of Levi's. Her hair, silky, blonde, was in rollers.

"Are you selling something?" she inquired nervously. "Because my husband doesn't want any."

"Is he here?"

"No, but he doesn't like me, you know, talking to salespeople."

For some reason this rule made Melissa more aggressive than she'd been able to be with anyone else.

"I won't take much of your time," she said persuasively. "I think it's something you'd really be interested in."

"I don't know." The woman touched her hand to her rollers as if checking for dryness. She was incredibly young to be married, seventeen or eighteen at the most. Her cheeks, though pale, still had a baby fat roundness.

"What's your name?" asked Melissa, coming towards her.

"Jill . . . Jill Peters."

"Jill, you don't mind if I come in for a minute, do you? I'm really not going to try and sell you anything you don't want."

"Well, just for a minute. . . ."

Walking into Jill's house was like walking into a version of Melissa's parents' house, or their house of twenty years ago. Even the smell was the same: stale, cigarettey, sad. There were snapshots taped to the wallpaper, a bowl of wax fruit on the table, a few *Sports Illustrated* and *Family Circle* magazines carefully arranged in a basket. The TV, underneath a plastic doily and a jar of dried weeds, was the center of the room; in a cage by the window peeped a lone canary.

"Been married long?" was all Melissa could think to ask.

"Only three months," Jill said, beginning to unwind her long soft hair from the rollers. "Larry's a student. I'm planning to take some classes too," she added. "When he gets finished. I just found out I'm pregnant, though."

She tried to seem happy, but her round face looked wan and almost ill. The blonde curls fell gently to her bare shoulders. "Can I get you some coffee or anything?"

"Coffee, sure. Thank you." Melissa followed Jill out to the tiny kitchen. It was spotlessly neat, again like her mother's. All those macaroni and cheese dinners, eaten by the light of the Mickey Mouse Club and the Evening News. All those peanut butter sandwiches gorged down at the old plastic table with the shiny checked tablecloth. She could almost remember the pattern of the plates, colored flecks in them like candy.

"What are you selling?" Jill asked, setting a kettle on to boil.

"Encyclopedias."

"That must be fun, going around to people's houses."

"It's all right. This is my first day." Melissa stopped herself from explaining anything more. Better get started, better start with the spiel. She suddenly glimpsed her head in a mirror over the sink. Could this heavy-set, mature-looking woman with the gray and white streaks in her hair be herself?

"What's your husband studying?" she asked instead.

"Oh, just general for now. He doesn't really know what he wants to do. I want to be a nurse . . . someday," Jill said, sitting down and twisting a lock of hair in her fingers. She was polite to Melissa as she would be to any middle-aged woman.

"That sounds good," said Melissa.

Conversation had suddenly faltered. Melissa stared at her hands, trying to avoid the mirror over the sink. What had made her ask to come inside? Jill seemed to be wondering the same thing.

"I don't think Larry would be interested in an encyclopedia. I mean, he does all his studying at the college and everything."

What about you? Melissa could have demanded. Christie would have, even though she was no feminist; she would have started right in convincing Jill that she was able to make a decision on her own. But Melissa, for all her politics, couldn't seem to do that. If, by some miracle, she got Jill to agree, she'd have to live with the thought of what Larry would do or say when he came home. He'd be furious with Jill, just as Melissa's father had been when her mother bought that vacuum cleaner on credit or when she'd enrolled in a correspondence course for bookkeeping. He'd always acted as if her mother were too stupid to take any independent action; she'd ended up believing it herself.

Melissa stood up, murmuring, as if she were frightened of something. "Thanks so much. I won't wait for the coffee."

"All right," said Jill helplessly. "Well, good luck. Have a nice day."

She leaned on the door watching Melissa walk to the sidewalk, twisting and retwisting her long blonde hair in her fingers, a slight figure against the shabby duplex.

I can't let this get me down, Melissa told herself, walking furiously across the street. I can't start empathizing with every woman I meet. Why couldn't I have treated her differently? She expected it. I could have been warm, friendly, authoritative, the graying, mature woman in the mirror. Jill was lonely, it would have been a snap to sell her.

Something nagged at Melissa as she stood on the street corner, wondering which house to try next. Henry Mandell. Someone she hadn't thought about for years, and wouldn't have now but for Jill and the absent Larry. It had been the summer before college, when she and Christie had hung around the community pool, flirting with lifeguards. He'd wanted to get engaged. A tall, muscular boy with a silvery fall of hair across his brown forehead, the handsomest boy she'd ever known. What if she had married him? She might have had three children by now, be what Jill would become in another fifteen years—what her mother was now, a tired, frowsy housewife who was afraid to open the door to strangers, afraid to have a thought of her own.

If it hadn't been for Christie, for the feelings she'd had about Christie even then. . . . "Don't throw your life away, Melissa. Think of everything we want to do."

Melissa found herself at a halt in front of a small house at the end of the block. She couldn't recall where she was in relation to the Ramada Inn any longer. She did want to be able to say to Christie that she'd sold at least one encyclopedia set. She went up to the house and knocked.

A young man in jeans and a Budweiser T-shirt answered the door.

"I wonder if I could take a minute of your time to tell you about something that will change your life?" Melissa said eagerly.

Fifteen minutes later she was still there, still talking vigorously and, she thought, on the point of making a sale. Rob and his wife Sarah were definitely interested. They thought it might be an investment for their two pre-school boys. Unfortunately, Melissa found herself talking more and more to Sarah, telling her what she had been too hopeless to tell Jill. "Think of this as something you can use all your life, something that will help keep you in touch with the world."

At that suggestion Rob put his foot down. "I don't think we'd be able to swing it." His eyes were suddenly suspicious and hard.

Sarah, a quick, curly-haired redhead, said, "But Robbie. It sounds so great. Melissa is a librarian, and Grandma and Grandpa might. . . ."

"I said *no*, honey. Thank you very much for your time, Ma'am, but I don't think we're ready to make that kind of outlay."

Melissa forced herself to smile. "Oh, sure, I understand."

Before the door was quite closed, though, she heard him

mutter to his wife, "If she's a librarian, what's she doing selling encyclopedias?"

What did I do wrong? But Melissa knew, as she walked with counterfeit briskness away from the house and toward a series of vacant lots that led up into the pine-sprinkled hills. She'd acted as if Sarah were a person too. If she'd continued to direct her spiel towards Rob she might have made it. It hadn't been consciously intentional—she had almost liked him at first. She was just so used to talking only to women. And now she hated him. Fucking pig, controlling asshole. They were all the same: Henry, who'd wanted her to give up college and marry him; Taylor, who'd expected her to follow him all over the country while he looked for work; Glenn, who'd answered her questions about his job with a 'you wouldn't understand.'

Melissa slowed down, puffing a little, and began to search for a spot to sit on the hillside. No, that part of her life was gone forever, and had been for years, ever since she turned up in Eugene, still smarting from Glenn's rejection. And she was glad it was gone. Whatever her problems with women were and had been, they never centered on the male ego, on the differing balance of worldly power. Painful as her partings had been with women lovers, difficult as some of their arguments and disagreements, she felt they'd pushed her forward, in some way, toward honesty and a better understanding of what she wanted and needed—and never toward self-hatred, the continuing legacy of misogyny.

From her sunny, needle-strewn seat on the hill, Melissa regarded the mobile homes and rag-tag houses and duplexes. She wondered idly what Robbie would have done if she'd declared herself a lesbian. Thrown her out on her ass, probably. "It's important to make a point of it to everyone," Debra had said. "To let them know we're everywhere, that they can't keep making their stupid heterosexist assumptions. If they know or suspect and you still don't tell them, you're playing right into their hands, don't you see? Letting them see you're ashamed and afraid of their opinion."

Once it had been enough just to come out at all—to yourself, to other women. They'd understood why you didn't want your parents to know, or some of your old friends, or most of your co-workers and neighbors. They would only be upset, they wouldn't understand. Melissa leaned back on the carpet of warm, sweet-smelling needles and looked up at the mountain blue sky. She closed her eyes and saw it again, that dream she'd had just before waking the other morning.

There was a dinner party, in a restaurant, a Chinese restaurant with big, round, black-lacquered tables that reflected the light. Many of the people at the tables she knew; they were relatives, they were old friends, some from very far back. Old boyfriends were there, her first grade teacher, her mother, her father, her two older brothers, Christie of course, Christie the way she used to be, with long, sun-streaked brown hair and an eager, determined face.

There had been a lot of toasting and laughing, and finally Melissa herself had stood up with a glass in one hand, raising it high, saying, "Yes, it's true, yes, it's true. I am. I'm a lesbian."

Then what a clapping and murmuring and delighted sighing there had been. It was as if she'd said she just won the Nobel prize. She had looked at them, everyone, recognized them, loved them, and in turn, felt their acceptance float up over her like warm steam from a bath, had seen the love on every face.

Melissa lay drowsing on the hillside for a while longer, drugged by the warmth and pine smell, making her decision. When she finally sat up, it seemed very still and hot in the dry mountain air. She was dazed but certain; she would start with Christie.

It was just sunset as she approached the Ramada Inn. The sky was pale rose and peach, the air mild with a hint of wood burning. Crickets chirped softly and for a moment Melissa felt happy in spite of her tiredness. She and Christie would have a quiet evening, talking things out. Maybe they'd take a drive to watch the stars. A few were already out; soon the southwestern sky would be full of them.

She found her friend in the cocktail lounge, standing at the bar with two men.

"Melissa, over here," Christie called loudly. "Want you to meet two super guys."

She was more than a little drunk and already somehow physically entangled with one of them. George was his name; he was a strapping fellow about forty or so, with the bold offensiveness of the natural salesman. He was wearing a Hawaiian tie and a gaudy turquoise and silver ring. The other man, Bob, was even slimier, dressed in a blue polyester suit and a pink, striped shirt. He was the short, wizened kind of man who always made Melissa feel huge.

"I didn't do too well," Melissa said, trying not to show her dismay. "Only one sale." It had been to two Kuwaiti students who spoke minimal English and offered her mint tea. They had been very polite and surprised by her visit. One of them wrote out a check while the other chattered on about America and Americans. "You are so free here, you girls. In my own country the girls do never go out."

"Well, that's one more than me. Hell, I gave up after the first ten minutes. I knew I wasn't up to it." Christie's turquoise eye shadow was smeared and her lipstick had run into the fine lines around her mouth.

"You gave up?" said Melissa, thinking, and you let me trudge around all day by myself?

Christie was oblivious. She lit another cigarette though she still had one going in the bar ashtray. "Some days it's just like that."

"Yap," agreed her companion. "Some days the bar is the only place for us."

"What are you drinking?" asked the small, skinny man, with a repulsive nudge of familiarity.

Nothing, Melissa almost said. Screw off. But she settled for a beer. She didn't know what to do. She'd been, without realizing, desperately looking forward to talking with Christie about the people she'd met, about their shared past of poverty. "Was it really so awful?" she wanted to ask. And, "Did you have the same feeling of escape I did?" "How can you bear to be reminded of your childhood all the time?"

Now a part of her already knew the answer. Christie couldn't. That's why she was drinking. She'd probably been drinking since she dropped Melissa off.

Mingled pity and anger surged in Melissa's plum-jacketed chest so that she could hardly hear Christie's next words, cajoling, intimate. "No reason we can't have dinner with these fellows, is there? Not when fate's thrown us together and all."

It was what she'd said when they had been in the cafe in Barcelona. "Melissa, come and meet Arnold. He's staying in the same apartment building we are. It's fate!"

"Count me out," said Melissa. "I'm exhausted. Do we have a room yet?"

"Hey, don't be a spoilsport," said George, hanging over Christie's thin shoulder. "Gal here says you're visiting her from Oregon. Remember you're on vacation."

"Please, 'Lissa. Just dinner, and then we'll go to bed."

"Har, har," laughed George. 'I guess you didn't mean that like it sounded."

Melissa felt like she was going to be sick. In Barcelona Christie had giggled, "Arnold asked me if we were lesbians or something. Can you imagine?"

They were all looking at her. "Well," said Melissa, forcing herself. "Just dinner then."

In Barcelona, in the beginning, they had been so happy together. Melissa couldn't remember when it began to change. She herself had been easily satisfied, following a routine of study in the morning over *café con leche,* visiting the sights in the afternoon or leisurely reading the *Herald Tribune* at sidewalk cafes, traipsing from bar to bar in the evening. It was her first real taste of freedom. No more classes, no more books, no more teachers' dirty looks. Just the warm September sun lighting up the Plaza de Cataluña, with its flocks of white pigeons and children in short pants and pinafores . . . the delicious taste of puddingthick hot chocolate with little fried donut rings . . . the late nights when, full of Rioja wine and *tapas* of squid and sweetbreads, she and Christie had strolled back to their flat through the feathered trees of the Ramblas, under moonlight shining on ornate baroque scrollwork.

They had held hands sometimes, had sung old folk songs, and Melissa had felt Christie's long soft brown hair on her cheek, the sweet smell of her, California roses and Spanish Maja. She hadn't minded much when Christie first got to know Arnold and his friends. Manuel and Fernando were Spanish; they'd taught her jokes as well as giving her poetry to read. And after all, she and Christie had always had boy-friends, from high school through college. None of them had stood in the way before.

It was just that, for the first time, Melissa was beginning to feel something different about her friend, something new and exciting and terrifying. It might have been because they were in a foreign country together, freed from the restraints of home—the worries about money and getting good grades, the need to fix on a career, the depressing family visits—that it was happening. Or it might have been happening inside Melissa herself. Perhaps she'd always been attracted to Chris-tie. Perhaps their adolescent involvement with each other had been something more than shared narcissism. Melissa didn't know, but something inside her urged her to hope.

When occasionally Chrisite expressed dissatisfaction: "We're not meeting anybody"; "Do you think we should travel around a little?" Melissa had always agreed. Was it her fault then, that Christie had discovered Arnold? And yet it still might not have come to anything if Melissa hadn't gotten sick.

It had started with a cold caught in an unseasonal rain and it hadn't gone away. Day after day she'd lain in bed, sneezing, then coughing, feverish, and with a growing pain in her side. It was too much to expect that Christie should always stay with her. Christie had brought her medicine and then a doctor who said Melissa had pneumonia and needed to go to the hospital.

Christie had visited her there up until the day of her release. Then the nurse had brought a letter.

"Melissa, don't be mad. I just couldn't hang around here any longer. Arnold has to go back to London and I've decided to go with him. But I expect you to come and visit us before you go home. Hear? This trip was the beginning of my whole life. Thanks for being such a great friend."

Bob, the weasely salesman, was sullen but pushy. Perhaps he was emboldened by the sight of George already fondling Christie's knee under the table. Bob kept offering to buy Melissa another drink, though she still had most of her beer, and trying out possible conversations while wolfing down steak and fries. He knew all about Eugene, he said. "Not too much night life there. What do you do for excitement?"

"I don't do anything for excitement," Melissa told him, moving her salad around in the bowl. She had stopped trying to catch Christie's eye; her friend was too busy describing her life in London to George. "I was a designer for a very important ad agency. We had the Mary Quant account and lots of others. I'm really an artist. David Hockney called me one of the best American painters to come out of the seventies. I just thought selling would be fun for a while."

Take Louise Nevelson, Christie had said. Take Georgia O'Keeffe. Still prolonging the lie that she could become anything but what she was, a cheap, flashy, alcoholic, second-rate.... No, Melissa couldn't judge her. Too many memories still tugged her back: Christie at thirteen, practicing ballet in her mother's living room, absurdly dressed in tennis shoes and a baggy old swimsuit; Christie at fifteen, winning an art prize for her self-portrait; she and Christie swearing eternal friendship at sixteen, on the way home from school one day; testing each other on French verbs, sharing countless pizzas and confidences, discussing methods of birth control or how to scrape up money for a job-hunting dress, planning their trip to Spain.

She was my best friend, thought Melissa, staring at the thin stranger with the frizzy hair and loud, hectic laugh across the table. I'll never have another. Not Debra, not anyone. But why didn't she share my feelings? Why did she leave me for Arnold just when I was learning how to love her?

"I hate to say this," said Bob to Christie. "But your friend here isn't giving me a whole lot of help."

Christie and George looked over and Melissa saw George give Bob a beefy wink. Christie smiled at Melissa impatiently.

'Oh, 'Lissa's a serious girl. Librarian. Dark, mysterious type, you know. Opposite from me."

"Maybe she doesn't like you," said George to Bob. "Maybe you're not her type."

"Yes I am," asserted Bob, half angrily. "Any woman's my type." to prove it he put his hand on Melissa's thigh.

"You get your fucking hand off me," Melissa said evenly. She stood up and moved out of the booth.

All of their faces looked up at her, surprised and un-sympathetic.

"Whassa matter?" Bob finally said. "You don like men?"

"No," said Melissa slowly, holding on to the edge of the round black table. "I don't. I like women. I'm a lesbian."

She stared straight at Christie as she spoke and for a moment Christie, robbed of her drunkenness, met her eyes. She knows, thought Melissa; she's always known. It was as clearly as they had ever looked at each other, and as finally.

"Good-night," said Melissa. As she stumbled through the dining room she heard Christie's slurred but ringing voice, "Don't ask *me*. I hardly know her, haven't seen her for *years*."

In the emptily comfortable, regulation-appointed room of the Ramada Inn, Melissa sat for a while on one of the single beds, staring at the phone and at herself in the huge wall mirror. The graying, mature woman looked shaken, but somehow more familiar, even resolute.

"We can be anything we want," she and Christie had always told each other. "We can do anything we want to." It was the chant that had carried them through their adolescence into college and into the world. The litany that had saved them from the lives of their working-class parents. The lie that had left them unable to recognize the strengths and weaknesses they already had, believing that identity was a mask to be put on and taken off at will, nothing to do with who you really were, with what you really wanted from life.

Debra answered at the first ring. "Melissa, I've been trying for days to get you. I've been so worried."

"It's good to hear your voice."

"But where are you? This sounds long-distance. Oh, I've been kicking myself ever since I left. I really didn't mean everything I said. And then I heard you lost your job. . . ."

"No, you were right. It's time for me to choose. I've chosen."

There was a pause; Melissa could hear Debra stop breathing and realized she didn't know what Melissa was going to say.

"I came out," Melissa told her, and the words didn't scare her. "Girl, did I come out."

"But where are you?" Debra's breath came back in a rush of warmth. "When are you coming back?"

"I'm in a Ramada Inn in Flagstaff, Arizona, looking at myself in a mirror. Yeah. But I am coming back. Tomorrow. I'm going to fight the lay-off and whether or not I win, I'm going to leave Eugene for a while." She found herself smiling at the woman in the plum pantsuit. "I'm going to Spain, to Barcelona. I just realized I never finished my trip. . . . Want to come?" she asked.

Phantom Limb Pain

The professor of Russian 101, Evening Section, leapt in front of his demurely fidgeting class that first night like a dissident ballet dancer making his entrance upon the Western stage. Expecting accolades, contemptuous and eager, he stalked towards the casement windows and flung them open, though it was still early spring and seven o'clock in the evening. A shiver ran through his captive audience, but no one protested. In his cheap foreign suit, wearing an oddly spotted tie, he made them feel small, huddled.

He sprang, he paused, he introduced himself. What? His wrists were bone and sinew under frayed cuffs. His hair stood up like a stiff hat of gray fur, brilliantined. His jaw was hacked, his eyes slits of granite shot with mica. He was terrible, frightening, queer.

Although no one besides himself had dared to speak, he announced that tonight was the last time they would use English. Was he speaking English even then? His accent gulped and smeared their language almost beyond recognition. From now on, he said, swinging to a seat on his desk, a giant in momentary repose, it would be Russian, Russian, русский язык.

The class of thirteen, now utterly dismayed and hopeless, shivered again, and those who had sweaters pulled them down to cover their wrists.

Up again, bounding among them, he demanded their names. Six inches of index finger leveled at each in turn, a christening. They would have Russian names now, and not

only that, but patronyms. Patronyms, he said, suddenly illuminating the confusions of Tolstoy's novels, were the names of
their fathers, with an ending.

Thus Cheryl became Sasha Andreievna. I'd rather have my
mother's name, she wanted to say. Or nothing. My own twice.
Long ago she had dropped her father's legacy for a newly
minted surname. Williamson had become Will. It jolted her to
be reminded of her father; she brought out "Andrew" without
thinking, then remembered she hadn't written to him in years.

When all were introduced and reintroduced as double-
named Russians, their professor repeated his own name. This
time she caught it; Ivan Ivanovitch, Ivan, son of Ivan, Son of
himself. "Ivan the Terrible," he said.

Some of the students didn't get it, were already looking
huntedly towards the door, but Sasha couldn't help laughing.
Half angry, half amused. He was so conscious of his own
power, oh yes, he knew his impression. A typical male. I'll
leave at the break, she thought.

He stared at her appreciatively, seeking a bond. He's
frightened, she knew suddenly, and looked away. But already
he was moving again, to front stage. With nervous contempt
Ivan Ivanovitch noticed that some of his students had their
books already open to the first page. Dramatically he slammed
one of them shut.

"Tonight," he said, "we begin with memory."

A cool April wind whistled lightly through the brilliant
classroom as Ivan Ivanovitch began to chant what was obviously the first line of a poem: "Я вас любил. . . ."

He recited it through, paused at the end as if to accept a
burst of applause that the students were too timid, too boorish
to give, and then turned somber, pedagogic.

"Pushkin," he breathed with stern reverence. "And this is
his loveliest poem of all." Ivan Ivanovitch did not offer to
translate it for them but instead produced from an expensive
but worn briefcase a clutch of badly mimeographed sheets.
"You will memorize this by next week."

There was by now a stunned quality to the silence in the
room, as each student took a page and saw the rows of com-

pact purple hieroglyphics.

"Excuse me, sir, Ivan, Ivan... ," a young woman said faintly. "I thought this was a beginning Russian class." She closed her notebook as if prepared to slink away on the spot.

"Da, da, of course it is."

A thirtyish engineering type in the front row exploded. "But we haven't even learned the Russian alphabet. Surely you can't expect us to read this."

There were murmurs of agreement. Sasha Andreieva took heart. They wouldn't just sit there, lumpish and intimidated. "We can't read this," she echoed, pushing the smudges firmly away.

"Read?" he sneered back at them, snatching the challenge up in his enormous fists. "Who says something about 'read?' I say, 'memorize,' and you hear 'read.'" He paced before them, through vast steppes. "Memory, memory, memory. You Americans know nothing about the memory. Without History, without Culture, you grow up watching your teevee. Every eight-year-old child in Russia knows this poem. They know Pushkin and Lermontoff, all the greatest poets. By their heart. Da, it is expected." He heated this subject up excitedly, running his fingers through his brisk hair. "Expected, da, expected. But American schools do not teach memory. Recite to me one poem you have learned." Ivan Ivanovitch paused a fraction of a second, scanning contemptuously. "Hah! You see? You Americans do not even know your own Declaration of the Independence. Now," he proved. "You understand?" He suddenly jumped on to the squat desk behind him, becoming nine feet of messianic zeal. "Repeat after me."

His arms flung north and south, he implored them.

"Weird," muttered Sasha Andreievna, dropping into a chair across the living room from Edie.

Patient, ready to be enlightened, Edie looked up from her sane British mystery and repeated, "Weird?"

"This teacher...." But how to explain him? Sasha hadn't gone home at the break; he hadn't given them a break, had

only pushed them on and on through the rigors of the still un-
translated poem. At ten, all thirteen students had rushed
wildly for the door. Would any of them come back? Sasha
would not, oh no. Chalk up a wasted evening to . . . experience?

"Well, Russian. . . ." Edie said, marking her book with a
finger and dreamily regarding Sasha. "What a thing to study.
Ten years out of school and you working all day, too. I'd be
exhausted."

Yes, Edie would be exhausted, Sasha thought, regarding
her lover pocketed in the chintz like a kangaroo, a plump cat
of a woman with soft paws and large vague eyes. Work flat-
tened Edie, movies and plays laid her low, politics enervated
her and friends most of all. She read gothics and mysteries to
be soothed and slept ten hours a night. Weekends she pottered
and napped.

It amazed Sasha now that she ever could have been taken in
by Edie's lethargy, that she had found it amusing, endearing.
"My sleeper, my dreamer," she called Edie, resting her head
on Edie's plentiful breasts, her cushioned stomach, allowing
herself to reinvent her mother's caresses.

"Weird," she repeated now. "A madman. All evening he
had us memorizing a poem in Russian. By Pushkin. I don't
even know what the hell it means. Yah vas lubiel . . . I can't get
it out of my head now. But he's crazy, Edie, big and jumpy
and something in his eyes like fear. He's punishing us, I'm
sure of it. A tyrant, a petty tyrant, just like my father. A
stupid Russian man making us take our father's names."

"You should have taken that dance class," Edie murmured,
straying back to her mystery. "You like to dance. Maybe it's
not too late to change."

"But I've always wanted to learn Russian . . . I need to do
something with my brain. . . ." Sasha kicked off her shoes.
"It's him, he's nuts. Any other teacher . . . oh shit. . . . How
was work today?"

Edie sighed, a fat morsel of blonde in the mouth of the
chair. "Oh, busy. Phone ringing off the hook. Mr. J. complaining, I think his stomach was bad today. Some of the sec-

retaries want to organize. How can we? I told them. So few of us. But we could use the money. . . ."

Edie sighed on, her blonde hair beading into light under the lamp's glow. I could never ever be a secretary, Sasha thought, irritated, pitying. Lucky that nursing is more organized. We're professionals, at least, though we don't get near enough money compared to the doctors. Still, it's a challenge. Always something to learn, emergencies where you can really help. And no male bosses. The doctors descend and ascend like fake dei ex machina. We run the show.

Why then study Russian, or anything? It wasn't that medicine lacked interest. Only that, after ten years, it wasn't quite enough. Every two or three years she'd changed floors: medical, surgical, a stint in intensive care, but that was too hectic. Now she was back where she'd started, on a surgical ward, as assistant head nurse. All the same, mere efficiency had begun to bore her. Hadn't she seen it all by now? Limbs and organs cut away, repaired, reinserted. Sutures and dressings, sterile and disposable, hiding the mystery of healing, the surprise. Then, how like a clock the body was, always hopeful, always eager to get back on schedule, pathetically ready to tick again. Only individuals kept it all fresh, the mind suffering in new ways with the knowledge of mortality. Psychology alone made work interesting, working with people, around people every day. And yet you couldn't afford to get too involved. There was death. And all the complications of loss.

"You're always studying something," Edie said, a little envious, mostly disapproving, and opened her book again. "Last semester it was economics. . . ."

Sasha walked over and kissed her lover's smooth forehead, trying not to show, not to feel her frustration. "You look tired. Want me to make your lunch for you tonight?"

"Oh, would you? Make tuna, we haven't had that for a while."

"You should have see him, Edie. A complete madman." In spite of herself, Sasha began to smile.

*

Six students reappeared the next class session, Sasha

Andreievna among them. Embarrassed, complicit, pleased at
not being put off so easily, they spoke hesitantly to each other.
Students and workers, a retired dentist, a woman who had
been around the world. "Did you manage to memorize the
poem?" they whispered. "Yes," said Sasha. She hadn't been
able to forget it, though she still didn't know what it meant.
Yah vas lubiel, she'd sung as she injected pain killers and
changed bandages.

Ivan Ivanovitch loomed in the doorway like an uninvited
guest. Sardonic and sad, his eyes counted them. What did you
expect? Sasha wanted to say. You drove them away. Her
heart, fickle beast, went out to him. But he wouldn't have
sympathy; with a lunge he was among them, keeping his
promise: No English.

His hair was gray and gleaming, a rakish tall cap. She
noticed his fine eyebrows this time, his angled cheekbones. In
the cheap black suit, his shoes glistening like bowling balls, he
pranced and strutted. In Russian, in русский язык, he
pointed and spoke. There was no mention of the grueling
poem, though they waited, hopefully, to shine. Instead Ivan
began with the basics. Tables and chairs had names, so did
pencils and windows. Becoming sentences and questions,
the objects in the room danced with Ivan Ivanovitch.
Где карандаш ? *Where* is the pencil? It is *here*, it is *there*. He
opened his backdrop, the window, and blasted them with
spring. They struggled, dutifully, in confusion, to keep up,
fitting their tongues around the awkward words, pushing
them out louder into the room, ever louder. He had them
shouting with his trick of cupping an enormous hand to a
small, well-shaped ear.

Then, suddenly, he seemed satisfied and pointed to the
clock. In a voice so normal it sounded like a whisper, he announced a break. His students were astounded, disappointed.
Knowledge had seemed so near, mastery impending. With
reluctance they stretched themselves and followed Ivan
Ivanovitch into the hall.

There the corridor was swelling with other students, smoking and chattering. Ivan Ivanovitch positioned himself near

the stairwell and brought out a pack of Camels. In a whispering clump, his students remembered their poem. This, this was how the class should have started last week. The naming of concrete objects, their useful arrangement. But had the memorization been for nothing, then? Sasha, assistant head nurse, used to assuming authority in unclear situations, appointed herself representative and approached the stairwell.

Seeing her coming, Ivan Ivanovitch proffered a Camel, courtly, inscrutable. She shook her head, drove straight to the point, ignoring the depth of his mica-flecked eyes.

"What about that poem you had us memorize last week? Don't you want to hear us recite it?"

Ivan Ivanovitch affected extreme amazement. "You memorized it?"

"Well, of course." She was indignant. "You *told* us to."

He laughed and she faltered slightly. "I don't know what the words mean."

"Tell me," he said, "why you bothered?"

Forty, fifty, Sasha couldn't tell, though she judged age every day at the hospital. His wrinkles were few, his eyes very tired. Close up she felt a stoop in his tall body; his breath was ashy, rasped.

"You said we couldn't memorize. That's not true."

"There were thirteen last week," he stated.

"You wanted to drive them away."

"They were not serious."

"How do you *know?*"

Ivan Ivanovitch smiled, showing false and mottled teeth. He bent closer to her, with a thick charm that offended. "Say the poem."

"Here?" Embarrassed, Sasha tossed her head and saw her fellow students peering discreetly.

"Why not?"

The urge to show him was stronger than any restraint. She began, "Yah vas lubiel . . . ," only to be interrupted.

"The 'L,' the 'L,'" he said. "You are missing it entirely. What we have in Russian is the 'dark L,' it glides the top of the mouth, from the back to the teeth. Listen."

She listened, missing it, and tried again. She saw him steeling himself, in sadness, in amusement, and tried harder. Faster.

"Very good," he said noncommittally.

She was furious with him, wanted to turn on her heel. What did he expect? Perfect pronunciation? She had memorized it, hadn't she?

"What is your job?" he asked abruptly.

"Nurse." She was brief, eyeing his reaction. If he were impressed or contemptuous, he didn't show it. Politeness fell seamlessly across his expression. He dropped his cigarette and ground it with a shiny shoe.

"Time to get back," he said.

"Any better tonight?" Edie asked.

"Christ," Sasha muttered. She remained standing by the door, emptying out the contents of her bag on a table, separating stethoscope from car keys, paperback from Russian text. "Who is he, anyway? One of the decayed aristocracy from the way he acts. A White Russian general. You know that poem I killed myself to memorize for tonight? He'd forgotten all about it. We didn't get a chance to say it. He as much as admitted to me that he'd used it to get rid of most of the class." She threw herself the length of the red tweed couch. "The first half of class was all right," she allowed. "But then, when we went back, we didn't learn anything. Instead, he went on a long diatribe against American teaching methods, the university system, American culture, everything. He's obsessed with the idea of TV, thinks it's our ruin, et cetera."

"Well, you don't like TV," Edie pointed out reasonably.

"I'm not *against* it . . . it just bores me. . . . And who is he to criticize us anyway? He came here of his own free will, didn't he? He was probably a cab driver in Russia. I'd like to know what makes him think he can teach this language. I could learn more from just reading the book."

"Careful, your chauvinism is showing."

"It's his chauvinism, damn it. I'm not used to sitting captive, being lectured to by some man. The way he looked at me!"

"Try being a secretary sometime," Edie said without irony.

"I don't know how you stand it."

"What else can I do?"

Sasha was silent. It came over her suddenly how very tired she was of her own job. She had been tired of it for a long time.

"Why don't we just move to another country, throw everything up and start over?"

"Move . . . you mean pack up and leave?" Edie's soft eyes swept the room fearfully. "But we're so comfortable here."

"*You're* comfortable. . . ." Sasha stopped. There was no use in arguing. Edie did not like arguments, they only made her cry.

Edie went back to her only mode of escape, a gothic set in a far land. Sasha knew, if she looked up from the pillow where she had buried her head, that she would see Edie mouthing some of the words. Once it had been endearing, then irritating, now it no longer mattered. When had love changed, what had it changed into?

Drifting now, Sasha forgot about moving, Edie, even Ivan Ivanovitch, and remembered a case at the hospital that day. The man in 317 screaming with pain because his leg hurt him. Only his leg was no longer there; it had been amputated the day before. A recognized phenomenon, written up in textbooks, studied for generations. Phantom limb pain, they called it. A remembered sensation in what now no longer existed. No pain in the cutting off point, the wound, but pain further down, where memory insisted. Not imaginary, but real.

Sasha's cheek scraped the rough red tweed of the couch as she turned to stare at Edie mouthing her book: pencil, window, where is the table, where are you?

"It must be hard to live in a world where no one really knows who you are, not to be able to prove that you have, you had another existence."

"No one ever said it was easy to be a lesbian," Edie looked

up briefly from the novel where she was transposing the sex of the hero.

But Sasha had been thinking of Ivan Ivanovitch.

Yah vas lubiel, lubov yehsho, bwitz mojet... I loved you once, love you still, perhaps.... Now that Sasha had read the translation of Pushkin's poem it would not leave her alone. It went through her mind constantly at work, interfered with her concentration. She forgot to give a routine medication, had to be called at home, late at night. She let one of her patients go home with his stitches still in. There had to be a way to leave Edie without hurting her, but how, Sasha didn't know. She found herself dreaming of adventure, traveling to Russia perhaps. She had the money, it would give her a chance to really practice the language. Ivan Ivanovitch could tell her what to visit.... But Edie wouldn't come, and then, Sasha had never much liked travel, the mechanics of it. She liked being in one place, never mind the comfort, but she needed some sense of being useful, responsible. Maybe she should go work in a clinic somewhere, in some underdeveloped country. Edie wouldn't want to go there, either.

Unable to speak, to act, Sasha buried herself in her work, in her Russian class, resolved to master the language better and faster than anyone else. Not for *him,* though think it he might, in his male pride, his foreign arrogance, but for herself.

The class was down to five now. "The Masochists," they called themselves, as if they were a secret society. But Ivan Ivanovitch had to be a masochist in his own right. Why else would he subject himself to the torment of trying to teach "this beautiful language to a class of ignorants?"

They had sunk deep into the grammar and were foundering badly. Ivan Ivanovitch occasionally put out a hand to help, but more often he perched furiously on his island of a desk, like a lighthouse whose beam glares steadily off into the night above a raft of shipwrecked sailors. In some essential way he seemed to be against his students, willing them to fail.

Yet he was perfectly comfortable, it seemed, when haranguing them about the state of their culture. Sometimes, when in a good mood, Ivan Ivanovitch would even intersperse his diatribes with stories about his last trip to Moscow, ostensibly to show how American culture had infiltrated the world.

One night he told them about selling blue jeans on the black market. "When I arrived I have my suitcase full of blue jeans, five, six. Every day I put on a pair and go to the streets. The people they come up to me whispering, 'How much you want for those blue jeans?' Then we go to a place and change trousers. When I came back I am richer and I have these many pairs of Russian trousers."

That explained his tacky wardrobe. But what had he done with the money, then? And wasn't there something disturbing about his pandering to the base desires of the Soviets for Western commodities?

Sasha didn't know how to put the question into words, however, feared his flashing eyes. There must be something she was misunderstanding. She saw him looking at her then, with a curious intensity she found so unnerving, and blurted out, "What did you do there, when you lived there, I mean?"

The class held its breath. He had never spoken to them about his early life in Russia. Among themselves they had postulated the wildest, most romantic theories: he was a dissident, a Jew, he had suffered . . . in the Gulag perhaps; he could have been an Orthodox priest, or anything. Sasha continued to suspect that he was a noble of some sort, with that carriage and that head—until she was angry with him, when she returned to the cab driver theory.

"I was a schoolboy, of course," Ivan Ivanovitch snapped, lifting his head high to stare balefully at them all. When he drove them back to class after their break he used the excuse of their too friendly curiosity to give them a test on verb endings. He was especially hard on Sasha, singling her out for the most difficult forms.

After class he stopped her, the last one out the door. "Locomotion and conveyance," he said. "I am afraid you do not understand the difference between the two."

She was putting on her sweater and gathering her books.

Wearily she answered, "I know there's a difference in going somewhere yourself and going somewhere with a, a book, for instance, or another person. But I'm damned if I understand what it is."

Ivan Ivanovitch had never looked stiffer, though he tried to smile. "The difference is that instead of locomoting by myself now, I would like to convey you to have a cup of coffee."

He had been born in Kiev, in 1935. All his early memories were of war. "Although we from Ukraine hated the Soviets and first welcomed the Nazis, we soon saw the mistake. Many many people died. I was taken and put in a camp. Only later do I find my mother again, but my father was shot for a partisan. One uncle he went to Turkey and there we went also when I was thirteen. At night, on a boat. We wanted to come to the United States but it was at first impossible. That was my mother's hope, that we would come here for my schooling. She wanted me to be a doctor. But all the years of my schooling were passed in Turkey, that useless place. When we finally came I am thirty, and how could I be a doctor?"

His thick voice had all the embarrassment of confession and his eyes were so intense that Sasha had to stare very hard at his enormous hands, laid out flat as corpses on the table. Against her better judgment they had not gone to a coffee shop, but instead to "a very special place I know." She doubted now that he had ever been here before; it was too expensive with its plush booths and lantern-lit tables, and they were obviously out of place, he in his ill-fitting black suit and worn cuffs, she in jeans and a sweater.

It wasn't that she was exactly frightened of him, or even that she mistrusted him. Only that the faint flush of romance she had invested Ivan Ivanovitch with had totally dissipated, and instead she was only saddened, immeasurably saddened by the sight of this great broken man beside her drinking vodka.

She had wanted to know the mystery of his life, but had stupidly expected more excitement from it. She wasn't prepared for the paralyzing rush of pity she felt hearing him recite the trials of the countryless. It reminded her of a long and sordid illness, leading eventually to amputation. It wasn't a fairytale, not even a gothic; how could she have imagined that he would hide his life if there had been anything marvelous in it?

"Is this supposed to be a student-teacher conference?" she'd cracked nervously as they entered the lounge, and perhaps she really had had some idea that they might discuss her progress in class. She had longed for encouragement like any school child. But if anything were clear now, it was that her earliest intuitions had been correct; he despised teaching, felt it only slightly less humiliating than being a bookkeeper. Yes, he was a bookkeeper during the day, it turned out, not a professor at all. He had only been hired to teach this evening class when the regular professor broke both legs in a skiing accident.

Sympathy did not come easily to Sasha, not towards herself nor towards the hundreds of patients who had passed under her hands. She had steeled herself to cheeriness against the misery of the world; still, in this dim room where the organ hummed like a live beast in the corner, she found herself drifting deep into his failures. After another glass of vodka he told her that he lived with his mother, in a small apartment by the lake, and suddenly she saw it all, saw his exile illuminated as clearly as the small hot lamp on the table.

A refugee, too, she saw herself standing in the snow before a barbed wire fence that bordered on a heavy white forest of birches, saw herself taking secret passage in the dank hold of a cargo ship to Turkey, saw herself in a glaring, smelly bazaar bartering the samovar from home. She saw herself sharing a bathroom with a frail and whining old woman, who could only speak in Russian and refused to have a TV in the house. She saw herself bound by duty and pain to resurrect each day a life she had only known by hearsay. For Ivan Ivanovitch, to be Russian was to be perpetually a refugee, to be destined to hate every country with a hatred so strong it was only surpassed by ignorance of his own. Even the long-awaited visit to Moscow had taught him nothing except that even there he was seen as a foreigner. His mother had taught him everything. She would read Pushkin's poems aloud to him at night, in the sweltering towns of inland Turkey, conjuring up his history and prophesying his future, but powerless, powerless. After the trip to Moscow, nothing seemed real to him.

Sasha understood now his bravado and desperation in class; he was afraid of being found out. Russian meant much more to him than he could ever convey. He could not teach the only thing he had.

Sasha's own crop of stories seemed suddenly rooted in hard and stony ground. She pulled at memory like a weed, but only the top came off in her hand. When Ivan Ivanovitch pressed her for details, there was little she could say. And yet, she too had a well of sadness inside her. She told him about her mother, who had run off with another man when Sasha was eight, then had died and been buried in some distant state. She had never gotten over hating her father for not telling her about her mother's death until many years later.

"I see now that he made the decision to cut her off to save himself. He refused to remember her. But to leave me for so many years thinking her alive, thinking I would find her someday."

It must have been the vodka, for Sasha was crying a little now, and Ivan Ivanovitch put his big hand over hers. She felt his rough, ashy breath on her shoulder and pulled away. He must not think this intimacy was anything more than the chance sharing of sorrow.

She told him about the clear sun of California and the beaches where she swam out to sea. Her lack of friends, her decision to become a nurse and to move away.

It had really been because of a woman she had moved, of course, but Sasha was still sober enough to know not to tell him that. All the same, stronger than anything she had recounted, the memory of her first night with Edie rose up in her. It had been the bed more than anything, the bed as soft as a dream, covered with pieced quilts in worn and fancy patterns. In the morning the sun had slipped in through lacy curtains and Edie had wrapped a quilt around her fullness to make coffee. She hadn't known, when she followed Edie up the coast to make a new home away from both their families, that Edie would never want to move again, that the softness in her would come to be an obstacle instead of a resting place, and that there were other ways of losing people than having them die in a distant state.

"I have a roommate," Sasha said, "We're not getting along so well right now. We're different."

It was far easier to tell him about the hospital, how the work challenged and drew her and was still not enough. "I've had this notion," she said before she knew it, "of working in another country, running a clinic maybe, being more to the patients . . . healing them, I don't know. . . ." She stopped, embarrassed.

"My mother," Ivan Ivanovitch said into his glass, "says that only God can both give and take away, and that even He will not bring back what is gone. All that the men can do is try to heal."

"I'd like to meet her," Sasha said impulsively, leaning towards him slightly.

"She would not . . . no, we cannot go there." He grabbed her hand almost roughly and Sasha was amazed, alarmed even, to see a predatory look come into his gray eyes. "I thought . . . we can go to your house."

Sasha jerked away from him, upsetting her glass, but she couldn't be angry as she mopped at the table with her napkin. "My roommate. . . ."

Ivan Ivanovitch tried to take her hand again. Even in his drunkenness he was stiff and courtly. The hunter's look was gone from his eyes; she wondered if she had imagined it. "Please," he said.

"No." But she didn't withdraw this time.

"When I see you in the class first night. . . ." He stared at her like a dying man, but she felt the life in him coursing through his rough fingers' grip. She didn't think him ugly now, or even odd. His silvery eyes burned into her like the eyes of someone in a platinum photograph, a relative disappeared, an exile, a mother who had died so far away. And for an instant Sasha almost wanted to give in to him, to drown her sadness in his, to resuscitate some forlorn hope that life was more than a series of losses and leave-takings.

But only for an instant. "No," she told him firmly, becoming abruptly the assistant head nurse, the independent woman who knew her own heart too deeply to pretend that such distances could be bridged. She loved women, even if her feelings for Edie had changed. She would find someone else, she would find something else.

"American women have no passion," Ivan Ivanovitch muttered, jerking to his full height in a burst of masculine pride.

Sasha did not argue. Whatever had been between them, whatever for a moment had seemed possible, was gone forever. Let him think what he liked. She had never understood her father and could not pretend to understand the sexual vanity of any man. It could only reduce her to try. Yet in some obscure way she felt grateful to Ivan Ivanovitch, almost as if he had freed her from something. Within this suddenly tawdry and very typical scene she had found the strength to move ahead again.

She left him there drinking, morose and ungainly, his hair stiff as gray bristles, his head between his hands. She left him with his past and with a part of hers, and went home to tell Edie what she planned to do.

Edie cried, but some of her tears were necessarily of relief, that Sasha had finally realized what she herself had known for a long time. Having never experienced death, Edie could not fear loss or understand the forced, painful finality of Sasha's decision. Partings had never threatened Edie; she cared only that they remain friends, had only worried that Sasha would take it all too hard. Edie's quiverings of romance were confined to books, and unlike Sasha, she seemed to believe that life never really changed as long as it continued.

Sasha, who had expected to be the one to comfort, had been comforted instead. They decided that, when Sasha found a job in a clinic in Ecuador, Edie would visit her. Edie became almost animated, seeing in this plan no disappearance of affection, only greater comfort for them both, an end to conflict.

"After Russian, Spanish should be a snap for you," she said cheerfully. "I may even try to learn Spanish myself. I could take a class."

Sasha knew that Edie never would. Yet she could picture her with a Spanish book, lying underneath the pieced quilts of her soft bed—this bed where they lay now, touching each other gently—and mouthing the words, *Where is the jungle, where are you?* And for a moment she clung to Edie with all the emotion of a frightened child, knowing suddenly and with a terrible hopelessness that she would always feel abandoned, even if it was she who did the leaving.

"You're such a strong person," Edie soothed her. "You'll do fine. And so will I," she added, almost in surprise.

"I won't forget you," Sasha promised fervently.

"Why, how could you?" Edie laughed, then yawned and closed her eyes, still stroking her friend's hair.

"You will forget your Russian of course," Ivan Ivanovitch said stiffly when he learned her plans. He was awkward with her now in class, self-protective. It was difficult, and Sasha too didn't really want to remember that for one evening, their eyes and hands had met, that they had, for an instant, been one in sorrow and loss. They had taken refuge again in the roles of student and teacher, with a slight change: sometimes, in the midst of his withering scorn and bravado, Ivan Ivanovitch seemed to recall that Sasha knew what he was—a bookkeeper, without a TV—and then a shy, almost quizzical look would creep into his flashing eyes and he would go back to the lesson.

Smiling a little tensely, Sasha began to quote him the Pushkin poem, but broke off abruptly, understanding for the first time what it was she said, and that they were speaking in a language he had given her.

"The 'dark L'" he couldn't help snapping, while his old gray eyes burned into hers with a loneliness he did not try to disguise. "You still have not got it."

"I can't," she said sadly, then turned so that he couldn't see her face.

On the last night of class Ivan Ivanovitch solemnly presented her with a samovar, thirty years old, from a Turkish bazaar. His mother, he said, holding it tightly for a moment in his huge hands, had said he might give it to her.

"You won't forget me?" he asked again, his eyes once more those of a dying man.

She could have told him that the past is never lost as long as there is someone to remember it, just as a body knows the limb is there even after it is gone. If she could have, she would have placed her hands on his strong hands and healed him. She would have healed herself if she could. But she already knew that healing is not the same as bringing back, and she knew that he knew it, too.

The Hulk

"If you have a color TV it's even better," Nina says. "He's green."

"I'm glad Lisa doesn't," I respond with some feeling. "This is bad enough. That guy has too many muscles for his own good. It's not healthy."

"You intellectuals," she scoffs. "I bet you don't even have a TV."

It's true, but I don't tell her that. I've never liked being called an intellectual. Hell, I never finished college and I'm starving on food stamps. What's so smart about that?

"Ooo, there he goes," she says excitedly. "He's turning into the Hulk. He can't help himself."

I stare at her in real amazement. She's not kidding, she is truly thrilled and stimulated by his transformation from ordinary guy to raving maniac. In spite of having spent the last four days in her company I wouldn't have believed it.

But then, I don't know her at all. It's been one of those awkward situations where you're mad at your lover and want to get away, so you think of your old friend Lisa who says please come to L.A., I'd love to see you, and then she turns out to be having a desperate and passionate affair with someone you never meet and meanwhile some other acquaintance is crashing in her apartment. So it ends up not really a visit to anyone, just a kind of protracted limbo in the company of somebody you don't know and probably don't like and it's three days before Christmas, your lover is calling you collect begging you to come back and here's this guy foaming at the fangs, two stories tall, with a torso like sixteen tightly rolled sleeping bags lashed together, throwing people out the window.

"Ooo, ooo," says Nina; "oh, ouch." Then, seriously to me, "The really tragic part about it is that he doesn't like doing these things. He's always remorseful and they're looking for some way to cure him. It's like a parable of mankind, you know?"

In spite of both direct and round-about questions I have not yet been able to discover what Nina usually does, or how she makes a living or any of the normal things you might want to know about a person you're ending up having to depend upon for complete emotional support. She isn't young, I know that. Her hair is going gray and it's permanented into curls that she heaps forward on her crown like a 1940's comedienne (though it may be the latest style for all I know). About thirty-five, I'd say, maybe older; indifferent about dress, usually wearing voluminous pants and a tube top that flattens her large breasts like an ace bandage. She has spidery long fingers and feet the same, a round kind of face devoid of expressions but not of mystery. In fact, I find her extremely mysterious, though somehow familiar looking. Where did she come from? How did Lisa meet her? What is she doing staying here?

I haven't had a chance to pose these questions to Lisa. In with a hug, out with a kiss, meanwhile changing her clothes and ruffling through the bills.

"Heard from A.J. yet?" she asks. Her large brown eyes regard me with what momentarily appears to be concern.

"Four times in the last two days. She doesn't want to talk about it on the phone, all she wants is for me to come back. *Then* we'll talk about it, she says, but I know that once I go back...."

"Give her my love," Lisa smiles warmly, vaguely, and then: "Gotta run, *he's* waiting."

Lisa, my dearest high school friend, how can you do this to me? Remember the locker we shared, the little notes you wrote me with x's at the bottom for smooches, how your mother let me run away to your house when things got bad at home? And how we've kept in touch all these years, over ten years, in spite of living in different cities and you being a successful screen writer and me just a hopeful nothing. It was you I came down to see, I even thought that maybe . . . but no, *he's* waiting. Christ, in the eleventh grade you would have been ashamed of yourself.

"Have you ever met this, uh, friend of Lisa's?" I ask Nina.

She is reading the huge bulk of the *L.A. Times,* inch by column inch, with close-up concentration.

"Nnnn," she says.

I think, she can't be as stupid as she seems if she reads the paper so thoroughly. I try, "What's your opinion on the hostages?"

"Uhhnnn," she says.

I leave her. It's not like I have nothing to do. I brought five books with me to read and a notebook to fill up and a short story or two to work on. It's not like I have to sit around making conversation with this woman or wait for Lisa to turn up or A.J. to call again. I have my fucking life to figure out!

I write in my notebook. I pace the floor. I go out, down to the Mexican restaurant at the bottom of the hill, along Sunset visiting the Cuban grocery for a mango ice. I come back and sit in the garden with Volume Three of Virginia Woolf's *Letters* and stare out through raggedy palms at the Hollywood Freeway. I hate being alone but I can't concentrate (I tell myself) with Nina always around.

She never goes anywhere.

First she gets up and reads the paper. This takes about two hours. Then she washes her hair and works on her curls with an electric wand. Then she lies, fully dressed, in the sun for a while and finally puts on a record, does a few exercises and settles down to watch TV. She doesn't do dishes because she never cooks. She eats sunflower seeds and fruit and drinks kefir out of the carton. She is actually very tidy. All her possessions are in one box; she never takes them out for long, simply rearranges them when she finishes her toilette. She sleeps on top of Lisa's bed in a sleeping bag. . . .

But I'm making it sound as if we don't talk at all, when, in truth, we have exchanged some bits of conversation. Not about the hostages or Lisa's hot stuff or my worries or hers, if she has any, but strange pieces of dialogue—meaningful, if you could understand them.

For instance, yesterday she says to me, "Do you think the world is going to end pretty soon or not?"

Astonished, all I can mutter is, "I don't know."

"I hope it doesn't," she says, and a faint blush of sadness slips across her round face, so unwrinkled, so incongruous under the pile-up of graying curls.

It makes me feel sad too. All this quarreling and feeling and hoping for nothing. So I say gently and with sympathy, "Don't worry about it. No use worrying about it."

"Oh, but I have to," she says earnestly. "I'm thinking of going to Santa Fe, you know."

Confused, I think she means she knows of some top-secret bunker there where she can hide from the nuclear destruction. I want to ask her if she'll give me the address, but suddenly she says, quite cheerfully, "Santa Fe's a nice place. It's hot there."

Most of our conversations take place, not during commercials, as you would expect, for then Nina sits rapt and solemn, watching the antics of flying candy bars and yodeling housewives, but during the shows themselves, when she is moved to offer some comment about the nature of the universe as expressed through a sit-com or adventure.

She laughs, she oohs, she groans, her normally expressionless face becomes animated; she turns to me and says thoughtfully, "Do you believe in good and evil?"

"Just evil."

"Oh, I think there's always room for improvement," she says seriously.

And so we are sitting watching the Hulk, now a regular chump again and indeed full of remorse at having been pushed too far and gone large and destructive, when the phone rings.

I answer it, prepared for the operator.

"Will you accept a collect call from Alice Jones?"

"Go ahead," I sigh. "Well, what now?"

"Oh Cary, I miss you so much. When are you coming back?"

"I'm not coming back until you get your head examined."

"But that will take too long. You have to come back before then. The cats miss you. Fred isn't eating his kibble."

I steel my heart. Poor Fred. "There's no use us discussing this, A.J. I'm prepared to make changes. But you have to make them too."

"What changes?" she says eagerly, as if the subject had never been broached before.

"You know what changes." I'm starting to get worked up. "I've told you over and over that I can't stand you shouting at me and calling me names. Then claiming you had a nervous breakdown and don't remember anything."

"What names? Cary, I never call you names."

"What do you think egotist is then?"

"It's not a name. It's a description."

"Description of you, you mean. I'm perfectly happy working and writing by myself. I don't need your companionship day and night. I don't need someone to pay attention to me all the time."

"You don't love me," she chokes. "That's it, isn't it?"

"Oh Christ." I slam the phone down and tell it, "And don't call me anymore either."

Nina's eyes are devouring a disembodied hand rolling two different kinds of anti-perspirant across a piece of glass. I stare bitterly at her shoulders emerging from the tube top. She has beautiful skin, but not so beautiful as A.J.'s dancer's silk.

"Is he going to turn into the Hulk again?" I try moodily but not without some desire for reassurance.

"Nnnn," she says. "He only does it once a show."

"I've got to know, who is she?" I whisper the next morning,

following Lisa out the front door. She's been here five minutes, long enough to grab a notebook and put on a clean shirt.

"Oh, Nina? She's just somebody I know."

"From where? A trip to the moon, maybe?"

"She is kind of spacey, isn't she? You'd never guess she was a pretty well-known TV actress as a kid, would you?"

"Lisa! You're shitting me."

We are almost to the car where *he* is waiting. I can barely make him out behind the wheel, can only see that he has large hairy hands and sunglasses. The early morning sunshine suddenly strikes me in the pit of my stomach.

"I don't know the whole story," Lisa says absently, her brown eyes glowing at the sight of him. "Something about she was going to get her own serial and her husband threw her out or maybe he beat her, I forget... I met her at Sally's.... We'll all have to get together for dinner one of these times."

"When?" I'm desperate, want to hang on to her, drag her back inside.

"Oh, *soon*," Lisa says brightly and pops into the car.

In the living room Nina is doing her spidery long nails over in a thick and plummy lacquer. She waves them about while she studies the business pages. Her face, as usual, reveals nothing, though now that I know she was—is—an actress she looks both more interesting and more beautiful. I try to think what show I could have seen her in as a child—*Wagon Train? Father Knows Best? Leave It to Beaver?* ... and I am suddenly, and uncomfortably, aware of her large breasts; unrestrained for the first time by the tube top, they hang like twin eggplants, meaty but with a thin, satin finish, under a loose, unbuttoned shirt.

Has someone hurt you? I feel like asking. Or, Do you think people are responsible for everything they say? Did he really hit you? Oh, look at me. What happened to you?

"Lisa tells me you're interested in acting.... "

She doesn't even glance up. "Uhhnnn."

*

I think of writing a story about A.J. except I remember how she screamed at me, "You fuckin' egotist and now you'll probably put that in a story too." It's not worth fictionalizing, she's not worth it, but all the same I wonder if I could get into words what I used to feel about her and how it changed. How her anger changed everything.

At first I was amazed and guilty. What had I said, what had I done to make her lash out like that? I would stand in a freezing sweat watching her face thicken up and her words gnash out, "You always," "You never," "You can't do this to me." Going for the throat, the most wounding phrase. "You bitch, I'm sick of your smartass shit. You think you're so great, you can't even get a grant."

She could get mad at me for anything, and it would be over as soon as it came out. "Oh Cary, I'm sorry. I don't know what came over me. I don't even remember what I said."

She would be refreshed, happy as a little buddha. When I would try, in my torturously painful fashion, to reason through her feelings: "Are you angry because I have to spend a lot of time alone? I know it doesn't seem like working to you, I know it doesn't bring in much money . . . I don't mean to be selfish. . . . "

"Oh Cary, I understand. I really do. You're going to be a great writer someday and I want to help you."

"But you just said. . . . "

"Oh, don't think about that. I'm just feeling a little crazy today. It's my period." Or "my job." Or "my parents." Or almost anything.

If I continued to press ahead with my guilt and desire to do right by her, she would burst into tears. "Oh, I'm so worthless, I'm so unhappy, I don't know what I want to do, I had a terrible day at work."

The sight of her tears always made me remorseful, eager to comfort. It was my fault that she stopped being a dancer and became a bus driver. And god knows, nobody's life was easy, everybody could break down sometimes with tension, look for someone to blame. . . .

But I learned one thing pretty quickly and that was not to

cry in front of her myself. Both times I did, driven by complete despair, I watched her eyes widen with victory, with delight. She didn't come over and take me by the shoulders, whisper that it was all right, that she loved me. She only smiled greedily and went in for the kill.

If I was strong she respected me. If I was weak, so much the worse.

The only solution was to keep silent, to let her blow herself out. But who would go on like that forever? We went on for five years.

Lisa turns up on Christmas Eve, quiet and carrying two bags of groceries.

"*He*'s eating with his family," she announces. "I thought we could do something with a ham."

Certainly Lisa feels abandoned, but after an hour or so she regains her cheerfulness, cutting up vegetables, boiling potatoes, stirring up an eggnog batter. Besides, she's going to sleep with *him* tonight. It's not so far away.

We drink some eggnog, even Nina, and suddenly nothing is quite so bad, it's Christmas after all, and Lisa is brilliantly reminiscent, "Remember that turkey Mr. Harris and his toupee in French class?"

"Oh, Jean-Jacques Rousseau, and his slides of sailors in Marseilles." We grow hysterical. "Remember, remember?" I think I haven't been so happy in a long time. Lisa is all shining brown eyes and peachy mouth and I remember the first time we kissed, and she says, "If only you weren't so moral about writing for the movies."

I don't get insulted at all. "Oh, I don't know. I think I could write a pretty good script for the Hulk."

"The Hulk!" she shrieks. "Oh my god, have you been watching that? Isn't that the trashiest thing?"

"I like it," Nina speaks up.

"It's like a parable of mankind," I hoot.

"That's right," she smiles, and for the first time I think, I *do* like her and she likes me.

"You two," sighs Lisa.

We beam all around, but just then the telephone rings. It's bound to be the Hulk, so I get up and answer it. No, it's *him*, unable to make it through a single evening without Lisa. Strangely enough I am jealous handing the receiver to her, watching her face go dreamy and expectant.

They murmur back and forth. I hear her whisper, "I miss you," and, "Yes, in an hour," and my pleasure vanishes.

I'm simply a bit drunk and more than a little unhappy. What can A.J. be doing tonight? Is she alone, does she miss me? Or is she out with someone I might not even know, is she thinking of going to bed with her? Has she given up on me completely?

"More eggnog?" says Lisa.

I think I could actually jump up and start screaming at her.

Now it's later and she's gone to fuck and be fucked. Nina and I sit in front of the television, watching a special. But even she doesn't have her heart in it. When the phone rings she jumps up as if it's for her, and it is.

"Hello. Yes, hello. Yes, fine."

I try not to listen. Her husband, mother, children?

"No, nothing."

"Uhhh."

"No, I can't. . . . How are. . . . "

She gives me a quick glance, half turns away. Where have I seen her before? I go into the bathroom and think about my Hulk script.

It could begin as a sit-com: two roommates (of course you don't say they're gay), both *artistes*. One gives up dancing and finds a job as a bus driver because she doesn't want to be poor. The other struggles through low-paying part-time jobs and writes, and never worries about money and is happy when she isn't feeling guilty. It's sort of like the Odd Couple. The writer is at home, either forgetting to wash the dishes or cleaning everything up in a frenzy of neatness (both connected with writing). The other is angry about having to go to work all day and comes home . . .

Suddenly turns into the Hulk, breaks the dishes, throws the writer's typewriter in the trashcan and. . . .

Suddenly it doesn't seem so funny.

Nina is off the phone when I come out, with no expression on her face to show what has passed. However, she is drinking rum straight out of the bottle, a bad sign.

Naturally, I join her.

We sit in front of the TV with the sound turned down on some people singing carols.

"So, when are you going to Tucson?" I ask.

"I'm not going anywhere." Nina regards me with equanimity and, I notice abruptly, a little something extra. Interest? Sexual interest? The tentative beginnings of lust? I hope it's not just my imagination, but something seems to have opened up between us, something warm and zippy. *Rawhide?* I wonder. *The Donna Reed Show?* The line of her tube top is low on her chest, the cleavage deep and swelling. I begin to have terrible fantasies of pulling it down, just to see the way the lovely eggplants would pop out.

The Hulk is a monster in all of us, I think solemnly. I could want to turn into a beastly thing, grow two stories high and carry her off to bed.

Of course it all turns out much differently. I don't think I could ravish someone if I tried, and I am back to wondering, *The Ozzie and Harriet Show? Bonanza?* when she says calmly, looking me straight in the eye, "Want to go to bed?"

It isn't, all expectations and rum to the contrary, completely satisfactory. Nina's response to passion seems to consist only of gripping my head between her legs and muttering, "Go on, go *on*."

I *am* going on, at least as best I can under conditions of extreme claustrophobia. I try to imagine myself in a nice hot place, inside an oven with a loaf of baking bread. Bread, yes, Nina is like a soft, spongy loaf, from the sweet dough of her bumpy thighs to her yeasty stomach. She is also, in spite of my best efforts, as dry and hot as unbuttered toast down there. For some reason I keep recalling that Nina was famous once and I saw her, I watched her on TV, and this upsets me. I mean, not knowing for sure, which show. It's not really that much of a turn-on for me to make love with someone I know nothing about.

At least part of me feels that. The other part is longing desperately for A.J., for her mossy pebble in its spring-fed pool. For the first time I truly understand the meaning of the term "dry as a bone." Nina's cunt is arid as a tiny desert and it's sucking the saliva right out of my mouth without leaving a coating.

"Go on," she clamors, but her tone is hardly aroused, much less arousing. She sounds, instead, embarrassed. I raise my head and stare at her. She's not sweating but a kind of sun-lamp heat seems to radiate off her body. It's cooking me too.

"Are you all right?" I whisper dryly.

She opens her eyes and I see how dilated the pupils are and, slow as I am, it occurs to me that Nina must be drugged. All child stars turn into drug addicts, you know. Immediately several things become clear, her drifting gaze, her sluggish responses, even her occasional manic energy while watching TV and the slightly philosophic bent of her thoughts.

But even as I stare at her, horrified, her pupils seem to contract into something like a normal look, half shy, half despairing, and when she speaks her voice is perfectly calm: "I guess I can't come."

I sort of roll off then into Lisa's pillows.

"My husband always told me I was a lesbian, and I always wondered, but I guess I'm not."

Faint groan from me, disguised as a cough.

"Are you mad?" she asks.

I recover my voice. "No, I'm not mad." But even to my own ears I sound that way: disgruntled, angry, disappointed. How can I explain that that's how I'm feeling about myself this minute?

"You don't have to perform for me," I tell her. "I'm not a man."

"Maybe if we just lie here," she says hopelessly.

It's the last thing I want to do. My heart is crippled with sadness and desire for A.J. It's all I can do not to jump up and try and call her. But I don't. It would only be the same if I went back, I know that now more than ever somehow. So we lie here, side by side, not touching, until Nina asks,

"Have you ever been hit?"

I shake my head. "No, just words."

"Oh, words," she says, vehement. "I hate words too. But when it turns into hitting, that's the worst."

I don't even need to ask, do you want to talk about it, because the story comes spilling out. It's an old story and a new one and it gives me the creeps because it's so much like my own. Nina's husband only hit her a couple of times (only) but he spent a lot of time telling her he was going to. He had been a child star too, in the same serial (that famous one, now I remember, *Dad's Kids*) and he'd gone on acting for a while, though he never got very good parts. He'd wanted Nina to stay home and have children and she couldn't and after a few years he'd gone into real estate and she'd started drinking and then she'd stopped and she'd tried to get some acting jobs and had been offered one and that was when the violence began.

All the time she's telling me this I'm remembering more and more clearly the cute little teenage brother and sister on the show and how I loved them, Cathy and Bob. And I'm remembering that the first time A.J. really screamed at me was when I had a story published in a good magazine and how guilty I felt, knowing she had given up, and suddenly Nina and I are clinging together, crying as if our hearts would break.

That seems to damp everything down and when we try again to make love it's wet and thick and warm as a beach towel drying in the sun, half soft, half rough and completely comfortable.

The next morning, Christmas morning, is very eventful. First Lisa comes breezing in with *him*, Rodney, "call me Rod," and proceeds to make breakfast for him.

"There was nothing at *his* house," she explains breezily, tunneling back into the refrigerator past Nina's kefir and my stale tortillas to the ham, and leaving me and Nina to make conversation with him.

We discuss Jerry Brown and the hostages and he has a lot of opinions as befits an up-and-coming screen writer. He is also very hairy, and it's not just his hands but large areas of his body: chest, arms, legs (all uncovered, this is L.A.). I take a deeper dislike to him and so does Nina when he suddenly says, "Say, weren't you little teenage Cathy in *Dad's Kids?*"

"Uhhnn," she says.

Unlike me he is persistent. "Well, weren't you?"

Fortunately Lisa calls out, "Come and get it," and, not mistaking the invitation to include us, Nina and I slink off to the bedroom. I feel very much in love with her this morning and pull down her tube top less with beastliness than with the desire for reassurance that those satiny eggplants are still there.

When we come out Lisa and *he* (I mean, *Rod*) are having an argument, their first, to judge by Lisa's alarmed looks. It has something to do with the screenplay they are writing together.

"Women don't talk like that," she is trying to reason.

"What do you know about it? My first wife used to talk exactly like that." He looks at us unpleasantly. "Ask little Cathy, she used to talk like that too. 'I'm so proud of you, Daddy' and she's thinking 'Go fuck yourself, Daddy.'"

"Go fuck yourself, *Rod*," little Cathy says calmly.

This enrages *him* even more, the sight and sound of all these women who are not talking like they're supposed to, and he snarls, "Say, Lisa, who are these girls anyway? What are they doing here? Is that why you haven't wanted me to come over? What are they, your dyke friends or something?"

I would like to be able to report that the three of us, Lisa included, turn into Hulks, or better, the Furies, right then and pummel him to supertenderized beef, but instead we just stand there, embarrassed, and hot and hairy Rod seems to realize that even without lifting a finger towards him we are all just too much and stalks out the door. And I would like also to be able to say that Lisa shrugs her shoulders and goes back to writing the first feminist car-crash epic by herself, but instead she lights out after him with scarcely a look at us. And a minute later we hear the car zoom off.

The second thing that happens this morning, just as Nina and I are getting comfortable in bed together, is that the doorbell rings and it's the other *him*, Nina's husband, aka little Bob, the innocently sexy, wimp-curled boy who once threw me into a frenzy of desire at ten. Needless to say he's quite changed by now, though he still looks younger than Nina. He too is extremely hairy and (dare I say it?) rather Hulk-like.

He says more or less the same things as Rod but they're all directed at me (it's true my zipper turns out to be undone): "Who is she? She looks like a dyke." Etc. I find I am getting tired of this. I mean, what is this radar they have? My own aunt, the noted spiritualist, doesn't have a clue. And I say, borrowing little Cathy's secret lines, "Fuck off."

Never did I suspect what a powerful phrase this is. First *him*, then *him*, both turned away by those magic words. I wonder why I never used them on A.J.

So little Bob leaves too (with a little additional encouragement from Nina, who stoically claims she will call the police) and right then the third thing happens.

A.J. walks in the door.

"Cary," she says, tearful and carrying her suitcase, determined not to notice the former child star cursing and stomping past her, "I had to come."

"Nina," I say. "The Hulk."

Then I have to sit down. It's been a hectic day (Christmas, what Christmas?) and I know that nothing is going to drive A.J. away, short of a complete confession, and maybe not even that.

"Uhhnnn," says Nina. "Hi." And gives me a piercing look before retiring to the bathroom.

A.J. doesn't even ask who she is. "I just flew here on the spur of the minute. I had such an awful time last night. I couldn't stand to be alone."

If only she were angry; I could deal with her like the men

who'd just passed through the living room. But instead she's in one of her most abject and frightened moods. She's going to go through with the scene whether I want to or not. All I can do is get her outside, into the little plot of garden overlooking the Hollywood Freeway. It's not that I don't love her; yes, I do, and she looks better than ever, with her dancer's strong and graceful limbs, her perfectly symmetrical features. You wouldn't guess to look at her that that face could ever harden up like wall spackle in a mask of complete hatred and contempt. You wouldn't guess that this sweet and loving voice, saying, "Cary, Cary, how I've missed you," could ever say, "I hate you, you bitch."

"Well, aren't you glad to see me?" she asks, as we stand watching the lovely vision of an almost empty freeway on Christmas morning while the sun shines down out of a clear and hardly smoggy sky. "I've come all this way to tell you I'm sorry, I'm really sorry, and I need you back."

I'm touched. Who wouldn't be? But it's somehow no longer enough. Even the thought of her little frolicking, moss-covered pebble is no longer enough.

So I just say, "Uhhnnn."

Naturally A.J. didn't give up easily. There was plenty to promise—a new schedule, she'd get back to dancing, damn the money, do what she really wanted, we'd been happier then, it was important that I keep writing, she wouldn't call me names, she'd *understand*, and she did understand. . . . And plenty to reproach me with—my egotism, my indifference, all she'd given up for me, how I took everything so seriously, our five years together, she never thought I'd leave her. Eventually she found out (I told her, I mean) that I'd slept with Nina (once so far) and all hell broke loose—I was a traitor, a liar, what did I see in her, Nina was a jerk, had been terrible as little Cathy, was old now and could hardly put a sentence together.

She stayed two days, yelled half the time and cried the other half, while Lisa called to ask how long I'd be staying (not that she wanted to drive me out because we were really such good friends, remember that French class, but *he* was just wondering), and while Nina quietly made reservations for Sante Fe. For two.

And when A.J. finally left, we left too, if not to find a place where the world wouldn't end, then to protect ourselves a little from people who wanted to destroy us, and, maybe, to prevent ourselves from turning into Hulks too.

We're still here. Lisa writes us sometimes—she's still with *him* and claims she's unhappy, without seeing any way out —but as Nina was saying the other day backstage at the Santa Fe Women's Theater (I wrote the play, she's starring), there's always room for improvement.

Hearings

The threshers came in from the fields and he a small boy then, not more than six or seven . . . but how well he remembered it . . . the rough trestle tables laid end to end under the oak trees . . . for naturally the kitchen couldn't hold them all, and the heat . . . three women, his mother, no, his aunt and two neighbor ladies cooking all day on a wood stove, pies and biscuits, fricaseed chicken, basins of mashed potatoes with gravy, pitchers of milk so cold it stung your hand to hold them, frothy beer and even coffee in all that heat . . . four times a day they ate, early breakfast at four, late breakfast, then dinner and supper . . . and they were big men, these farmers, with arms like knotted tree boughs, coming in from the fields of wheat, up to the pump to splash their sunburned faces. . . .

I never thought I wouldn't be a farmer. . . .

His daughter murmured something and he turned his head irritably.

It's not my fault, she thought. How am I supposed to remember if it's his right or left ear? Christ!

"This looks like the place, Dad," she repeated.

"Hmmm."

What a stupid idea this all was. But what else was there to do on a visit but be a tourist? And she had suggested it. "Remember that place you and Mom took us . . . once, I can barely remember it. Trees and plants and oh, a wonderful tram with red-and-white-striped awnings. Kevin and I thought it was fantastic."

"The Los Angeles Arboretum," he'd said promptly, surprising her. Had she thought it was a dream?

He was not such a cold man, after all, she decided. She would stop short at calling him tender. What was it he'd put in his last letter? A list of people who'd influenced him: a teacher, her mother, a friend, his second wife. Then he'd mentioned his cat, the cat she'd fucking given him one year long ago when she left the city. And at the end, a P.S.: "I haven't listed either you or Kevin because I feel you've had no influence on my life."

All these years she hadn't seen him and still it hurt. She'd joked about it with her friends. "His cat, for Christssake."

And not me.

She pulled into the parking lot. "Okay, we're here."

That was the trouble with Kate. Always so abrupt. "Okay"; "All right"; "So what?" "Come on." He didn't know where she'd gotten it from. This new job she had, what did she call it—coordinator?

"So you're the boss?" he'd asked.

"No, I'm not the boss. We don't have bosses. It's a collective and coordinator is a revolving position."

Exasperation mixed with triumph, that was Kate all over. And how could he keep up with any of it? When they invented a word a week. But they were too self-conscious to be directors, governors, presidents any more.

All the same he remembered her as a little girl, his peanut Kate. "My Daddy's the President of the California 'Counting Soci-ety." At conventions she had jumped in everyone's lap, had stood on the table and sung a little song.

He didn't dare remind her of that.

She watched him get slowly and painfully out of the car, straighten up inch by inch.

Oh god, he's old.

She remembered his voice on the phone. "I guess I've had a stroke."

He had sounded exactly the same, only a little weaker. He wasn't paralyzed, was he?

No. It was just the hearing in his left ear. Some blood vessel had burst, blocking the tympan membrane. He'd lost his equilibrium briefly. It had come back. So would the hearing, he hoped.

She had never known her father to complain; he wasn't that sort. Whatever happened, he went on.

Still, this was serious.

"Do you want me to come down?"

"No, no. It's really not necessary. I'm fine."

"I want to. Please."

The dictionary said the tympan membrane "closed externally the cavity of the middle ear and functioned in the mechanical reception of sound waves and in their transmission to the site of sensory reception." It was the eardrum; the thin sheath that kept the outer and inner separate, in balance.

Preparing to leave she had talked about it to her friends. "My father had a stroke!"

It was her first intimation of old age. It wasn't fair that it had come to her so early. She hasn't accomplished anything yet . . . she didn't have anything she could call her own. She'd be an orphan if he died . . . an orphan at twenty-nine, no, she supposed not. But she was frightened.

He couldn't die before she'd seen him, told him . . . what?

He was wearing a natty blue polyester suit with a red string tie. His face was firm, though pale, and his hair was entirely white.

"This doesn't look familiar at all," he noted, looking around.

He followed her through the turnstile, watched her scrabble in her pocket for the admission fee she insisted on paying herself. Always so proud; almost thirty and no career. But she had been like that, doing what she wanted, he'd had nothing to say about it.

He felt timid around her.

She wasn't like her mother at all. And in an instant . . . yes, the arboretum, once they got inside, was just the same . . . he saw Polly, dimpled and shy, in a blue serge suit with padded shoulders, exactly the way she'd looked when he first met her at the dance. He'd cut in, could still remember the big, warm sound of the Jimmy Dorsey tune, "You're a Lucky Guy" . . . it was just after the war, in one of those salty old halls down by the amusement park, torn down now, urban renewal and a string of condominiums. She'd been a schoolteacher. A good family and he couldn't say that hadn't helped him get where he was going . . . "You're a Lucky Guy," she'd sung along with the music . . . and the war was over . . . they'd both come out to California to make a new start. "My diamond in the rough," Polly used to call him. But he'd made a good home for her and the children . . . more than he'd ever hoped to do for himself back on the farm when his mother first and then his father had died, forcing him to find a job to get through school . . . but he had done it, and when he heard he got a scholarship he had walked across Illinois to the college because he hadn't had enough money for trainfare . . . "You're a Lucky Guy" . . . they did the foxtrot then and he had stumbled . . . Polly had changed his luck . . . she had expected him to lead and he had . . . he had . . . but where was Kate taking him? She was walking too fast.

She wanted to find the tram. Oh, she remembered it clearly, with its open sides that let you just sail along, looking at everything. She couldn't have been more than ten, at the most, and probably younger, because after her mother got sick they'd never gone anywhere anymore. Not as a family, at least; it had been neighbors and friends taking them along, in cars filled with dozens of kids, no special privileges, the pocket money doled out firmly and "Make sure you go to the bathroom first." Kevin had been lucky, Jimmy next door was just his age, but she had been lonely, taking a book with her everywhere and feeling too good for the rest of them.

Even then.

Pity for her child self struck her. She'd been so glad to finally become an adult... but what had she done with it? Time had seemed to stretch out before her... she remembered being twenty forever, longing to be twenty-one... and twenty-five had felt like a watershed, the moment when she would finally...

"Don't walk so fast," her father told her grumpily. "Didn't you say there was a tram here? I don't remember it...."

You could have been a grandfather, she almost told him, and suddenly she could have cried, though she hadn't cried at all at the women's health clinic. There'd been some blue-grass music on the radio and posters on the walls celebrating and defending women's right to choose. Would she have chosen differently if she'd known her father was going to have a stroke? But who could know... who could have predicted that the thought of him dying could have affected her like this... make her feel about ten years older overnight and full of the saddest kind of anxiety about his life, her life, the things they had never done or said. And she was forgetting anyway, he already was a grandfather.... Kevin's two, the third one coming in a few months. Where *was* Kevin, if it came to that? She could have used his support at a time like this. He was their father, their only father...

"Oh!" she said involuntarily. It was the tram. "But it's so small and faded."

It was all coming back to him. They had gotten off the tram and walked over a bridge. A kind of lake, with ducks, and at its edge, an old Victorian-style house.

"No, there can't be a house here, Dad," Kate told him. "This is all part of an old ranch or something. There might be some adobe houses, somewhere. Yeah, I think there were... Kevin and I played Indians...."

But he was sure of it. Because he remembered that at the time it had reminded both him and Polly of her parents' home

by the lake in Michigan, all gables and curlicues, the house
where they had gotten married. She'd come down the stairs,
she'd been carrying Lilies of the Valley and in her dark hair
she had worn a wreath, a wreath . . . and without wanting to,
he saw her in the coffin, surrounded again by flowers. No, I
don't want to die . . . that had been his first thought when he
came to at his desk, blood drumming in his ears and a weightless, numb sensation in all his limbs. He'd tried to stand, had
fallen onto the carpet . . . this is death, was all he could think,
and it couldn't help surprising him, that it was both so easy
and so final, that it had come so quickly. The doctor said now
he could live another twenty years if he were careful . . . it had
been a blood disorder as it turned out, too many red blood
cells, he had forgotten the medical name, but the cells had
built up and built up until they clogged. The doctor a woman
with a sense of humor he did not appreciate, compared his
veins to a faulty sewer system . . . and now she was saying that
he might never get his hearing back . . . but she had said he
might always have to walk with a cane and look at him now . . .
of course he did get tired easily . . .

And Kate was urging him off the tram. "Let's go see the
herb garden."

She thought it might cheer him up. Honestly, he was starting to look a little down in the mouth . . . she supposed they'd
have to go soon, and really, what did it matter? They weren't
going to be able to talk, they never had . . . she didn't feel like
shouting into his good ear, "What was your life really like?
How did I fit in? What made you give up on me and Kevin?
It's true you never tried to tell us what to do, but maybe we
could have used some advice. . . ."

The herbs were sweet and pungent. She couldn't help press-
ing her nose into a bunch of warm sage, breathing in the dry
mountain smell. And for a moment she could have cared less if
they talked. Maybe it was just enough to be together like this,
walking in the sunlight, noticing the world . . . why should she
always feel a sense of failure with her father? He seemed to ex-

pect nothing of her ... she knew he loved her ... it was just that she didn't impinge upon his own life anymore, if she ever had. ...

That time when Robin had accused her of harboring a death obsession and she had denied it ... but she had been trying to finish her first novel and had developed a strange fear of crossing the street ... she used to stand for minutes at a time staring carefully and hopelessly in both directions, sure that the moment she stepped into the crosswalk a car would appear out of nowhere, racing at a hundred miles an hour to mow her down. She had imagined it vividly and repeatedly: the moment when, rooted to the spot by horror, she would be thrown under the wheels and dragged into bloody pulp.

In that case, of course, she would be unable to finish her novel.

Robin had said, "That's the craziest thing I've ever heard." But where had she gotten that paranoia from? That paralyzing fear that surfaced every time she took a risk, accepted a challenge, pushed herself to accomplish something?

Her father sneezed convulsively and blew his nose.

Some weed or other ... it was getting on hayfever season ... made him miserable his whole life, starting as a boy in the wheat fields ... they'd had to send him home finally, useless and ashamed. If not for that, well, he might have been a farmer after all ... it would have been a different life, healthier, not so sedentary. ... His cousin, Jack, had the old farm now, back to see him once ... at first he'd been excited to see everything as it had been, the swing in the tree, the barn in need of paint, horses like the one he used to ride ... but he and Jack had had nothing to say after the first hour. ... "An accountant, eh, make a lot of money, eh, well, I see you've done well for yourself, West, eh?"

He and Nan had been out of place in their city clothes and shoes and Nan had embarrassed him by holding her nose in the yard ... he'd left her with Jack's wife in the kitchen, hoping they would get along ... but afterwards, driving back down the dirt road, Nan had joked about hayseeds, and "honestly, no one would ever suspect you came from that kind of background...." But Polly had never minded, Polly had loved the country... it had been one of their plans to move back there one day, after the kids were grown, get a small place, a farm... it was Polly who had made it possible for him to marry a woman like Nan, a classy woman, a gourmet cook, a party-giver, a woman who had taste... and if she was a little high-strung and drank a little too much, well, that went along with it....

Nan had found him on the floor that day... no, you couldn't ask for more in a woman... she'd brought him flowers every day and made sure the nurses took good care of him... and if occasionally she'd gotten on his nerves... she wanted him to get a hearing aid, but he was damned if he was going to accept it... how would it look to his clients? A hearing aid like some old fogey? He still had his pride, he was only sixty-two, and if he was careful to get on the right side....

Most people didn't move around as much as Kate. Or was she forgetting on purpose?

"Sorry, I said...." She was conscious that she was shouting, and reduced herself to a gesture... this way was out. She'd completely forgotten about his hayfever... it was getting late anyway. Maybe they should be leaving soon. She thought of the relief it would be to get back to the motel and turn on the TV... let Nan take care of him... she knew how....

But how could he have married her? That she could never understand. "A man gets lonely," he'd said... and she knew what loneliness was, she expected to feel it her whole life. But Nan. "She's so different from Mom." "There's no one like your mother," he'd said simply. Still, getting married again meant he was forgetting her... forgetting Kate.

She followed him out of the herb garden, aimlessly, down a path trellised by roses. They had both lost their momentum... he seemed to have forgotten all about that lake, that house he'd been so excited about before. She looked at him from the back, trying to see him as just a man, a stranger, someone with no ties to herself. He still had some photographs of himself growing up. She even remembered the stories that went along with them: the farm in Illinois, left to his cousin after his father died . . . a blond, thin boy on a horse . . . a photo of his mother and father's wedding . . . "Sixteen, she was only sixteen!" she'd cried out. "And I look like her." Dead at twenty in childbirth, her third child. His father was handsome, stiffly old-fashioned in the style of the times . . . a Scotch immigrant . . . too fragile-looking to have made a good farmer . . . "He tried hard, but he wore out, died at twenty-nine. . . ."

He hadn't had a scrapbook, not like the scrapbook her mother had kept of her and Kevin's baby pictures, family trips, birthdays and Christmases. His photos were few, stuffed into an old college yearbook, Illinois State . . . even then he'd looked reserved and important . . . a straight-A student and he'd held down a part-time job as well, no time for sports or fraternities. When she had stared into the tiny eyes of the yearbook's class photograph, she had seen that he was a hard worker, a survivor, someone who already knew that he had to get ahead or starve.

He took it all for granted. "Yes, I knew that life wasn't easy and that not everyone made it, and that some people fell by the wayside." Yes, he had actually used that phrase, "fell by the wayside." It had a fated, almost Biblical ring to it, she remembered. And she'd felt a strange chill, almost as if it were an accusation, a prophecy.

She and Kevin had always thought him so old-fashioned, even as children . . . his fair, easily burned skin, the hayfever that kept him inside in summer, the suits he always wore, even around the house . . . he never played baseball with them or took them to the beach . . . but he had let her use his adding machine, had pulled out a book from the shelf called *Mein Kämpf* and told her its author was a "very bad man" . . . he came in his pajamas and got her when she'd screamed in the night, "There are bears in the closet," and he hadn't said no, but had carried her to the rocking chair and rocked and rocked her back to sleep.

"Daddy," she called softly up to him, trying out the word again.

His white head turned slightly, as if he strained to catch an unaccustomed tune.

The hearing played tricks as well as the mind. Just now he thought he'd heard Kate say, "Daddy" ... a little girl trailing after him in a pink flowered dress ... sometimes he thought it was coming back ... the clear, piercing call of a bird at dawn ... the threshing machines whirring in the fields of golden wheat ... his mother calling out his name, "West, dinner!" ... Jimmy Dorsey's singer, "You're a Lucky Guy" ... then he would remember that those were old sounds, old words crackling in the left ear like a broken gramophone. ... He'd told Nan once, "It's as if that ear is always listening to the past." "You should get a hearing aid," she'd told him.

"Daddy, Daddy." Kate would never call him that now ... he had tried to be a good father, he just hadn't known how, he'd had no models ... oh, it was easy when she and Kevin were little, so trusting ... later he hadn't known what to say to them ... "Your mother's dead" ... he had done everything on his own, no parents to help him ... what was a man supposed to do when his daughter moved in with some young fellow and then called him, crying, asking him to help her move? He really preferred not to know about Kate's life, it made him uncomfortable ... it would have been so much simpler if she'd gotten married and had children ... he liked being a grandfather to Kevin's kids, knew the exact relation he stood in in regards to them, Grandpa with the candy ... but he always felt from Kate that she wanted something from him, he didn't know what ... she refused to grow up, was that the problem? He didn't really know what she did, how she lived ... oh, she said she was a coordinator, and she wrote ... and she was probably involved with somebody or other ... she had said long ago that she would never get married, didn't want to have children ... but to continue to live with one man after another. ...

And again he thought of the house by the lake, the wedding and Polly with her lilies ... it had to be around here somewhere.

She composed words to his back: You never listened, you never knew what to say, you never cared. When you helped me pack up my things and drove me away to a friend's, you never said, "Why are you leaving him? What happened?" When I told you I was going away to forget you never asked, "Forget what?" You didn't tell me you were going to marry Nan. You never wanted to influence, be influenced. If I told you that I'd broken up again with someone, that I'd had an abortion because I was afraid of raising a child alone, afraid of how it would interfere with my life, you wouldn't know what to say. You never let us interfere with your life.

And yet she remembered the way he had held her as a child, had held Kevin's babies, the way he had taken her cat from her when she left and talked to it and scratched its ears.

He kept his head cocked now, always ... made him look curiously alert, yet dreamy ... he must think of the past, of his life, wonder what it had all meant, losing so many people who had been important to him, those who had influenced him ... and there it was again ... she had simply not been important to him once she grew up. It was futile to ... but he was moving quickly now, striding down the path with unusual eagerness.

"What's the hurry?" she called. He didn't hear her ... she had forgotten about the house ... and yet there, in a minute, it stood, exactly as he'd described it, "a Victorian house by a small lake" ... and he was climbing its porch and looking in all its windows like a boy of six.

What satisfaction ... that one thing from the past still remained intact, exactly the same ... he turned to Kate and for an instant was checked... where were her pink flowered dress, her glossy brown curls, her trilling, childish voice? Thin, anxious-looking, she watched, as a mother might watch a child, fearful that he would fall, afraid to say anything.

"Your mother," he said, hardly conscious that he spoke, unable to hear himself, "lived in a house like this. We were married there."

She opened her mouth, but no sound came out.

The Back Door of America

The flight from Seoul to Seattle was late; customs delayed Kevin even longer. While Kate waited for her brother to appear through the door marked NO ENTRY, she watched the other passengers and their friends and relatives.

The Southeast Asian refugees were first; they had nothing to declare, came through in groups, all boys and young men, small, shy, bewildered, each one appearing at the customs door as if it were a stage entrance, and he were a stand-in not sure of his reception from this foreign audience. "Over here. Come on, that's right." A boldly kind, big, busy woman had set up a card table piled with down jackets in thin plastic wrapping. She was calling out names, checking off lists, handing out jackets. Were they boat people, Vietnamese, Cambodians? How long had they been in the camps and where were they going now? "Nugen-Phu, okay, here you go." Soon the waiting area was full of the young men with black hair and black eyes and eager or frightened expressions, all wearing puffy new down jackets and suddenly taking up more room.

Kate watched, shifting the heavy photo album in its paper bag from hand to hand. There were others waiting with her, just as anxious, some of them holding rough sheets of paper with names on them up to their chests—MINH HO, MARY-ANNE DOHERTY—offering them to each emerging passenger, then, embarrassed, letting them drop slightly again as the traveler's eyes moved past.

There were Korean and American and Japanese businessmen, well-dressed in blue or black suits, in pairs or alone or sometimes with an attractive Asian, always Asian, woman. Other single men strode out, one by one; they were tall, square-jawed, purposeful, with closely clipped hair, wearing jeans and knit shirts, sometimes a sports jacket. They were military personnel, traveling on the civilian flight. Any of them could have been Kevin. Kate winced to think of it, for she had a horror of these men, with their steady eyes, their clean-shaven faces, their thickening necks. She believed they were all CIA agents; they *looked* like CIA agents.

Kevin didn't appear with them; he had a lower rank, after all, wasn't an officer, just a technician, or so she always reassured herself. A regular person, who'd needed a job, who'd stayed in for ten years, still needing that job, and who'd stay another ten, until he could retire.

"Kim, this is Mary and Diane," a white woman was greeting a little girl with straight black bangs across her forehead. "Your new sisters."

"Hi, Kimmy! Hi, Kimmy!"

Kim nodded noncommittally and was led away, a tiny, sturdy figure in the midst of her large white adoptive family.

Tailored Korean women burst out the door with hatboxes and Gucci flight bags, embracing relatives who were equally glamorous. Flash bulbs crackled; there were decorative tears, exclamations and laughter.

And still no Kevin. Kate moved closer to the NO ENTRY door, trying to get a glimpse inside the next time it opened. She'd called the flight information desk, had made sure he was on this plane. He only had two hours—closer to one hour now —in Seattle before going on to Montana to spend his leave with his family.

A couple of teenage girls with droopy Farrah curls and oily red faces rushed out and into a motherly woman's arms. They shrieked and laughed and one of them cried. Other teenagers followed, boys and girls. Kate realized they were all wearing blue vests, red skirts and white shirts. *People to People* their name tags read. They looked very Christian.

"Oh, I'm so *glad* to be back," one girl weepily proclaimed.

"I *loved* Korea, but . . . "

"Home is best!" finished another.

"Oh, you *guys*. I'm going to miss you so *much*."

"I know, I *know!*"

"But we'll write . . . "

"We can call . . . "

"Hi," said her brother. "Waited long?"

He was wearing jeans, a knit shirt; his gaze was steady, his hair short, his jaw remarkably square.

They decided to have lunch in a coffeeshop after confirming Kevin's flight to Billings. Details kept them from being shy; Kevin broke the inevitable silence when it came by saying, "Remember that time in Chicago at O'Hare . . . changing planes to Michigan, Grandma's?"

"I'd gotten those cigarettes on the plane and was smoking them, I was only thirteen, being grown-up . . . "

"Ignoring me."

"You got lost," Kate recalled.

"You dumped me."

"God, that's right, and I was panic-stricken. The flight was leaving and I couldn't find you and then I heard my name, 'Will Miss Kate Fink call the information desk, please?'"

"I could have told them 'Ratfink,'" Kevin said. "But then they might have guessed."

They'd been in this airport together six months ago, when Kevin was just leaving for his year of duty in Korea. One of Kevin's friends had been with them then, a Black man named Hans, son of an American G.I. and a German mother. Hans had been to Korea before; he said it was a terrible place. But he didn't seem overly concerned about going back. They'd smoked a joint with him out on the flight deck and later had a couple of drinks in the bar. Kevin had pumped him for information and groaned at everything he said.

"You see much of Hans now?" Kate asked, over turkey and

swiss cheese sandwiches.

"He's got a Korean girlfriend," said Kevin. "She used to be a prostitute, I think."

"What?"

"There's a strip that starts right outside the base. A quarter mile of little houses—rooms no bigger than your kitchen—just a bed, that's all."

"You . . ."

"I'm not the type to be attracted to Asian women."

Rascist bastard. But she was relieved, of course. "So you don't see much of Hans then," she murmured lamely.

"I take classes at night," explained Kevin. "Besides, it's different. I'm married."

After they finished eating, she showed him the photo album she'd brought along.

"Dad sent it to me," she said, "but I thought we could share it, that you could have it for a while."

She saw his jaw tighten. Their father never sent anything to Kevin, nothing he thought important anyway. He hadn't realized yet that Kevin was far more stable than his older sister Kate. Kevin had a wife, children, a job; Kate had two cats and her stubbornness.

"Anyway," Kate said. "You're the one who looks like him. I thought it might be fun for you to see what he looked like at your age."

They opened the album with its crumbling leather boards and black pages out in front of them. The first photographs were of tombstones: his mother's, his father's. Then came a long series of photos of people who had taken him in during his childhood and adolescence. "The Mullers." "Mr. and Mrs. Davidson." "Uncle John."

Many of them seemed to have had daughters. "Jo Muller, who was like a sister to me." "Mary, the Davidson's daughter, a real sweetheart."

The photographs had often been taken outside wooden frame houses; they all looked the same, even though the

names of the Illinois towns varied. Sometimes their father was
among the Mullers and Davidsons, sometimes he stood alone
—a handsome boy with wavy brown hair, dimples, a cleft chin
and glasses.

"He was pretty good-looking," Kevin admitted, peering
closely. "Too bad I didn't get the dimples."

"Wait till you see what's coming," Kate said, turning over a
few pages. "I never suspected he was such a ladies' man."

These photographs had no inscriptions written under them.
Instead they were more recently annotated by tiny slips of
paper that said, "From the Desk of A. West Winter." Most of
them read, in their father's small, accountant's handwriting,
"I can't remember this girl's name." Or, "I don't know who
these people are."

The photographs showed their father in remarkably care-
free, unfamiliar poses: lifting girls up in his arms, swinging
them from side to side, sitting perched with them on auto-
mobiles, picnicking. The young women were invariably very
pretty, with sausage curls, padded shoulders and wide, lip-
sticked smiles.

"Another girl I don't remember." "Can't remember this
one's name either."

Kate and Kevin began to laugh, laughed until tears came.

"It's just that it's so like him to make these notes," Kate
finally managed.

But it was sad, too. And sad for them. They were looking at
a happier, younger person than they had ever known. And
somehow they felt cheated, robbed.

They turned the pages, came to the war.

"Here's where you look the most like him," Kate said. "It's
that military glow."

Their father had circled his face in a group portrait of his in-
fantry battalion. In all these pictures he was wearing a uniform, several uniforms, in fact. He'd been in the Army, the
Marines and the Air Force. He used to joke that no one
wanted him. He'd ended up teaching flyer trainees how to recognize enemy aircraft. "The Battle of Santa Ana," he called it.
When they were very young, Kevin and Kate firmly believed

there had actually been a skirmish fought in nearby Santa Ana, California.

Here were more young women, WACs and WAVs. Kevin began to look uncomfortable. "It's really weird he doesn't remember any of their names."

"Wait till you get to be sixty-five," Kate said, then recalled that Kevin only took pictures of his family. He must have hundreds of thousands of Patricia and the children.

"Yeah," said Kevin, unconvinced. His Puritanical streak had surfaced. He hadn't gone with many girls before he married. Kate, on the other hand, had had forty-nine lovers, male and female; last year she'd counted them up and added a few more, just in case she'd forgotten any. She had a feeling that in thirty years she might have a hard time identifying photographs, too.

Kevin closed the album with a disapproving snap and shoved it back in the paper bag. He decided to have a beer. "Want one?"

When he came back to the table she asked him more about Korea. She had literally no image, no impression of it at all. Just some kind of bleakness when she thought of her brother there.

"It's filthy," said Kevin. "I hate to say it, but the Koreans are very dirty people."

"That's not true! That's your American standards—white suburbia, sterility!" It was somehow a relief to get angry, to fall into political self-righteousness.

"It is true," said Kevin decisively, with the air of a man who has been there and doesn't want to argue. "They pee and shit everywhere, in the streets, out in the farms, right on the crops. I don't like it there." He added unnecessarily, "I hate it there."

"You should get out of the Army then. Now, while you're still young enough to get a good job."

"Someone has to defend this country," he said, as if it didn't concern him.

"Bullshit. I don't believe you really believe that. You just needed something to do ten years ago and you stayed in without thinking about it. Now you've let yourself be brainwashed."

"The Russians would be all over South Korea the minute the U.S. pulled out."

She did not feel like agreeing to disagree. It was suddenly intolerable to her that her little brother should have turned into a man six foot tall with a hard square jaw. Calibrations! That's what he did—tested the instruments that tested the missiles.

"You probably think the U.S. has a right to be in Central America, too," she said, beside herself.

"You're goddamn right—that's the back door of America. The Russians have a foothold in Nicaragua and now they're exporting revolution to El Salvador."

"For your information, you can't export revolution," Kate sneered, hearing and hating herself. She lectured him, "Don't you know anything about the conditions in Central America, how the United States has supported the dictators and ruined the economy? If the U.S. government wasn't so hysterical about supposed communist influence they'd see that all the El Salvadorans want is to control their own country."

"The Russians are behind it," said Kevin. "We can't allow them to get in. First Nicaragua, then El Salvador, Guatemala, then they'll be in Mexico and then . . . "

"Then you'll be fighting the battle of Santa Ana, in a last ditch stand to defend Los Angeles."

They looked at each other. Smiled tentatively.

Kate said, "I don't really have anything against you. No matter what you think, I'll still . . . "

"It's easy to be brainwashed in the Army," he said, almost meditatively. "All you get to read is the *Stars and Stripes*. The news on the base TV is just as bad. And then they have these ads all the time, you know, people in the States singing songs, saying, 'We're behind you boys all the way.' But no one's behind us, no one cares. I know that."

"I could give you different things to read," Kate said eagerly. "I subscribe to a million things. At least you could read them, get a more balanced view . . . Here," she pulled out her new issue of *In These Times* from her bag, the one with Daniel Ortega on the front page.

"Ortega," said Kevin warily, taking it. "I don't know."

"At least listen to his side."

"All right," he said. "I'll read it on the plane to Billings." He looked at his watch. "Better get moving."

She didn't know if he were humoring her or if there were any way she could ever change him. Her anger had disappeared as suddenly as it had come, leaving an aching feeling. When they were little they had snapped at each other with wet towels in the bathroom. Once she'd pushed him into a doorknob and given him a bloody nose; once he'd broken her eyelid open with a sharp stick. She still had the scar.

"Any other news?" Kevin asked. "Anything special?"

"Just that I'm pregnant," she said. She'd been worrying about this moment from the beginning. "I don't live with the father," she went on bravely. "I don't know the father." She couldn't bring herself to say *sperm donor* . . .

Kevin didn't argue. She still had the authority of being older; she always had, ratfink or not.

"Dad know?" he asked finally as they came to the gate.

She shook her head.

"It's carrying it on, anyway," Kevin said.

They both knew what "it" was. The little lineage they had. Their own connection. Someone to give a photo album to, even if they didn't remember the names of the people in the pictures.

To some of her friends Kate had been able to joke, "I've gotten more and more allergic to my cats. That's why I have to have a baby instead."

But to Kevin she could only tell the truth, "I want some family too," she said. "I couldn't wait forever."

He nodded, turned brisk. "Well, I'll be back through in a month. Give you a call or something. I can give the album back then, after Patricia sees it."

"No, you keep it. He's your father too, you know."

"Where's that goddamn ticket anyway?" Kevin found it, presented it, was given a non-smoking window seat.

All of a sudden the crowd of refugees from the Korean flight appeared in their puffy down jackets, herded by their sponsor, the big, busy woman with the lists. She was checking their tickets, pushing them forward, getting them all safely on the plane to Montana.

"Don't you recognize them?" said Kate to her brother, who was trying to squeeze in front. "From your flight."

He shook his head, he didn't even really see them. "Bye," he said, hugged her and vanished quickly into the portable funnel.

"Bye," said Kate. "See you soon. Bye. Bye!" she called again, but ended up waving to the refugees, who smiled, and nodded back.

Miss Venezuela

There was a boardwalk once, surfacing through the sand only to disappear if you tried to follow it. Gray rough timber made porous by the salt air, it was hotter than ordinary wood, much hotter, Rhonda and Eric agreed, jumping on and off with tender young feet, and screaming loudly if they caught a splinter.

The boardwalk belonged to an earlier time; if you looked up at the mural over the entrance to the Long Beach Municipal Auditorium, you could puzzle out which era—unless you were a child, that is, and could ask your mother everything.

"Why are those girls wearing shorts in the water?"

"They're not shorts, they're bathing costumes."

"They're funny," said Eric, but Rhonda always looked and wondered. She liked the mural very much; it was faded but still colorful, like an old advertisement painted on a barn. It depicted a crowded seaside scene, all blues and yellows. Two young women with strong thighs and muscular arms disported in the shallow waves. Their hair was clipped around smiling faces and the costumes were sheer and black, looking painted on, as indeed they were.

"Bathing beauties," said Helen, their mother, and laughed a little, possibly because neither woman was particularly beautiful.

That was left to a few gorgeous creatures in the background who waved parasols with bamboo handles and Chinese fans against the summer heat. Modishly wasp-waisted and refined from every angle, the women still looked pale and droopy to Rhonda compared with the frolicking swimmers in the water.

"I bet the ones in the long dresses wish they could take everything off and go in the water," she observed once.

"Oh, I doubt it," said Helen.

"But they're not going to have any fun like that."

"Beauty never does," sniffed her mother. "That's not what it's there for."

Dolores María Angelus Otero was born in Caracas in 1940. Her father, Rafael Otero, was a *mestizo* from the Sierra Nevada de Mérida. For helping to organize a student strike he had been exiled with hundreds of others in 1928 under the dictatorship of Juan Vincente Gómez. He fled to Costa Rica, where he married the daughter of a butcher, Eva López Angelus. The two of them, with Eva pregnant, returned to Caracas in 1940. There they worked with Rómulo Betancourt and Acción Democrática until 1948, when Major Marco Pérez Jiménez brutally took power. Rafael Otero was jailed for the political crime of trade unionism and sent to the infamous Guasina Island camp in the jungles of Orinoco. He may have been tortured to death, though the certificate read that malaria was the cause.

Dolores Otero grew up after 1948 in a squatter's shack on the hills around the capital. They had a dirt floor and no running water, but Dolores had a good education. Her mother read her the novels of Gallegos, the poetry of Martí and Darío and Neruda, and gave her the oral history of resistance in Venezuela, starting with Simón Bolívar, the Great Liberator. Eva told her daughter that when Betancourt came to power again the foreign oil companies would pay for what they had done to Venezuela. Meanwhile, in Cuba, a group of bearded men and brave women were fighting in the Sierra Maestra against their dictator. Eva, though not Dolores (who was by this time attending the university), was among the crowd that stoned Richard Nixon, American vice-president, in 1958, during his visit to Caracas.

Eva died shortly after, of tuberculosis, ironically just months before Pérez Jiménez was driven from office and Betancourt, her old friend from exile and Acción Democrática, formed a new, democratic régime.

Dolores had no brothers or sisters, and only a few relatives she had never met in Mérida and Costa Rica. She was a brilliant and independent girl, however, strikingly beautiful and something of a troublemaker. She wanted both to make a lot of money and to change the world. She was also fatally unsophisticated, and before she was nineteen had had two abortions and had lost her place at the university.

Near the Municipal Auditorium there was a long pier, where you could walk out and have clam chowder or fritters or buy abalone ashtrays or shell-studded box purses. It was lined with people in windbreakers, fishing, hooking their lines with raw bait from a tin bucket and catching tires and bottles and sometimes sea bass. There was a smell of oil and tar, a tang so fierce and fresh it almost burned. Sunsets, seen from the pier, were orange and red in winter, pastel in summer. And sometimes you cold see Catalina Island, a low dinosaur on the horizon. There were no large waves anymore, though Long Beach was once known for its surf. The word "breakwater" used to confuse Rhonda, for how could water break?

The ocean water was always a little dirty and hardworking from the port and navy base, and full of bits of wood and big kelp bubbles. Rhonda and Eric, with Helen watching from the shore, still swam and bobbed in it, talking about sharks to scare each other, but never seeing any, seeing only jellyfish, rounds of white transparency, like slices of albino fruit. At intervals along the shore, as they walked back to the car, were the longlegged lifeguard stations, chapped by the wind and deserted in winter.

There was the Pike, before they cleaned it up, when it was still adult and rough and smacking of war. In later years

Rhonda and Eric would dare each other to go there, among the tattoo parlors and the blood banks and the side shows of freaks and animals and the fun houses, among the pawn shops and cardhalls and shops selling souvenirs for wives and girlfriends of the sailors, to the rickety calligraphy of the roller coaster, the one they said threw people off into the ocean as if they were dead fleas flying from the coat of a running dog.

Helen and Bob, their parents, had met at the Pike during a wartime dance, but they avoided the place now. Helen explained that the water in the pool called The Plunge was half pee and half spittle. And as Helen and Bob were themselves moving up in the world, so they all moved up geographically from the low life of the pier and the Pike to the fresh glamour of the bluff and Ocean Boulevard, with its divider of green grass, tall palms, its half-timbered mansions interspersed with neat little pink and yellow hotels called SeaView and Ocean Breeze.

They moved up to the Pacific Coast Club.

Dolores' first lover was the son of an oilman. Eva would have been shocked if she had known. Ever since the oil deposits had been discovered in the Lake Maracaibo basin and Gómez had awarded lucrative contracts to foreign developers, Venezuela had been in the hands of Gulf, Standard Oil and Royal Dutch Shell. The native Venezuelans who embezzled with them grew rich too, built villas around Caracas and vacationed in Europe on the graft money. Hermann's father was white, a *caudillo* turned businessman who had gone to Yale and who knew the Rockefellers intimately. Hermann had grown up mostly in New York, attending private schools, and had spent his summers in Maine and his winters in Switzerland.

To be honest, Hermann was not as bad as he might have been. A short, rather serious boy, he was too romantic, too generous, to be a good playboy. He was genuinely intrigued by Dolores, whose rich dark beauty had attracted him from a chauffeured car on a Caracas street. He was only eighteen, a year older than Dolores, and this was his first real foray into Venezuelan life. The fact that Dolores' father had been a member of the Generation of '28 and that he had been persecuted by Pérez Jiménez, the same man who had helped make his father rich, gave her additional glamour in his eyes. Without the knowledge of his family, he arranged meetings with her in a highrise apartment building and began to tutor her in the ways of the wealthy.

Dolores took to the life immediately. She was old enough to have a contempt for everything Hermann represented and young enough to long for it desperately. While arguing politics with him she consumed four-course meals; with money discreetly left in a drawer she bought clothes and took English lessons. To assuage her guilt she also bought presents for her classmates and handed out dozens of bolivars every day to beggars.

In the end she grew fond of Hermann who, after all, was always so kind to her. When she became pregnant, Hermann said he would go to his father and ask to marry her. That was the last she ever saw of Hermann. A woman who said she was his mother came to the luxury apartment, welcomed Dolores into the family and said she was taking her to the doctor for a check-up. Under anesthesia, the baby was aborted. When Dolores woke up she was in a dark room and bleeding. Hermann's mother was gone. Her own mother she never told.

Dolores was more careful with her next lover, a businessman who traveled frequently. She continued attending the university and decided on a career in law. She did not live with Ricardo, even after her mother died, but she accepted willingly his gifts and dinners. When she became pregnant again she knew what to do and did it. But something changed inside her after that: there were complications, an infection set in, and when it was cured, the doctor said she was sterile.

It was 1959 and Castro and his fellow revolutionaries had just overthrown Batista, but Dolores's university career was cut short by her inability to explain her long absence from class.

※

The Pacific Coast Club was a brown sandcastle of rather fantastic appearance, built on the side of a bluff. It had a turret, stained glass windows, a red carpet leading from the sidewalk through the gold-leafed doors and a lobby complete with doorman, leather book to sign in and huge fireplace. Off the lobby was a patio restaurant, with a marble pond owned by three very large old carp and supervised by waiters in white jackets who didn't like children.

Though the lobby was plush with old leather and humidors, the beach at the base of the club was strictly tropical. A bamboo fence surrounded it; there was an outdoor cafe where people in bright sarongs and polo shirts sipped tall pink and orange drinks. There were umbrellas and striped lounge chairs laid out in rows. Here you could see older women the color of walnuts and oily as fish lying hour after hour in their bikinis, with two little white half eggs shielding their eyes.

Although they, Bob, Helen, Rhonda and Eric, passed through this private beach on their way to the ocean, it wasn't a place any of them lingered in, any more than they did the lobby.

"Too fancy," sturdy Helen said, while privately yearning. Both Helen and Bob were nondrinkers as well as a little pale and stout. They looked best in their roles as Mother and Father, and sought out those like themselves at the club, rather than the heirs to oil fortunes and orange groves around Disneyland.

No, their sphere was the level in between lobby and beach, the physical family world of the Ladies' and Men's Locker Rooms, pool and gym. The pool, Olympic-sized, was ostensibly the reason for joining the club in the first place. Helen and Bob, who were bringing up their children in California as if it were their own Midwest, on canned vegetables, snowflecked Christmas trees and tales of hardship, religion and struggle, nevertheless insisted early that their children learn to swim—not as they had, fearfully dipping and plunging in summer waterholes and rivers, or later, by the shores of Lake

Michigan, learning the awkward, head-elevated breast-stroke— but really learn to swim. This did not mean an occasional dip in the urinated, snotty waters of Pike's Plunge, but special swimsuits and classes—beginner, intermediate, advanced— and for Rhonda, finally, the swim team. It meant that Saturdays were swim days at the club—eyes smarting from chlorine, ears clogged and muscles pleasantly heavy. It meant, eventually, dozens of boring laps, swim meets with whistles blowing and terrifying views from the high dive. But it also meant, always, the Ladies' Locker Room.

Dolores Otero had both a common and a distinctive beauty. She was on the short side, with large breasts and a nipped-in, curvaceous figure. Slightly bowed legs only gave her a more provocative stance, as she habitually leaned on one hip to compensate. Her hair was black, her skin was gold. All this was attractive and very Venezuelan. Where she differed was in the high cheekbones and the great Egyptian eyes, accented with a curling wave of eyeliner. Her nose was straight and delicate; her lips formed a naturally red ridge over small white teeth.

"Elegant, but sexy," approved several judges.

"Nefertiti," said another.

Dolores, in the course of looking up a professor who she hoped would intercede for her in the matter of her dismissal, had wandered into a beauty contest.

The ten other young women, one of whom, an almost natural blonde, had thought she had it in the bag, watched carefully as Dolores sauntered through the room.

"They told me Professor Carlos Guerrera was here?"

"Name?"

"Dolores María Angelus Otero . . . have I made a mistake?"

"Not the daughter of Rafael?" exclaimed one man, jumping up to embrace her. "We were in Costa Rica together. And Eva?"

"Eva's dead. . . ."

Such sympathy in the room. Daughter of a hero—in '59 you

could say it—a distinctive Venezuelan beauty—an orphan
now. All at once the men began to explain the advantages of
being Miss Venezuela. The money, the chance to travel, the
opportunity to represent the new democratic Venezuelan state
to the world. She was a patriot certainly, the daughter of
Rafael couldn't be anything else. But it was the promise of a
scholarship that swayed Dolores most. For if she had a scholarship, surely she would be able to return to law school.

To Rhonda, at seven, the Ladies' Locker Room was huge,
as big as an underground city, with streets and avenues of tiny
rooms, cubicles for dressing and undressing, each one with a
shower and six lockers. The ceiling was high, though the walls
dividing the rooms were low; the floor was entirely cement,
drained at intervals by sieved holes. There were no doors, only
white cloth curtains that never quite closed.

The Ladies' Locker Room had a very special smell, the
combination of ripe femaleness and water. It was the odor of
women undressing in small spaces, struggling with their
girdles and stiff brassieres, panting a little, giving off eddies of
perfume, talcum powder and deodorant as they got into their
wire-stiffened cotton swimsuits and tucked their hairdos under elastic caps, stiff white helmets embossed with sea-floral
designs or softly shirred pastel wigs. It was the smell of women
coming back from the pool, chlorinated water dripping from
between their legs, from their fingertips. As they got into the
showers there was the smell of hot water, soap, complete
cleanliness dried by fresh rough towels—then more perfume,
deodorant, hairspray, cosmetics, but never enough to completely eliminate the smell of chlorine and of wrinkled damp-
ness.

It wasn't just the smell that fascinated Rhonda. It was also
the sight of women. Eric, being younger, dressed with Helen
and his sister if Bob didn't come along. Those were the times
he and Rhonda liked to go crazy, running up and down the
little streets of white curtains, tugging them back, twitching

them, pretending to push each other inside, generally being bad, and sometimes, as a kind of reward, getting a glimpse of a huge, pink, wrinkled ass half-congealed into a girdle, or a pair of brown-nippled breasts falling out of a rigid ivory brassiere.

Eric eventually moved on permanently to the male world of jock straps and Brill Cream—the Men's Locker Room—while Rhonda remained, with her fantasies that grew both more circumspect and more daring. By the time she was eleven she no longer raced through the streets and alleys of the locker room, flicking aside curtains in the hope of surprising a woman's body. Instead, she practiced posing, shoulder strap casually falling off to reveal a small bud of breast, or towel draped artistically over her hipless form. She flung back her head, straddled the wooden bench and squirmed pleasantly. She stared at the two pubic hairs around her soft pink petals. And she waited.

Waited, not for some creepy kid to run up and down the corridors, but for a woman to make a mistake and come in.

Meanwhile, up in the lobby, Helen, so heavy now that she never bothered to come downstairs, tapped her foot and eyed Rhonda penetratingly.

"It seems like it's taking you longer and longer to get dressed."

"Señor Columbus made his discovery in 1498 and also chloromycetin was discovered by a Venezuelan. We have thirty-two species of eagle and eighty percent of the goods made by Sears, Roebuck and Co. are made here. The River Orinoco is one thousand six hundred miles long and has a big mouth at the Atlantic Ocean. The highest uninterrupted waterfall in the world is here. It is Angel Falls and is named for Jimmy Angel, an American pilot who crashed in it. Caracas is our main city and it is three thousand one hundred and thirty-six feet high. Its average temperature is seventy degrees so it is very pleasant. . . ."

Dolores paused, discouraged less by her bad memory and

worse syntax than by the complete irrelevance of what she was reciting. These English lessons, these facts to be memorized, all useless, watered down to be picturesque and non-threatening. When she tried to do research on her own, into how much control the foreign oil companies exercised over the political situation, into why Bethlehem Steel and U.S. Steel had gotten such a foothold on the iron ore industry, she was told she was being provocative and ungenerous. Venezuela had the highest per capita income in South America and all this was due to American development. It was true that certain industrialists had sometimes misused their power . . . but times were changing. Betancourt was in power again.

It was curious. A month ago she'd been both ignorant and powerless, a nineteen-year-old ex-student and ex-mistress. Now she was suddenly viewed as the representative of the country. She'd met Betancourt, exchanged platitudes about her father. All her life she'd been taught to revere this president, as a man who'd spent twenty-one years either in exile or in prison in defense of his ideals. But now, he was in power and he was so frightened of the military on the Right, the Americans in the middle, and Fidel Castro on the Left, that he hardly dared take a step in any direction. He was a shrunken, tired-looking man who couldn't help letting his hand slip accidentally from her shoulder in friendly greeting to her full breast.

"The per capita income of Venezuela is the highest in South America. Besides oil and iron ore our principal income derives from the export of cacao and coffee. Along the coastal zone production is bananas, fish, and there are beach resorts. In the *llanos* or middle plains there are many goats and cattles. Coffee grows in the Andes as well as some wheat and potatoes. The government is in the process of di-ver-si-fying, what is called 'sowing the petroleum'; meaning we like to put our money into other things to make more money some day. . . ."

There was something very wrong with all this, but Dolores wasn't quite sure what to do about it, other than to follow, with greater than usual interest, the triumphs and problems of the new government in Havana.

✳

Every year, at least since 1952 when Catalina Swimsuits had set up its own alternative to the Miss America Pageant, the far more exotic Miss Universe Contest had taken place in Long Beach, California. Rhonda's family was a great supporter of the pageant. Not only did they sit on the curb of Ocean Boulevard and watch the parade, but they followed the events on television as well, from the very first national anthem introductions through the swimsuit and evening gown competitions, right up to the final palpitating moments when the announcer opened the last envelope, the music surged expectantly and the newest Miss Universe burst into happy tears.

Nobody thought there was anything strange about this spectacle at the time. Rhonda's family certainly didn't. They used to compare the women fiercely at dinner and in front of the TV, both physically and geographically. Bob, a former information specialist in the Army and now the owner of a carpet store, liked to drop in bits of history and anthropology, perhaps to disguise his natural interest in the beauties' figures. Helen could be a little cruder; she sometimes made jokes about the sizes of their busts. Rhonda's own was hardly developing, a fact which seemed to please Helen, so obsessed these days with weight. "I never had this problem before I married," she would sigh, over the two huge mounds that covered her chest. "I was as flat as Rhonda."

When Rhonda looked at the foreign women she felt a glow and a wonder. What were they like, each one of them? What were the places like that they came from, that round, chin-tilted one from the Philippines, for instance, that tall lithe one from Iceland, that strapping freckled redhead from Australia.

Most years she got a chance to mingle with them in person, for there was always an overflow from the Lafayette Hotel into the Pacific Coast Club. Some years, damp and fresh, she'd run up from the Ladies' Locker Room and find the lobby full of mysterious women in suits and corsages, wearing wide ribbons: Miss Uruguay, Miss Canada, Miss India.

When she had been a child, they had sometimes stopped and smiled at her, stroked her head. At twelve Rhonda was awkward and yearning, with too much intensity.

Her mother found a picture of a naked woman in Rhonda's room. From now on, she said, Rhonda was too old for slumber parties.

If only she were beautiful—not Miss America, but something else, someone else. In school they offered Spanish or French as an elective. Rhonda signed up for both.

Dolores' roommate was from Sweden and could not have been more opposite, both in looks and in temperament; leggy, fair, careless and cheerful, Brigitte claimed she had starved her healthy body for weeks to win the contest, but that the money was worth it. She wanted to continue her medical studies in London and afterwards open up a clinic for women in Africa.

She introduced Dolores to Miss Portugal and Miss Sierra Leone, both of whom she'd met on the plane. Miss Portugal, a dimpled, satin-cheeked eighteen-year-old from Oporto, was the only one who was not anti-American or embarrassed at being in a beauty contest. Carmen ate her steak and salad at the welcoming lunch, wide-eyed and quiet, as the others discussed the de Beers diamond mines in Sierra Leone and Standard Oil in Venezuela. Brigitte mentioned that Long Beach, California, was an oil town too.

It was true. After lunch that first day the contestants were taken about the city on a tour bus. They saw the beaches and the amusement park, the harbor, the Douglas Aircraft plant and the new state college. They were even taken up to Signal Hill, an unincorporated outpost in the middle of the city that looked like a huge disheveled refuse heap. It had no wide boulevards fringed with palm trees or pink-and-green-stuccoed houses covered with bougainvillea, only row upon row of oil derricks and funny machines pumping up and down like rocking horses. The roads here were rough and dirty, the very air smelled of petroleum.

In spite of Dolores' late consuming interest in the oil industry, this was the first time she had seen a working oil field. She
wanted to stop and walk around, to take pictures with her new
camera. The chaperone, the former Miss California and now a
stylish matron in a little blue hat and white gloves, masked her
disapproval with trilling laughter.

"Well, just for a moment. . . ."

She watched helplessly as Dolores scampered about, photo-
graphing and thinking about industry's place in a socialist society.

Rhonda got up stiffly. The last float had gone by, the last
white-gloved waving hand. She must be getting older; she felt
a little silly this year as she made her way along through the
crowds, evading Helen and her brother. Who in their right
mind would wear long white gloves and high heels with a one-
piece bathing suit? And you had to admit, the whole international thing was pretty hokey: having Miss Holland pose in
wooden shoes, a white winged cap and a striped apron, while a
tape recorder whined out a little dance.

All the same, it was still the one place where it was okay to
stare. Ever since her mother had found that picture, Rhonda
had been self-conscious. Her mother wouldn't even understand that they'd all been looking at it at the slumber party. It
was Nancy's brother's, from his *Playboy* magazine. They'd
spread it out on the floor in the middle of the night and practiced the same pose, draping bits of sheet over *that place*. It
was a *joke*, Mom, Rhonda wanted to say. All the same it was
Rhonda who'd taken the *Playboy* picture home with her, nobody could deny that; and maybe it was only Rhonda out of all
the girls who had that funny feeling when she looked at the
woman lying there smiling, smiling with her nice soft breasts,
as if she were inviting Rhonda to touch them. Her mother had
looked so funny when she found the photo: "*What* are you

using this for?" she asked. Not even, Where did you get this?

And she'd snatched it from the drawer and torn it right in half, right through the breasts.

She didn't understand that Rhonda needed to know... what? Well, what they giggled about in gym class. That story about the woman who found the mouse in her closet, but it was really something to do with a hole in the wall and a man next door. She never understood that. And some girls talked about other girls who went all the way, like Jean who wore the thick lipstick and whose mother still let the older boy next door babysit because she didn't know what he and Jean were doing. But Rhonda didn't like boys very much. She just liked looking at women, even though she now knew that somehow it was bad.

She returned to the Pacific Coast Club, went downstairs to the Ladies' Locker Room. It was quiet today, for a Saturday. All the changing rooms stood open, their white curtains slack and sad in the thick, moist air.

Dolores was explaining the Cuban Revolution to Brigitte. It was the night after the swimsuit competition and they both needed to erase from their minds how it had felt to walk through the middle of a crowded auditorium, elevated on a runway like a turkey on a conveyor belt, wearing nothing but a white swimsuit, long white gloves and high heels.

"For some reason it's the gloves I hate most of all," said Brigitte. "Why cover up the hands, except to make us look like we can't resist, that we're clean goods as well?"

"Have you heard of a woman Celia Sánchez?" asked Dolores. "No? But she was up in the mountains, the Sierra Maestra, with Fidel Castro and the others. Knowing the way, leading and fighting. That is what I would like, *sabes?* I read their speeches now and the doctor's too, Che Guevara, and I am so happy, excited. For a people to be taking control. Soon they say they nationalize the industries, and give the land to the *gente* back from the *latifundistas*. And make everyone learn to read. What work there is to be done there, if one has the will to struggle. But struggle with others, not against them."

"When I become a doctor," said Brigitte, inspired, "I'll go there and work for them."

"Is it possible?" said Dolores. "To give up everything and start again? Better this time?"

*

Rhonda had escaped from her mother and Eric for a few moments, claiming that she had dropped her small purse on the beach and needed to retrieve it. It was the end of a boring day spent with the family, an entity she was coming more and more to despise. If it wasn't her brother kicking and pinching her, it was her mother remarking on everything with that sour smirk of unhappiness and condemnation. Why was she so unhappy, why so suspicious that everyone was cheating them or lying? And why did her father ignore her or believe what Helen said about her? Helen had probably told him about the *Playboy* picture. . . .

Rhonda walked along the edge of the water. It was getting on late afternoon; the sky had that white, blowsy feeling it got sometimes before sunset, when the ocean turned skittish and cold, the sand flared up under your feet. Seagulls cried hopelessly, callously.

She was thinking about the woman whose breasts her mother had torn in half. She couldn't help it, she still thought about them. And that funny feeling kept coming into her *place;* lately she had taken to rubbing it, not just on a bench or with a towel, but with her hand. She would die if anyone ever saw her, she knew that no one else ever did it, but more and more she wanted to. It felt so good, it felt like something built up, she didn't know what, because nothing ever happened. She would do it for a while, until she almost started to feel uncomfortable or in pain from the tingling and the want. And then she would stop, feeling unsatisfied and strange but also excited.

And now she was doing it again in her mind, thinking of the

breasts and wondering how whatever happened, happened. But what? But what? And suddenly Rhonda was overcome by the immense weariness of being a child. It wasn't fair never to understand, and to be pushed around and made to feel bad about everything.

She was approaching one of the lifeguard stations. Having completely forgotten, though perhaps intentionally, about Helen and Eric waiting in the lobby of the Pacific Coast Club, Rhonda decided it would be fun to climb the wooden ladder to the platform and to sit for a while. And think.

Dolores had escaped from the pageant temporarily, from her chaperone and the various officials. She was definitely not interested in the planned trip to Disneyland and so, during the flurry of boarding the bus, she had slipped away, back to her room to grab a scarf, dark glasses and coat. Thus disguised she'd come down to the beach to walk and to wonder what would happen if she suddenly flew straight from Los Angeles to Havana. Miss Venezuela was a full-time job; they had appearances scheduled for her all year in Caracas and around the country. A life waited for her there, though it was not, if it had ever been, her life.

She had climbed onto the platform of the lifeguard station and was sitting against the wind with her back to the warm, weatherworn door, when she saw the head of a young girl pop up over the side. The girl's eyes widened so comically that Dolores had to laugh.

"Don't be afraid, *chiquita*," she said. "I won't eat you."

The girl hesitated, then bashfully continued her climb. She was a gangly, awkward thing with big brown eyes and cowlicky hair. Her arms were rather muscular; she had a scrape on her knee, and elbow as well. She was wearing a skirt and sandals and carrying a white cardigan sweater. She seated herself at the far end of the platform and asked, "Are you in the contest?"

Dolores shrugged and with some embarrassment, then decided to be sophisticated. "Miss Venezuela, Dolores María

Angelus Otero, at your service."

"Gee," said the girl slowly, staring hard and turning away, beet red. "Gee," she repeated.

"Please," said Dolores, a little impatiently, but also kindly, "What is your name?"

"Oh. Rhonda. Rhonda Metcalfe. Wow," she said. "You're really from Venezuela?" And she seemed suddenly to have recovered the use of her tongue. "What's Venezuela like? I don't know anything about it. I mean, I know about Mexico, we went to Tijuana once anyway. I'm taking Spanish, you know. I mean, how could you know, but I am. *Cómo estás?* See, that's because I want to travel and do everything when I'm older. I can hardly wait, I can't stand being twelve, I mean, sometimes I don't feel like I'm twelve. I don't know, I feel so old sometimes but they treat me like a baby all the time. I wish I was as old as *you*. I wish I could be like you, it must be so *neat* to wear all those dresses and maybe get to be Miss Universe and meet everybody from other countries. . . ." Rhonda broke off. Dolores was staring at her in bewilderment. "Do I talk too fast?" she exclaimed solicitously.

Dolores burst out laughing and removed her dark glasses. To Rhonda she looked less like Nefertiti than Sophia Loren, redolent of sex and mystery and luxury. Dolores said, "It is just that, I am not so much used to, you are talking about very many things all at once. But you are a nice girl," she added.

Rhonda sighed and dropped her eyes for a moment, breathing hard. Her mind was busy with impossible schemes: asking Miss Venezuela to dinner, seeing if she could stay with them during her visit; dropping in on her someday in Venezuela. She was so excited that she could hardly think straight. "Do you have a little sister?" she burst out.

"I have no one," Dolores said, and her gaze swept the sea tragically. "I am now planning to be a revolutionary."

"Can I be your little sister?" Rhonda asked and then was aware of how ridiculous this sounded. She blushed again, up to the roots of her cowlick.

Yet for the first time Dolores really seemed to look at her and a soft yet spirited expression came into her large painted eyes. "I will be your sister, little one," she said, as if making a promise. "In my heart I will think of you. That we will both have better lives from this day forward."

It was so wonderful, her saying that, that Rhonda could hardly believe Miss Venezuela was talking to her. Perhaps Dolores was just being friendly, perhaps she was making some deeper vow to herself alone. At any rate Dolores suddenly reached over and took Rhonda's hand and squeezed it.

"Just be careful, my young friend, with the boys. Watch out," Dolores said, eyes narrowed.

It was on the tip of Rhonda's tongue to exclaim that she didn't even like boys anyway, but she didn't want to spoil the moment. She yearned into Dolores' lovely face, murmuring, "Okay."

This was the scene, then, that met Helen's eyes as she approached the lifeguard station in the course of looking for Rhonda all over the beach and fearing the worst: her twelve-year-old daughter holding hands with some dark, foreign-looking woman in a raincoat and scarf.

"My lands!" she gasped, standing stock-still in the windy sand.

"Who's that lady with Rhonda?" Eric said, and his piercing young voice carried over to the lifeguard station so that Rhonda turned around with a jerk of horror.

"My mother," she muttered to Dolores.

"Rhonda, you come right down off of that platform. Right now."

"Good-bye," said Rhonda, tortured, to Dolores, with one last look.

Dolores put her sunglasses back on and looked mysterious. "Good-bye, Rona," she said, squeezing the girl's hand. "*Que tengas una vida muy feliz.*" She ignored Helen and the yapping Eric at her heels.

"Who is that woman?" Helen hissed when Rhonda crossed slowly over the sand to them. "Just who is that woman you were holding hands with, Rhonda Metcalfe?"

"Miss Venezuela," sighed Rhonda. "*Just* Miss Venezuela, that's all."

And for once her mother had nothing to say.

❋

For years afterward, long after she could quite remember Dolores' liquid gaze and firm grasp, Rhonda cultivated a special fascination for the country of Venezuela. She dressed up as a cowgirl from the *llanos* for a skit on different countries once; she wrote a paper or two on Venezuela in school. She continued taking Spanish all the way through college. And naturally she nursed a secret preference for dark-eyed women who looked like Sophia Loren, though she ended up with a perfectly nice woman from Kansas, a freckle-face named Mary Sue.

When Rhonda went into the Peace Corps she was stationed in Bolivia. She managed to visit Venezuela several times, to sit on a bit of beach overlooking the sea, to smell the strong, familiar tang of salt and oily water, to feel a little silly but somehow at home.

Of course she never ran into the former Miss Venezuela. Dolores had jumped bail as the country's queen long ago and had moved to Cuba. She became a lawyer, married, and adopted three children, one of whom she named Rona. It might have been coincidence. It might have been how she kept her promise.

Walking on the Moon

I

It seemed so different at first. Almost as if I'd never been here before. The train station, for instance—they were renovating the Düsseldorf Haupthahnhof. Instead of stepping off the train from Hamburg and following the crowd to the spacious lobby with its numerous shops and newsstands, the way I remembered, I was shunted with the other passengers along rickety overhead corridors and stairways directly to the exit. I found myself unexpectedly outside the massive construction work, staring at the city without the slightest sense of recognition.

But then, it had been twelve years.

All my life I've loved rainy weather. As a child I was always happiest—broodingly happiest—on those infrequent days in Southern California when winter storms flooded the streets and everyone else stayed inside. I recall carrying my family's one umbrella down swollen pathways in the park, standing under dripping trees, reciting Edgar Allan Poe. Later, as an adolescent romantic, I discovered Rilke: *"Whoever you are, go out into the evening / leaving your room, of which you know each bit; / your house is the last before the infinite."*

It was raining when I arrived in Düsseldorf and it rained

steadily throughout the spring I spent there. The German grandparents of a high school friend had found me a job in an Evangelical Girls' Home, a Mädchenheim. I was to work a half a day cleaning in exchange for room and board and a hundred marks a month. I arrived with my suitcases packed with books and spent my traveling allowance the first week on the collected works of Goethe, Rilke, Mann and Hesse. I hardly spoke any German but expected to progress very rapidly on my own. I was eighteen and had graduated early.

The twenty or so other girls in the Mädchenheim were almost all dental hygiene students and most were, like me, away from home for the first time. They wore white stretch knee socks and mini-skirts and giggled a lot. In the beginning they invited me to their rooms, showed me photographs of their families and their vacations in Yugoslavia and invariably asked me why I had come to Germany. I had no photographs, wore embroidered jeans and no bra, and said I wanted to be a writer. After two weeks they left me alone.

It didn't really bother me then. I was much happier outside the Mädchenheim, exploring the city with its churches, bookstores and museums. I bought an umbrella and caught a perpetual cold in the damp Hofgarten, sitting on soaked benches, feeling a delicious sadness in the knowledge that I was far from home, was friendless and would probably die of pneumonia.

Of course I, like all the others, had a roommate. Her name was Edeltrude and she was also a dental hygiene student. She had bleached canary yellow hair, a rough crop of acne and an insatiable appetite for women's magazines and chocolate. Our narrow room was divided straight down the middle; her walls were covered with cut-out pages of fashionable models, her shelves held dozens of stuffed animals and dolls in Bavarian costume. I had only books and scraps of paper full of poetry and case endings.

Edeltrude and I never talked much. Every day after her morning classes she'd return to fling herself on her bed with a new assortment of magazines and a few candy bars, and there she'd lie for the rest of the afternoon, turning pages, melting chocolate on her thick pale tongue and picking at her face. I

read or wrote at the table by the window, painstakingly looking up every third word in *Siddhartha* and staring at the rain
that beat against the glass.

More often than not I went out.

I liked to stand on the banks of the Rhine, quoting Rilke
softly: *"As one who has sailed across an unknown sea / among this
rooted folk I am alone";* or wander through the narrow,
cobbled streets of the Altstadt. I dreamily watched the swans
in the canal or hunted up picturesque cafes where I could sit
for hours undisturbed, writing in my journal (*"We are all
strangers in this universe"*) or jotting down poems (*"We are all
strangers in this universe. . . ."*).

If I was at all disappointed in Düsseldorf it was because it
was not the pastoral Germany of my real and mental picture
books. After being half-leveled by Allied bombs during the
war, it had been built back up into a modern city with wide
boulevards and fashionable arcades. Tourist literature referred
to it as the "Paris of the North," but I would have preferred a
village in the Black Forest. I usually tried to avoid the city center in favor of the romantic park, but occasionally found myself hurrying past one of the expensive show windows on the
Königsallee with their often futuristic displays. It was 1969,
the year of NASA and the astronauts' Apollo flight. One department store, I remember, had a window lined with foil,
with silver-skinned mannequins dressed in hot pants and helmets flying weightless through the air.

My job at the Mädchenheim was simple. After breakfast I
was supposed to put the chairs on the tables and sweep and
wash the floor of the dining room. I then scrubbed the upstairs
hall and watered the plants. Before lunch I usually helped cut
up potatoes or slice vegetables in the kitchen. Finally I set the
tables and carried dishes out to them for the noontime meal.

That was all, but I hated it. I managed to get away to my
room each morning for an hour or two, to pursue my grammar
and to get out from under the eye of the housekeeper, Frau
Kosak. I called her the Cossack to myself. She was a refugee

from East Germany and she had heavy, stumpy legs wrapped entirely in flesh-colored, elastic bandages. Over these she wore hose with a black seam up the back. Frau Kosak was a hard worker and disapproved of me. She had a tread like an industrial robot, however, so I could usually get out of my room in time to be busy in a corner.

The names of the two women in the kitchen I don't remember. I don't even remember what they looked like. But they had a half-witted helper who still sticks in my mind. Called Anneliese, she was six feet tall, with tangled black hair and two raisin-purple eyes, intently insane. Her speech was garbled and rough. From the moment she saw me she took a liking to me and often tried to touch my face. I usually met her in the cellar where she worked scrubbing potatoes or washing linen. It terrified me when she loomed up out of a dark doorway; I believed her capable of anything.

Upstairs all was harmony and *Gemütlichkeit*. The manager of the Mädchenheim was a full-bodied, placid woman by the name of Frau Holtz. She tried to take a motherly interest in me, was always suggesting I go out with the other girls or take German lessons. When I resisted her efforts, with mingled arrogance and embarrassment, she began to look sorry for me. I used to go down to see if there were any letters only when I knew she was out of the office.

Usually there were no letters. My mother wrote once a week; my friends were more erratic. They were still in high school, getting ready for college by smoking a lot of dope. What did they care about my melancholic ecstasies over rain and Rilke? They might have been interested if I'd been meeting German hippies, but they were definitely not excited about an Evangelical Girls' Home filled with dental hygiene students, or a life that was lived—more and more half-heartedly—through word-by-word translations from the dictionary.

My self-induced sadness began to feel more like loneliness, my angst like mere homesickness and my explorations like the pacing of a prisoner.

I decided I needed a friend and I looked around to find one.

✳

I came to Düsseldorf today from Hamburg, where I'd been staying with two friends, Nathalie and Clara. I don't know them well, and before this trip I hardly knew them at all.

I met them last summer in Canada. I was sitting on a bench in Vancouver's Stanley Park, watching the sunset and thinking on and off about my life in Seattle. I wasn't on vacation, just taking a day or two off from work and friends. Nathalie and Clara were down by the water's edge, throwing in stones and sticks, and chasing each other, laughing. It was pleasant to see them against the rose and yellow of the sky, the one woman so light and snub, with electric blonde hair, the other olive-skinned and brunette, with an oval face and sloping shoulders.

I watched them for half an hour and returned their smiles. I was glad when I saw them coming towards me, then taken aback. The accent of their greeting was strong and obvious.

They were German.

Neither Nathalie nor Clara could tell I was an American. They hadn't learned to distinguish a mild West Coast intonation from a Canadian accent. I found it ironic when their faces changed; no, they weren't too fond of Americans. Two months they'd spent traveling across Canada. They were due to fly out of Vancouver's airport the next day and it had never occurred to them, apparently, to take a side trip south of the border.

"But you seem different," they told me carefully.

And Nathalie, snub-nosed and elfin, assured me, "We like you."

We spent the evening together and before we parted we agreed that when I came to Europe this year I would visit them in Hamburg. For some reason I never told them that I had lived in Germany once, a long time ago, had lived and worked in Düsseldorf for six months, in an Evangelical Girls' Home.

✳

There had always been a girl at the Mädchenheim who interested me. Although I never talked to her—I never talked to
any of them by now—I often watched her. She was a little
older than the rest, with an awkwardness that made her shy
away from furniture and objects as if they were obstacles to
her uncertain progress through the world. I had heard her
called "the Duck" and, sad to say, it fit. She took small, almost mincing steps that made her look like she was waddling.
This effect was emphasized by the breadth of her behind and
her narrow, forward-thrusting shoulders. She was always out
of alignment, always looked as if she were carrying a burden.

Her face was mannish, at least I thought so at the time and
with repugnance. It was square and heavy at jaw and forehead.
The skin was downy brown; she wore her hair clipped like a
boy's, with a straight part on the left. When she laughed she
shook all over and put her hand to her mouth. She never made
a sound.

I had noticed from the first or second day that she had no
friends. She would stand apart as we all waited outside the
dining room for the dinner or lunch bell to ring. At meals she
gobbled her food and left early. She was the only girl in the
Mädchenheim to have a room by herself.

Her name was Käthe.

It was about a month after my arrival at the Mädchenheim
that we first spoke to each other. It was a wet April evening
and I was returning after hours spent wandering in the Hofgarten. I was soaked beneath my umbrella, having let it down
romantically, but unwisely, to feel the rain on my face. I was
melancholy and hungry, since I'd missed lunch and probably
dinner; my only hope was that Edeltrude might give me some
of her chocolate. As I walked along the street I saw the Duck,
hunching and waddling her way towards me. She, too, carried
an umbrella; she, too, looked damp underneath it. Her short
hair was slicked back on her head like seal's fur. She protected
a book in one hand.

At first I thought I'd cross the street to avoid her; she must have had a similar idea, for she paused, jerked spasmodically, turned, then turned back again and came straight on. I couldn't run away after that performance; it was too clearly an unconscious imitation of my own. I came straight on as well. We met at the Mädchenheim's outer door.

"*Guten Abend,*" she said in a low voice.

"*Guten Abend.*"

I saw her break into a smile and wondered for an alarmed minute if she were going to start her silent, hysteric laugh. Then I noticed that she was staring at the book I held in my hand. It was the same as hers: a bright yellow paperback copy of *Also Sprach Zarathustra*. Hers was just more dog-eared than mine.

"So," she said. "You are reading Nietzsche?"

"Yes." We were both surprised. The American girl, the dental hygiene student—both reading Nietzsche?

"But can you understand it?" she asked.

"Well, some. I read it in English first. That helps."

I had not been reading it at all that day, or any day. It was filled with too many hard words. I only liked to carry it around because it made me feel scholarly and important.

"Nietzsche is our greatest poet," she said humbly.

I thought I was misunderstanding. "He's not a poet, is he? He's a philosopher."

Käthe looked amazed at my ignorance. Opening her copy to a heavily underscored and scribbled page, she read aloud:

"*You must discover a love which will bear not only punishment but all guilt as well! You must discover a justice which will acquit everyone excepting the judge!*"

"That," she concluded rapturously, "that is poetry. What a soul that man had. He understood so much."

Now it was my turn to be humble. "You've read him very thoroughly." I didn't want to admit I'd hardly comprehended a word of it. It was her margin notes that had impressed me.

Abruptly the suppressed, mouth-covering laugh shook her. I noticed that her eyes were bluegray, very large and clear. They seemed to be unconscious of the gyrations of her lower face; they looked sad and far-away.

"Have you missed dinner too?" I asked nervously.

She nodded, still twitching, but as if the fit had passed.

"Do you have any food?" My question popped out unexpectedly. Was I that desperate for company? Especially when I could see that she was more than a little strange?

"Come," she said and started through the door. "I will feed you."

We went inside and up the stairs and I was grateful not to meet anyone. Her room seemed larger than mine, but that was because it had only one bed. Everything was very neat. The top sheet of the bed was folded back severely, a pair of pajamas lay across it like a rigid human form. There was a small library standing straight and dignified on the table by the window: novels, poetry, more Nietzsche and one volume of astronomy.

Once inside her room Käthe grew calm and hostess-like. She went right to a large cupboard and revealed a miniature grocery store and kitchen. Crackers, cookies, sausage, cheese, even a half liter of milk. And a hotplate that, she informed me serenely, was illegal. I was surprised but pleased at the change in her. She wasn't so odd, after all, if she could put on some water for soup and start carving sausage and cheese. She even seemed to have discovered a maternal tone.

"Sit down, please. Let me get you some milk. I didn't see you at lunch. Did you miss that too?"

"I get tired of that dining room," I admitted. "Everyone talking about stupid things."

"And I too," she said. "I often eat here. I like it better."

We smiled at each other for the first time. I was relieved to see that when Käthe smiled she looked completely ordinary, even warm. Not a trace of hysteria.

I drank the milk carefully, obediently. It had a tepid, sweet taste that I found comforting. I liked being here, I decided all at once. And it was definitely better than begging a candy bar from Edeltrude and watching her cut her toenails.

I turned to Käthe's books, pulled the astronomy volume out of its strict alignment. Big and beautiful, though a little worn, it had full color plates of galaxies and solar systems. It made me remember an astronomy book I once had and a game I used to play with it. When I was sad as a child or trying hard to settle on who I was and what I loved, I'd open my book to the diagram of the planets and position myself out among them, a satellite, an angel, a flying speck of feeling. Only when I had safely left Earth behind could I let myself return, sometimes slowly, falling with faint gravity, sometimes leaping over meteors and asteroids, round Saturn's rings and Jupiter's moons, past the hot red sands of Mars, the cold windy craters of the moon, our moon, so different up close, so forbidding. At that point the earth would seem very welcome, now familiar, its continents revolving from brown to green to white, its oceans swimming dark blue to light. From space I would choose again my country, my city, my friends and family, those I remembered, those I loved, those that told me, *home is here*.

"Are you interested in astronomy?" I asked quickly, to stop myself thinking of how far away home really was.

Käthe turned back to the cupboard, busied herself arranging crackers on a plate. "It's my brother's," she said, as if I were trespassing. I put the book back.

Abruptly she said, "You are lonely. Am I right?"

I hadn't yet admitted that, to myself or anyone. "It's not so easy, always, being here. I guess I miss my. . . . But I'm learning a lot. Everything is very new and interesting."

The Duck gave me a penetrating bluegray look as she set the plate down in front of me. "Eat, eat," she urged, and then, with hardly a change of tone, "All people are lonely."

"Oh, I don't know." I filled my mouth so full I could barely articulate. "I'm not lonely right now."

"All people are lonely," Käthe insisted. "It is their fate."

I nodded politely and stole a glance at the copy of *Zarathustra*.

"Are *you* lonely?" I ventured.

Käthe stirred a packet of soup into the boiling water. Her shoulders began to heave and for an awful moment I thought she was sobbing. But it was only her laugh, silent, compressed, epileptic. I thought of telling her that to laugh like that was probably unhealthy. My grandmother used to tell me that about suppressed hiccoughs. "Let them out, Elizabeth," she would say. "Or else you'll get an irregular heartbeat."

"Do you really want to be a dental hygienist?" I blurted.

"Ha." Käthe stopped laughing and sneered.

"I suppose it pays well."

"Ha."

"It seems funny to think of you, I mean, you don't seem like the kind of person who, I mean, like Edeltrude. . . ."

Käthe stirred the soup violently. "Do you think I want to be studying the insides of mouths? Do you really think I am like the rest of them?"

"No."

"And yet, what should I do?" She began a waddling march around the small room, stopping to look at me after each sentence. "I am twenty-three. My parents took me out of school when I was fourteen. They put me in a shop to work. It was so my brother could go the the University. To study physics. They said I wasn't smart enough to go to the University. That I was a girl. It was not necessary." Käthe suddenly stared at me suspiciously. "You have been to the University?"

"Next fall." I wanted to explain that in America it wasn't such a big deal. Lots of people went. Lots dropped out too. I had already been thinking of dropping out.

But Käthe interrupted me. "All this," she said, waving to her Nietzsche books, "I have done on my own. Studied on my own."

"But," I fumbled for the words, "couldn't you have gone to the University when you got older?"

She glared at me quickly, then her eyes turned clear and far-away again. They were really wonderful eyes.

"It's too complicated," she said. "Other things happened."

Nathalie is a secretary, takes dance and judo classes in the evening, organizes against NATO and nuclear power, studies Italian and sews her own clothes. She's come out since we met in Vancouver, a process that was detailed in the long, intensely written letters she sent me over the past year. She fell in love with a woman in one of her political groups.

Clara, who only mailed a postcard or added a P.S. from time to time, works as a gardener for the city of Hamburg. She's been married and divorced and is, like me, now unattached. Unlike me she's never loved a woman, but she wonders if she might, someday. She is in therapy and sometimes sings and shouts to loud rock music in her room, swaying back and forth with anger. Otherwise she is a quiet and modest woman who likes plants and art books.

They don't seem so different from the women who are my friends in America. And, in fact, Americans and Germans have much in common: not only are we held in contempt by the rest of the world, but we despise each other's nationality as well. I can't be in Germany without sometimes thinking of the Jews and their destruction. They can't hear my American accent without remembering Vietnam or being reminded of the military bases full of soldiers and nuclear missiles that overrun their country now.

And yet—we're women. We're feminists. They tell me stories of smashing porn shop windows in Hamburg's red light district. I talk about spraypainting sexist billboards. We share feminist magazines and books, complain about all the meetings we go to, discuss abortion rights, gay rights, racism, the growing problem of violence against women, rape and battering. We talk and talk and have everything to say.

The only thing we don't share is language. They talk to me in English. I answer in English. Yet when they talk to each other in German I sometimes understand them. I don't want them to talk in German; it reminds me of things I'd forgotten.

"And so, you know, our group was . . . it was like our whole political group was in a. . . ." Nathalie turned to Clara in frustration. "*Was ist Niedergeschlagenheit auf Englisch?*"

"Depression," I said automatically.

They both stared at me.

I had to explain. "Well, I studied a little German once, a long time ago. There are a few words I remember...."

Clara and Nathalie laughed, surprised. "You never told us! Now we have to be careful how we talk about you?"

I laughed too, repeated, "I only remember a few words...!"

Yes, some words, very well.

I used to meet Käthe outside the dental hygiene school and we would walk for hours. In the evenings we retired to her room to eat cheese and crackers and discuss philosophy. All through April and far into May we sat at the table staring out at the rain while Käthe helped me with my German by setting me translations of Nietzsche.

I remember we discussed, among other things, the concept of *Heimweh*. Homesickness. I said I missed particular things sometimes—the beaches back home, a favorite picture on the wall, a tune my mother used to play on the piano. Käthe accused me of being literal-minded. *Heimweh*, for her, was a universal condition. She said she didn't miss people or objects she'd left behind; rather her yearning was for some state of mind she obscurely believed was possible.

"What state of mind?"

"Freedom."

Because German is a language that capitalizes all nouns, I even heard them that way: *Freiheit, Angst, Heimweh*. All were strange and meaningful and out of reach. Käthe's conversation sometimes sounded to me like a poem of Rilke's, lonely, aching, suggesting the saddest possibilities. I didn't argue with her that she was already free, but instead read aloud to her my favorite Rilke poem, ending:

> *"To you is left (unspeakably confused)*
> *your life, gigantic, ripening, full of fears,*
> *so that it, now hemmed in, now grasping all,*
> *is changed in you by turn to stone and stars."*

"Exactly," Käthe said. "Full of fears."

Of course, most of the time she drove me crazy. I hated to
see her furtive shakes of laughter. I hated the way she
waddled, the way she hovered uncertainly, toe to heel to toe,
on the edge of a curb, waiting for the light to change.

"It's no good," I tried to tell her. "The light will change
when it's ready. You'll only get yourself run over."

She rushed me through sites I'd already visited—the museums, the churches, the Altstadt, pointing out a history she
barely understood herself with a dictatorial and frantic air. She
demanded the right to buy me useless little souvenirs, insisted
on feeding me at every possible opportunity. She dragged me
into cafes to fill my plate with strudels and *Apfelkuchen*. She
would grow moody, sighing and urging me to eat, then suddenly, a fit of animation would strike her. She would ask,
"What does the *Übermensch* mean to you?"

Flippant, irritated, I answered, "The astronauts."

"*Genau*," she said seriously. "What an act of will to think of
reaching the moon."

"Oh, come on," I muttered in English.

But Käthe would not be dissuaded. "I love to think of
them, alone in space. How brave they must be."

I was glad that none of my real friends at home would ever
meet her, especially when she talked like this. At other times I
almost clung to her, feeling she was the only one who understood me now.

I knew, for instance, that Käthe and only Käthe could appreciate the beauty and significance of the four statues outside
the Kunsthalle. The four women stood in two couples; one
pair held hands, the other had their arms around each other's
shoulders. They were all of marble, Grecian in form and face,
with flowing robes. One carried an artist's palette, another a
book, one a temple and another a lyre. They were Muses of
course, but I saw them as creators, strong, forward-looking,
loving each other and their work.

"I would like them to be my gravestone," said Käthe the

first time I brought her to see them.

I felt the same. I said, "Oh, don't be ridiculous."

II

I said to myself, It's cheating to get a map, but I got one anyway. I didn't look at it, stuffed it in my pocket. A part of me insisted, You'll never forget. Another part wavered, It was so long ago, so many things have happened in the meantime.

I kept standing in front of the boarded up Düsseldorf Hauptbahnhof. It was warm for early April, sunny and dry. Midday. Finally I tied my sweater around my waist and started off. I was going to the Mädchenheim but I had no idea what I was looking for.

It wasn't so far from the station. I had walked to the Hauptbahnhof often enough, to mail letters, to buy American books and magazines, to take the train to Cologne to see the cathedral. Now I was only walking the way back to the Mädchenheim. I didn't really recognize any of the stores, or the street names or even the city's general configuration. Still, I didn't have to look at the map. The sidewalk began to speak to me. The sidewalk, hot under the spring sun, said, "You were so unhappy here." The sidewalk remembered my homesickness; a sad taskmaster, it instructed me where to cross the street, where to turn. My heart beat rapidly, painfully, and my breath stuck in my throat. I didn't know the way but my feet remembered it all. This way. Now this.

It was no more than ten minutes away, on a street I suddenly recalled as having been bombed-out and never rebuilt on one side. Now there was a parking lot there. On the other side of the street was a row of thick houses and walls with heavy doors. I couldn't remember the number but I recognized the door. Right in the middle of the row; it said, Open me. I walked into a corridor, a courtyard. There was the Mädchenheim, with a garden. It all seemed so much smaller. I looked up and saw an open window on the second floor. I told myself, "That was Käthe's room."

Near the end of May there was a holiday, a long weekend, when Käthe asked me to come home with her to meet her family. She said her brother was coming.

"I thought you didn't like him?"

We were sitting in her room on a mild spring evening, in front of the open window. Below us, in the garden, the dental hygiene students crossed and recrossed, laughing, arms linked. their white knee socks shone like birch trees in the twilight—sturdy, but somehow transparent. That evening it made me sad to see the girls, with their pleasure in each other's company. They were Käthe's and my age, but they seemed so much younger. They were all younger than I had ever been. I wouldn't have been caught dead at home with my arm around a friend.

"I never said that," Käthe protested.

I shrugged and lit another Attika. I'd taken up smoking in the last few weeks, to make myself more interesting. "Not that I blame you," I exhaled. "Didn't you once tell me that he was the reason you couldn't finish school?"

"Don't ask me such questions. It was not his fault. Anyway, I've forgiven him."

Käthe leaned out the window so I couldn't see her face. After a minute she said dreamily, "I want to fly. Down in the garden among them. Shall I try?"

Her broad behind stuck out ludicrously, rectangular as a box of laundry soap turned sideways. Go ahead, jump, I thought, yet I almost put my arms around her waist to stop her falling.

"You never talk about your childhood," I said, jostling her at the window, letting my ashes drift down into the blossoming cherry tree beneath us. In the garden Edeltrude was walking with another girl. She looked up at me and Käthe, waved, then whispered something to her friend. I waved too, casually, and took a step backwards.

"But if I take you there to see it?" Käthe still stood looking out. She seemed oddly insistent.

"Come back inside, they're talking about us," I said. "Yes, I'll go." I added in a slightly bitter voice that it might be a welcome change from the Evangelical Girls' Home.

It was late when we arrived at the small town north of Dortmund; nevertheless Käthe's mother insisted that we eat something. She didn't embrace her daughter or make any sign of affection other than a worried twisting of her broad forehead. "So you're all right, then?" it could have meant. Or, "The same as usual, I see."

Käthe's mother was a big woman, not so much fat as lumpy, as if she had pebbles under her skin and rocks tucked into her faded cotton dress. The twisting of her forehead was habitual with her; it marred what otherwise might have been a handsome face. For it was broad and strongly molded, the eyes the same shade as Käthe's, a light bluegray, the color of a lonely pond in autumn.

Frau König led us right to the kitchen, roomy and bright, almost painfully clean. Out of the small refrigerator came milk and orange juice. From the pantry she brought liverwurst, Jarlsberg and fresh butter. Thick slices of bread she cut for us, holding the firm loaf to her chest.

Käthe gobbled stolidly as she always did, intent on her food, silent. Her mother plied me with coffee and with slow, distinct questions, as if I were deaf, a lip-reader: "How do you like Germany?" "What do you do here?" "How many in your family?"

Her forehead twisted as if a pellet of pain were planted between skin and skull. From time to time Frau König put a hand up to smoothe the wrinkling, but her voice continued steady: Was I studying? What did my father do? Was I staying long in Germany?

I began to feel that the questions, in spite of being directed at me, were a means of circumscribing her daughter. Like nets they drew closer and closer, like warnings they took on an ominous tone: How had I met Käthe? Did we spend much time together? When was I leaving Düsseldorf?

Stumbling over even familiar German words, I found myself lying in the effort to staunch Frau König's curiosity. I gave more information about my family, not to mention my impressions, my plans, my memories, than I ever had to Käthe . . . and I gave them entirely new meanings. Oh, I was just a student who'd finished high school early, over here to get to know the language better. My father taught data processing at a technical school, my mother was a housewife who enjoyed the piano. I had two younger brothers, both football players. We lived in a three-bedroom house with a two-car garage, though we only had one. . . . I really liked Germany very much, though of course I would be glad to see my family again. I hoped at the end of the summer to do a little traveling before I went home. I'd love to see Munich and Salzburg and Zurich. I had heard so much about them.

I naturally said nothing about wanting to be a writer or about having run off to Germany to immerse myself in poetry and melancholy. Instead I talked of Düsseldorf—such a cultural city—and of the Mädchenheim—so many nice girls. I didn't look at Käthe as I talked for fear of seeing my betrayal in her large eyes. But what had she expected? That I would tell her mother stories of evenings spent discussing Nietzsche? You didn't talk to anyone's mother about your real feelings and thoughts. You tried to seem disgustingly normal, in the hope she wouldn't probe deeper. It seemed very important, as Frau König stared at me with her forehead twisting and as Käthe spread yet another slice of bread with butter, that I appear as unthreatening, as cheerful, as innocent as possible.

"So," Frau König said finally, satisfied or perhaps just tired of my ingenuity. "My Käthe has found a friend."

"*Ja, ja.*" I nodded my head up and down vigorously. "She's teaching me German."

Käthe ate silently on.

✳

Clara was talking about her group therapy. How she fell in love with a sensitive man after he came into the circle and described how he could never follow up on his attraction to a woman. He would feel initially infatuated, but after a few meetings, a few nights, suddenly he couldn't stand her.

"So what happened between you?" I asked.

"After a few nights he couldn't stand me."

We were sitting in her room with a pot of tea between us. Clara was wearing a light Indian shirt and her dark hair was pulled into a short ponytail. She smiled at me.

"And then he *talked* about it, about us, in front of the group. Was I embarassed." Growing serious she said, "They asked me to talk about my side of it and all of a sudden I was going on and on about how much I hated my father, how he never treated me with respect, how in fact he *disrespected* me."

Nathalie whirled in. "Oh, tea, good. What a day I've had. I finally told that boss to leave me alone. I suppose I'm out of work soon."

Clara and I had to laugh at this juxtaposition. "Have you ever had therapy, Nathalie?" I asked.

"Of course, of course. *Natürlich,*" she said, pouring herself tea and opening a parcel filled with cream cakes. "When I first became aware of my attraction to Agatha, that's exactly where I went. To the psychiatrist." She paused to stuff her mouth with cake. "Delicious, my favorite kind! so of course he tells me I hate my father. I tell him, sorry, no, it's my mother I don't get along with. My father went off a long time ago."

Clara interrupted, "He tells her she hates her father for abandoning her. While my therapist and group say, 'Oh, you don't really hate your father. You're just mad at Heinrich. He's the one who has problems, you should have tried harder to make him get over his dislike for you!'"

We all started laughing then, mouths full of crumbs and cream.

"Have you ever had therapy?" they asked me.

I shook my head. "No, I hated myself and my parents about equally. It all balanced out in the end. I like them now. My mother went back to school and got a degree in music. My dad retired and goes fishing. They're divorced of course."

The visit to Käthe's home was marked by many meals, each more awkward than the last. Käthe's father turned up at lunch the next day. He was unremarkable, except for his gnarled hands, out of character in one who worked in an office. They were bent and discolored, like lumps of glass unblown and melting. I was fascinated in a horrible way, staring at them clench their way towards dishes and bowls, wounded animals groping over the white tablecloth.

We ate sauerbraten and carrots and potatoes with thick gravy, and cucumber salad with sour cream and apple torte with whipped cream, course after course, ending with chocolate and coffee. I had never eaten so much or been so polite in my life. I praised each dish Frau König brought to the table and followed her constant injunctions to eat, to eat, with enthusiasm. I wanted to please her, I wanted her to like me, if only to make up for Käthe's firm silence.

After lunch Frau König took us shopping while her husband napped. In the car I sat in the front seat while Käthe huddled monosyllabically in the back. Frau König drove with surprising speed and expertness and pointed out the few sites of interest: a fifteenth-century church, an auto parts factory, a heavy wooden cross on one of the hills to mark the site of a munitions plant that operated during the war; the same plant, Frau König told me simply, where Herr König's hands had been burned.

It was a small and perfectly quiet town. The square stone or stuccoed houses were laid out in neat rows around a central block of stores. There were trees and flowers everywhere; they were meticulously planted and cared for. Nothing in the town seemed out of place; it was modern but not at all fashionable, charming but not at all quaint. The women in their neat cotton dresses, the shopkeepers in their white aprons, the children in short pants or short dresses playing docilely in the yards, were all sturdy and tidy and a little sullen. They all said, "*Guten*

Tag," when we went by.

I asked a lot of questions, out of nervousness. I could see that Frau König was beginning to tire of my anxious gaiety, as well as of Käthe's stubborn refusal to talk. Frau König's forehead twisted more than ever. I could almost see the little bubble of pain darting under the skin. Käthe noticed it too, for suddenly, as we paused at a stop sign, she was asking her mother if we could walk home from town.

"It's going to rain," warned Frau König, but she couldn't help looking relieved.

"We won't be long," said Käthe. "I want to show Elizabeth something."

As soon as her mother's car had turned the corner Käthe started walking me rapidly towards the hillside. "A shortcut," she said.

"Is your mother all right?" I asked helplessly.

"Migraine."

"Oh, no wonder," I said. "And there I was, talking and talking."

For the first time since we'd arrived Käthe smiled. "No, she likes you. I can tell. She thinks you're a nice girl."

I waited a moment, then burst out, half in remorse, half in anger, "I don't know what's wrong with me. Home was never that great. My father has a girlfriend and my mother drinks too much. They're always fighting. My brothers can't wait to leave either. None of them care about me. They were glad to see me go."

We had reached the top of the hill and stood panting with exertion. It was cold and windy in the late afternoon; the grass was turning a color I'd never seen before, a dark green, with an iridescent undertone. For a moment, the light seemed to shrink entirely out of the air and invest itself in the land, so that we appeared to be illuminated from below, as if each shard of grass were equipped with a tiny spotlight, a radiant point at the root that traveled up to meet us.

"I knew you were lying," Käthe said softly, as if it didn't matter. "The only way not to lie is to be silent, to think about other things."

"Why did you want to come?" I said. "It's so terrible."

I couldn't see her face clearly but I felt Käthe turn towards me, ungainly but solid above the carpet of illuminated green.

"You know," she said. "I wanted to see my brother."

"I thought you wanted to show me where you grew up, so I could understand."

"Maybe that a little too. Yes, maybe that most of all."

There was a sort of crackling in the air and then the light was drawn up out of the land again and flew across the sky. Lightning flashed a few miles away; in the seconds before the boom it was very silent.

"Look," said Käthe, pointing to a group of white buildings down in the valley on the other side of town. "That's the hospital where I stayed." Her voice was so calm that I didn't bother to ask why. When the great shuddering crash of thunder came, with the rain just behind it, we took off running, fast down the easy slope, and holding hands so we wouldn't fall.

"My therapist," said Nathalie, "spent all his time trying to persuade me that being a lesbian was sick. 'This is 1980,' I told him. 'No one believes that anymore.' I just wanted some help adjusting, figuring it all out. Finally I stopped going to him. I found a lesbian support group."

"I'd like to stop going too," said Clara. "I wish I had the courage to tell my father what I think of him to his face. He made a lot of money in the war, do you know what that means? How afterwards he felt and how he punished himself and us? When I remember my childhood. . . ."

"I don't know if it's worth it ever to go back and to re-experience anything," I said. "It can only be painful."

"Silence is painful too," said Clara softly, and Nathalie added, "We grew up knowing not to ask questions, being taught to forget what we had never learned. We want to remember now, even when it hurts."

※

The next day, Sunday, Käthe's brother Peter, the astro-physicist, arrived from Berlin. He wasn't at all what I'd expected. In his late twenties, tall and muscular, wearing light wool pants and a black turtleneck under a tight jacket of fawn suede, he looked like an Italian male model. Peter was richly, elegantly masculine, from his expensive boots to his fine Swiss watch, from his longish, carefully styled hair to his aviator glasses.

I stared rudely as he came breezing in, smoking a small cigar and carrying a leather satchel and camera case. No wonder Käthe resented him. It was obvious whom fortune had shined on in this family. Yet when I looked over at Käthe I found her to be overjoyed. She rushed to him, less like a duck than a puppy, wiggling up and down, inviting and shying from a hug. Käthe's shoulders shook, her bluegray eyes widened to ponds of love.

Peter took it easily. Cigar dangling from his lip like a tiny stick of dynamite, he slapped his sister on the back, shook his father's misshapen hand and hugged his mother with filial indifference. When we were introduced he gave me a charming and comprehensive smile, as if to say, "Families, aren't they ridiculous? But you and I understand each other."

Suddenly the bleak atmosphere of the house had changed. Frau König brought out Kirsch, Herr König offered Peter his chair and Käthe... Käthe, who I'd been positive held a deep and lasting grudge against her brother... she was the most devoted of all. She took his satchel and hugged it unconsciously to her breast, she rushed to put the footstool under his sleek boots, she hung over his chair giggling laboriously, a fish gasping for air.

Peter patted her hand and looked at me. "Glad to see me, then?" Through his tinted glasses I could see that he was winking. I couldn't help winking back.

At first I told myself that I liked Peter because he spoke

English to me. I hadn't realized how much I missed the sound of my language in the air and on my tongue. After having struggled sincerely and intensely for almost three months to speak German and only German, after having worked my way through the entire grammar book, through *Siddhartha* and *Tonio Kroger* and *Zarathustra*, after having had my pronunciation corrected daily by Käthe, I now—suddenly and overwhelmingly—gave in to the desire to speak English and only English.

Käthe, amazed and uncomprehending, could only stare as I unleashed a flood of previously unspoken thoughts and feelings. The relief of not having to choose between verbs nor grammatically construct my every small subtlety was enormous. I became, on the spot, instantly more relaxed; my jaw muscles loosened and my tongue quickened.

Not only did I find Peter a good conversationalist, I also thought him attractive, brilliant... and kind. He had the lubricative kind of personality that went right to the trouble spot, the center of this family's creaky machinery, that oiled it and soothed it and made it run easily.

He was sympathetic to his mother, for instance, in asking her about the neighbors and the garden. Yet he also placed his hands on her twisting forehead one afternoon, smoothing out by gentle force the migraine pain. He talked to his father of politics and the economy, arguing without contradicting. The older man became quite talkative at meals now, brisk and opinionated.

Peter's friendliness towards me and his obvious concern for Käthe made me ashamed I'd ever thought badly of him. Of course it hadn't been his fault that Käthe had had to leave school, or that she'd had to work in a shop. He'd only been eighteen or nineteen then, with a brilliant future before him. Should he have said no? It was only to his credit now that he still cared what happened to his sister. He asked her questions about Düsseldorf and her studies, chided her for not seeing more plays and films, gave her several books to read, and joked that her friendship with me had broadened her horizons: "Next you'll be traveling to America!" he told Käthe.

"No, seriously," he said to me, in his British-accented English, "you will be good for our little Katey. She doesn't go out enough."

I didn't tell him that neither Käthe nor I went out at all, preferring to spend our time in her room discussing the fine points of philosophy. By the second day of his visit I was trying hard to forget that I even knew Käthe. My entire energies were concentrated on making Peter like me.

I didn't know if Käthe realized the extent of my disaffection. I felt her sometimes staring at me, but I never responded. I answered half-heartedly when she addressed me, and made deliberate mistakes.

Peter laughed, "Look, Elizabeth is forgetting her German already."

I did notice, however, that the calm and quiet dignity Käthe had shown with her parents had vanished with Peter's arrival. I didn't blame it on him; I didn't know what to blame it on. I only knew that I had been on the verge of seeing her in a new light, the Nietzschean, sky-splitting light of that evening on the hill; and now all that was gone. Käthe was again the awkward, embarrassing acquaintance—I refused to call her friend—of the Mädchenheim. I couldn't believe that I'd gone around with her for almost two months, that I'd allowed myself to feel sympathy for her, that I'd tried to share my thoughts with her and that I had even begun to long, sometimes, for a greater closeness between us.

"I think my problem was going to a male therapist in the first place," said Nathalie, leaning back against Clara's knee and letting Clara run her fingers through her light and frisky hair. "Something happens when you're around a man, especially a professional. A desire to please, to impress. You're talking in his language, letting him set the rules. . . ."

"A woman counselor can affect you in the same way," Clara argued. "It depends on the person."

"I think I know what Nathalie's saying," I broke in.

"Haven't we all betrayed a woman for a man sometime in our lives?"

"I don't think I'm saying that," said Nathalie.

"I think Elizabeth is," said Clara.

They looked at me with curiosity. I laughed, a little painfully. "Sometimes I wonder if we don't all treat the women's movement like a new religion. I mean, once you're converted, you're absolved of all previous sins. We're all so very righteous about our former lives. It wasn't our fault, *they* made us do it. And yet, all our actions had some effect. We were affected too, still are. Can you ever be forgiven, forgive yourself?"

Clara brought me within their circle. "Are you crying? Don't cry, Elizabeth."

Nathalie hugged us both. "Only, I wish I could speak English better. It's hard for me sometimes to understand, to say what I mean."

"It's hard for me, too," I said.

Peter lit my Attika cigarettes and smoked his tiny cigars. We sat up late, he and I and Käthe, after their parents had gone to bed, on lawnchairs in the neat backyard, watching the stars in the spring sky.

Peter talked, mostly in English, with hurried translations for his sister, about his work in Berlin, about his imminent departure for Peru. Eclipses were his specialty; he was going to the Andes to view one next month. He would visit Machu Picchu, climb the Inca Trail.

We all stared up at the sky. Käthe said something about the astronauts, the moon shot.

"The frontiers of knowledge are indeed opening up," Peter told her in German. "Incredible that in another month there will be men walking on the moon." He turned to me, with that blend of irony and interest I found so seductive, and lit my cigarette. "You must be so excited, Elizabeth, knowing that it's your country about to make history."

"Oh yes," I said. I glanced at Käthe, glad she didn't understand my little burst of national pride. I had so carefully squelched any conversation about the Apollo flight with her.

Peter went on in German, "The amount of preparation, of scientific trial and error it's taken to achieve this feat is nothing short of astounding. Here we have three men, three ordinary men, blasting off from earth with enormous rocket power, then loosing the rockets and traveling up and onward in a small, a tiny capsule. . . ." He described each detail as if he personally had imagined the flight and had overseen it every step of the way. Yet there was something more disarming than arrogant in his description. In spite of the flood of very Germanic grandiloquence, Peter continued to look like an advertisement for elegant southern European men's wear. He was still wearing his blue-tinted aviator glasses. I wondered idly if he could really see the stars he was pointing to above. I wondered even more if he could see me. And I especially wondered how I could make him like me enough to make him want to see me again.

Then I glanced at Käthe. Her square face was rapt, almost exalted. By the look of her she was traveling up with the astronauts, letting go one rocket after another, soaring into the stratosphere.

Peter looked at her too and his tone immediately changed, became easy bantering. "Now Käthe here, what does she know about space? She broke that little telescope she used to have, didn't she?"

Käthe blinked, fell and burst into silent laughter, covering her mouth.

It was pitiful.

Peter took Käthe and me to the train station after dinner Monday night and while Käthe was buying a magazine and some chocolate, he said, "You have known my sister a long time now?"

"Six or eight weeks, that's all."

"How much has she told you about her life?"

"Well. . . ." I hesitated. It seemed an odd question. "I got the idea she was cheated out of going to school and had to go to work instead. I don't know how much I believe that anymore." I wished we could talk about something else. It was the first time we'd been alone together, even for an instant. I wanted him to ask for my address, to say he'd enjoyed meeting me, anything personal.

"Whatever happened," he said, "it was necessary."

"She said she forgave you," I remembered, but I didn't really understand what he was talking about.

"Did she? I don't know. I hope so. I forgive her." And for some reason he took off his aviator glasses. My impression of him changed immediately and unfavorably. His eyes were a weakish pale blue, his jaw overlarge without the balance of the wide frames. But the strangest thing was a white hairless scar on one temple, not a duelling scar, but a thick crescent of flesh near his eye. He looked like a bad Nazi from a war movie. I shivered automatically and said the first thing that came into my head.

"We're not really friends, you know, Käthe and I. It's just because we're at the Mädchenheim that we know each other."

That made Peter smile. He put his glasses back on and his voice resumed its playful tone; he was again the worldly Italian model. "Oh, you're too young for all of this. You can't be more than sixteen, can you?"

"I'm eighteen. I'm going to college soon."

He gave me a peck on the cheek as Käthe came up and then pressed her ungainly body to his elegant one for an instant. She clung to him. She said, "Visit me. Visit me. Visit me."

There was a note of hysteria in her voice that seemed to alarm him. He held her firmly at arm's length. "Good-bye, Käthe. I'll write you and see you when I come back. You must study and work hard. No dreaming. Elizabeth will keep an eye on you."

He winked at me from behind his sky-blue glasses as Käthe and I boarded the train.

III

I didn't have a plan. I certainly didn't plan to walk inside the Mädchenheim. Yet I did. Two girls sitting at a table looked enquiringly at me. I stuttered, "Do you speak English?"

"*Nein.*"

I knew this room. I knew it all. There was the desk, the office. But so small.

I didn't really believe I could still speak German but I could. I said, "I am an American who lived here twelve years ago."

One of them stood up. "Let me get Frau Holtz."

She was still here. I hadn't counted on this. On seeing her again. She came down the corridor from her room, rubbing her hands together, staring at me. She was only a little older, a little bonier.

"I'm Elizabeth Michaels," I said. "I lived here twelve years ago. Worked here."

"American?"

"Yes."

"I don't remember." She shook her head. "I suppose you did."

Shortly after our trip to Käthe's parents', a new woman joined the staff of the Mädchenheim as an assistant to Frau Holtz. Fräulein Schmidt was slender and flat-chested, very tall and very brown-skinned, with a black mole the size of a dime at the corner of her mouth. Her shirts were crackling crisp and always tucked into belted dark pants, but her general air was less formal than alert and warm. She was almost too confidential, the sort of person who leaned on you when talking and fixed you with a sympathetic stare. Also, her breath was bad.

One by one, she arranged conferences with all the girls to talk about their problems and plans for the future. I was initially suspicious of Fräulein Schmidt and, when my appointment came around, grew defensive at the idea of explaining my literary aspirations, much less my now severe bouts of homesickness. But she listened gently, offered a few suggestions and, before I knew it, had me sitting in on an art history class at the Kunstakademie.

In spite of having resisted all Frau Holtz's efforts to make me more sociable, I fell in with this new scheme with something like relief. Through the class I started to meet some new people—an older woman painter from Brussels and a sculpture student named Hans. When he became my regular boyfriend, my status at the Mädchenheim went up considerably, and I forgot I'd ever considered the dental hygiene students unworthy of my company. I began to make friends with some of them, going out for a beer now and then or to a disco. I sat with them at mealtimes, and even Edeltrude and I found more to talk about. She redid my eyebrows and loaned me white knee socks, and one evening we went walking in the garden where she linked her arm through mine.

Both my reading and my writing sputtered out; I stopped memorizing Rilke and, when I took long strolls in the park now, it was with Hans to feed the ducks. I didn't ignore Käthe completely, but our torturous conversations about Nietzsche were a thing of the past. I became polite and friendly and after a week or two wasn't even making excuses not to see her. She accepted my changed attitude without asking any questions. Perhaps she even expected it. We never discussed the visit to her parents, my stories about my family, or how we had both acted with Peter. The evening I walked with Edeltrude in the garden I suddenly looked up at Käthe's window and saw her watching us. I waved and, after a minute, she did too.

Part of the reason it was so easy not to see Käthe was that she was more and more taken up with Fräulein Schmidt. It began shortly after their scheduled conference and continued, with greater and greater intensity, all through June. You never saw them apart; either Käthe was hanging around the Fräulein's office or the Fräulein was up in Käthe's room. You would have thought they'd known each other for years, the way they talked and laughed. It seemed to me that Käthe had found a much better friend than I had been; I was frankly relieved, and when the rumors started, was the first to deny them.

Gretchen said the Fräulein and Käthe hadn't come down to lunch one day, and when Eva had gone up to fetch them she'd discovered them holding hands.

That didn't worry me, but when I heard that Fräulein Schmidt and Käthe had been spotted in the Hofgarten with their arms around each other, I got nervous. I wanted to say I thought it was all right—German women were always linking arms, weren't they? How was I supposed to know when it was serious and when it wasn't?—but I was afraid of being laughed at, afraid the others would remember how much time Käthe and I had spent together back in the spring, afraid they would think she and I were...

"*Lesbisch*," they whispered and giggled now at mealtimes, at the table, sneaking looks at the two of them. Stories of finding the Fräulein and Käthe in the shower together, in bed together, were circulated flagrantly. I began, in spite of myself, to believe them. I thought I understood now why Fräulein Schmidt's close, bad breath and sympathy made me uneasy. They were lesbians, with their short hair, sexless bodies and strong faces. Käthe had probably even been attracted to me. There was that time we'd held hands running down the hill, that time we'd stood close at the window. I shuddered to myself remembering and thought how lucky I was to have escaped. If Peter hadn't come for a visit I might still be Käthe's friend.

That the scandal didn't blow up was due to its being by now the end of June. Finished with their term at the dental hygiene school, the girls departed one by one for their homes in Stuttgart, Bonn, Cologne. I exchanged tearful farewells with several and promised to visit when I could. I was already planning my own vacation—a trip to Munich and Switzerland—before I returned home to begin the fall quarter. My parents had sent me two hundred dollars and told me to stay away as long as I liked.

By July most of the girls were gone. Both Frau Kosak and one of the cooks went on vacation too. Frau Holtz left for two weeks in France. Only a few, including me and Käthe and Fräulein Schmidt, stayed on. There was a ghostly quality to the Mädchenheim now, an almost secretive quiet that hovered in the halls and nearly empty dining room and that made me want to be outside as much as possible, in spite of the fact that it was very warm that summer. The streets were like cookie tins and even the tree-shaded park was drenched in humidity and lassitude. I spent most of my time with Hans in the deserted studios of the art school, helping him fire his clay figures. A few times I stayed the night with him and no one noticed. But in early July he left too and I was back on my own.

It was then that I began to feel jealous of Käthe and Fräulein Schmidt, just as the summer was reaching a point of unbearable heat and splendor. I couldn't remember any longer why I had ever disliked either of them, why I had thought them ugly—Fräulein Schmidt so crisp and warm, with her mole like a tiny black moon, and Käthe with her big, earnest bluegray eyes. Seeing the two of them together, happily chatting in the office, or working in the garden, I started to feel left out, to feel, furthermore, that I had never appreciated Käthe.

What had happened between us, anyway? I couldn't remember. We certainly had never fought about anything. No, all I recalled now were those rainy spring afternoons when we'd trudged through the streets arguing about *Heimweh*, or those cozy evenings in her room drinking tea and reading philosophy.

I began to write poetry again and it was full of bitterness, lost affection, melancholy. I took out my old copy of Nietzsche and sighed over it. I bought the *Herald Tribune* and read about the approaching moon shot. I started smoking seriously, a pack a day. I wrote letters to my parents that I didn't send, asking them why we all lied so much. I said it would serve them right if I stayed over here forever, that they didn't have any idea of how much I missed them.

*

One morning Fräulein Schmidt found me standing in a corner of the garden, at a loss to know what to do with myself. She walked quickly towards me, smiling, wearing one of her stiff shirts, unwrinkled in spite of the heat.

"So, Elizabeth," she addressed me without preliminary. "Your friends are all gone now, what do you do with yourself?"

"Nothing," I muttered.

"Lonely then? Homesick?"

The garden was a well of green, damp and sunflecked. I looked at her cheerful, strong face and wanted to cry, *Nobody understands me.*

"You must spend more time with me and Käthe then," Fräulein Schmidt urged. "We've had some delightful picnics in the country. Please come with us sometime."

I did cry then. I sobbed and sobbed, urgently at first, then comfortably, burying my face in her crisp shirt front. She smelled of pine soap, a little of bad breath. The last woman I had hugged had been my mother at the airport; underneath the Jean Naté fragrance she always wore had been the scent of buoyant good-bye cocktails.

"When are you going?" I finally asked.

Fräulein Schmidt laughed and held me out at arm's length while she applied a handkerchief poultice to my tears. The black mole danced on her lip.

In less than an hour Käthe and I were packed into Fräulein Schmidt's Volkswagen with a basket of food and headed out of the city. It was a brilliant day, hot but fresh, with white clouds twining themselves around the sun from time to time like airy cats around a fat yellow cushion. I can't remember what we talked about in the car. I was so completely grateful to Fräulein Schmidt for taking me along, to Käthe for acting as if I had never stopped being her friend.

Yet I remember that afternoon, in fits and starts, very well. Partly because I was the happiest I'd been for many weeks, and partly because, after it, nothing was the same. We drove about twenty miles out into the countryside, past an historic castle and several small towns. We stopped at none of them, however, and instead Fräulein Schmidt—who was now urging me to call her Monika—pulled up near a wooded stream.

"Swim first and then eat," she suggested. But although the day was hot, the water was chill and bubbling. We contented ourselves with rolling our pants legs up and wading back and forth, building dams and skipping rocks. Monika was the ringleader. I still recall her firm brownish calves, the water reflecting up on them, making rainbows through the dark hair. Käthe was awkward and fell in twice, but she only laughed and took off her shirt to dry in the sun. We all took off our shirts then, and sat down to eat. It didn't seem strange to me, perhaps because the two of them were so casual.

We ate fresh cheese with pumpernickel and pears and hard, fatty sausage and drank beer. The beer made me sleepy under the sun. Whenever I opened my eyes I saw Käthe's white skin and Monika's brown nipples, but soon I kept them closed, feeling only the grass sweet and soft under my cheek. And I thought, before drifting off, "The important thing is not to lie, ever. But is silence the only way?"

It didn't even make sense to me at the time.

When I woke up the two of them had their shirts back on and were discussing the Apollo flight, due to begin that evening.

Monika said, "Whenever I think of men on the moon I get a picture in my head. Of bugs beating senselessly against a light bulb. Buzz. Buzz. And then they burn up."

"Do you think they'll die there then?" I asked.

"Perhaps. The moon is a woman, you know, in every language but German. Maybe she'll grow angry when they try to land, maybe she'll burn them up with her light."

"I always think of the moon as a terrible cold place," I said. "Like a dusty bathtub in a deserted house."

Käthe said dreamily, "I would like to go there someday. Perhaps I have already been. Sometimes it all seems so familiar to me. How you could walk like a feather on the surface, so light you hardly touched. Sometimes I think I may have done that."

"In a dream?" I asked.

"No, in my life."

I giggled, suddenly thinking of the mannequins in the show windows along the Königsallee, flying through the air, silver stick figures. "Oh, Käthe, you're just crazy." I reached out and touched her arm. I felt closer to her than I had in weeks.

There was a short, constrained silence, then Käthe laughed, in the old way, hysterically but silently, with her hand pressed to her mouth, and Monika reproved me, "Please don't say things like that."

"It's an American expression," I floundered. Idiomatically, I supposed, my German still left something to be desired.

Yet we had a wonderful time on the way home. I asked Käthe whether, now she'd finished the dental hygiene course, she'd stay on in Düsseldorf and get a job.

"But we haven't told you!" said Monika. Her hair was damp from the heat and her forehead glistened. More earthy now than crisp, she was driving with the window down, at high speed. "Käthe, tell her. We are going traveling. We want to go to South America and do something there. We don't know what, something interesting."

I wasn't prepared for this, but was able to quickly endorse the idea. "But won't it be awfully expensive?"

"Oh, I have lots of money," Monika said, and her black mole sat on her smile like a licorice drop. "And Käthe will go to the University there."

"In South America?"

Käthe smiled, enjoying Monika's enthusiasm. She was rolling her window up and down absentmindedly. "I don't expect much," she said strangely.

Monika chided her. "Oh, it will be wonderful. We'll start completely over. I promise you that."

It didn't occur to me to ask why they would need to. "Well, if I'm ever in Argentina, I'll look you up."

"Peru," said Käthe. "Peter says Peru is beautiful. You can

see the sky better than anywhere from there."

"Peter won't be there then," Monika reminded her, passing a car with dangerous speed. Then she leaned out the window and waved back at the car. The hot wind blew her short hair flat on her head. "Will he?" she asked.

"No, I suppose not," said Käthe.

"You're not calling yourself a lesbian yet?" asked Nathalie one evening while we sat together in her room drinking Moselle.

"Well, I've only just started, you know, being attracted to women."

"Oh, I doubt that," she laughed.

"If I could just fall in love, it would be easier."

"You seem to me the lonely type," she noted. "Like Clara."

"It's not just that," I said, and then, abruptly. "Do you ever feel afraid?"

I was thinking of my first real sexual affair with a woman, last year. Before that, a sister among feminist sisters, I used to be able to hug and kiss women friends in public without a qualm. After I got involved with Lucy I was far more nervous, wondering what her neighbors and my own would think, what my family and co-workers would say, how my "sisters" would react. As it turned out, it had all been over within a month anyway, and hardly anybody knew.

"Not so afraid," said Nathalie, shaking her lively hair. "But if I ever break up with Agatha I may be. I was like you before, wondering, and then—I met her and *knew*. But I don't have too much experience finding women like I used to find men. And sometimes I feel there are so few of us, us lesbians. It's isolating."

"Much better than the old days."

"And still, still so much the same." She drank more wine and brought out a book. "Now look at this." It was about the women's clubs in Berlin in the twenties. The *Damenklubs*. "They came from everywhere: England, America, Scandina-

via, France, Germany of course; they had such a strong culture of their own. Books, journals, music and cabaret and
theater, even a film, *Mädchen in Uniform*. Look at these
photos, how they dressed, their faces. I wish I'd known *that*
one, she's so nice-looking. . . ."

"What happened to those clubs, those women?"

"You know," Nathalie said. Her bright face shut down for
an instant. "They were killed or they pretended or they left
the country."

I thought of a book I'd read about the Pink Triangle, the
homosexual equivalent of the yellow star the Jews were made
to wear. Naturally the book concentrated on the men, lesbians
invisible, not taken seriously, as always. But if that meant
more of them had survived? *Had* more survived? And what
had it meant to survive by becoming invisible?

"I think I am a lesbian," I told Nathalie.

"Now are you sure? Don't make a mistake!" she teased and
then more seriously, with a hug. "It doesn't matter to me what
you or Clara call yourself. It's not so important."

"But isn't it?" I said trying to imagine myself in Berlin fifty
years ago, hanging out in the *Damenklubs* while it was fun and
disappearing when it wasn't. "If they started taking gay
people away again, what would you do? What would any of us
say we were?"

"Not this time," Nathalie said, putting her arm firmly
around my shoulder. "No, not this time. We'll fight. We're
fighting already. Can't you feel that?" Her voice shook a little
but she held me playfully. "I'm doing judo, after all, and I'm
not going to be taken anywhere I don't want to go."

We were in Frau Holtz's sitting room, just off the foyer,
watching the take-off from Cape Kennedy that evening, when
the door to the Mädchenheim sounded with a disconcerting
ring. Nobody wanted to answer it; it was the countdown.

"I suppose I should go," said Monika.

The bell rang again, twice, insistent.

The rockets flared white on the screen, filled its small square with roiling plumage. The German announcer's voice shot up too, less practiced than convulsive. The Apollo team had made it. They had left the earth. They were gone.

Käthe got up and went into the foyer to answer the door. Almost immediately we heard her cry, "Peter!"

Monika gave me a startled look. I thought, am I really going to see him again? Monika stood, pulled back her shoulders; the black mole went up like a battle flag. Very deliberately she took me by the hand and led me into the foyer.

"Elizabeth," said Peter, continuing in English, "How very charming to see you again."

"Yes," I goggled. He was handsome as ever and beautifully dressed in tassled leather boots and a Peruvian embroidered shirt open on his chest. His aviator glasses wrapped around his lean face like a semi-transparent blue bandage.

"Fräulein Schmidt," said Monika, holding out her hand.

"Ah, a new director?"

"A new assistant. Frau Holtz is away on a trip. She will be back tomorrow."

"*Ach so,*" Peter nodded, turning to Käthe. "Go on, get your coat, Katchen. You want to hear all about my trip, don't you?"

Käthe, without another word, rushed upstairs. Peter watched her go, smiling faintly.

"She's already eaten, we all ate early so we could watch the moon shot... ," Monika began with a kind of desperately controlled politeness, but Peter interrupted her, clapping his hand to his styled hair, though not enough to derange it.

"It's happened already? I thought it was later tonight."

"It was wonderful," I said, rather stupidly. "You would have liked it."

"Dear little Elizabeth, our little American friend. You saw this important historical event then. Don't you feel proud?"

"You just missed it," said Monika, "not five minutes ago." She seemed slightly more sure of herself. The sight of Peter's elegance must have amazed her just as it had me. Soon, I thought, she'll realize how kind and sympathetic and brilliant he really is.

Monika went on, "It will be on the news again. If you and Käthe care to stay I can make coffee. We have a torte as well."

I held my breath, hoping he would say yes.

"You could tell us all about Peru," Monika continued, now smiling in her warm, confidential way. "I'm sure Elizabeth would love to hear about your travels."

"I would. I'd just love it."

Käthe came barreling back down the stairs with a sweater and her purse, face alight. She hardly looked at me or Monika. "I'm ready."

"Why don't I take you all out?" suggested Peter. "We can come back here later and watch the news."

"An excellent idea," said Monika. "I have a favorite spot."

"So have I," said Peter.

It was a beautiful evening, clear and balmy as California. The streets were crowded, the shop windows and signs had never glittered more brightly, the canal was a river of light crisscrossed by shadowbridges. We went everywhere, we went to half a dozen places I had never been before. It should have been one of the high spots of my entire stay in Germany. I didn't know why I wasn't enjoying myself very much.

I kept feeling left out somehow, even though Peter occasionally took my arm when we crossed a street, even though Monika bent her head to talk to me from time to time. I might not have been there, for all that Käthe noticed me, but the other two bothered me more than she did. It wasn't fair that I couldn't speak German as well as Monika, that I couldn't seem to hold Peter's interest the way she could. I knew I was a much more fascinating person. He'd seemed to understand that once, now he was only curious about Monika. He wanted to know all about her, where she'd grown up, what she'd studied in school, what she wanted to do in life.

He said she looked familiar to him. She said, "I have that sort of face." She said she'd spent most of her adult life in Denmark. She'd taught German. She expected to go back there eventually. She made a joke about the Germans being too repressive.

I expected that Monika would tell him all about the trip to South America, or that Käthe would. I didn't think anyone would mind then, if I brought it up. I added that I hoped to visit the two of them sometime.

We were by then in an expensive little restaurant in the Alt-stadt. It was Peter's favorite place. I could see how he would like it. It was modish and restrained, more French than German, with white linen tablecloths and fine china. There were lanterns at every table, round and plump and of blue glass, so that the candles flickering inside them gave off a pale cool glow, like the color of Käthe's eyes sometimes, a light lunar blue.

"What's this?" asked Peter, staring at his sister. "You're going to Peru?" He didn't seem angry, only amused, ironic, like the time he asked Käthe, "What do you know about space?"

"Just an idea," said Monika, before Käthe could answer.

Käthe started to laugh, then caught herself. But her face still twitched nervously, with guilt and fear and even anger. "You went," she said. "Why can't I?"

"Oh, I have nothing against it," he said, lighting a tiny cigar from the lantern. "But all the same, two girls traveling alone in South America, it's ridiculous. You don't know what it's like there."

"It's true we're not famous physicists," said Monika testily. Her mole was quivering on her upper lip like a dying fly. I watched it, fascinated, suddenly beginning to understand that she hated and feared Käthe's brother. Yet I felt helpless to do anything. It was the same when my mother and father fought, neither of them raising their voices, but still managing to put furious anger into their words. I always wanted to stop them, but when I tried, they said, "But we weren't fighting, dear."

"What was it like there, Peter?" I asked desperately in English. "Did you see the eclipse? Was it a good one? I saw an eclipse once, my mother and father took me to see it. We went to Griffith Observatory, that's in Los Angeles. It was the only eclipse I ever saw, but I was so young I didn't really understand it. It got so dark and cold suddenly, like a nightmare, and no one said anything. I couldn't understand what had happened to the moon, where it went. My father told me it didn't go anywhere, but I didn't believe him. Make it come back, Daddy, I said. Make it come back."

My hands were shaking. I tried to laugh sophisticatedly. "Isn't that absurd? 'Make it come back!'"

"This was an eclipse of the sun," answered Peter in German, coldly. "We gathered a great deal of important information."

Then I, too, felt frightened of him.

IV

"Would you like to look around a bit?" Frau Holtz asked.

I numbly nodded, followed her upstairs. Everything was the same, down to the plants in the windowsills. I recalled that I used to water them.

"Elizabeth Michaels?" she mused. "Do you remember your room?"

I led the way.

"Who was your roommate?"

"Edeltrude."

"From Bad Ems?"

"Bad Godesberg, I think."

"Hmmm."

She opened the door to someone's room, the one Edeltrude and I used to share.

"Only one girl to a room now," Frau Holtz said.

Even one to a room it looked tight. No wonder Edeltrude and I hadn't gotten along.

Frau Holtz gave me a good look. I became acutely conscious that I was wearing one gold hoop and one pearl stud in my ears.

"And what do you do now?" she asked.

"I'm a writer." I wanted less for her to be impressed than for her to recognize that I had grown up.

"I'm sorry I don't remember you," she sighed.

We were passing the corridor off of which Käthe had had her room, when Frau Holtz suddenly asked, "And who were your friends?"

"I only had one," I told her. "Käthe König."

"The girl whose brother was the doctor?"

"No. The girl who killed herself."

"Yes, that's the one."

That evening with Peter must have been the day before Frau Holtz came back because the next thing I remember was her asking me to come down to her office. I went, if not willingly, then with no real apprehensions. The worst I could imagine was that she might reprimand me for not doing my work during her absence. My thoughts centered especially on the unwashed upstairs hall and I wasn't at all prepared to hear her say:

"I received a telephone call from Fräulein König's brother this morning."

I waited, puzzled.

"He told me some disturbing things about Fräulein König and Fräulein . . . Schmidt."

The French sun had tanned Frau Holtz's corrugated skin to the color of an overripe banana peel. Somehow she no longer looked so placidly maternal to me, but almost coldly militant, gathering up the reins of her authority like a general who'd been on leave.

"Such things do not happen in the Mädchenheim. I will not allow them."

"What things?" I finally managed.

Frau Holtz's yellow-brown skin began to blotch violet around her ears and neck; she grew pinched and dry about the lips. "I want you to tell me what you've seen while I've been gone."

"I'm hardly ever here."

Frau Holtz made an effort, and the violet gradually disappeared from the banana. She coughed and began again in a gentler voice, "Fräulein König's brother is very concerned about her friendships. As one who has been primarily responsible for her here in Düsseldorf, naturally I am also concerned. It has been a source of satisfaction to me that Käthe, Fräulein König, has done so much better while she has been at the Mädchenheim."

"But she didn't do better," I blurted out unwisely, "until. . . ."

"Until Fräulein Schmidt came, you mean?"

"You don't understand," I said. "For the first time in her life she's been happy."

"Elizabeth," said Frau Holtz firmly, severely compassionate now. "I am not accusing you of anything, if that's what you think. You are a simple young American girl. You were lonely and had not many friends. . . ."

Suddenly a terror arose in me that she *was* accusing me, that she did suspect me of something. "What are you talking about?"

"I am talking about Käthe König, a girl who has a history of mental problems and abnormal . . . fixations. I am talking about a girl who spent some years in a hospital for treatment. I am talking about a girl who tried to kill her brother when he intervened. I am also talking about a woman who lied about her qualifications and her background in order to become my assistant."

I couldn't take it in. I couldn't seem to understand why Frau Holtz was so angry. "But what have we done?" I wailed, for the first time implicating myself along with Monika and Käthe.

Frau Holtz shook her head. "You're not helping me, Elizabeth."

"But what have we *done?*"

Frau Holtz suddenly looked discouraged. "If it's true you've done nothing you needn't worry. But Fräulein Schmidt must leave today. As for Käthe, her brother is coming to get her tomorrow."

Clara invited me to share her bed one night. "So we can talk."

She told me that if it had been hard for Nathalie to tell her that she'd become a lesbian, it was hard for her too. "She was my best friend, then suddenly I felt... overrun, is that the word?"

"Superseded maybe... but are you sure? Lesbians need best friends too."

"But maybe only other lesbians. Did she tell you I may move out?"

"No. Why?"

"Oh, Elizabeth, I think I'm jealous."

We held each other and I felt my attraction to her turning hot and sweet.

"I wish I could," Clara murmured, "I wish I could. I wish I had more love in me, not so much fear and hate."

"What are you so afraid of?" I said, kissing her cheek, her forehead, stopping myself. "Don't be afraid, don't let them make you afraid."

"It doesn't come from them," she cried. "It comes from me."

"It comes from them," I said.

I didn't see Monika go and I didn't seek out Käthe. I spent the day out of the Mädchenheim, walking through the streets of Düsseldorf. I remember it was very hot, without a breath of air to leaven the heavy stone sidewalks, the weighted buildings. I wondered why I had ever come to this city, out of all the places in the universe. It still seemed foreign to me, worse than foreign, unfamiliar.

In the Hofgarten the red clay of the paths burned like fire against the too-green grass; the sky bristled angrily with heat.

A blue sky, turning black and violet. A thunderstorm was coming. I could feel it building in the prickly air, like a series of sobs in my throat, choking me.

Käthe was not crazy, I should never have used that word. There was a difference between insanity and fear. I had seen my father bring his hands down on the white and black keys of my mother's piano; I had heard my mother clinking ice in a glass at midnight, waiting for my father to come home. These things frightened me; they were not insane. In between there were picnics and trips to the beaches, there was my mother sewing in the kitchen and my father reading us parts of the newspaper.

I had wanted to get away from them so badly.

I sat on a bench in the park, smoking cigarette after cigarette, and tried to imagine myself far out in space, alongside the astronauts looking down. Only when I did that, looked down from a place near the bitter cold moon, all I could see was myself, a tiny stick figure, full of *Heimweh* for nothing and nobody real, poking out from a round, hot, blue and green ball, like a marble, a marble spinning in blackness, spinning and spinning.

When the thunderstorm came I stood by a tree. I saw the earth and sky separate, expand with a bolt of lightning, contract with a charge of rain. Everything was purple and red and green, like a wound being washed clean. I was glad, then, that I had never loved anybody much, that I was beginning to be old enough to be free. I would never go home to my parents' again. I would stay here or go somewhere else, a rainy place. I would have a little room by myself, read poetry and write. I would learn to write what mattered, draw a line around craziness and keep it out. That wouldn't be lying, it would only be silence sometimes. And in the evening I would go out into the streets and look at the moon, raining or not. It would always be there, cold and white and distant, less like a memory than a stone marker in the night.

It wasn't me who found her, though it could have been, but

Anneliese, the witch of the cellar. She came screaming up into our breakfast the next morning and no one could understand what she said. Finally the cook went downstairs to see what had frightened Anneliese so, and she in turn came shrieking up.

She had seen Käthe hanging, she had seen Käthe dead. She said it was a sight she would never forget.

"Clara, Nathalie," I said. "I don't know what you'll think of me when I tell you this. . . . I have been to Germany before. I lived here once. There were things that happened. . . . I didn't come to visit you intending to relive any of it, but it's so close now, it's all so close. . . ."

Clara came into the bathroom. "Nathalie. . . . Oh," she said, seeing me at the mirror. "I thought it was Nathalie in here. I thought I heard German."

Nathalie came in behind her, sat on the toilet sleepily. "What shall we do tomorrow? It's Saturday."

"*Ich muss nach Düsseldorf fahren.* I have to go to Düsseldorf," I added in case they hadn't understood.

"I told you," said Nathalie to Clara. "There was something."

"Do you want company?" said Clara, touching my arm.

"No, I mean—when I come back. . . ."

"We'll be here."

Peter came immediately. I didn't see Monika until some days after the funeral. Peter made all the arrangements and wept at the funeral, taking off his aviator glasses so that the crescent scar shone smooth and white. Monika didn't even go to the funeral. Peter gave me Käthe's much-marked Nietzsche collection; he said his sister was a bright girl who could have led a normal life eventually. Monika made a reservation for Buenos Aires. Peter said he hoped Käthe had finally found peace. Monika said Peter would have to live with this his whole life long.

Peter took me out for coffee and confided the story of Käthe's mental illness.

"We were very close as children, but even then I could see that in spite of her intelligence there was something not quite right with her. She was awkward and plain, slow in school; she didn't have any friends. She depended quite a lot on me. At first I didn't mind, it was flattering to have her reading the same books, trying to study what I studied. That's where her obsession with Nietzsche began. I was very fond of Nietzsche as a boy. But then I went away to school, to the University. . . .

"Käthe always needed someone. She formed a romantic attachment to one of her teachers. It was reciprocated. Of course that couldn't be allowed. You know our small town. There was talk. The only thing to do was to take Käthe out of school. The teacher was dismissed. I took care of all that. . . . Käthe used to write me letters full of Nietzsche. When I began my course on astronomy she saved up money and bought a telescope, a pitiful little thing. You could barely see the moon in it. She sometimes stayed up all night watching the stars. I think it began to affect her mind. She talked of flying, of being two people, one above looking down. She said she was always watching herself to make sure she didn't make any mistakes. My parents couldn't handle her, they were afraid she might hurt herself. Fortunately there was an excellent treatment center not far from us, in the valley. Käthe spent five years there. She came out quieter, except for that nervous laugh. We thought she was completely cured. I suppose no one can ever be completely cured. . . ."

Peter looked pensively at his coffee. A small cigar was between his elegant fingers; he rolled it back and forth a few times before striking a match to it.

"But she tried to kill you," I said.

"It was an accident, I'm sure of it. She didn't know what she was doing. Sometimes I've doubted that she remembered it. . . . For the last few years we've been, we were closer than ever. I did all I could for her. I got her into the dental hygiene school. She was really a very bright girl, in her way, she could have had a normal life eventually."

I went to see Monika in her new room to tell her I was leaving sooner than I'd thought for Munich. That's when I found out she was leaving too. She hadn't even bothered to unpack when she'd moved from the Mädchenheim. Everything was in boxes and suitcases and she was wearing an unironed shirt. There were dark circles under her eyes; her mole looked dried out as a raisin from the force of her bad breath. She frightened me as much as she attracted me

"I changed my name. I went away to England for a while after it all happened, then to Denmark," she said. "I never expected to see Käthe again. At first I hardly recognized her. She was much different when she was younger, when she was my student. She had a clear, fresh mind, the sort of mind a teacher hopes and longs to find. She was terribly honest, she never lied about anything. I suppose that was a clue right there to what was to happen. *Mein Gott,* you've seen her parents, and Peter. What use did they have for someone like her? And yet they couldn't leave her alone. She idolized her brother. She didn't understand that she got nothing back from him, that he took everything from her. She could have gone on to the University. She wanted to study philosophy. But everything was for him, for Peter. Her parents wanted to take her out of school. That's when it all came out, about her and me. Käthe could never keep anything back. You understand, it was not a sexual thing, not yet."

Monika watched me light another cigarette. A touch of the teacher was in her voice as she murmured, "That's bad for you, Elizabeth, to smoke so heavily at your age." Then she went on:

"I wasn't sure if he recognized me until Frau Holtz called me in and told me she knew my real name. But I didn't mean any harm. I would never have taken the job at the Mädchenheim if I'd known she was going to be there, Käthe. A student of dental hygiene, what could be more depressing? She never blamed her brother, she was so guilty about having tried to kill him that she loved him even more. More than me, more than herself. I know she was never crazy, or if she was, that he made her, her parents made her that way. I should never have abandoned her then. I thought I was doing the right thing, no . . . I was afraid for my reputation. Peter threatened to tell the school, to make it impossible for me to work again. And Käthe was so young. It was impossible."

Monika stared at me, almost angrily. "But what do you know about this? You never really knew Käthe, how could you understand her? You were not a good friend to her."

"That's not true. I mean, she got on my nerves sometimes, the way she laughed and everything, but I always find something about a person I don't like, I mean. . . ."

"*I* could have helped her, she trusted me. If we had gone away as we planned, if you hadn't mentioned Peru. No, it wasn't your fault, I'm sorry. Peter was her guardian. I know now since he claimed the body. We would have had to deal with him. But I should have killed him for her this time. I should have been courageous instead of so afraid. Instead of letting her turn it against herself. I won't see her again.

"This time I won't see her again."

Frau Holtz took me down to the kitchen. It was just midday and the meal was almost finished. She said doubtfully to the cook, "Here is a girl from America who worked here many years ago. I don't suppose you remember her."

I didn't remember the cook at all, though I recalled every expression and gesture of Frau Holtz's.

"*Ja,*" said the cook simply, glancing at me as if it were a few weeks, instead of twelve years that had passed. "*Die kleine Elizabeth, sie weinte so viel und hatte so viel Heimweh.*" The little Elizabeth, who cried so much and was so homesick.

I laughed awkwardly. "Yes, that was me."

"You won't stay to lunch," invited Frau Holtz.

"No, thank you. But thank you. I'm sorry."

"I wonder why I can't remember you," she said. And seemed truly puzzled.

"It's safer to be invisible," I answered. But perhaps I didn't say it correctly, for Frau Holtz just smiled, shook my hand and showed me the door. My whole visit had taken just under fifteen minutes.

I stood in the garden a few moments longer, exhausted, and to give myself an excuse, took a picture of the Mädchenheim. I began to wonder why I hadn't asked after Käthe's family. What had happened to Peter? And to Monika? And why hadn't I explained or disputed anything? Even Frau Holtz's one memory that Käthe's brother had been a doctor instead of a physicist.

Yet not for worlds would I have gone inside again.

The little Elizabeth, who cried so much and was so homesick.

Early the morning after Käthe's funeral the astronauts starting walking on the moon. It was three or four o'clock in the morning and the cook woke me up to come down and see the great event on television. I sat with her and two other girls, Heidi and Eva, in the gloomy dining room, watching the ghostly shadows take their first steps. I didn't want to be impressed and I wasn't—still, it almost hurt to hear their faraway American voices describing the marvels that they saw, the marvels that to us were only shivering gray and white images on a small screen.

I wished that Käthe could have been there, to see that they were not *Übermenschen*, but tiny, almost weightless figures bounding back and forth in their bulky suits, trying to get a toehold on the shifting surface, completely dependent on the fragile support systems that linked them to this earth. They were brave, I could have told Käthe, but at the same time there was something wrong with them, with the picture that flickered so strangely on the screen.

The way they talked, a jumble of code words and boyish delight. Pleased with themselves, yet detached in tinny, lingering voices. As disconnected from each other as from the control center, the earth with its countries, cities, friends and family. My stomach started to ache, it was the homesickness and the sadness beginning again.

It was the fear I had watching the astronauts walking on the moon that they wouldn't get back alive. And that I, too, after having been through space and time to walk another surface than my own, would not return to tell the story of what I'd seen.

I had planned to stay in Düsseldorf a few hours. I glanced at my watch after leaving the Mädchenheim; it had only been forty minutes since the train pulled into the Hauptbahnhof. There was time enough to stroll around the city again, the city I had once known so well.

I turned right down a street of shops and walked a few blocks to the Hofgarten's far end. In the canal were ducklings, this spring as always.

I was lightheaded and speedy, as if I'd just drunk a cup of strong coffee. How could Frau Holtz not have remembered me? Had Edeltrude really been from Bad Ems? Had Peter really been a doctor? I had never tried to remember before.

After I left Düsseldorf that summer I traveled for two blank weeks in the Alps, then returned home to San Diego. I never went back to live with my parents, who, in any case, divorced shortly afterwards. My brothers stayed with my father and my mother went back to school. She and I became good friends about a year ago.

I, meanwhile, moved north to finish my degree in another state. I worked, I wrote, I lived with a man and then alone. I became a feminist, an activist; I wanted now to become a lesbian.

I had never told anyone about Käthe. I'd never thought of her from the day I left the Mädchenheim, twelve years ago.

Now, passing slowly through the Hofgarten, on paths my feet remembered better than my mind, I began to feel that I was walking somewhere, for some reason, that I was even in Düsseldorf for some reason, in Germany. And yet, I was also very sure that if I hadn't met Clara and Nathalie that day in Stanley Park, I wouldn't be here. I would never have come back.

I had survived. That had been enough until now.

I came to the other side of the Hofgarten, crossed under the busy street to the Altstadt. The first thing I saw when I turned the corner were the four statues, the four Muses in two pairs.

On the pedestal of one pair someone had scrawled a feminist slogan in red paint.

I thought that Nathalie and Clara would like this scene. I took out my camera. Tears ran down my face.

All unconcerned a group of three young women students was sitting at a bench to one side. They looked up casually to see me photograph the marble women.

One pair holding hands. One pair with their arms around each other.

About the Author:

Barbara Wilson is the author of four novels, including two feminist mysteries, *Murder in the Collective* and *Sisters of the Road*, as well as several collections of short stories. She has also translated the short stories of Cora Sandel and a novel by Ebba Haslund from Norwegian. She lives in Seattle and London.

Other Selected Titles from Seal Press

Fiction

BIRD-EYES
A powerful exposé of a teenaged lesbian runaway's psychiatric
treatment in the 1960s
by Madelyn Arnold $8.95

LOVERS' CHOICE
Stories that chart the course of women's lives and relationships
by Becky Birtha $8.95

GIRLS VISIONS AND EVERYTHING
Lesbian-at-large Lila Futuransky is ready for anything
by Sarah Schulman $8.95

AMBITIOUS WOMEN
A political drama about women caught up in a grand jury
investigation
by Barbara Wilson $8.95

THE THINGS THAT DIVIDE US: STORIES BY WOMEN
Sixteen stories exploring racism, classism and anti-Semitism
edited by Faith Conlon, Rachel da Silva and Barbara Wilson $8.95

Mysteries

STUDY IN LILAC
A fast-paced feminist thriller set in contemporary Barcelona
by Maria-Antònia Oliver $8.95

FIELDWORK
A witty suspense featuring Marsha Lewis, amateur sleuth
by Maureen Moore $8.95

MURDER IN THE COLLECTIVE
A member of the print collective is murdered and Pam Nilsen tracks
the killer
by Barbara Wilson $8.95

SISTERS OF THE ROAD
Pam is back, investigating the murder of a teenaged prostitute and
runaway
by Barbara Wilson $8.95

Seal Press also publishes the *New Leaf Series* on domestic abuse, the
Women in Translation series and a variety of women's studies titles.

For further information, write to The Seal Press, 3131 Western,
Suite 410, Seattle, Washington 98121.
Please include $1.50 for postage and .50 for each additional book.